Time
Journeys

by

Richard Veit

WingSpan Press
Livermore, California

Published in the United States and the United Kingdom by WingSpan Press, Livermore, CA

The WingSpan name, logo and colophon are the trademarks of WingSpan Publishing.

First edition 2021

ISBN 978-1-63683-011-7 (pbk.)
ISBN 978-1-63683-028-5 (hardcover)
ISBN 978-1-63683-989-9 (ebook)

1 2 3 4 5 6 7 8 9 10

The most effective way to destroy people is to deny and obliterate their own understanding of their history.

George Orwell

Time Journeys

Logan Gramm was aboard a subway train, commuting to work from New Jersey. A charming brunette stood not six inches away from his right leg, her hand gripping the overhead strap. He wanted to offer the girl his seat, but eighteen grueling months in the Big Apple had taught him to refrain from calling attention to himself by showing common decency. When the enchanting creature exited, two stops before his own, Logan's eyes wandered from his iPhone to her slim posterior. Not many young women wore dresses these days, and hers was very becoming. Its hem swished from side to side, a couple of inches below the knee, with every step she took.

The restaurant where Logan waited tables was just a couple of blocks from his underground station, so it was clearly impossible that he could lay eyes upon the same vision of loveliness who had exited the subway so many miles back. And yet, there she was again, walking across the intersection directly ahead. He was sure of it, unless she had an identical twin sister who wore precisely the same clothes. A moment later, she disappeared into a jewelry store, and Logan forced himself to think of something else. It made little sense to obsess about this solitary female, no matter how attractive, when all the laws of physics told him that the two chance meetings were separate and unrelated.

Scotty's Steakhouse would not be described as a high-end establishment, but it did offer a wide variety of fried appetizers, sizzling cuts of beef, and four choices of innovative desserts. Gratuities for the wait staff ranged from adequate to dismal, providing Logan with a precarious living until he could secure a more stable position—hopefully teaching history or writing on historical subjects.

His favorite colleague at the restaurant was a server named Erin Duffy, who spoke with a distinct Irish accent and aspired to an acting career on the legitimate stage. There was nothing unusual about that on the island of Manhattan, where a substantial percentage of young people in food service were listed at theatrical agencies, in the forlorn hope of auditioning for parts. Erin certainly qualified in the looks department. She was a fetching girl of twenty, unabashedly romantic with two or three boyfriends at any given time.

"Did you see the curly-haired gentleman at table eighteen?" Erin asked.

Logan was standing next to her in the kitchen, both of them waiting for the cooks to plate their orders. His mind was far away, still contemplating those strange encounters with the subway girl. When he realized that Erin was talking to him, he snapped out of it. "Nope. What about him?"

"I think it's that actor who just hit Broadway after starring in a bunch of rom-com movies. I can't remember his name, but it sounds like him when he talks. He's got a very distinctive voice."

"Whose table is that?"

"Robert's, and I'll bet he gets a nice tip, too."

"No doubt."

When Logan left the kitchen, he was carrying a full tray, so he could not very well gawk at the customers. But the man in question did indeed resemble someone he had seen on the big screen. Turning the corner, he almost dropped his tray. Seated at table nine was the same girl he had already observed twice in the city, in rapid succession at two impossibly divergent locations.

Resolving to dismiss this figment of his imagination, he kept as far away from her as the day's work routine would allow. Still, when he heard the brunette raise her voice to say, "Excuse me, please," and motion to him as he passed by, Logan had no alternative but to obey her summons. He gulped and slowly approached the table.

"I know you're not my waiter," the girl said, "but I wonder whether you would mind bringing me another glass of iced tea."

"Certainly, ma'am," Logan said.

She grinned at him in a familiar way, friendlier than the occasion really demanded. Out of courtesy, he forced a smile of his own. When he returned with the beverage request, the woman was gone. She had left a note, hardly larger than a business card, concealed within a miniature envelope marked "L. G."

"Meet me across the street, at Java Bay," the message read. "My waiter said you get off at eleven."

From that point on, the workday seemed to drag, with Logan in a quandary between excitement and dread. The girl was a beauty, but how could he dismiss such a specter as those multiple sightings? There was something odd about her that he could not quite fathom. Most disconcerting of all was why she was so interested in making his acquaintance.

He clocked out and, finding a gap in the traffic, jaywalked to the all-night coffee shop that he knew so well. And there, at a booth near the entrance, sat the mysterious brunette, whose long, wavy hair was unmistakable.

"Sit down, please, Mr. Gramm," she said. "It's nice to meet you more formally."

Logan did as he was told, sliding across the seat cushion until he was directly opposite the young lady. "How do you know my name?" he asked.

"Lucky guess."

"Is that what the 'L. G.' stood for?" He waited for her to laugh at his quip, but she did not. Instead, she just sat there, idly blowing across her steaming coffee.

Logan gazed more intently at the girl's face, which was pretty enough to grace the cover of a movie magazine. She appeared to be around twenty-one or twenty-two, but certainly no older than twenty-five. For what it was worth, there was no wedding band on the left hand.

"Are you recruiting me for something?" he asked.

"In a way, yes."

"Well?"

"I'm not at liberty to say, at least not for a while yet. First, we need to get to know each other a little better." She took a sip of coffee, laid the cup down, and sighed. "I'm sure this must seem very strange to you, but everything will become clear soon enough."

Logan gave a nervous laugh. "So, what gives? Are you from another planet or something?"

"What makes you say that?"

"I've seen you four times now, and you seem to travel faster than a subway train."

The brunette's expression relaxed a bit. "I assure you that I am an Earthling, through and through. My full name is Tamara Renée Hansen, but you may call me Tammi for short. Tammi with an 'i'."

"Pleased to meet you—I think."

A male attendant brought Logan some coffee and warmed up the girl's cup with a refill. Tammi waited for the attendant to leave their table before saying another word. Then she turned to Logan and leaned forward. "Have you ever heard of ProGrade Kronotechnix?"

"No."

"Good. That'll make our project a lot easier."

"What project?"

"Yours and mine. The project that I'm facilitating."

Logan looked at the polo shirt she was wearing. It was a pleasant shade of fuchsia, with a small, stylized monogram in white that tastefully spelled out PG Kron.

"Is that your business attire?" he asked. "You're at work right now?"

"Oh, yes. Very much so. This is what I do for a living."

"Lounging around, talking to strangers?"

Tammi giggled. "There's more to it than that. You might say I'm here to solicit a professional favor."

Logan blew on the surface of his hot coffee and took a sip. "Now I'm even more confused."

She reached inside her purse and pulled out an electronic device. "Do you mind if I perform a little experiment for you?"

None too sure, he gave a slight nod of assent.

Tammi faced the device toward him, so he could view what was imprinted upon the various buttons. "Press your thumb against this identity sensor."

"Here?"

"Yes, please." He did so.

"This is only in demo mode," she told him, "but see what happens when I push the CURRENT key." A series of ten digits appeared on the electronic display. "That's the Unix Time code, the number of seconds that have elapsed since January first of 1970."

"What about it?"

She stood up and pretended to cough. "Watch as I point the device at you and press APPLY."

Instantly, Tammi was seated, just as before, but then she stood up and pretended to cough. And again she said, "Watch as I point the device at you and press APPLY."

Logan was dumbstruck, but there was no way to ignore the evidence. "Everything happened twice," he said.

"From your perspective, yes. You re-lived about four seconds of your past." Tammi gave a look of satisfaction, almost smugness, and settled back onto her seat cushion. "What's occurring, from here on out, is your new present, but with approximately a four-second delay. Think of it as a DVR signal that you've synched back upon itself."

Logan could not suppress a smile. "How did you do that?"

"I'm an intern rigger. It's what I'm training to do."

"What's a rigger?"

"Someone who facilitates a fine-tuning of the past—who corrects negligible deviations from what should have been the case. I'm only certified to adjust the most trivial events."

Logan raised his eyebrows. "What if I don't believe you?"

"No one does, right off."

"By nature, I'm a skeptic," he said. "Time travel is nothing more than sci-fi ... and the 'fi' stands for fiction."

"Do you feel any sensation of existing in the past?"

"Nope."

"Even though you're living four seconds behind your old present?"

He started to laugh but then recalled what he had witnessed—particularly the girl's ability to teleport herself across town. "What if I decided to stay in the past permanently? Would that be dangerous?"

"Impossible. The return time is programmed into your algorithms," Tammi said. "PGK would be out of business in a hurry if we didn't return our clients to the present." She pressed RESUME, and his consciousness returned to that precise point in time when APPLY had taken him in the reverse direction. Tammi, in fact, was still standing.

Logan remained unconvinced. "How come I can remember the first occurrence and also the 'rerun'?" he asked. "Why was my memory not restored to the present, with the duplication erased?"

"Because you're in our system, temporarily. The thumbprint identified you as a permissible client." She looked around the coffee shop. "You and I are the only people in this room who experienced that aberration."

He, too, looked around. Just as she suggested, none of the diners seemed mystified by anything out of the ordinary. "That's pretty amazing—if it's true."

"It is true, and what you saw was only a small sampling of what we offer," she told him.

Logan took another a sip of coffee. "We?"

"PGK." She pointed to her PG Kron monogram. "We've been around for seven years now, mostly experimental until the past four. The complete name is ProGrade Kronotechnix, Inc."

"Are you in management for this company?"

She laughed. "Hardly. I'm just a lowly recruiter, but I hope to become a rigger pretty soon—one of about eighty in our firm.

I have less seniority than most of the other trainees, so my boss calls me 'rookie'."

He glanced toward the electronic device, which she casually held in her left hand, as if it were a common remote for surfing TV channels.

A female attendant approached their table and inquired whether they cared for any dessert.

"No, thank you," Tammi told her. "This coffee is fine." The attendant smiled and walked away.

"Don't time travelers have to eat?" Logan whispered.

Tammi smirked at him. "You'll recall that I just finished a meal at your steakhouse. Doesn't that entitle me to human being status?"

"All I know is that you ordered another glass of iced tea. Then you skipped out when I brought it."

"For your information, I had a New York strip steak, with asparagus and potatoes au gratin. Ask Kevin, my waiter. He'll back me up."

"And how'd you pay for it? Do you carry interplanetary plastic?"

"My company has set up a very generous account for me at a well-known bank—one I'm sure you'd recognize—so I use a debit card to make purchases. It's all perfectly lawful." She took her final sip of coffee. "I like shopping in Manhattan when I'm off duty."

"Why here and why now?"

"This is my territory—all five boroughs. What you regard as 'the present' just happens to be the period of time that I'm currently assigned for recruiting purposes. Otherwise, we never would have met."

"When are you going to tell me why I was chosen to be your next guinea pig?" he asked.

"Guinea pig?"

"Isn't that what I am?"

"Not at all. You, Mr. Gramm, are a prospective client of ProGrade Kronotechnix."

"Hah! Then you're barking up the wrong tree. I barely earn enough to pay my rent."

"You misunderstand. No money will be exchanged between you and me. PGK is an independent contractor for the Department of the Interior."

"So, you work for the feds."

"No, I work for a private corporation—which works for the feds. There's a difference."

"How so?"

"We operate at a profit, like any other successful business, whereas DOI is a bureaucracy, beholden to politicians and the taxpayers."

"Why should they care about fiddling with the past?"

"They don't—not in the slightest," Tammi said. "DOI is called 'The Department of Everything Else' because of its random purview. Probably some lobbyist or special-interest group weaseled a grant from them, and that funding has stayed in the budget. But PGK sure isn't complaining."

"What if I say no?" Logan asked. "What if I'm not interested in being your client?"

"That's entirely up to you. But I can't believe you'd turn us down. It's a win-win proposition—for you and PGK. You don't receive a penny from us, but neither do we charge you for all-expenses-paid visits to an unimaginable past."

He idly circled an index finger inside the handle of his cup. "Tell me more."

"Tomorrow. This meeting was just an introduction. If you're willing to pursue the matter a bit further, I'll give you all the details—including what you stand to gain from putting your name on the dotted line."

"So, this involves a commitment from me?"

"Yes, indeed. Once you sign up for our services, you'll be obligated to follow your appointments to their natural conclusions. Rest assured, most of them will be quite positive."

"How can you be so sure?"

"Because of our little talk here tonight."

Logan smiled. "Meaning ... ?"

"You've learned something about me, Mr. Gramm, but I've also learned a great deal about you."

♦ ♦ ♦

The PGK agent and her potential client agreed to renew acquaintances the following morning at ten o'clock in Grand Central Terminal. Logan Gramm was already there when Tammi Hansen finally showed up at almost a quarter past the hour—out of breath from rushing the final two blocks on foot. She looked quite stunning to him, even given the shapelessness of her conservative business suit. Beneath the loose-fitting jacket was her fuchsia blouse with its PG KRON monogram.

"Sorry to keep you waiting," she said, "but I entered the wrong coordinates and didn't bother to recalibrate. I figured you'd probably be late anyway, so thirteen minutes and forty-seven seconds might not make much of a difference. How long have you been here?"

Logan smiled. "I was about five minutes late, but I beat you by nine."

Only a hundred or so travelers were milling about the cavernous Main Concourse at this particular hour, but such a public venue provided a welcome anonymity for the meeting. After all, it was much easier to find seclusion in a city of nine million than in a hamlet of ninety.

They went downstairs to the food-court level, where no one was likely to recognize them. There, seated next to Logan at one of the round tables, Tammi proceeded with her presentation. "Last night was just a taste of what to expect," she told him, "should you choose to sign on with our company."

"But why me?"

"For one thing, I'm aware that you intend to become a historian, whether in the classroom or as a writer. According to our scouts, you have the temperament and emotional stability to function well under duress. Believe me, I'm thoroughly versed in your habits and inclinations. You're the right person for the job."

"And you're enlisting me to change history?"

"Could be, but only in a microcosmic sense. We're not allowed to tackle the big issues ... like Lincoln's assassination or Pearl Harbor. Our tinkering won't change the broad course of world history. Not only are we forbidden to do so, but any such attempt would be rejected by natural forces, causing a non-consequence. Things remain just as they were." She glanced around the dining area, as if planning her next move. "Want to see something interesting?"

"Sure."

Tammi reached into her purse and brought out the hand-held device that she had shown him the previous night. She allowed him to eye it more closely than before. It was metallic silver in color, and one corner displayed a golden logo of "PG-13."

"This is the latest PROGRADE model, number thirteen."

Logan glanced from the device to her face. "Is that a joke?"

"What do you mean?"

"To us, PG-13 stands for 'Parental guidance is advised—may not be suitable for children under the age of thirteen'. It's a rating system for movies."

"Nope. Just a coincidence," Tammi said. "I carried a PG-11 until last week. Never did have a twelve."

She surveyed the lunch room and spotted a likely foil. "See that man with his tray of food?"

Logan nodded his head.

"Watch what happens," the girl said. She pressed the CURRENT key, and a series of ten digits displayed on the electronic display. "After I activate the PG-13, move that chair a couple of feet away from the table." She pointed the device toward Logan and pressed APPLY. He stood up, walked over to the adjacent table, and slid the chair back a little.

When Tammi pressed RESUME, Logan found himself seated again. The man with the tray stopped for a moment, narrowly avoiding the repositioned chair. Baffled, he pushed the chair forward with his foot and laid the tray on the table.

Prank accomplished, Tammi returned the peculiar device to her purse. "You just made a miniscule change of history," she told Logan, "but so minor in scope that it was fully accepted. Had there been a more drastic consequence—say, if the man tripped over the chair and broke his arm—rejection would have occurred, returning you instantly to the present. It's almost foolproof."

"Almost?"

"Well, I've never seen it fail. Let's put it that way."

"I still don't understand why you've chosen me for this project."

"I didn't choose you, Mr. Gramm. That came from the upper echelon at PG KRON. I'm just a recruiter, following instructions. They've sent me out on assignment, so here I am."

"Where's your company located?"

"I'm afraid I can't tell you that."

"Why am I considered to be the right person for this job?"

"Well, for one thing, you have some military experience behind you."

"Just two years, stateside. And I never saw any combat."

"Still, you're somewhat familiar with firearms, and presumably you know how to obey orders." Tammi paused for a second before continuing. "Also, it helps that you're single."

That took Logan by surprise. "What difference does my marital status make?"

"There is a small amount of risk involved, so—all things equal—my superiors prefer unmarried subjects."

"Are you saying it could be dangerous?"

"That's always possible. Traveling through time inevitably presents a certain element of the unknown."

"What if I decide not to participate?"

"That's entirely your prerogative—until the completed paperwork is processed by PGK. You'll need to sign a release."

Logan was staring at her purse. "Are you going to show me how to program that gizmo for myself?"

"I'm afraid not," she told him. "Programming is the exclusive job of riggers."

"Meaning you'll be going along with me?" He grinned.

"Nope. I'm just an intern. Besides, the device tracks one person's Unix Time number back to a pre-determined second, which makes it impractical to travel in tandem."

That came as a disappointment. "Couldn't you use an additional device—but programmed alike?"

"Out of the question, Mr. Gramm. Riggers are expressly forbidden from traveling to their own destinations, except for business purposes—which is how I happen to be in New York City right now. Unauthorized recreational usage is just cause for termination. One of my girl friends got the sack that way."

"Where did she travel?"

"Paris, 1927—to watch Charles Lindbergh land at Le Bourget. Kristen was one of the 150,000 people there to celebrate. She went deliberately, too, knowing that the trip would cost her job. She was about to resign anyway because PGK doesn't believe in maternity leave."

Logan nodded his head. "I can think of quite a few famous events I'd like to see, first hand. If I agree to participate in this venture, do I have my choice of destinations?"

"You're granted one preliminary, recreational trip of your own choosing, but it needs to be of little historical consequence. Be thinking where you might like to go."

"I already know."

"Oh?"

"I'll tell you later—if and when I sign up to take the plunge."

"Speaking of which ... " Tammi said. She pulled a small stack of papers from her briefcase. "All we need is your signature on a few lines, and then we'll be ready to proceed. Does this sound like something you might like to explore further?"

Logan's face darkened a bit. "I can't help feeling that there's a hidden catch."

"I can appreciate why you might feel that way, Mr. Gramm. In fact, we get that all the time from our recruits. 'What's in it for PGK?' they wonder. 'Why should they be investing a small fortune in technology so I can joy ride to the past?' It smells of a scam."

"Well?"

"As I told you yesterday, our company is a subsidiary of the Department of the Interior, which is charged with fine-tuning minor inconsistencies in the past. That's just a negligible line item for DOI—a few paltry billions, disguised in the budget—but it must be acted upon nonetheless. And you get to reap the benefits. Should you decide to enlist in this program, there will be a training period, followed by your recreational trip and then a commitment of five additional missions—or more than that, if both parties agree. You've been chosen because of your demonstrated skills in the field of intellectual research. We believe that you will be sensitive to the exigencies of historical manipulation."

"And if I disagree with what I'm asked to do? Can I refuse to accept an assignment?"

"Absolutely. PG KRON wants you to be pleased with whatever operations you consent to pursue. Each will be fully explained at a briefing prior to launch. Either you consent to go or not. It's up to you. Declining a mission will not be held against you in any way—you are, after all, essentially a volunteer—and someone else will be selected for the job. Yours will be one name among dozens on a roster."

"No strings attached?"

She shook her head. "Either party can abrogate the contract at any time, should one become disenchanted with the other. I think you'll find that PGK runs a loose ship, rather informal, and strives to keep its jobbers happy. It is a symbiotic relationship. You are able to visit intriguing epochs, almost to your heart's content, while PGK fulfills its mandate to correct imperceptible flaws in the progression of history."

Logan stared at the girl. "You know, you're very good at what you do. This is nothing but a sales pitch, and I'm swallowing it—hook, line, and sinker."

Tammi's smile seemed sincere enough. "Should I take that as a 'yes'?"

"I suppose so," Logan told her. "I can't think of any reason why not. How do I enlist?"

She spread three sheets of paper in front of the young man. "Simply sign on the bottom line of each page. I encourage you to read the verbiage first, to satisfy yourself that everything is just as I described it."

"Can I bring the forms home with me and return them to you tomorrow, signed?"

"Sorry, but no."

"Well, I hate to waste so much of your time."

"Listen, I've got all morning to serve you. The enlistment of Logan Gramm is my one and only project for today—besides shopping."

Logan did indeed read over the documents that very morning and—finding everything to be in proper, indecipherable legalese—he applied his signature to the requisite lines. Come what may, he was now an unpaid employee of PROGRADE KRONOTECHNIX, INC.

"We will contact you shortly to arrange the recreational trip of your choosing," Tammi Hansen said. "Once you tell me the dates and place, I'll personally see to it that the proper coordinates are registered to your mission log."

"Did you say 'dates'—plural?"

"Yes, the beginning and end dates. You are entitled to stay up to seventy-two hours."

"Any restrictions?"

"None whatsoever. But we encourage you to remain within the modern era and the civilized world. No caveman tours, for instance. We surely don't want to lose you on your maiden voyage." She chuckled, but Logan detected nothing funny in what she said.

"Is it possible to get killed in the past?" he asked. "Or is there some kind of cosmic insurance, which won't allow that to happen?"

"Our clients are subject to the physical laws of nature, just like anyone else, so being killed in the line of duty is a distinct possibility. That said, in the unlikely event such a mishap occurs, the PG-13 is programmed to interpret your death or major injury as an excessive repercussion and thus abort the mission. You will return to your APPLY time with no ill effects, except for an unpleasant memory and wounded pride. Bear in mind, however, that three strikes and you're out, so don't let it become a habit. Don't be foolhardy. You're not bullet-proof, and you will feel the pain of death or injury before revival."

Lips pursed, he gave that some serious thought. "Does scrubbing the mission kick in pretty quickly?"

"Not bad. We're working to limit the response quotient to a bare minimum—just a matter of fourteen seconds, max."

"Fair enough," Logan said. "When do I start?"

"A qualified instructor will provide you with two half-day sessions of intensive training, but you won't be on the clock until leaving for the first of your five official missions in the contract."

"Will I be seeing you again?"

"To be honest, it's very doubtful that our paths will ever cross after today. Sometimes I do meet up with one of my recruits, but only in the most dire of circumstances—court cases, body identification, contract infringement, and so forth. In other words, you probably won't want to see me again."

"Can I request you for my instructor?"

"Not qualified, by a long shot. My background is in sales, not the physics of Einstein's space-time continuum."

"Do you know who my instructor will be?"

"Could be any of thirteen—eight men and five women—none of whom I know by name. They all come from HQ, whereas I'm based at one of the four branch offices. I graduated from college two years ago and fell into this position when my husband joined the firm in research and development."

"So, you're married?"

"Oh, yes." She studied his face. "You seem surprised."

"You're not wearing a ring, so I assumed that you were ... "

"Available?"

Logan blushed. "Well, single."

"Nope. I'm no longer in circulation. And I have a little boy to prove it." Tammi stood up, quite abruptly, signaling that this session was at an end.

Logan rose to his feet, too, although feeling that many questions still remained to be answered. "You've been my sole contact so far," he said. "What happens next? Who's going to tell me when to report for training?"

"You'll receive a message directly from HQ—by email or whichever system you prefer to use. We offer every conceivable form of communication, and they're all time-corrected, so we can correspond back and forth."

"I guess email would be the best way to reach me. My email address is logramm1@bucco.net."

She entered his contact information into her wristpad by means of a voice-recognition program. "Our people should notify you within twenty-four hours, and they'll try to arrange a slot that is mutually convenient."

"Will this be a one-on-one workshop?"

"Yes. An agent travels to your present, and all instruction is given in your own time frame. You'll need to have an entire day off from Scotty's Steakhouse."

"I'm not scheduled to work this coming Sunday."

"I'll let HQ know, and they'll be in touch." Tammi looked at him for a moment and smiled.

"I hope to see you again," Logan said. He extended his right hand, and she shook it ever so lightly, as women often do.

"Thank you for your willingness to participate in the project, Mr. Gramm. I think you'll find that PG Kron makes historical refinement a very fulfilling experience." Her voice, in affirming the company line, sounded almost robotic.

◆　◆　◆

Just as Tammi Hansen had suggested, Logan received an email message from Heidi Franks, who identified herself as an instructional associate for PROGRADE KRONOTECHNIX. She, in turn, pledged to dispatch an agent named Frederick Backhaus to guide Logan through "the essentials of modern time travel," as she put it.

On Sunday morning, just after 8:30, Logan met Backhaus in a seminar room of Stevens Institute of Technology. Such a space had been utilized previously, according to the PGK agent, but Logan was not quite sure whether it had been cleared with SIT officials beforehand. In any case, the campus was quiet and relatively deserted on weekends, so no fuss was made of their impromptu usage of the facility.

The two training sessions, morning and afternoon, were fascinating in the extreme, and Logan could not believe his eyes whenever he consulted a clock. Like his favorite subjects at college—in which captivating professors spoke on topics that fired his imagination—he hated to see this workshop come to an end. He scrutinized Frederick Backhaus's expertise on the PG-13 with uncommon interest, despite the fact that Tammi had assured him that all such programming decisions would be handled by others, rather than by the time traveler.

Backhaus identified the ten-digit numbers as Unix Time, a system for tallying the quantity of seconds that have elapsed since midnight, Coordinated Universal Time, on Thursday, January 1, 1970. By convention, scientific endeavors in such fields as computational operations had adopted this method to describe points on a linear time scale. Events that pre-dated the Unix Epoch could be represented by counting down in negative values.

Beyond the basic precepts of time distortion and quantum teleportation, Logan's instructor touched upon such practical concerns as finite co-existence, precursory kinesis, ripple effect, speculative historiography, phantom shock, and emergency abort. The latter, he said, was of utmost importance—potentially life saving. Although authorized technicians always uploaded the termini of an excursion prior to launch, conceivably there might arise extenuating circumstances that called for quick action to negate those coordinates. That explained the reason for a PANIC button.

Backhaus pulled a hand-held device from his briefcase. "This is your PG-13 for the recreational excursion. Keep it with you. It has been programmed by someone with an exemplary record, so don't worry about being sent to the Somme River in 1916." He paused for a laugh that did not come. "The PG-13 will activate at the START coordinate and deactivate at the END coordinate. All you need to do is log in with your thumbprint, which is already on file in the unit, and then press APPLY."

"So, I can push the buttons now and nothing will happen."

"Nothing. It's a built-in safeguard," Backhaus said. "Same thing after you return to the present. Outside the window of coordinate times, the device becomes a humble conversation piece or paperweight."

"Why are there two sets of START and END buttons?" Logan asked.

"This top tier represents your point of embarkation—the here and now, so to speak—and this lower tier is for your destination in the past. The digital displays can toggle between Unix Time and the more recognizable common time. You'll only be concerned with the latter."

"What about locations?"

"Geographical coordinates are sealed into the device by our riggers, and you'll have no reason to view those."

"Are they numerical, too?"

"Oh, yes—incredibly long strings of digits that would mean absolutely nothing to the untrained eye. But they are accurate to within five inches of the target placement."

When the all-day workshop concluded on Sunday at 4:45, the agent was nearing his programmed terminus. Ever businesslike, Backhaus gathered the scattered paperwork and placed it into his briefcase. Then, without further ado, he told the student, "Be prepared for your initial trip on Thursday morning at seven. This is the recreational excursion that you signed up for when you enlisted."

"Thank you. I'll be ready."

Backhaus glanced at the clock display on his PG-13. "I'm out of here in exactly one minute and twelve seconds. Best of luck on your travels, Mr. Gramm. What's your destination?"

"Pienza, Italy."

"And the time?"

"Pretty recent. This is just a lark."

"Good. That's exactly what your RecEx is meant to be—sort of a welcome to the team."

"Where did you go for yours?"

"Forbes Field in Pittsburgh, seventh game of the 1960 World Series."

Logan's face looked pained. "Mazeroski."

"I had a lousy seat—upper deck and way down the right-field line—but it was awesome to watch Ralph Terry throw that final pitch."

"Not for a Yankee fan."

Backhaus patted him on the shoulder in commiseration. "Listen, maybe we'll run into each other again somewhere down the road. Probably not, though." After shaking hands, the instructor walked over to one of the wooden chairs and, holding his briefcase by its handle, sat down, perfectly relaxed. Without a further word, he was gone.

Logan collected the PG-13 and his belongings—notepad, pen, instructional booklet, and cell phone—and walked from the seminar room. He was due to work the next three days at Scotty's, but soon thereafter he would be passing into an alien world, in terms of both time and place. He went home, packed a suitcase, and reviewed what little he knew of the Italian language.

✦　✦　✦

Someone by the name of Frieda Cole was entrusted with programming the new recruit's itinerary. According to a short biography in the employees' manual of PROGRADE KRONOTECHNIX, she had worked there for four years, the last three as a rigger, so Logan Gramm could feel confident that plenty of experience was ensuring his well-being. An email from Ms. Cole advised Logan to anticipate departure at precisely 06:36:17 on Thursday morning. Then he would be on his own in Pienza, Tuscany, for the ensuing three days. It crossed his mind that emails and the internet were probably antiquated technologies for personnel at such a futuristic company as PG KRON. No doubt they were conversant with any and all systems that were necessary for communicating with their clients. Going back far enough, that would include faxes, telegrams, and even handwritten letters in stamped envelopes.

Logan tossed and turned in bed for most of the night, until his alarm awakened him at 4:55. He showered and then willed himself to eat breakfast: a pair of toaster waffles with syrup, accompanied by a glass of orange juice. That was followed by a cup of strong coffee while he sat in an easy chair and peered at the digits of his wristwatch. 6:05 ... 6:16 ... 6:21. When he touched the thumbprint sensor and APPLY button, a slight *ping* of activation was heard. 6:27 ... 6:32 ... 6:35. Gripping the suitcase's handle, he closed his eyes and waited. If all went as planned, soon Logan Gramm would become a witness to—or even an extra in—the filming of his favorite motion picture, Franco Zeffirelli's 1967 production of *Romeo and Juliet.*

The transition was painless and imperceptible. Had he not opened his eyes, he would have been unaware that anything occurred. And yet, the evidence was unmistakable. He looked around and saw that it was mid-afternoon in a scenic European locale. Lying about 125 miles to the north-northwest of Rome, this was Pienza, in Siena province, Tuscany, a town of some two thousand inhabitants. The analogue clock on a tower showed it to be 3:22. Air temperature had climbed by almost thirty degrees, a function of being shifted from spring to summer.

Logan's single piece of luggage withstood the transition unscathed. In keeping with his new surroundings, he made sure that the suitcase was an obsolete style, with no rollers on its base. He also brought with him a period 100,000-lire bank note (Banca d'Italia, 1967), with a portrait of novelist Alessandro Manzoni on its face. That should be more than enough money to cover his brief stay.

He spent the balance of the day arranging hotel accommodations and then making his way, on foot, to the ultimate prize of all, Palazzo Piccolomini. If director Zeffirelli's schedule was transcribed accurately, at least two of the next three days would be devoted to shooting one of the most important scenes in *Romeo and Juliet*, the masquerade ball at the Capulets. That is why the American visitor chose this particular day to arrive.

Logan tried to familiarize himself with his new surroundings. According to a guidebook that he carried with him to Italy, Pienza was the birthplace in 1405 of Enea Silvio Piccolomini, who was elevated to Pope at the age of fifty-two and took the name Pius II. It was he who inspired the transformation of Pienza into a model Renaissance town. In 1459, Pope Pius II commissioned the famous architect Bernardo Rossellino to design a Duomo, a town hall, and a papal palace for himself and his cardinals and court. A major feature of Palazzo Piccolomini was the splendid view, from its triple-arched rear loggia, of the soul-stirring Val d'Orcia and the slopes of Monte Amiata.

Even at a glance, it was obvious that this picturesque, fifteenth-century settlement was in the midst of a good deal of turmoil, with the vehicular traffic of cars, vans, trucks, and buses everywhere, in addition to great masses of heavy equipment and scores of people congregated around the palace. No exterior filming was taking place at present—that seemed clear enough—but there was certain to be an ant mound of liveliness within the grandiose, sandstone walls.

Logan walked over to a friendly looking workman and asked, in English, "Excuse me, sir, but when is the call time for extras?"

"No more shooting today, mate," came the answer, and the man's accent was decidedly insular rather than continental. "There were some takes this morning, but the on-camera blokes have been here since 5:30, so they're long gone by now."

"What's the schedule for tomorrow?"

"You'd be a Yank, then?"

"How can you tell?"

"Because of the way you say 'schedule' with a 'k', I 'spose." He stepped back and studied the stranger's appearance. "You certainly do look the part for this picture—right age and size and all—and anyway I'm partial to our Allies. Fought alongside your lot at Anzio, January of '44."

"Oh?"

"Nearly bought it there, as a matter of fact." He pointed with his tobacco pouch toward an open doorway. "Why don't you go see Mr. Scavello? Could be he's got something for you."

"Should I mention your name?"

"Go ahead, not that I carry much weight around here. Tell him Geoff Tinker sent you, for what little that's worth."

"Thanks."

"They don't pay much. Just a few quid and lunch—that's about it."

"I'm not here to get rich," Logan said. He grinned and nodded goodbye.

"Ta-ra." Tinker pushed his two-wheeled dolly over to a liftgate box truck, across the side of which was painted B.H.E. PRODUCTIONS—VERONA PRODUZIONE.

Nothing was happening inside the palace but set-ups, and it was all Logan could do to stay out of the way. The room's ambiance seemed eerily familiar to him, as if he had stepped out of a dream and into a fantastic reality. One crewman spotted him and asked, "*Cosa vuoi?*"

"*Signor Scavello, per favore,*" Logan said in his best approximation of the local tongue.

He must have been rather convincing, too, because immediately the man began speaking quite rapidly in his native language, leaving Logan at a loss. Shrugging his shoulders in bewilderment, the American could only repeat, "*Signor Scavello?*"

"*Vieni con me,*" the crew member told him, and he led Logan to a makeshift office area with a large desk and a half-dozen chairs.

A tall, brooding man with long sideburns stepped forward and raised his eyebrows. "*Sì? Posso aiutarti?*"

"Are you Mr. Scavello?"

Missing nary a beat, the man switched over to perfectly idiomatic English. "Yes, that's right. How may I help you?"

"My name's Logan Gramm. Mr. Tinker sent me—Geoff Tinker. He said you might be in need of another extra."

"Actually, we could use five or six more. We've got the wardrobe but not enough warm bodies. When can you be here to start?"

"Right now, if need be."

"We can get you fitted today, but there won't be any shooting until nine tomorrow morning. Extras show up at 5:30. Okay?"

"Yes, fine." Logan shook Mr. Scavello's hand and then followed him through a maze of rooms to wardrobe. Fittings for him and about ten other latecomers took less than one hour, and then Logan was finished for the day. He walked across town toward a distant tower whose clock face was back-lit for nighttime viewing.

The American's hotel, Il Giardino Segreto, was a restored eighteenth-century structure with—as its name might suggest—an attractive inner garden. It stood at Via Condotti 13, in the southeastern section of Pienza, only about a mile and a quarter from Palazzo Piccolomini. He counted himself extremely fortunate to find such agreeable lodgings, especially with so many foreigners in town for a major film production. After asking the hotel staff to telephone him at 3:30, he also set his own alarm by using a pocket calculator, which he brought along with him for the trip but planned to keep hidden from curious eyes. It had cost him $4.95 in his own world, and yet 1960s inhabitants would no doubt be willing to part with a hundred dollars or more for such a technological marvel. Or filch it for free.

Again he could not sleep well, remaining restless until well past midnight. At long last, though, he dozed off and made it fitfully through the next three hours of darkness. The telephone rang a couple of minutes before his calculator had the opportunity to beep him awake, suggesting that this hotel's staff was more dependable than many he had encountered over the span of his young life. That assurance was nice to know because he would be staying an additional night as well.

Logan was the first extra to arrive at the palace, and by a wide margin. Evidently, a 5:30 call for acting talent meant 6:00 in the relaxed climes of the Italian peninsula. Still, that gave him a valuable opportunity to wander about the grounds in solitude and savor the architectural splendors of Palazzo Piccolomini and the adjacent Duomo. A night watchman shined his flashlight toward the intruder, but Logan was able to convince him—in his fractured Italian and the guard's fractured English—that he was connected with British Home Entertainment Productions, if only in a lowly, superfluous role.

Wardrobe and makeup consumed two full hours of the morning preparations, and Logan's attire, labeled "L. Graeme" on its collar tag, consisted of colorful Renaissance tunic and tights with an operational codpiece. After costuming was finished, a brief rehearsal, complete with recorded music, accounted for the other hour before cameras were finally readied for action. Though this was all new to the latest arrival, it served as a second rehearsal for most others in the crowd, those who had reported for work the day before. Logan's menial status relegated him to a position at the rear, but so many takes were captured on film that he did feel a constituent part of the performing troupe.

The segment at hand, when edited, would depict one of the most stirring moments in the dramatic literature, the initial meeting of Romeo Montague and Juliet Capulet in the great hall. This scene was the epitome of love at first sight—romantic, sentimental, innocent, amorous, and coy—and its visceral impact depended wholly upon the two stars who were asked to bring these conflicting emotions to life.

Franco Zeffirelli was present on the set—in charge of every nuance, as any good director will be—and he guided his two adolescents through their paces with the apparent mastery of experience. This was a bit illusory, however, for he himself had only supervised one previous cinematic production, that of *The Taming of the Shrew*, with Richard Burton and Elizabeth Taylor. Both features may have been Shakespearean screenplays, but that is where the similarities stopped. Youngsters Leonard Whiting and Olivia Hussey could hardly be treated with the same toughness as Dick and Liz in their prime, so gentle allowances were made for the two stars' teenaged insecurities. All things considered, they held up quite well under the stress and delivered their Elizabethan lines with true understanding and in a conversational tone.

Drifting far beneath the rarified aura of Shakespeare's principal roles was an anonymous Veronese citizen of Capulet heritage. He was consigned to a remote camera view, content to revel with other partygoers in the shadows. While there, his assignment was to chat amiably, maintain a fourteenth-century bearing, and, above all else, not be visibly aware of the star-crossed liaison that was developing before his very eyes. This generic townsperson, played by an American named Logan Gramm, was careful to remain in character, but nonetheless he discreetly gathered in much that was happening around him in the palace ballroom. He heard the director's instructions and also the Nino Rota/Eugene Walter music, with actor Bruno Filippini lip-synching Glen Weston's pre-recorded rendition of "What Is a Youth?" He noticed the blaze of colors, the frequent camera movement, and the occasional repositioning of lights and microphones as the situation dictated.

More than anything else, he stole repeated glances at a sweet actress named Olivia Hussey, who was every bit as lovely in person as he had imagined her to be from countless vicarious encounters through the medium of motion pictures—in this film and in *All the Right Sounds*, which was shot a year later. During the long stretches between takes, Logan was free to gaze toward the girl and fully appreciate her stunning beauty. It goes without saying that he would never be able to meet her—the chasm separating star and extra being insurmountable—but perhaps that was just as well. She was, and always would be, his ideal conception of Juliet.

From what he could judge at a distance, the real Olivia Hussey had an endearingly sassy personality and playful sense of humor, but it was a fragile charm. In defiance of the VIETATO FUMARE signs, this pretty sixteen-year-old would casually light up a cigarette while on the set and smoke like a woman twice her age. But so what if her off-camera persona did not quite live up to the impossibly lofty image that he had created in his mind? That was not a fair standard of measurement for any human being, much less a teenaged actress with the pressure of a major film production resting upon her delicate shoulders.

Another early-morning call led Logan to the papal palace the following day, but this time he showed up at 6:00 instead of 5:30 and was still the first extra to arrive for duty. This session consisted of a few brief retakes and some new footage that did not require the presence of Miss Hussey and Mr. Whiting. Their characters would be filmed separately, alone in a curtained antechamber, where they would at last speak with one another and share their first kisses. For the sake of continuity, extras were asked to assume, as precisely as possible, their former positions in the Capulets' great hall, and twenty-two-year-old Bruno Filippini again took center stage for the mouthing of the Rota song, both in wide shot and close-up.

By noon, the young American's contribution to *Romeo and Juliet* was at an end. He collected his meager wages—in either pounds or lire, his choice—and departed for Il Giardino

Segreto to pay his hotel charges and retrieve the suitcase. Logan wondered where handsome Leonard Whiting and beautiful Olivia Hussey might be at that moment. He had heard that the couple were on affectionate terms away from the camera, as well as in front of it. Perhaps that explained why, quite apart from their unquestioned acting talents, the chemistry between them fairly crackled on screen. With the adorable Miss Hussey haunting Logan's thoughts, all he could think of was, "See how she leans her cheek upon her hand. Oh, that I were a glove upon that hand, that I might touch that cheek."

The essential coordinates had been pre-programmed by rigger Frieda Cole, so Logan was free to relax for a few minutes, suitcase in hand, outside the entrance of his exquisite hotel on Via Condotti. One final time, he soaked in the pleasant sights and sounds of Pienza. Then, as the PG-13 approached 14:10:04, he shut his eyes, and the change must have been instantaneous. Upon re-opening them, he was standing in the living room of his familiar Hoboken apartment, having squeezed an incredible three-day Italian sojourn into one single day away from work.

But the return was a bit discouraging, too. All he brought back with him, besides the suitcase of belongings, was an exciting memory that he would be unable to share with any friends or relatives. The only people he could ever tell were those who had arranged his journey in the first place, and surely it would mean little to them.

◆　◆　◆

The next communication that Logan Gramm received from PROGRADE KRONOTECHNIX was not an email but a text message. He had forgotten to set his iPhone to SILENT, so it chimed at him on a Tuesday night in Scotty's Steakhouse, just as he was accepting the food selections for a party of six. Order submitted, he viewed this text while helping the busboy clear off a table. The message read, <Contact PGK at once. Your Op-1 has been arranged.>

Logan was not certain how best to respond. Should he acknowledge it by email, by texting, or through the social media? Probably it made little or no difference to the recipient at PGK. Regardless of the chosen platform, Logan's answer was sure to be accessed with the ease of child's play. The rep might even be unaware of the system used because any reply would automatically convert to modern standards. Logan decided to text back and almost immediately received instructions to meet agent Henri-Pierre Villot at a specified Dunkin' Donuts shop, no later than 9:30 on Thursday morning.

Despite this emissary's three French names, his dialect was idiomatically American English. He was of western European stock, but his native language was clearly that of the New World. Moreover, he spoke with the crafty assurance of someone who knew far more than he let on to new acquaintances. From where Logan sat, this Villot resembled an arrogant fraternity man from Dartmouth, Princeton, or one of the other Ivy League institutions. Even his coffee preference reeked of affectation, insisting that the shop's attendant concoct a quirky mixture of Turbo and Hazelnut blends. Logan was distrustful of him at once but soon discovered that the man's abrasive nature was an honest reflection of his competence.

"Well, Gramm, are you ready for that first big leap of faith?" Villot asked.

"Don't forget my trip to Pienza."

"That hardly fits the bill."

"How so?"

"Recreational excursions are, by definition, elective in nature. Nothing was changed for the positive."

Logan grinned. "Yesterday I saw myself on a DVD of *Romeo and Juliet*—when I hadn't been in that film before. I'd say that's pretty cool."

"Cool?" Villot was looking down his nose at him.

"Awesome ... exciting ... amazing. You know."

"Sorry. Thankfully, that definition has dropped out of the lexicon." The PGK agent took a sip of coffee and reached for his shirt pocket. "Is it permissible to smoke in here?"

"Not inside any public building."

"Why is that?"

"I don't know. Second-hand nicotine, I guess. The danger of getting lung cancer." Logan studied Villot's face. "Is cancer cured where you come from?"

"Can't say that it is."

"That's a shame. I was hoping—"

The emissary shook his head. "I mean I can't say yes, and I can't say no. We're not permitted to disclose anything about what might represent the future to our clients. It's one of the tenets of our employment with DOI, a gag rule that's rigidly enforced."

Logan took another bite of his chocolate frosted doughnut. He, too, was drinking coffee, but his was the more straightforward Original Blend.

"Let's get started," Villot said. He glanced around the room and, seeing that their conversation would be reasonably private, felt free to forge ahead. "This is your Op-1, so I'm open to anything that you might wish to ask."

"Thank you."

"But let me pose a question to you first."

"Shoot."

Villot brought his hands together, fingers spread with their tips touching. "How is your grasp of the American Civil War?" he asked. "This dossier claims that you were a history major in college."

Logan cocked his head to determine what the agent was holding. "Is that my curriculum vitae?"

"Among other materials, yes. It's all here—everything from honors and awards to social misdeeds and even a few civil transgressions."

That made Logan wince. "I don't recall having any of those."

"I beg to differ. Believe me, nothing is too trivial for us to investigate."

"And yet, PGK hasn't written me off."

"Obviously not, and that's a good sign," Villot told him. "We don't make a habit of wasting the company's time, nor the department's money."

"I guess I should be proud of myself for making it this far."

Evidently, that was not worthy of a response, for Henri-Pierre Villot continued without changing expression. "It's the late spring of 1864, and there's a young widow in Georgia named Rebekah Olney—living just to the northwest of Marietta. She must be saved from Sherman's marauding troops."

"Why do you speak like it's in the present tense?"

"Because it is in the present tense—for you—and I'd advise you to begin thinking about the op in those terms. The sooner, the better."

"How do I find this Rebekah Olney person?"

"The coordinates will take you directly to her."

"Will Frieda Cole program them for me?"

"Who?"

"Frieda Cole. Isn't she the rigger who loads coordinates onto my remote?"

"We have dozens of riggers—too many to know by name, I'm afraid." Villot chuckled under his breath. "And it's not called a remote, as you so charmingly put it. Hereafter, the device must be referred to as a PG-13. It's the latest model, a prodigious advance over the old PG-12 that served us so well for over a year."

"I'll try to remember that," Logan said. He sipped the coffee.

Villot leaned back in his chair. "Better ask me some questions now. I won't be there to hold your hand."

Logan thought for a moment. "How old is Mrs. Olney?"

"Eighteen."

"And already a widow?"

"Nothing unusual about that—not in those days."

"What was her husband's name?"

"Nathaniel—or Nate."

"When were they married?"

"November of 1861."

Logan's eyes widened. "Rebekah was only fifteen?"

"Almost sixteen."

"Any children?"

"One, a girl named Amanda. Nate was killed at the Battle of Fort Pulaski, so he never even saw his daughter."

"Amanda is now three?"

Villot gave a smirk. "It's not just a simple matter of arithmetic, Gramm. Little Mandy was conceived in wedlock—which was also common in those days—so there's a nine-month gestation period to consider. The child is still short of her second birthday."

"And what's so important about Rebekah Olney?"

"There's no reason for me to reveal that. Typically, our clients are kept in the dark about the big picture. Just accomplish your task, and the context will take care of itself. PGK has designed this mission to alter the future in a very surgical manner—minimally invasive, you might say. Unless you botch the effort royally, I doubt that you'll ever notice what happened."

Logan registered his confusion by squinting at the agent.

"History will thank you," Villot added. "The world will be an ever-so-slightly better place for your having visited Acworth, Georgia, on June 8, 1864."

"Will it be dangerous?"

"We've arranged for you to avoid the skirmishes, as much as possible. You'll be unarmed, which might put Mrs. Olney at ease—especially with so many Union soldiers roaming the area."

"How long will I be there?"

Villot consulted an electronic device. "Only three hours. We can't risk having you stay any longer than necessary because you'd give yourself away for sure." He used his left leg to slide a piece of luggage toward Logan. "Inside this suitcase is your wardrobe for the trip. Period clothing is all you'll need to take with you."

"Not a blue uniform, I hope."

"As a matter of fact, either Union or Rebel would be precarious on that day."

"How come?"

Villot searched for the right words. "Because of the anarchy all over Cobb County, anywhere near the Western and Atlantic railroad line."

Logan stared at the suitcase. "How do you know these clothes will fit?"

"Everything has been altered for you—thanks to a hologram and 3-D printer—and the style has been researched to blend into mid-nineteenth-century culture."

"Is it safe for a military-age male to be dressed as a civilian?"

"Hardly. Try to make yourself scarce, or you could be shot as a spy."

"What's the name of the town again?"

"Acworth."

Logan picked up the coffee cup, his hand a bit unsteady, and downed the final gulp.

Villot seemed to notice. "Above all, don't show your nerves," he told him. "That would make you more conspicuous than whatever else you could say or do. People can sense that. Understand?"

"I think so."

"Remember that anything you happen to accomplish will not be earthshaking or immediately noticeable. You won't be splitting the atom, so it should be easy to maintain a calm demeanor."

"You make it sound like a walk in the park," Logan said.

"Not at all. To a select group of people, your presence will be very significant—indeed, life-changing."

"I'll keep that in mind."

On the table lay a small box, and the PGK rep now opened its lid. "Here is your PG-13, along with an owner's manual. Commit it to memory, from cover to cover. You depart in just under forty-five hours, Saturday at 6:45 AM. Be dressed and ready to leave." Henri-Pierre Villot grinned at his pupil. "You might also plan a last-minute stop at the restroom, unless you happen to be partial to relieving yourself in the great outdoors."

♦   ♦   ♦

The alarm on Logan Gramm's cell phone awakened him at 5:15 on Saturday morning, cutting short his sleep at roughly three hours. Throughout the night, until finally dropping off, he experienced difficulty in ignoring the excitement that this day was sure to bring. After eating a quick breakfast of two granola bars, he tried on the drab clothing that agent Villot had given him on Thursday. The woolen breeches and shirt felt rough to the skin, but they fit reasonably well, as did the boots.

Into the shirt's hidden interior pocket he slipped the PG-13. By now, he was familiar with its functions, though today's excursion would require nothing more than authentication with his thumbprint. All details of time and place had been pre-programmed by a faceless rigger whom he would probably never meet. In essence, he was placing his trust in the unverified expertise of an unnamed technician from the unknown future. By 6:40, Logan felt as ready as he would ever be, so he made his way over to a chair in the kitchen, activated the device, and sat with his eyes closed.

The first thing that aroused his awareness was the distinctive smell of gunpowder, perhaps wafting toward him from a recent battle several miles away. There was no sound except for birds chirping and wind blowing through the trees. He opened his eyes and gazed upon a rural flatland with rolling hills in the distance. Gentle, blue waters of the Etowah River lay just ahead, identifiable from his perusal of an Acworth website the night before. A hundred yards to the northeast was a modest farmhouse, presumably the habitat of Mrs. Rebekah Olney and her little daughter, a toddler by the name of Amanda.

Logan reached for his PG-13 and noted that 02:58:13 showed on the countdown display. It would be vital to check the time remaining as often as possible, whenever the situation permitted.

He re-buttoned the hand-held device inside his shirt pocket and began venturing toward the house, not knowing how friendly or hostile his reception might be. Halfway there, a shot rang out, and he could hear a bullet whizzing through the air, much too close for comfort. He fell headfirst onto the prairie grass. Was it a Union or Confederate soldier who fired at him? Conditions were so chaotic at this stage of the war that speculation was pointless.

He lifted his head far enough to see a woman coming around the side of the ramshackle barn. She was holding a rifle at her side and shouting something that he could not apprehend from such a distance. Logan managed to raise his hands a bit—not easy from a prone position—in the hope that this universal gesture might convey a peaceful intent. Hearing no loud report from her firearm, he slowly stood up and began edging toward the house, hands high above his head. The woman now held the rifle in front of her, as if in a defensive posture.

Logan persisted in advancing forward, but the moment he lowered his hands, the woman trained her rifle directly at him. Again his hands went upward, and yet he continued to walk toward her. By now, he had come within hearing range of what she was yelling: "Are you a Yankee?"

"No, ma'am. I mean you no harm."

"Who gave you permission to trespass on my property?"

"I want to help you. Please listen to what I have to say."

"Stand right where you are—not an inch further."

Logan did as he was told. But even with his hands high above, as if in surrender, she persisted in aiming the rifle at his chest. "Would you kindly lower that piece of artillery?" he asked. "As you can see, I'm unarmed."

"What were you plannin' on doin' here—before I stopped you?"

"Nothing, I swear," he told her. "I have a message for you, and I pray to God that you'll take it to heart. You're in imminent danger. Believe me, there is no time to lose."

The woman scowled at him and took a step forward. "Who are you?" She spat the words out with a deep loathing. "You are too a Yankee! I can hear it in your voice."

"It's true that I hail from New Jersey, ma'am. I won't deny it. But I'm the farthest thing possible from a Union soldier. How can I convince you?"

"By leavin' my property."

"I can't do that, Mrs. Olney. Not until you're safe."

The woman stared at him for several seconds. "How'd you know my name?"

"That's not important. What is important is that Sherman's men are just beyond those trees. You and Amanda need to leave right now. It's a matter of life and death ... or worse, if you understand what I mean."

Rebekah lowered the rifle to her side, brushing some stray hair from her eyes. She looked a good ten years older than her true age but was still rather attractive.

"These men are Union renegades," Logan told her. "They'll do anything they please to you, without blinking an eye."

Rebekah glanced warily at the tree line, off to the northwest. Four men with weapons were trudging across the pasture, one of them limping badly. Their bluish uniforms were tattered and in disarray. They were deserters, she figured, the worst of all the Yankee swine—answering to no one and living off the spoils of war.

"How do I know that you're not one of 'em?" she asked.

"Because dressed like this, I could be shot as a spy—by either side that captures me."

That made sense to her. "It appears, sir, that I have no choice but to believe you."

"Get your daughter, and come with me. And try to keep out of sight, as much as you can."

She entrusted her rifle to the stranger and ran to the house, crouching low. A minute later, when she came back out, Rebekah was carrying the little girl in her arms.

"Can't she walk yet?" Logan asked.

"Just learnin' how. She'd only slow us down."

Logan peered around, toward the river. "Give her to me." He exchanged the rifle for her daughter, whom he hoisted to a shoulder. "Did those stragglers spot you?"

"I don't know."

"Could be they just want to ransack the place for food, but we can't take the chance. As you can see, we'd be outnumbered, four men to one—and I have no great yearning to be hanged as a Rebel spy."

Her eyes widened. "Is that what you are?"

"No, but that doesn't mean they wouldn't enjoy stringing me up, just for the sport of it."

The three of them—man, woman, and child—fled to relative safety, concealing themselves amidst some trees along the river bank. From there, they watched as the four renegade troops, firearms raised, kicked down the door of her farmhouse and burst inside.

The child began to cry, and Rebekah said, "Hush, Mandy! We'll be goin' home soon." She pointed to the stranger. "This nice man is our neighbor, Mr. ... "

Logan bowed at the waist, something he assumed a chivalrous gentlemen of that epoch might do. "I'm Mr. Gramm. Mr. Logan Gramm."

" ... and Mr. Gramm wants to be our friend," she added.

Grinning, he squatted down and touched Amanda on the tip of her nose. "Mandy, I'll wager that you're a very good helper around the house."

The girl's face brightened. "I help Momma."

Minutes passed, growing into an hour or more, and still the bedraggled soldiers remained entrenched. Logan strolled about thirty feet away from the woman and girl, pretending to view the flowing waters. There he retrieved his PG-13 and was astounded to see that the numerals had dwindled to 01:17:48.

"Maybe they fell asleep," Rebekah said. She was standing behind him.

Without turning around, Logan slipped the device into its hiding place—not that such caution made much of a difference. She could have no conceivable grasp of what it might be.

He faced the eighteen-year-old woman and gave her a reassuring smile. "The important thing is that you weren't there."

She shuddered visibly at the thought. "I'm appreciative of what you've done for me, Mr. Gramm. And for Mandy, too."

"Is there anyone who could take you in? Any relatives near-by?"

"Not on my family's side."

"So, you're not from around here?"

"I was born in Buford, forty miles to the east. This is my dear husband's land." Her jaw began to tremble. "Nathaniel was killed two years ago." She took a deep breath, eyes filling with moisture. "And now these same murderers are plunderin' the house that he and his father built with their own hands."

"Why did you stay ... all by yourself like this?"

A single teardrop trickled down each cheek. "No Yankee skunks are gonna steal Nate's property. Not while I'm still alive to defend it."

Little Amanda, who had been playing in the dirt with a small stick, now wandered over to the others. "Momma, dose men kill?"

She wiped away the tears. "No, honey, of course not. We'll be goin' home soon. You'll see."

Logan knelt down and tickled the girl's stomach. "We won't let anything bad happen to you." Amanda giggled for a moment and then resumed scraping in the chalky soil.

Rebekah, too, seemed more at ease. She stood very near to Logan, their arms almost touching, while they both kept a watchful eye on the house. "What made you come here to help me?" she asked him. "Are you a friend of someone I know?"

"I can't tell you that."

"You knew my name, so you must be familiar with these parts."

"I'm just here to help."

Suddenly, as if from deep within, a glow of awe flashed across her face. She dropped to one knee and whispered, "Are you my guardian angel?"

Logan was tongue-tied. Staring down at her, he shook his head ever so slightly. But his denial was unconvincing.

He realized that this imperiled woman's reckoning was—in every sense that mattered—quite true to the mark. "Please stand up," he said. "I'm as mortal as you are, nothing more."

Scarcely ten minutes later, with a scant 00:31:06 showing on Logan's PGK device, the four Yankee deserters, apparently satisfied by their pilfered meal, crept from the temporary shelter of the Olney farmhouse. They headed in a southeasterly direction, passing to the onlookers' left and away from the advancing division of General Sherman, whom they loudly (and drunkenly) disparaged as "Uncle Billy." In the circumstances, they probably had cause to fear him even more than they feared the Rebels.

"Do you keep strong spirits in the house?" Logan asked the young woman.

"Two bottles, which my father-in-law gave to Nate."

"Sounds like they're empty by now."

After the renegades disappeared into a thick underbrush, hopefully never to be seen again, Logan ushered Rebekah and Amanda back to the violated sanctity of their house. The battered front door now hung askew, ripped loose from its lower hinge. Logan forced it aside far enough for entrance, and Rebekah took a visual inventory of the cabin's interior. The fugitive soldiers had broken two chair legs, eaten all of the foodstuffs from the pantry, drained two whole bottles of Kentucky bourbon, and (from the smell of it) urinated against the rear wall. It was chilling to contemplate what they might have done, had Mrs. Olney not been whisked from the reach of their prurient appetites.

A distant sound of horses could be heard, so Logan rushed to the east window to determine whether their riders were friend or foe. (How odd it was for this New Jerseyan to consider himself a Confederate.) Three civilians could be seen, racing their mounts at top speed toward the cabin. Logan sneaked a glance at his PG-13, aware that time was running very short. The countdown displayed 00:12:29.

Rebekah joined him at the window. "It's my brother-in-law ... Daniel!" she said. "I don't recognize the two men with him, though. Could be farmhands, I 'spose."

"Where does Daniel live?"

"With Nate's parents, over in Oak Grove."

"Can they take you and Mandy with them?"

"I don't know, but they sure do seem willin' to try." With a prettily smiling face that Logan had not seen before, Rebekah began readying Amanda for their short trek to Cherokee County. "Daniel's only fourteen, too young for military service," she said.

Again Logan went to the window. The galloping horses were raising clouds of dust, which naturally threatened to attract the attention of enemy eyes. And yet, that could not be helped. The lives of a stranded woman and child were of prime concern. He checked the countdown one more time: 00:08:57.

All three of them—Logan, Rebekah, and her little daughter—went outside to greet the rescuers. "Daniel!" the young lady shouted. "Am I happy to see you!"

"Howdy, Becky," the teenaged boy told her. "This here is Herbert Royster, and that's Micah Dempsey." Both men tipped their hats. "They're wranglers for the Rebs." Daniel beamed with grown-up pride.

"There's a shortage of horseflesh just now," Royster said. "That's why we had to bring these nags."

Rebekah motioned toward her new friend. "This is Logan Gramm. He's been a god-send to me and little Mandy. Just seemed to fall from the sky." Politely, the men nodded to each other.

"How come you're not in uniform?" one of the wranglers asked.

"Don't worry," Rebekah told him. "He just rescued me from some Yankee vermin."

"That so?" Daniel said.

Rebekah nodded her head. "Can Mr. Gramm come along, too? He saved me and Mandy from—"

Logan stopped her in mid-sentence. "I'm due to the south in short order. Hot action brewing down there, I think."

That sounded odd to Dempsey. "You're afoot, Mr. Gramm?"

"I can cover more ground that way, through the woods. And nobody can track me."

"Well, collect what you need," Daniel told his sister-in-law. "Figure on bein' gone for several weeks."

"Best of luck to you all," Logan said.

His shunning of the contraction "y'all" brought a chuckle from Rebekah, who announced that her friend was from New Jersey.

"We won't hold that against you," Royster told him, "considering that you're not wearin' blue."

Tears came to Rebekah Olney's eyes as she walked over to say goodbye. "May the Lord bless you, Mr. Gramm." She kissed him on the cheek. "I'll never forget what you've done for me."

"My pleasure, Mrs. Olney," he said.

"Do me a favor."

"Ma'am?"

Call me 'Becky' once, before you leave. That will seal our friendship."

"Okay ... Becky." He gave her a brotherly wink. "And you can call me 'Logan'."

"Very well ... Logan." Rebekah smiled at him, and for just an instant she was a blushing teenager again, instead of a war widow living far beyond her years.

Then they turned aside from one another forever.

Logan could sense that his allotted duration in 1864 was growing dangerously short, so he hurried around to the rear of the cabin's perimeter. Sure enough, the PG-13 had counted down to 00:02:07. The sound of horses' hooves could be heard, but he chose not to watch Rebekah Olney ride out of his life. He preferred to remember their brief moment of closeness and the touch of her sweet kiss on his cheek.

Just over two minutes later, Logan Gramm was standing wide-eyed in his Hoboken apartment, dazed by the novelty of time travel. It astonished him to think that he had actually set foot in Civil War America—while his temporary contemporary, Abraham Lincoln, was governing from just 550 miles to the northeast.

And yet, a festering doubt remained. Hard as he tried, he could not shake the suspicion that his symbiotic relationship with ProGrade Kronotechnix was just a bit too good to be true.

◆　◆　◆

The Wednesday night crowd at Scotty's Steakhouse was larger than its mid-week norm, so Logan had little opportunity to speculate about what challenges his next mission might bring or even what century he might be asked to confront. PGK clients were never invited to suggest their favorite epochs—nothing of the sort. All destinations were predicated upon the whims of staff researchers, of which there were said to be nearly three dozen. Now that he thought of it, that would be an interesting job for someone with his historical curiosity, but he was born countless years too soon.

Erin Duffy was second in line at one of the restaurant's six computer screens, waiting to input a food order before she brought a tray from the kitchen. Logan sneaked up from behind and tapped her on the shoulder. "Guess who."

She turned around. "Hey, Logan, did you ever think of that actor's name?"

"What actor?"

"The movie star who was eating in here a while back. The *Times* made such a big deal about his belated Broadway debut."

"Can't help you," he said. "I hardly ever go to the movies, and I've only been to one Broadway play in my whole life. Too expensive."

Erin took a deep breath, choosing her words with care. "I've been thinking about your social life lately. Don't take this wrong, but we should go see a show together sometime."

Logan squinted at her. "I'm not so sure that's a good idea."

"My goodness! Thank you very much."

"You know what I mean."

"It doesn't have to be a real date, if that bothers you," she told him.

"What also bothers me is a dire shortage of cash. My apartment rent is astronomical."

"Even over in Jersey?"

"Yep."

"Well, it was my idea, so I'll pay."

"Nope. Only if we go Dutch. I've got my pride, you know." His grin broke the tension.

"Okay then, Dutch it is." She stepped up to the computer screen.

"Incidentally, I hope you're talking about a movie, rather than a play," Logan said. "Broadway can cost a hundred bucks or more."

"Your choice. I'm a huge fan of both."

"And that's where you want to be someday, right? In front of your adoring public, either on the screen or on the stage."

"Both would be perfectly acceptable."

"Then I can tell everyone, 'I knew her when'."

"When I was hustling for tips at Scotty's," she said. "Anyway, keep it in mind, if your calendar isn't already full."

"I'll check. Maybe I can squeeze a date with you into the mix."

"Aha! So you *do* want it to be a date." She began prodding the touch screen.

He smiled at her, but she was looking the other way.

On Tuesday of the following week, both Logan Gramm and Erin Duffy had the night off from Scotty's Steakhouse, so they decided to take advantage of their mutual freedom to attend a show of some sort. She preferred Broadway, but he nixed that idea because of monetary concerns.

"Just a flick, if that's all right."

"I'll pay," Erin told him.

"Nope. Dutch or nothing."

And so they settled for a highly regarded movie that was screening at the closest multiplex to where they worked. The plan was to be outside the theater at 5:30. Logan was there on time, but Erin was not. He called her cell phone and left a message.

It was 6:15 when she finally made her appearance, out of breath from running. "Sorry! I was in a meeting. I saw that you called, but I couldn't answer or even send you a text."

"The movie started a half-hour ago," Logan said. "Do you want to go in late?"

"No, I never do that." Erin gave him a sheepish grin. "It's against my cinematic principles. Maybe there's something else playing."

"What kind of meeting was it?" he asked.

She grasped his arm and beamed. "I got a job!"

"In show biz?"

"Yes! Well, it's just as an extra—but on Broadway. Can you believe it?"

He smiled back. "Is it a musical?"

"Nope. Straight drama. It takes place in the early 1930s, and my role is to get out of a car, walk a few steps, and throw my hat into the air."

"Do you get to say anything?"

"I have three lines, so that's not exactly a supernumerary."

"What made them pick you?"

"Don't know," Erin told him. "I guess because I can walk and toss a hat in one motion."

"I'll bet looks had something to do with it."

She blushed. "I doubt that. You should have seen some of the girls who auditioned. Three or four of them were knockouts."

"You caught somebody's eye."

"Actually, one of those gals got a pretty major role. A lot better than mine. But still … "

Through a process of elimination, they finally settled upon the 6:35 showing of some romantic comedy, starring two of the hottest names in Hollywood—not that this was any guarantee of quality. As they stood in the ticket line, the lobby's oppressive air nearly made them swoon from the odor of buttered popcorn.

A troubling issue crossed Logan's mind, something buried in all the excitement. "You'll be staying with Scotty's, won't you?"

Erin looked away. "I'm afraid not. There are seven nightly performances—plus the Sunday matinée."

That hit Logan hard, but he tried not to show it. "Is this a full-time position? I mean, can you live off what they'll be paying you?"

"No way. And then there's the union dues. I'll need to find a part-time job to make ends meet."

He forced a smile. "At least it's a foot in the door. A star is born! Congratulations."

"You need to promise that you'll come see me."

"When does it open?"

"Not for five weeks yet. But they're already constructing the sets, and rehearsals start on Monday."

"Do you like the people?"

"I haven't met any of the cast—except that one girl—but the producer is a wonderful, gray-headed gentleman, and the stage director is very funny."

Logan and Erin went into the auditorium and endured what seemed like a dozen movie trailers. They sat next to each other, of course, and his arm went around her shoulders almost at once. She did not object, so he kept it there until the arm began to tingle from lack of circulation just before the main feature.

The rom-com was a real turkey—formulaic throughout and with inane, manipulative dialogue. No one in the real world spoke like that. This flick must have been written by a committee of ten. Still, Logan had reason enough to enjoy it. Who knew when, if ever, he would sit alongside Miss Erin Duffy again? He was sad to see the final credits roll.

"Let's get some Chinese take-out," he said.

"Isn't it too late?"

"Nope. I know a place that's open until eleven."

"Here or in Jersey?" Erin asked. She studied his reaction, which was evasive.

"Come on. I think you'll like it," Logan told her. "And you don't have to get up early in the morning."

"How did you know that?"

"Because you're scheduled to work the two-to-eleven shift tomorrow, and you haven't resigned from Scotty's yet."

Erin gave that some thought. "Just remember this isn't a real date."

"Scout's honor. I'll be on my best behavior."

"By the way, when's the last train back to Toidy-toid?" she asked him. "I don't want to get stranded in Hoboken."

"Not until 10:55. And the trip only takes about fifteen minutes." He was amused by the way she pronounced Thirty-third, impressed by her comedic flair for dialects.

Through the darkness they traveled by subway and PATH train to Logan's suburban neighborhood west of the Hudson River. After purchasing two Chinese dinners, they carried them up the steps to his third-story apartment. Immediately, he opened the curtains to reveal a postcard panorama of Manhattan, far off in the distance.

"Gorgeous view!" Erin said. "I never get to see the city from this angle."

"I'm certainly paying for it, which is why I may have to leave after my lease expires."

"Bummer! How come?"

"I expected to have a better-paying job by now."

"Doing what?" she asked.

"Teaching history—or writing about it. What a pipe dream that's turning out to be."

"You studied history in college?"

Logan nodded his head. "Unfortunately, a liberal arts degree isn't worth the sheepskin it's printed on these days."

"Well, maybe something will turn up. In the meantime, of course, there's always Scotty's."

He hoped what he said next would not come across as syrupy. "It won't be the same there without you."

Erin took it at face value. "I'll miss some of the good times we had," she told him. "But thinking back, it was mostly just drudgery, and the tips were not great."

"I can attest to that," Logan said. He began walking toward the refrigerator. "What goes well with Chinese?"

"Do you have any wine? This is sort of a celebration."

"Nope. Just soft drinks—Coke, Dr Pepper, Sprite."

"You pick. I like them all."

"Incidentally, the restroom is over there, if you want to wash up and/or use the facilities."

She did both and then came out holding what she thought was a TV remote. "You left this in there." It was the PG-13 from PROGRADE KRONOTECHNIX.

Logan tried to act nonchalant. "Oh, thanks." He held out his hand, but she was curious about the device.

"Why does it say 'PG-13'?" She giggled. "Does it censor adult programming for you?"

"I guess that's just a model number."

"And 'PG KRON' is the brand name?"

He nodded. "Korean, I think." Again he reached for the PG-13 in vain.

"What are these buttons—APPLY, RESUME, CURRENT, REFRESH, EMG FLR, PANIC, FLYWHEEL, CANVAS? Those don't seem like television terms."

"That's because it's not for a TV. Actually, this is a controller for a video game I play."

"I didn't know you were into gaming."

"Not very heavily. Someone gave it to me." Logan disliked telling falsehoods, but he had no other choice. Fortunately, Erin accepted his explanation without further comment and laid the PG-13 on the kitchen counter. Logan had no trouble maintaining his composure through this ticklish situation because he knew that nothing calamitous could possibly happen, even if the girl accidentally pressed a button or two. The identity sensor would protect the device's integrity, and Erin did not have a registered thumbprint to launch the operating system. Still, he was irked at his own carelessness for leaving the intriguing device in plain sight.

They ate their Chinese food at a table facing the bay window. Although it may have seemed that Logan concocted the cozy setting as a romantic lair, such was not the case. This was where he always dined, whether alone or in the company of friends. Somehow, it made him feel engaged with the Big Apple, while not having to pay a king's ransom for the privilege.

Logan walked Erin back to the PATH station too late to catch the 10:07, but another train for 33rd Street would be along at 10:22. The longer they waited on the platform, the more strained their conversation became. They would be seeing each other at work the next day, but after that, the future of their friendship was up in the air.

"When do you plan to tell Danny your news?" Logan asked.

"Tomorrow, right after I punch in at two. I'm sure he'll understand."

"Maybe, but that won't make it any easier on him."

Erin looked baffled. "Because the night shift will be short-handed?"

"No. I think he has a 'thing' for you."

"Really? I hadn't noticed."

"And so do two or three guys on the wait staff."

She blushed at the flattery. "Anyone I know?"

"Could be."

"Well, I hope they'll come to see me in my role on Broadway—negligible though it is."

"They probably will," he said, "if they don't want to lose contact."

Erin noticed a headlight far down the track. "Anyway, thank you for the movie and dinner."

"We went Dutch, remember? I should be thanking you just as much."

"But you supplied the table and chairs—and that awesome view of Manhattan. It topped off a very enjoyable evening." Erin looked up at him, wondering what would come next. But they did not kiss. When the train pulled into the station and slowed to a halt, she told him, "See you tomorrow at Scotty's."

"That'll be a sad day for all of us," Logan said, "but I'm happy for you."

· ◆ ◆

Several of the restaurant's television screens were carrying the Yankees game, and Logan paused from his duties as often as possible to keep track of the score. It was a good night at Camden Yards, what was shaping up to be a lopsided victory over the Orioles. That would stop a three-game skid and perhaps keep the Yanks within striking distance of the AL East lead.

Logan was filling some drink glasses for a table of eight when Erin caught his eye. "Well, I told Danny," she said, "and I don't think he was too pleased with me."

"He got mad at you?"

"A little. Maybe you were right about him. I could sense a personal vibe going on there—something beneath the surface."

"He didn't make a play for you, did he?"

"Oh, please! Danny Hibbert? I don't think he's ever spoken a complete sentence to any girl, unless it was to scream at her for spilling a tray."

Logan turned aside, intent on delivering the drinks. "Hey, you, don't leave without saying goodbye. Promise?"

"I won't. What kind of a pal do you think I am?" She winked at him and grinned.

For an instant, Logan imagined a personal vibe of his own, but he was too busy to give it much thought. Besides, he would probably never see her again after today.

In the end, Erin was as good as her word. Late that night, she walked up behind Logan as he was mopping his assigned quadrant of the dining room floor. Chairs were poised upside-down on the tabletops, and post-game recaps were showing on most of the screens.

"I suppose this is it, then," she said. "I'll be going now—for keeps."

He placed his mop back in the bucket of soapy water. "I hate for you to leave us, but I know this will kick start your career."

"I can only hope."

"When do you report to the theater?"

"Monday morning at nine. We'll be having a read-through and also do some blocking for the cast. That part will be easy for me—upstage, center—but of course I need to sit in on everything that happens."

"Have you ever acted before?"

"Not for a paycheck," she said. "Just some amateur stuff in high school and junior college. And two summers' worth of master classes in Upper Michigan."

"Where will you look for a part-time job?"

"Anything but food service, I guess."

"Burned out?"

"Not really, but the hours don't work very well—at least while my current gig is still on the boards." She smiled at him. "One of these days, I'll come back to eat at Scotty's and give all the customers a thrill. Big celebrity, you know."

"Ask for Logan Gramm because it looks like I'm stuck here. Are you a generous tipper?"

"The worst."

"On second thought, don't ask for me."

They both laughed, but then Erin became quite serious. "Well, goodbye, Logan. It was fun working with you." She held out her hand, and he shook it.

"Goodbye, Erin. I suppose this is when I'm expected to say, 'Break a leg'."

"And I may just do that, climbing out of the gangster's car every night." She pointed at him. "You must come see the play. It's your moral obligation ... to demonstrate your support of the arts."

"I'll do that. Please leave me a free ticket at the window ... to demonstrate your support of the poor."

Erin giggled at the remark, but only for an instant. With a sigh, she turned to leave, and Logan wondered whether he would ever see her again.

Just as he suspected, morale at the steakhouse declined with Erin's absence from the wait staff, and Logan was not the only one who suffered the dispiriting effects. Besides himself, a handful of the other servers—not to mention the night manager, Danny Hibbert, and his assistant, Derek Bowles—appeared to be downcast for more than a week after her departure. But time heals all wounds, and gradually the work environment returned to normal. Even Logan had days when he gave the girl no thought whatsoever. Other days were not so easy.

One thing that occupied Logan's mind was concern over his obligation to PROGRADE KRONOTECHNIX. Three weeks had passed since the company last contacted him, and surely his next mission was in the offing. A text finally arrived in the early morning hours of a Tuesday. Logan heard no chime because he always switched his iPhone to SILENT overnight. Upon awakening at daybreak, he noticed a 2:11 AM message that was worded in the same familiar style as before: <Contact PGK at once. Your Op-2 has been arranged.>

He wrote back and, hardly sooner than he touched SEND, along came a text reply. It was from agent Alejandro Vásquez, who suggested that they hold their session at 10:30 on Friday morning in an iconic New Jersey spot—Frank Sinatra Park on the Hudson River.

Logan was already standing outside Blue Eyes Restaurant when a dapper man in his forties, with sunglasses and a neatly trimmed mustache, strode purposefully toward him. "How long have you been waiting?" the man asked.

"Five or six minutes," Logan said.

"Then you were six or seven minutes early," Vásquez told him. "It's 10:29 right now, and these time coordinates don't lie." In his right hand, he was holding a PG-13, which he slipped into the royal blue PG KRON sport jacket. "Let's go over to that bench. We only have twenty-three minutes."

"Who programmed it for you?"

Vásquez seemed surprised by the question. "I don't know. Some female rigger, but I didn't catch her name."

"I just thought it might be somebody I know."

"Highly doubtful."

They sat on a bench at the crest of the park's Amphitheater. Far off in the distance sprawled Midtown Manhattan, highlighted by a stunning view of the Empire State Building.

The PG KRON agent opened his briefcase and pulled out a dossier. "Before we begin, I'll need your expired PG-13, please. He glanced at the paperwork. "It took you to Cobb County, Georgia—1864?"

"Yes, that's right."

"Successful run?"

"Can't say for sure, but I hope so. A woman's life was at stake … and her daughter's."

"Those are the meaningful ones," Vásquez said. He looked wistfully at the skyline. "I remember a few of them myself."

"How many missions did you have?"

"Two sets of five each."

"Where did you go on your recreational trip?"

"I'm not allowed to tell you that."

"Why not?"

"Because it's still in your future."

"So?"

"So, you're restricted to the past. Don't you remember signing this contract?" He studied a piece of paper and turned it over to the back side. "With a counter-signature by … Tamara Renée Hansen?"

"Oh, that."

Vásquez chuckled. "Yes, that. Maybe you should pull it out more often to refresh your memory."

"Do you know Tammi? Pretty girl, don't you think?"

"Never heard of her, so I really couldn't say."

Logan thought it strange that no one from PROGRADE KRONOTECHNIX ever seemed to know each other. Either it was such a large firm that people could not learn their colleagues' names or there was a regulation that prohibited talk about internal operations.

does not matter.

"Time to get down to business, Mr. Gramm," Vásquez told him. Into the briefcase he reached. "Here is your PG-13 for Op-2. The specs have been programmed by an anonymous rigger. I say that because I knew you would ask."

Logan smiled at his comment. "Does headquarters consider me a troublemaker?"

"Not particularly. We have much worse. But your profile does caution me that you possess what is described as an 'unhealthy curiosity'."

"Well, pardon me for being a serious historian."

"Don't take it personally," the agent told him. "Just an observation from the higher-ups. I'm sure we all have black marks in our profiles."

"Actually, I accept it as a compliment."

Vásquez searched through some papers and found what he wanted. "That's neither here nor there," he said. "What we need to discuss now is Philadelphia, summer of 1928. Unless you decline the PGK offer, which you are entitled to do, your next excursion will be to the so-called 'Roaring Twenties.' Interested?"

"Very."

"I thought that might get your attention. But this won't be all fun and glamor—far from it. You'll be dealing, tangentially at least, with a crime syndicate that is quite powerful and ruthless. Two brothers and their wives are in the crosshairs and don't even suspect anything. One of these men serves on the Board of Aldermen."

"I need to save him?"

"If possible, yes," Vásquez said. "As always, the tampering with historical fact must be minimal, in order to avoid ever-broadening repercussions. Your objective is to detain a mercenary killer named Joseph Bonner Doake, who has been hired to eliminate the alderman by assassination."

"He's a hit man?"

"In the vernacular." The agent handed Logan a photocopy of the man in question. "Memorize his appearance. Unless something goes terribly wrong, you won't be physically confronting J. B. Doake, but you need to know what he looks like. Your only mission is to stop him from leaving the ballpark until at least seventeen minutes after the final pitch. That will give the two couples ample opportunity to return to their homes unscathed."

"So, I take it, this is a baseball game?"

"Shibe Park in Philadelphia."

"How am I supposed to hold Doake for that long? I can't tie him to the backstop."

"You'll only have to delay him about a minute. That's when the four people finally drive away. Before that, they are outside the players' entrance, talking with a friend named Howard Ehmke. He's one of the Athletics."

Logan squinted at the agent. "How do you know all of this?"

"Our researchers are very skillful, as you may already have noticed."

"I can't argue with that."

The PGK agent paused for a moment, allowing some people to walk past. "Any other questions?" he asked.

Logan had one major concern. "Isn't this J. B. Doake armed?"

"No. His weapon of choice is a 1926 Nash. Doake has been ordered to force the two couples off the road and down an embankment—i.e., no circumstantial evidence, no eye-witnesses. The fact that four innocent people die in this 'mishap' is unimportant to the mob. It's all a nasty matter of city politics."

"Who's the alderman?"

"That's not for you to know," Vásquez said.

"How can I save someone, if you won't even give me his name?"

"The man's identity is beyond your purview. By design, we only burden you with details that you need to know."

"But if I save his life—along with three others—why isn't the mission rejected as a non-consequence?"

"Because these people's historical statures are minor enough to pass muster. We're not talking about Gandhi or Kennedy here."

Alejandro Vásquez consulted his PG-13. "Our time is running short, Mr. Gramm. Any other questions before I go?"

"Assuming I'm successful, can't Doake try to kill them again some other day?"

"He's on thin ice with the mob. He'll not get a second chance."

"What about 1920s clothing?"

"I've delivered that to your place in Hoboken. And, of course, a period wristwatch. You'll need it."

"How'd you get inside my apartment?"

Grinning, Vásquez held up his PG-13.

"Silly me," Logan said. "By the way," he added, "will I be in Philly early enough to see the whole game?"

"Certainly. Arriving late would attract too much attention. Just blend in with the other fans, that's all. And don't start too much of a conversation with this Doake fellow, or you'll be courting disaster. The most important thing is to be aware of the precise moment when those seventeen minutes have elapsed."

♦   ♦   ♦

Logan Gramm opened his eyes to find himself standing upon an oil-stained slab of concrete behind a clothing shop in Philadelphia. It appeared to be a loading dock of some kind, but no trucks were there. For that, he could thank the meticulous researchers at PG KRON. Somehow, they had discovered that the clothier's weekly delivery came on Thursday, and this was a Monday—May 28, 1928.

Upon walking around to the storefront, Logan saw a ballpark in the distance. People were already flocking there for the Athletics-Yankees game, which was scheduled to begin in just forty minutes. This would be the teams' sixth meeting in an exhausting span of five days, having played make-up doubleheaders on both Thursday and Friday. Sunday baseball was not yet sanctioned in the city, so the Yankees had taken that day off, but the A's used their "day of rest" for traveling by train to the nation's capital and a game at Griffith Stadium, where Sunday baseball was permitted. The Senators beat them, 4-1, behind the two-hit pitching of twenty-three-year-old Bump Hadley.

Philadelphia's Shibe Park was a rather young stadium, having opened its doors just in time for the 1909 season. It occupied a large city block—bounded by 20th and 21st Streets, between Lehigh Avenue and Somerset Street. Logan purchased a premium ticket for $1.25 and made his way inside through the 21st Street entrance. That was the closest gate to the third-base dugout, where the Athletics held court and—more to the point— behind which Joseph Bonner Doake would be cheering for the home team before departing on his nefarious deed.

J. B. Doake was not difficult to spot. As the photocopy suggested, he wore muttonchops, a felt homburg, and wire-rimmed glasses. But contrary to Logan's expectations, the hit man seemed very friendly to those around him, not at all how a gangster would behave in the movies. And he knew baseball, too, observing the game with an expert's discerning eye.

"Bunt him over, Connie!" Doake would shout. "Can't you see how deep Dugan's playing?" And "That would've been a triple on good legs, Tyrus!" And "Lefty, you can't hang a letter-high curveball to Poosh-'Em-Up! You know better than that."

Meanwhile, Logan Gramm—himself something of a student of baseball history—could not believe his good fortune at being placed in this particular setting. The fabled New York Yankees were in town, closing out their six-game road trip to Philadelphia, and the "Murderers' Row" lineup included such household names as Ruth, Gehrig, Lazzeri, Meusel, Combs, and Durocher.

The Athletics were no slouches, either. Lefty Grove was on the mound, Mickey Cochrane behind the plate, and the outfield was probably the greatest ever assembled—in terms of Cooperstown credentials, that is. From left to right, they were Al Simmons, Tris Speaker, and Ty Cobb, though the latter two were well past their peaks of performance. And, as if that were not enough, a promising youngster in the person of third baseman/catcher/first baseman Jimmie Foxx would be available for duty as a pinch hitter.

So enthralled was the transient from New Jersey that, for several innings, he allowed himself to ignore his reason for being at Shibe Park in the first place. Could this really be happening? To experience the physical presence of Babe Ruth and Lou Gehrig was unthinkable for anyone born after the Hoover administration, and yet here they were. Ruth played left field for the Yankees on this day, a decision that manager Miller Huggins often made because of Babe's inability to follow a fly ball's trajectory through the blinding sun. That meant he stood a scant two hundred feet away when the Athletics were at bat. Logan could actually hear the Bambino shouting to his teammates and exchanging good-natured gibes with the rival fans behind him.

J. B. Doake heard Ruth's comments, too, and he was not polite in his response to them. Apparently, ballpark attendants in 1928 were more tolerant of unsavory language than they would become later in the century. This was a typically rowdy Philadelphia crowd, tempered only by a few soft-spoken women who were sprinkled among the boisterous, cigar-smoking alpha males.

The game itself had plenty to enjoy—if you were a Yankees fan. Combs and Durocher each collected three singles, and Ruth, Lazzeri, and Dugan had two hits apiece, including home runs by the latter pair. Gehrig singled, too, driving home an additional run. As for the vaunted Athletics outfielders, they produced an RBI-single by Speaker, a double by Cobb, and a three-run homer in the third inning by Simmons.

Joe Dugan's two-run clout came in the ninth off Ike Powers, and that gave New York a comfortable 11-4 lead. By then, Logan was only half-watching the action, determined instead to focus his attention on the mercenary's slightest move. When Yankee reliever Archie Campbell induced third baseman Jimmy Dykes to pop up to Gehrig for the game's final out, Logan consulted his wristwatch. The game had taken 2:26 to complete, about average for that era. His mission now was to make certain that Doake did not depart from the ballpark for something over a quarter-hour.

As the minutes passed, he began to wonder whether the PG KRON intelligence was accurate. Doake exhibited no inclination to leave his seat, calmly chatting with other fans while police officers secured the diamond and a two-man ground crew made their usual post-game repairs to the home plate area, pitcher's mound, and base paths.

Not until the eight-minute point did Doake finally ascend the aisle, and even then he appeared to be in no hurry whatsoever. Clearly, he was following four other fans, one of whom must have been the alderman. Logan did likewise, trying to act as casual as possible. Outside the ballpark went the hit man, passing through the same gate that Logan had entered some three hours earlier.

Doake proceeded along the perimeter of the mammoth structure, stopping amidst a large group of garrulous people. They were visiting with a ballplayer who lingered near some parked automobiles. Logan heard one of the onlookers say, "Mr. Ehmke," and the hurler nodded his head with a smile. Howard Ehmke was already in his street clothes, not having broken a sweat that day, for he was not due to pitch again until Wednesday in Boston. Some of those around him seemed to know Ehmke personally because their chatter was on familiar terms.

Logan joined in the chorus of admirers and was able to put his fore-knowledge to good use. Aware that he would be encountering this six-foot-three pitcher after the game, he had conducted some preliminary research to make himself sound more convincing.

"How are you and Cobb getting along?" he asked. "I know you weren't on the best of terms in Detroit."

Ehmke looked in surprise at him but did not reply. Instinctively, Logan changed his approach. "I still think you threw consecutive no-hitters, by the way. One of my friends was at Yankee Stadium in '23 and swears that first-inning grounder was an error."

That made Ehmke grin. "Thank you for the word of support, friend. Shanks still feels bad about it because the ball did hit his glove."

"Even Tommy Connally, the umpire, said as much."

Ehmke, a soft-spoken teetotaler, just shook his head and added, "Well, I made an error, too—so I can't complain—but I also got three hits to Howie's none!"

Logan glanced down at his wristwatch: one and a half minutes to go. When he looked up again, he saw that the politician—whom someone greeted as "Your Honor"—had begun climbing into a car with his brother and their two wives, while Doake was walking quickly toward his own vehicle. Suspecting nothing, the brother put his car into gear and then waited at the exit for the cross traffic to clear. Joseph Bonner Doake was not far behind, but with a respectable distance in between. Obviously, he planned to remain in visual contact until that split second when he could make his deadly move, causing the other automobile to swerve out of control.

Just as the first car pulled onto the street, Logan went into action—stepping in front of the second car with his arms waving. "You have a puncture, sir!" he shouted.

Doake hit the brakes.

Logan gestured frantically and shouted over the engine noise. "A puncture!"

The driver jumped out and ran to the left rear tire, where this considerate bystander had seemed to point. That was when Logan used his pocket knife to slash the tire that was diagonal to it.

"No, sir, the front right!" he shouted.

Sure enough, the inner tube was deflated, and this automobile was in no condition to travel beyond the nearest service station.

Logan contrived a suitable look of compassion. "Sorry, sir. I could see how low it was and didn't want you to get stranded."

J. B. Doake, the would-be hit man, responded with a sneering look. "Thanks a lot, kid," he said. "You've been a big help." Then he gazed into the distance, down 21st Street past Lehigh Avenue.

His prey had eluded him, and the Organization (as it was called) did not accept failure with a generous spirit. Now Doake himself had become a marked man, for bunglers were not granted another chance. Philadelphia was the big leagues in more ways than baseball.

The countdown display on Logan Gramm's PG-13 indicated that he would depart in precisely 00:06:17, which allowed him to amble back for a more leisurely look at the entrance to this innovative, steel-and-concrete stadium—something he would never again be able to do. Dominating the structure's ornate, French Renaissance style was an octangular tower that rose atop its southwest corner, near the office of owner/manager Connie Mack. It was a majestic sight, particularly since there were no light standards to mar the sweeping roofline. Night baseball at Shibe Park would not arrive for another eleven years to come, the first American League ballpark to have lights.

As Logan waited in a secluded alcove for the final few seconds of his Op-2 to expire, he pondered what this mission had accomplished, and an intriguing thought occurred to him. Now that the deaths of four innocent people were averted, any *Philadelphia Inquirer* article that once appeared in print about the fatal crash had instantly vanished without a trace. It never existed.

The mysterious properties of time travel continued to fill him with wonder.

✦　✦　✦

Following the last full day of rehearsals, the Hersey-Vann Theatre had gone dark for the evening, but there would be commotion aplenty when 8:30 PM rolled around again. Opening night was always the epicenter of Broadway excitement, and the unveiling of Vernon Arthur's play, *Murder at Wit's End*, was not likely to be an exception to the rule—particularly with philanthropist C. Archibald Finney's millions invested in a newly minted, failsafe triumph. The two stars, Haven Belling and Marjorie Anderson, had teamed up twice before and were on record as saying that their latest collaboration would be the best yet.

This particular premiere—just over twenty hours away— would also be Erin Duffy's professional debut, so a great deal rested upon her performance, even if the role was minor. She presumed that her mild case of stage fright was perfectly normal for someone so inexperienced. Maybe she could channel it into a positive force, building upon such nervous energy to generate a personal magnetism that might reach across the footlights. That was her plan anyway.

But tonight she needed some companionship, a friend who was able to shore up her confidence prior to the steady approach of curtain time. Erin had not seen Logan Gramm for over a month—ever since she quit her job at Scotty's Steakhouse—so now she texted him at work, wondering whether he might want to renew acquaintances on a short jaunt from the deserted theater to her underground station.

He texted back, <As soon as I wring out my dirty mop. Unlike you, I'm not in the glamorous world of showbiz!>

It was well after eleven o'clock as they strolled along Seventh Avenue that night, but the sidewalks remained heavily populated. "The city that never sleeps" was living up to its reputation.

"I couldn't get you a ticket for the gala premiere," Erin told him, "but there were a few left for our Sunday matinée. Not bad, either—twenty-ninth row, just right of center. Too far back to see many details, but at least you'll be in the house." She chuckled. "And I don't think there's a pillar directly in front of your seat."

"Just so I have an unobstructed view of the gun moll," Logan said, "or whoever it is you're playing."

"Actually, my character is a good girl—except kind of shallow in the head, if you ask me. It's hard to construct a personality on the basis of three lines of dialogue."

"No back story?"

"Not in the script, but of course a good actress will invent one to flesh out the humanity—making the person more believable to an audience. At least that's what my drama teachers always preached to us."

They climbed aboard the subway and passed by no fewer than seven stations before her stop. "This is mine," she told him. "Want to come in with me? I'm so stressed out that I can't sleep anyhow, and I could use the company."

He shook his head. "My last train to Jersey is 11:25."

"Oh, please do. You can have some coffee in the bargain, if you don't mind decaf."

"Where would I sleep?"

"The couch opens into a bed. My sister has used it before, and she says it's not too terribly uncomfortable."

They stepped off the train, and Erin escorted him for a block and a half to her tiny third-floor apartment. When she switched on the overhead lights, Logan saw at once that this girl possessed a decorative *savoir faire* far beyond anything he could ever hope to achieve. What the apartment lacked in square footage was more than offset by artistic panache.

Her favorite period was Art Deco, and that explained why the two rooms were filled with replicas of Depression-era paintings, posters, and sculptures. "Even the play I'm in fits that description," she said. "It's set in the early 1930s."

"Do you feel like you're living through those days?"

"No, I can't honestly say that. There's too much behind-the-scenes reality to remind us that we're still in the present—a shouting director, costumes that don't fit quite right, a prop or backdrop that doesn't function properly. Little things like that kind of ruin the illusion for us on stage. Sometimes I do wish I could go back, though."

That intrigued him. "How come?" he asked.

"I'm not sure. I think my personality just blends into that period of time, so I would feel at home there. Then again, maybe I'm just a sucker for the artwork." She gestured toward a table with eight sculptures. "Do you like any of these?"

Logan was ignorant of art history, but he did have a certain aesthetic sensibility. He stared at the *objets d'art* from every angle. "My favorite is probably that one," he told her. He was pointing at a sixteen-inch bronze figurine.

"That is *The Dolly Sisters* by Demétre Chiparus, a Rumanian sculptor who lived in Paris between the world wars. Supposedly, it depicts identical twins from Hungary who were a dancing sensation in the teens and twenties. It's one of my favorites, too, but don't ask me to single out one piece above the others. I would feel very disloyal in doing that."

They sat at the kitchen table with cups of hot coffee in front of them. On the CD player was Howard Hanson's *Romantic Symphony*, which Erin claimed to hear at least once a week, "just to keep my sanity." Hanson composed it in 1930, for conductor Serge Koussevitzky, to celebrate the Boston Symphony Orchestra's fiftieth anniversary. "A musical equivalent to Art Deco does not exist," she said, "but in my estimation, this work comes about as close as any other. Some people favor Aaron Copland's score for *The City*, but I'm not so sure."

"The Empire State Building is Art Deco, isn't it?" Logan asked.

Erin flashed a radiant grin. "Yes, indeed! How did you know that?"

"Just a wild guess. It resembles some of the artwork in here. So does the Chrysler Building."

"You have a good eye. Maybe there's hope for you yet."

Logan was impressed by how this girl's pretty smile could light up a room. That innate charisma would be a definite plus in her attempt to establish a career on the stage. Many an audition might be won on the sheer strength of charm alone, and perhaps that is how she landed her current role, despite the disadvantage of a thin résumé.

After the finale of Hanson's symphony came to a pulse-pounding conclusion, they devoted eighty-seven minutes to streaming a film—*Death at a Funeral*, Frank Oz's brilliant comedy from 2007. And then, as if sleep were an alien concept to them, the pair spent another hour playing the video game *L.A. Noire* on her PC. Again, the girl voiced a preference for bygone days, though she made no further attempt to articulate why she felt that way.

The clock showed 2:45 AM before Erin was finally ready to call it a night. Her eyelids became heavy, and she could not stop yawning. "Time for little girls and boys to go to bed." She motioned toward the couch. "Grab one end, and I'll help you unfold it." That accomplished, she disappeared into the bathroom without so much as a nod of farewell, leaving her guest to improvise his own accommodations. At least this skirted the issue of a goodnight kiss. Maybe that was her intent.

When Logan awoke at 7:50, after less than five hours of sleep, Erin was not to be found. She had left a handwritten note on the table where their empty coffee cups still sat. "Stay as long as you want, sleepy head. Feel free to eat some cereal. I'll be at the theater all day long. The entire company will have a light meal together—and then the WORLD PREMIERE of *Murder at Wit's End*. That's rather scary! Thanks for helping me make it through the night. Erin."

◆　◆　◆

Scotty's Steakhouse was crowded that evening, it being a Friday, so Logan did not give his friend's professional stage debut as much consideration as it probably deserved. At a quarter past nine, he wondered whether her three lines of dialogue had been declaimed yet. He knew it was a three-act play, but he could not recall which act was "hers," if indeed she had ever told him. Hustling for tips kept him too busy for much thought about anything else.

Upon opening the door to his apartment at five past eleven, Logan was startled to see a suitcase standing next to the coffee table. That was surely the work of PROGRADE KRONOTECHNIX, from whom he had not heard a peep in several weeks. Maybe this meant that his Op-3 was imminent. Curious about the grip, he clicked its latch aside and peeked at the contents. What he saw was 1940s attire—that much he could tell—but no other clue was evident.

He rang Erin's cell phone, but the only answer was her voicemail prompt. Depending upon how prolix Vernon Arthur had been when he crafted *Murder at Wit's End*, the play may not yet have reached its final *dénouement*. Some contemporary dramas were known to test their patrons' endurance for upwards of two hundred minutes. Allowing for that, Logan would try Erin again in an hour or so—hopefully after three or four waves of curtain calls had subsided.

Meanwhile, he heard the sound of a *ding*, signaling that a text message had arrived on his iPhone. In view of the suitcase, this sender's identity came as no surprise. Nor did the wording, which was impersonal and businesslike: `<Contact PGK at once. Your Op-3 has been arranged.>` He texted back and immediately received instructions to meet agent Deidra Hutchins at 12:15 the following afternoon in the Johnny Rockets restaurant at Second and Washington. He was also reminded to bring his expired PG-13, which could be recycled for someone else's journey into the past.

The nostalgic diner's interior harkened back to the malt shops of the 1950s, with black-and-white checkered flooring and fire-engine-red furniture. Jukebox players adorned many of the silver metallic tabletops.

"Logan Gramm?" a female voice asked. It belonged to a dignified lady in her fifties who was standing just inside the front door.

Logan walked over to her. "And you're Deidra?"

"Deidra Hutchins, yes. I've read a lot about you, Mr. Gramm." That seemed rather prosaic to Logan, seeing as how she was referring to the same stale résumé and biography that all PGK agents were issued before interacting with him. "Shall we go over to that booth?" she asked.

Logan nodded. "How long do you have? I know you PG KRON folks are always on the clock."

"Time is our job," Deidra told him. She smiled, proud of her clever remark. "To answer your question, I'll be here for another forty-seven minutes and twenty seconds."

He followed her across the room, and they sat facing each other in one of a dozen identical booths. A waiter brought menus, but Deidra was more interested in what songs were available on the jukebox. "Pardon me, Mr. Gramm, but I'm an amateur historian when it comes to popular music."

Logan looked at the titles. "These are even historical to me," he said. "Most of them are over sixty years old." He stared at Deidra for a moment and then glanced at the waiter, who was patiently watching them from behind the counter. Finally, Logan spoke up. "Are we going to eat, or is this just a business meeting with ice water?"

"We'll grab a bite of something, and I'll even pay." She continued looking at the music. "Not too extravagant, though. The federal government frowns upon profligate spending."

"Since when?" he asked. She saw no humor in the comment.

The waiter approached their table while trying to remain cheerful. "Shall I come back when you've decided?"

"Yes, please," Deidra said. After she finished thumbing through the selection of songs—swinging the pages back and forth within a glass case—she looked directly at Logan for a moment, studying him. "Now, down to business. Have you ever heard of 'The Battle of Los Angeles'?"

"Yes."

"Tell me what you know about it."

"A couple of months after Pearl Harbor, southern California was thought to be under enemy attack, so anti-aircraft units launched some heavy firepower."

"How would you like to be there when it actually happens?"

"Absolutely. What's my mission?"

"To save someone from a disfiguring injury. That's all you need to know."

"Why is PG KRON so interested in this person?"

Without a word, Deidra offered the same patented PGK smile that he had seen so many times before. It was almost as if the firm's agents took a qualifying course in how to remain enigmatic.

"Hungry?" she asked. Only now did she finally get around to perusing the menu. She ordered a hamburger, fries, and milk shake for each of them. "This is your third op, Mr. Gramm, so I don't need to go into great detail about what is expected of you. Just do your assigned task, and let the course of history take care of itself. You'll probably never know how successful you were."

"I'm getting used to that."

The waiter brought their meals to the table, and Deidra became silent until the young man was out of hearing range.

"By the way, don't worry about taking the suitcase I delivered," she said. "This will be a very short visit. You'll leave tomorrow at 12:32 PM, carrying with you this PG-13 and some identification that you might—"

"I can't leave tomorrow."

"I beg your pardon."

"I'm not available tomorrow."

She seemed annoyed. "Why is that?"

"I'm planning to attend a Broadway play tomorrow afternoon, and I can't miss it. This is a personal matter."

"Easily fixed," Deidra told him. "We'll just have your return time moved earlier, so nobody will even know you've been away."

"Sorry, but I need to see this Broadway show before I leave for the war."

Deidra shook her head and sighed. "All right. If it's that important. You are a volunteer, after all." She picked up her PG-13. "Let me log into these coordinates. Hang tight."

Logan watched as the agent pressed some buttons on the device. A split second later, she was no longer sitting in the booth but standing alongside it. "Oops, sorry," she said. "Pretty close, but I'm no rigger." She sat back down and put a couple of French fries into her mouth. "We're all set. I had your Op-3 switched to a Monday morning departure at 8:24." She handed Logan his reprogrammed PG-13.

"How long were you gone?" he asked.

"Just now?"

"Yes."

"About forty-five minutes. It took me that long to find a rigger who could adjust your departure time."

"The rigger didn't happen to be Tamara Renée Hansen, did she?"

"Who?"

"Tammi Hansen."

"I'm not familiar with that name."

"And you wouldn't tell me, even if you were."

Deidra grinned. "What do you think?" She took a sip of her strawberry shake.

◆　◆　◆

The Hersey-Vann Theatre was teeming with activity. Early buzz for *Murder at Wit's End* was quite favorable, with positive reviews in both of New York's major newspapers. One hailed the play as "a breezy, speakeasy romp," while the other saw it as "a *thug*fest of zingers and social commentary."

Logan Gramm's ticket—for the third performance in what promised to be a long run—placed him in the middle of the twenty-ninth row, between a gaunt gentleman who surely weighed less than ninety pounds and a plus-size matron whose girth barely squeezed between the armrests. His vision of the stage was unobstructed, for a tiny lady with a shaved head sat directly in front of him. That came as a pleasant surprise because usually he was behind André the Giant.

When the houselights went down, the realist set was bathed in a gray fog of Prohibition angst. The stage action began with a cop walking his beat, but he almost immediately passed from view, giving the streets over to the anarchy of everyday life. Costumes were topical: edgy, double-breasted pin-striping for the bootleggers, and slinky, waistless gowns for the bobbed-haired *femmes fatales*.

There was more humor in the dialogue than Logan anticipated from the online critics, who seemed to hear nothing but grim, bullet-ridden threats. Act One flew by in a flurry of scene changes that introduced the principal personae, wove a tale of jealousy and revenge, and awed the audience with some skyscraper backdrops that defied belief. No expense was spared in bringing a quality product to fulfillment, thanks mainly to financier C. Archibald Finney and his consortium of investors.

The first intermission prompted Logan to wander toward the aisle after stepping past the elderly man to his left. He mingled among the well-dressed crowd, many of whom took full advantage of the opportunity to visit one of the two wet bars. Logan even ascended the stairs, curious to see how the drama would appear from balcony level. Blinking globes, recessed into the ornate ceiling, alerted him that it was time to return to his seat, and he narrowly made it back there before the curtain went up for the second act.

Ten minutes later, an actual 1930s limousine, midnight black in color, entered the scene and halted upstage, center. Out climbed a sassy brunette who tossed her hat high into the air and hollered, "Eat your heart out, Bobby Creel!" Onlookers surrounded the girl, but she stepped atop the car's running board and spewed defiance. "There ain't a soul in this town who's gonna keep me from clawin' to the top—not Bobby or no one!" When somebody on the street cried out, "Hey, loudmouth, what makes you so special?" the girl pointed a finger at her accuser and spouted back, "Because I'm Tony Martini's best gal, that's what. Look at how his kisses smeared my lipstick!"

And that was it. She hopped down, submerged beneath the maelstrom of Manhattan life, never to be seen again. This character's name was not spoken on stage, but Vernon Arthur consistently referred to her as "Rosalind (Rosie)" in the cast list and stage directions, perhaps to facilitate union membership or actor credits. Evidently, the playwright of *Murder at Wit's End* was more practical than most others in his profession.

After the final curtain, it was a couple minutes shy of five o'clock when Erin Duffy finally came forward to the seating area and greeted the only person who had attended the play just to see her. "What did you think?" she asked. "Be honest, now. I can take it."

"Best Actress in a Supporting Role," Logan said.

"Oh, sure. Miss Rosie stole the show." She gave him a bashful smile. "Sorry to drag you down here for three measly lines, but it means a lot to me that you came."

"Glad to. And there's another show tonight?"

"At eight thirty. No rest for the weary. Maybe I'll get it perfect this time."

"You sounded fine to me."

"I felt like I was kind of mumbling. A 'Noo Yawk' accent doesn't come naturally to an Irish girl like me. Rosie Novello was born in the Bronx."

He squinted at her. "How do you know that?"

"The back story, remember? I made up a whole lifetime for her—orphaned at three, raised by a gangster named Novello, high school drop-out, shameless gold-digger, and diehard Yankees fan."

"Very professional."

"I'd better be, now that I've lost my amateur standing." She started walking toward the exit, and he kept pace alongside.

"Have you found a full-time day job yet?" Logan asked.

"No, and something needs to turn up pretty soon because my savings are getting depleted. There's really not much money in playing Tony Martini's best gal for a living."

"Maybe it'll lead to more auditions."

"That's my hope, but the theater is a fickle lady."

"How much do Haven Belling and Marjorie Anderson pocket?"

"More than enough to live on, I'm sure. That's where I would like to be in about five years."

"Playing opposite Haven?"

Erin pretended to gag. "Hardly. No, Marj can have him all to herself, for what little I care." A sudden thought caused her to stop. "Speaking of Haven, he's throwing a cast party tonight, and everybody will be there. Want to come?"

"Can't. I have an appointment in the morning."

"Early?"

"At 8:20."

"Is it a job interview?" She caught herself, embarrassed. "Sorry to be so nosy, but I've been hoping you could find something at a college—you know, in history."

"No such luck." He grinned at the irony. In a very real sense, this trip was to be the very essence of history—living it for himself.

Logan Gramm and Erin Duffy enjoyed a meal together and then went their separate ways, she back to the theater for a Sunday night performance of *Murder at Wit's End* and he back to his apartment's computer for some internet prepping on the Japanese air raid that never was.

♦ ♦ ♦

The last week of February 1942 was punctuated by a surreal incident that brought the war home to residents of southern California as no newsreels or radio reports could do. This outlandish phenomenon began shortly after 3:00 AM on February 25, a series of inexplicable developments that would come to be known as "The Battle of Los Angeles."

Nerves of Angelinos were already badly shaken. Only eleven weeks had passed since the bombing of Pearl Harbor, and the war news was bleak. Los Angeles, with its Pacific Coast locale, dense population, and industrial might, was considered to be a prime target for another air strike. A couple of hours past midnight on that Wednesday, ground spotters detected a flying object streaking across the sky from Santa Monica to Long Beach, and Army analysts suspected that this mysterious aircraft may have been of enemy origin.

Appearing in the vicinity at 2:47 AM was Logan Gramm, placed by PGK coordinates near the intersection of Hawthorne and Carson in the Los Angeles County settlement of Torrance. His instructions were clear: to prevent two automobiles from colliding on West Carson Street, about one hundred eighty feet east of Hawthorne Boulevard, at precisely 03:21:36. A blackout order had been issued, so traffic would be traveling in virtual darkness along the roadway, tempting fate with precarious driving conditions. Although a wartime speed limit of thirty-five miles per hour was in effect, motorists fell short of unanimity in abiding by that national statute.

Acting quickly, Logan stepped off sixty paces along Carson's asphalt shoulder and then waited, PG-13 in hand. He heard a vehicle of some sort approaching from the east, but he was unable to see it. This could not be one of the two ill-fated cars, however, because sixteen minutes still remained before the collision. Sure enough, the pick-up truck rattled by without incident.

There was an occasional display of thunder and lightning in the distance, well to the south, toward San Pedro. That was where an Army installation, Fort MacArthur, stood as a sentinel to defend the West Coast from enemy attack. But precipitation was not in the weather forecast, so this had to be something different, something man-made and far more foreboding. Suddenly, the skies illuminated.

Logan gazed upward at eight or ten searchlights, all of which seemed to be trained on a single moving object directly above. Almost simultaneously, the big guns from Fort MacArthur erupted with a vengeance, and tracers filled the heavens. Even so, the strange target persisted in flying across the darkness, southeastward along the shoreline, in the menacing direction of Terminal Island and its adjacent city of Long Beach. How could anything possibly withstand such a barrage of rapid-fire artillery?

That was when Logan noticed a faint clanking sound, like metal raining down from high above. The noise became progressively louder until a particularly jarring thud made him dive for cover. He was being bombarded by a shower of hot shrapnel, falling from what had become an apocalyptic sky.

The time traveler lay in a ditch by the side of the road, arms covering his head, until he sensed that this flying object's course was no longer drawing fire overhead. Logan's PG-13, toned down to its dimmest setting, told him that the minutes were running short. He could now begin to scrutinize the oncoming vehicles—of which there were very few in the wee hours—hoping against hope to save them from a deadly crash. For an extended period, nothing whatsoever approached, but then, at 03:20:58, he heard a suspicious sound from the east. This had to be the westbound car in question because another vehicle had just turned left from Hawthorne and was now proceeding in the opposite direction, out of its proper lane, down the middle of the road.

Logan had only a few seconds to respond. He pressed a button labeled EMG FLR and laid his PG-13 in the center of West Carson Street. Instantly, a sequence of strobe flashes and multi-colored beams burst forth from the unit. Were this an actual air raid, such a strategy might have been suicidal, but Logan's prior knowledge of the event assured him otherwise. And the plan worked to perfection. Drivers of both cars—alerted by the emergency flare to watch for impending danger—slowed down to under ten miles per hour and passed each other with plenty of clearance to spare.

But those two blessed souls, oblivious to their deliverance, were not the only motorists who observed Logan's warning lights. A squad car of the California Highway Patrol hastened to the scene as well, its uniformed driver determined to investigate who had so flagrantly violated the blackout restrictions. It was quite possible that this saboteur was attempting to signal the enemy aircraft, although exactly why the Empire of Japan would choose to obliterate a lonely stretch of pavement in Torrance was unclear.

When a flashlight shone in Logan's eyes, he realized that there was no way to escape. He raised his hands in surrender, was frisked, arrested, and transported to the nearest Sheriff's Department sub-station. Once inside, he was taken to a musty, windowless room, ordered to remove his fedora hat, and interrogated by two stern-faced CHP lawmen. Judging from the gruff tone of his inquisitors' voices, the sting of Japanese treachery remained fresh in their minds.

"What is this instrument I'm holding?" an officer asked.

Logan could see that it was the PG-13. "It's a highway flare, sir, used for emergencies."

"Is that what this was, an emergency?"

"Yes, sir."

"Explain."

"Two cars would have collided," Logan said, "badly injuring both occupants."

"How can you possibly know that?"

"Just an educated guess."

"And how does this thing work?"

"Press the 'Emergency Flare' button: E-M-G-F-L-R."

The officer declined to do so. "We'll have our demolition men take a look."

Logan knew that the device would not function anyway—not without his own thumbprint for re-activation. "It isn't a bomb, sir, if that's what you were wondering."

Across the shabby room, a detective retrieved the subject's identification papers from a state government envelope, where they had been placed by the arresting officer. "It says here your name is Logan Gramm," he said.

"That's correct."

"From Hoboken, New Jersey."

"Yes, sir."

"What brings you to Los Angeles?" He pronounced the city name with a hard 'g'.

Logan knew that all he had to do was delay for another six minutes, until 04:19:27, and he would be free. "I'm looking for work at an aircraft plant."

"Is that so?"

"Yes, sir."

"Which one?"

"Any that will have me."

"Why were you walking along West Carson Street in Torrance? Is there an aircraft plant there?"

"No, sir. I was getting some fresh air and thought the road looked dangerous to traffic."

"Do you always carry an emergency flare with you?"

"No, sir. That was just a fortuitous circumstance."

"A what?"

"Somebody's good luck—whoever was driving those cars."

The officer spoke up again. "Do you speak German?"

"No, sir."

"G-R-A-M-M is a German name, if I am not mistaken. Isn't that right?"

"I believe so, but I'm three-quarters English," Logan said. "It just happened that my paternal grandfather was of German stock."

"Be that as it may, do you hold any allegiance to the Fatherland or to the Führer?"

"None at all. Hitler is a criminal and should be shot."

"Are you a member of the German American Bund?"

"No, sir. I've heard of it, but I don't subscribe to its principles."

"Do you consider Charles Lindbergh to be a hero?"

Logan paused for a few seconds, careful not to blunder. "I once did, when Lindbergh landed in Paris," he said. "But I don't think so any more. He's an isolationist."

The detective shuffled through some papers. "You were only nine or ten at the time—of Lindy's flight, I mean—and yet you have vivid memories of it."

"What's so strange about that? I saw the newsreels. All of my family did."

"How many brothers and sisters do you have?"

"One of each."

The detective checked that claim and found it to be accurate. "Are your parents still alive?"

"Yes, sir."

"Both of them?"

"Yes, sir."

"Do they live in New Jersey?"

"No, sir. They live in Pennsylvania." That, too, checked out. "How come you're not in uniform? It says here that you're twenty-four and able-bodied."

"My number hasn't come up yet."

"And you did not bother to enlist."

"No, sir."

"Why not?"

"I'm in school."

"Oh? Where?"

"PCC, near the Rose Bowl—Pasadena City College."

"Never heard of it."

"I meant Pasadena Junior College. Jackie Robinson went there."

"Who?"

Logan closed his mouth. These breakneck questions were tricky, which was probably their design.

The detective's tone of voice eased a bit. "Care for some coffee, Mr. Gramm?" he asked. His words had become friendly and polite, perhaps to soften up the suspect.

"No, thank you," Logan told him, "but I could use your facilities, if that's permissible." Hearing no response, he added, "The restroom. I need to relieve myself."

The detective glanced at his superior officer, who gave a curt nod of the head. "But make sure his pockets are empty."

"They are." The detective pointed toward a battered door with chips of paint missing. "Make it quick. We need to get fingerprints and a mug shot."

"Yes, sir." Abandoning his fedora and the confiscated PG-13, Logan went inside a malodorous, square-shaped room and shut the door behind him. There was no lock.

By 4:15, "The Battle of Los Angeles" had ebbed to a close, but not until more than fourteen hundred projectiles were fired from shore batteries. Although Logan was not there to read them, newspaper accounts of the skirmish would fan the flames of fear. The *Los Angeles Times* carried a headline that proclaimed, ARMY SAYS ALARM REAL, and further editions screamed, L.A. AREA RAIDED and JAP PLANES PERIL SANTA MONICA. Five deaths were attributed, indirectly, to the presumptive air strike, three of them in car accidents during the blackout and the other two from heart attacks. Many onlookers were injured by shell fragments from the 12.8-pound explosive charges, which traced a forty-mile swath along the hurtling object's airborne course.

After sunrise on Wednesday morning, radio broadcasts breathlessly confirmed that Los Angeles had indeed been attacked by one or more raiders, perhaps as many as fifty aircraft in all, three of which were shot down over the sea. A report filed by the Seventy-seventh Street police station alleged that an unidentified airplane had crash-landed near Eighteenth Street and Vermont. Details on the battle were sketchy, which was not unusual for such a recent event, especially one that occurred overnight during a blackout.

Logan Gramm was back home, standing hatless in his apartment and happy to be released from the custody of law enforcement. As for the PG-13 that he left behind, it was cleared by demolition experts and would gradually be relegated to nothing more than an office curio, a conversation piece around the water cooler. Authorities conceded that it must indeed be an emergency signaling device of some sort—if only they could get the blasted thing to work.

♦　♦　♦

Erin Duffy drew closer to Logan Gramm as the weeks passed. She had not established a friendly relationship with anyone in her theater company, mainly because everybody else, particularly those in leading roles, considered the meager part of "Rosie" to be far beneath them. Erin sensed a definite hierarchy, unspoken but inviolable, that governed all facets of socialization among the players. Whenever two or more of the principals began chatting with each other, Erin suddenly became invisible to them, scarcely above custodial status.

Nor was she able to secure a more remunerative position to augment her income, despite repeated efforts to make contact with producers who could offer a pathway to success. One audition seemed promising for a while, and yet the part went instead to a SUNY freshman with no theatrical experience whatsoever, except for one summer spent inside a cartoon costume at Walt Disney World. Although the girl did have a lively personality, this particular character called for introspection and a melancholy spirit. How an utter neophyte landed the role came as a mystery to the other five finalists—even allowing for their normal lack of objectivity in such a competitive setting. But the decision had been made, and it was pointless to delve into hidden motives.

"I can hold out for about ten more days—maximum," Erin told Logan. It was a Tuesday morning, his day off for that week, and the pair were drinking coffee at a table in the shopping mall. "I'll be thrown into the gutter if I can't find something in a hurry."

"Care to be my roommate?" Logan asked. He made the statement in jest, but Erin seemed to accept it as a serious proposal of alliance.

"I would need to keep it a secret from my parents," she said. "Still, it might be a way for both of us to keep our heads above water."

He forced an uneasy grin. "Wait a minute. I was only teasing, and I figured you knew that." His clumsy attempt at damage control did little to divert her thoughts.

"I'm desperate, Logan, and it sounded good to me."

"What if I help you find a day job instead?" he asked.

"That's fine, too, but I've already tried, and the hours don't mesh with what I'm doing in the theater—daytime rehearsals and evening performances. Besides, I'm through groveling for tips."

That was a low blow. "Well, thank you very much," Logan said.

"You know what I mean. Now that I've got my foot in the stage door, I need to strike while the iron is hot." She laughed at herself. "To use a very awful mixed metaphor!"

"It wouldn't work, Erin—no way. Living together would wreck our friendship, and I don't want that to happen."

"Then let's not call it 'living together'. I don't like that term anyway because it puts too much pressure on the situation. Think of us as being on the same team. We're solving two problems at once, and we can give each other plenty of space. Do you have a rollaway or cot for me to use?"

"Nope. Besides, what would we do with all of your Art Deco statues?"

"I'll get rid of them, if I have to. I'm in no bargaining position, so I need to be flexible." Erin leaned toward him, almost whispering. "And I could chip in seventeen hundred dollars a month for rent. Would that come in handy?"

Logan's eyes widened. "You must be making pretty decent money."

"For most of the country, yes, but not for New York City." She took a sip of coffee and nodded her head. "You know, viewing Manhattan from across the river might be kind of nice for a change. And a lot less expensive."

"You're really serious, aren't you?" he said. "How long have you been hatching this crazy plan?"

"Just now."

"That's hard to believe."

"No, really. It didn't even cross my mind until you suggested being your roommate."

Logan could hardly believe his ears. "I didn't suggest it! I was making a joke. That's an important distinction, which you're conveniently ignoring."

Erin looked hurt. "So, the answer is no?"

"Let me think about it," he said. "I'd like to help you, but living with someone is a step that shouldn't be taken lightly. Especially with someone of the opposite ... gender."

"You make it sound so immoral, instead of what it would really be—totally innocent and ... " She pondered her vocabulary. "What's the word I'm looking for?"

"Platonic."

"Yes, innocent and platonic. I'll bet hundreds of theater people are living like that, to pay the rent."

"Theater people maybe, but not people who are sane."

Giggling, she punched him on the arm. "Someday, you'll come to appreciate your roommate a lot more than you do now."

Logan felt helpless to put his foot down, and Erin moved in to "their" apartment less than a week later. First, though, she used half a day to transport her collection of artistic bric-a-brac to Glen Burnie, Maryland. That was where her parents resided, in the same house that she had called home as a girl. When they asked about the move, she responded with honesty—to a degree. She and her roommate would share expenses, Erin explained, enabling both of them to stay afloat despite the horrendous cost of living so near the Big Apple. The fact that "Logan" could also be a female name was serendipitous but unstated.

Sleeping arrangements became settled without too much fuss. Logan retained his own bed, and Erin, being the interloper, did her best to make do with the couch. He offered to alternate days or weeks in the bedroom, but she firmly refused. "No. This was my idea, and I promised myself that you would not be inconvenienced at all—or as little as possible. The rent money I'm paying you is not enough to commandeer the bed." He felt selfish about it, but she would not budge.

Except for the girl's overnight blanket and pillow—stashed out of sight during the daylight hours—there was only one obvious change in the living room. Atop the coffee table sat a lovely specimen of Art Deco, the sole piece of statuary that Erin brought with her to New Jersey. It was *The Dolly Sisters*, the same figurine that Logan had singled out as his favorite. Although perhaps too tall for its spot in the room, this artwork added a nice, sentimental touch that was lost on neither of them.

With very little adjustment, a manageable household routine soon developed. Logan was generally home from Scotty's Steakhouse by 11:15 PM, while Erin never returned before midnight, departing at Hoboken from the Journal Square PATH train. This disparity gave Logan a head start in preparing for bed, which was opportune because of the shared bathroom. After shutting the bedroom door, he would turn on his sound synthesizer—waterfall, rain, or ocean waves—and seldom hear that she had entered the apartment. Then, arising to his alarm clock at eight, Logan would get dressed, tiptoe into the kitchen to make a pot of coffee, and wait for his roommate to join him at the breakfast table. On clear days, the Manhattan skyline provided an awe-inspiring backdrop.

Although Logan Gramm would never articulate it as such, even to himself, the sweet visage of Erin Duffy was rather breathtaking, too—and she was usually seated just an arm's length away.

◆　◆　◆

"PG KRON is paying for everything," Mariusz Wojewódzki said. "Even this fine Cuban Montecristo." The rotund agent inhaled a long draw on the cigar and blew smoke straight upward. "You act surprised."

Logan turned his look of shock into a smile, amused by the cavalier attitude. "Not much that PGK does surprises me anymore—after going through three ops on the receiving end. Your company doesn't seem to run a very tight ship, Mr. Wo … "

"Just call me 'Voya'." The bearded young man chuckled. "Appearances can be deceiving from a client's vantage point. We're not all that lackadaisical. I haven't had two days off in a single week for more than six months."

"Are things really that busy for manipulating the past?" Logan asked.

"You have no idea, Mr. Gramm." Wojewódzki lowered his voice before adding, "If you want my honest opinion, DOI has exceedingly deep pockets, and they need to justify their own existence."

The two men were inside the gazebo at Hoboken's Church Square Park, leaning back against the tubular railings. Around the exterior of this eight-sided bandstand, an elderly lady had been admiring the nameplates of composers, but she stopped long enough to give Wojewódzki an unmistakable scowl.

Taking the hint, Logan suggested to the agent that they walk over to an open patch of grass and continue their discussion there. "Lots of people don't like tobacco smoke," he told him, "particularly cigars."

"Well, there's no accounting for taste," Wojewódzki said. He leaned back, laughing like an operatic basso profondo, and waddled down the steps with his client. "We must be careful not to offend the most sensitive amongst us." The old woman glared at him but held her tongue.

Safely away from unappreciative nostrils, the PGK agent contentedly patted his plump belly. "Mr. Gramm, you would have enjoyed the prime rib that I ate this morning—medium rare, with more than a touch of fat for succulence. I came here early to take advantage of my *per diem*."

"You had prime rib for breakfast, Voya?"

"Actually, it was hardly an hour ago. Keep in mind that it's still morning for me. The restaurant was already serving from their lunch menu, so there was no alternative."

"And PROGRADE KRONOTECHNIX paid for it?"

"Oh, yes. We get a very generous expense account." He burped under his breath. "But back to the main topic, Mr. Gramm. I am available to entertain any questions that you may have."

"When is my next excursion—my Op-4?" Logan asked. "I have a roommate now, so that makes my absence more noticeable. I'll have to be extra cautious."

"Rest easy. We can have the rigger leave you with no discernible time away from home or work—wherever you desire. It's just a simple matter of tightening the time coordinates."

"I know, but there's always the matter of a suitcase, period attire, and other props that might grab her attention when I suddenly materialize out of thin air."

"*Her* attention?" Wojewódzki was grinning from ear to ear.

Logan's face turned red. "Listen, Voya. It's absolutely above board—nothing but a financial arrangement. We've never even kissed each other."

"Is she pretty?"

"Very much so—an actress. Why do you ask? Does this alter my contract with PG KRON?"

"Absolutely not. Whatever you do in your present is none of our business. You're only on the clock if an op is in progress."

"Can you tell me when that will be?"

"Your suggested departure is Tuesday morning at 10:43. Be ready to leave ten minutes before that—in your nineteenth-century costume."

That made Logan smile. "What year?"

"Early May of 1891, the inaugural concert at Carnegie Hall, just across the Hudson River from where we're standing right now."

"Tchaikovsky will be there, if I'm not mistaken."

"Yes, indeed. He was invited to headline the week-long festival, conducting some of his own music. Interested?"

"I should say so. Will I get to meet him?"

"No, I'm afraid not," Wojewódzki said. "All six performances are sold out—as you might imagine—and we've had a deuce of a time securing a ticket for the opening concert. Someone who once had a seat will be in the standing section."

"Sorry about that."

"Can't be helped. It's for the good of the world." Wojewódzki winked.

"This mission is that important?"

"No. I was being sarcastic. It's hardly worth your trouble, to be honest with you. But maybe it has larger implications down the pike. Giving you a definitive answer to that would exceed my job description."

"What am I expected to do?"

"At the opening concert, there will be an elderly gentleman sitting next to you. He will wear a monocle and spats, while flaunting a diamond-studded walking cane. Directly in front of this man will be a lovely woman, hair piled high, very regal." Wojewódzki took two leisurely puffs of the cigar. "Here's what happened in real life, Mr. Gramm, according to our researchers. During the intermission, the lady's purse disappeared—misappropriated by the elderly gentleman, who left the hall at once, carrying with him twenty-five hundred dollars in C-notes. That was a great deal of money in 1891."

"Was it ever found and returned?"

"Not as it stands now, but that's where you enter the picture. If you're successful, the cash would be used to keep an orphanage from closing its doors forever. This charitable institution, as I understand it, could then become the home of a notable humanitarian and patron of the arts."

"Can you tell me who that would be?"

"It's one of PGK's little secrets and not for us common folk to know. All the researcher told me is that this person would spread a lot of goodwill during his or her long life. I've examined the topic on my own—just yesterday—but I came up empty. Obviously, I don't have access to the sources that our company employs. They are truly mind-boggling, like nothing you could possibly conceive."

Logan gave the agent a mischievous grin. "Tell me this, Voya. Any chance that I could go on a tour of your physical plant?"

Again, Wojewódzki unleashed a massive belly laugh. "Dream on," he said. "Your field of play is in the past, not the future, and so is mine. It's just that I happened to be born into a much later generation, giving me more of the past to explore."

"How many generations separate us?"

The inscrutable PGK smile appeared. "Do you really expect me to answer that?"

◆　◆　◆

Horse-drawn carriages of every social class, from lower-middle to lordly aristocratic, filled West Fifty-seventh Street and Seventh Avenue on the evening of Tuesday, May 5, 1891. At the southeast corner of that intersection stood the Music Hall, an Italian Renaissance structure that was to be inaugurated with an eight o'clock concert by the New York Symphony Orchestra. In the audience would be the hall's chief financier, industrialist Andrew Carnegie. Guest of honor for the occasion was Russian composer Pyotr Ilyich Tchaikovsky, who had arrived in the United States nine days earlier aboard the French steamship *La Bretagne*.

Trying to fit unobtrusively into the busy scene was a twenty-first-century visitor by the name of Logan Gramm, who had abruptly appeared from nowhere at Jacob Wrey Mould's wooden bridge over The Pond in Central Park. A leisurely thirty-minute stroll separated him from the Music Hall. This stranger in town wore a black tailcoat, matching vest, dark trousers, white shirt with detachable collar and cuffs, a tall, black top hat, and floppy bow tie.

"Have you an extra ticket?" someone on Sixth Avenue asked him.

"No, sir." Logan kept walking.

"I'll gladly pay you a double eagle for subscription seating," the man added. Smiling hopefully, he held out a gold coin.

"Sorry, sir, but I cannot help you." Logan gave a polite tip of the hat but continued on his way. At least the New Yorker had judged him to be a concertgoer—a good indication that his apparel was suitable for such a grand setting—and again Logan felt in the debt of PG KRON researchers. They also contributed a trivial factoid: the Music Hall's architect, William Burnet Tuthill, was a fellow Hobokenite.

Logan surrendered his ticket at the door and allowed an usher to show him to row seventeen. Although a substantial percentage of the men checked their hats upon entering, he chose to carry his with him, placing it upon his lap for the concert. The nattily attired gentleman sitting to his left did likewise. He wore a monocle in his right eye, and there were spats over his shoe tops. Leaning against his left knee was a diamond-studded walking cane.

The chair in front of this elderly gentleman was vacant at the moment, but an attractive woman arrived to occupy it about ten minutes before eight o'clock. Her hair was arranged in a charming bouffant bun, and the black leather purse that she cradled between both hands was quite stylish in a tastefully understated manner. Logan watched this woman, who was about forty, lay the handbag alongside her in the seat—a bit casually, he thought, but perhaps that was influenced by hindsight. No doubt the man directly behind her was scrutinizing the purse's whereabouts, too.

On stage were several hundred choristers of the Oratorio Society of New York and, arrayed in a semi-circle around the conductor's podium, the Symphony Society Orchestra. Logan joined in the applause when twenty-nine-year-old Walter Damrosch strode briskly to the wooden stand and raised his baton. Opening the concert was the Doxology "Old Hundred" ("Praise God from Whom All Blessings Flow"), performed by chorus, orchestra, and organ. That was followed by a word of welcome from the president of the Music Hall's management company, Morris Reno, who then introduced Bishop Henry Codman Potter of the Episcopal Diocese of New York for a lengthy oration on "Dedication of the Hall." The national hymn, "America" ("My Country, 'Tis of Thee"), came next, borrowing its tune from the British anthem "God Save the King/Queen."

As Maestro Damrosch was leading Ludwig van Beethoven's *Leonore Overture No. 3*, it crossed Logan's mind that the lives of some of these orchestral players may well have overlapped that of Beethoven himself, who passed away sixty-four years earlier. *Leonore Overture No. 3* was a large-scale composition, about fourteen minutes in duration, and it elicited from the audience an appreciative response. Maestro Damrosch acknowledged the applause with several deep bows from the waist before retiring to the wings at backstage right.

When the hall's modern electric lights illuminated for intermission, Logan Gramm sensed that it was time to act. He immediately stood and, hat in hand, greeted the gentleman to his left. The man was reluctant to converse, haughty to the point of rudeness, and yet Logan persisted. By now, the lady in row sixteen was standing, too, chatting with her female companion to the right. Her purse lay flat, unguarded atop the seat cushion.

Just as the elderly gentleman leaned forward to capture his prize, Logan's top hat forcefully deflected the grasping hand off-target, which caused the walking cane to tumble in front of him. Logan apologized profusely for his clumsiness, but the man would hear none of it. His eyes were focused straight ahead, where the lady, still engaged in an animated conversation, reached down to take a cough drop from her purse. By the time Logan knelt to retrieve the man's cane for him, this heedless woman had tucked the purse under her arm.

The old man was seething with resentment. He turned sharply to his left and departed in a huff, knowing full well that there could be no second attempt. Indeed, the foiled larcenist never did return to his seat, so Logan was able to enjoy the rest of the concert without feeling the pressure of undue concern. Meanwhile, the lady in row sixteen remained totally unaware of the taut drama that unfolded behind her and how close she came to losing a small fortune in charitable funds.

Logan consulted his PG-13, which showed a countdown figure of 01:03:46. When the house lights dimmed, the audience returned to their seats, and to center stage strode a rather tall man with a neatly trimmed, grayish-white beard. This was Pyotr Ilyich Tchaikovsky, regarded as one of the three greatest living composers in the world, along with Johannes Brahms of Germany and Camille Saint-Saëns of France. There was a loud ovation that tested the new hall's acoustics nearly as much as did the chorus, organ, and orchestra at full volume.

Tchaikovsky had wanted to compose a new work for this momentous occasion, but his other commitments would not permit such an extravagance. Instead, he chose to conduct a march that he had written back in 1883 for the coronation of Alexander III as the new czar. Over the intervening eight years, this energetic, bombastic piece had acquired the title of *Festival Coronation March*, but the Music Hall concert presented it as *Marche Solennelle*—perhaps in the mistaken belief that people might think it a freshly composed work. If so, this ruse fooled few music lovers in the audience, for by now the American public had taken Tchaikovsky's *oeuvre* to heart and were familiar enough with his march to recognize its true origins.

The great Russian master conducted in an understated manner that was anything but flamboyant. And yet, he elicited an alert performance from Damrosch's New York Symphony Orchestra. The composer would later confide to his diary that "The March went by very well. Great success." When the piece concluded, Logan Gramm watched—with more than three thousand others—as Tchaikovsky responded to the thunderous applause with a series of quick, self-conscious bows from the waist. Almost clinically introverted by nature, he seemed flustered to be held in such adulation.

His public responsibilities met for the evening, Tchaikovsky retreated to the premium box of E. Francis Hyde, president of the "friendly rival" New York Philharmonic Society. From that privileged vantage point, he witnessed French composer Hector Berlioz's *Te Deum* for tenor solo (in this case, Italo Campanini), triple chorus, and orchestra. Although penned as long ago as 1849, this was its local premiere, and Tchaikovsky was less than favorably impressed. "*Te Deum* by Berlioz is dullish," he wrote. "Only at the end did I taste the intense pleasure of it."

Berlioz was notorious for conceiving his masterpieces on a broad canvas, and this weightiness made Logan Gramm rather fidgety in his seat. *Te Deum* was about fifty minutes in duration, which left him only a short time to join in the celebratory ovation, squeeze past as many patrons as possible up the aisle, and flee to a dark alley where he might slip from view.

As he ran for cover, Logan could not help but wonder why the riggers at PROGRADE KRONOTECHNIX persisted in cutting so tightly their clients' departure times. Presumably, there was some rationale for such madness, and maybe one day he would learn the answer. For now, though, he had to be content with sprinting around the nearest corner—hat in hand—so he would not make a spectacle of himself by vanishing from the public eye.

But Logan's problems did not end there. Although his formalwear was hardly noticed amidst the nightlife of 1891, such a garish display was sure to bring stares from casual onlookers in the present day. Worse luck, PGK's coordinates deposited him at the entrance of his apartment complex just as four college students in a Jeep Wrangler were driving up to the rolling gate for admittance. Flushed with embarrassment, Logan shouted to them, "Costume party!" Then he made light of the moment by giving them a courtly bow, top hat sweeping down to knee level. Fortunately, the students were cynical (and intoxicated) enough to dismiss his quaint behavior with nothing beyond a derisive laugh.

♦   ♦   ♦

All too soon, the idyllic pattern of Logan's home life in Hoboken threatened to come to an abrupt halt. Three weeks after Erin Duffy began sharing the accommodations, she received a part-time job offer from an unexpected source. This opening, while not in the world of theater, was so closely related that a theatrical booking agency handled the arrangements. Erin was to report to a photography studio for duty as an advertising model. Hours would vary, but the studio was willing to make allowances for her acting schedule. Many folks on its modeling roster held down concurrent positions on stage, so there was nothing particularly unusual about that.

Erin told Logan, "If everything goes well, you'll see me in *Cosmo* and *Elle* pretty soon—maybe within two or three months." Her eyes were gleaming with excitement.

"Sorry, but I don't make a habit of reading either of those."

She frowned. "That's not what I meant."

"Just kidding. Actually, I think it's great. When do you start?"

"Whenever I get an assignment. It's strictly on a stand-by basis, but Tanner says he expects to shoot me at least once a week. My pic will appear in his browsing gallery—at the studio and online—and if anyone likes what they see, I'll get a call."

Sure enough, Erin received her first "gig" within a few days. Then she began getting summoned three or four times a week, usually early in the mornings, and the sessions quite often lasted for up to six hours. This was the nature of posing for the demanding ad reps of New York City.

It was not long before she was tempted to rent an apartment of her own. Logan could not blame her, for she was now earning enough income to afford a four- or five-room flat in **the Big Apple**, thereby doing away with that crowded train ride to and from New Jersey. Her modeling aspirations had proven far more lucrative than her full-time position as a minor cast member in *Murder at Wit's End.*

One Thursday at noon, she and Logan had lunch together, something that did not occur very often because of their diverging work schedules. Erin invited him to join her at an Italian bistro, and she insisted on paying for both of their meals. This made Logan feel a bit ashamed of himself, envious of her burgeoning career while his was bogged down in the doldrums.

"Tanner thinks I have real potential," she told him. "In fact, he's going to send some proofs to a friend in Los Angeles."

"Modeling or acting?"

"Both, as far as I can tell. Tanner has some contacts out there."

"In the movie industry or advertising?"

"Advertising," she said. "But the two do converge quite a bit, so who knows what might happen? Tanner thinks L.A. is the place to be, and I wouldn't be surprised if he picked up and moved his business to the West Coast one of these days. He's even mentioned it to me during the photo shoots."

Something was annoying Logan, but he could not put his finger on exactly what. Maybe it was because Erin seemed to be gloating. "Who is this Tanner that you're always talking about?" he asked.

"He's my boss—where I work—Tanner Ammon Photography. I thought I told you that."

"Not that I remember."

"I'm sure that I did."

"You may have said his name a couple thousand times, but you never revealed who he is."

"Revealed! This isn't some dark secret. I'm quite open about it."

"Anyway, now I know who the great 'Tanner' is. Thank you so much."

Erin began staring at the wall-mounted television screen, which was showing a European soccer match. "If I didn't know any better, I might think that you're jealous."

Logan forced a laugh. "Jealous of what?"

"You have all the symptoms of being jealous of Tanner Ammon."

"I don't even know the guy. How could I be jealous of him?"

"That's what I'm wondering."

"Listen. I might be curious about who he is, but that's only because I'm interested in your welfare. If you ask me, you're spending an awful lot of time with him, and I don't think it's very healthy."

She gave a smirk. "Well, I appreciate your concern, and I'll try to be more thoughtful in the future. Shall I cancel all of my appointments, just to be on the safe side?"

"Be careful, that's all. He could be after more than a working relationship."

"What if he is? He's very nice looking and only six years older than I am. I don't see a problem."

"How close are the two of you?"

"I consider Tanner to be a good friend. We enjoy being together."

"Socially, or just in the studio?" Logan asked.

"During studio hours ... for now."

"Anything else you'd like to tell me about this incomparable boss of yours?"

"Yes. He drives a Porsche Panamera to his private parking space each day, and he lives on the thirty-first floor of a luxury high-rise."

"He sounds perfect for you. No doubt about it."

Erin took a deep breath and seemed to count to ten. "He's also a devoted husband, and the father of two adorable children—Deborah and Benjamin."

Logan glanced at her and then away. "Your Tanner is married?"

"He's not *my* Tanner. That honor belongs to Wendy Ammon, his wife of five years."

The ensuing silence was broken by Logan's clearing of the throat. "I guess you're sort of upset with me, huh?"

"That was a rather immature display of jealousy," she told him.

"Why would I be jealous of a married man?"

"Don't give me that! I didn't mention Tanner's marital status until much later in our conversation."

"I just don't want to see you get hurt, that's all." He paused. "And I also don't want to see you leave."

"The apartment or New York?"

"Both. I've sort of gotten used to having you around. It wouldn't be the same without you."

"You'd miss our early-morning talkfests over coffee?"

"Among other little niceties," he said.

Erin grinned at him. "Niceties? What's that supposed to mean? I wasn't aware that I had any niceties."

"Sure, you do. You're full of niceties, as a matter of fact. I can't even count all your niceties."

"Name one."

"Let's see ... niceties, niceties." He squinted at her. "Okay, how's this? You squeeze your toothpaste tube from the bottom. You can't get much more noble than that. It's almost heroic."

"You're easy to impress."

The waiter arrived at their table—a portly, gray-haired gent of about sixty, with a white apron tied around his waist. He may just as well have come from Central Casting. Laying their savory meals before them, he said, "*Signorina ... e Signor.*"

Confused, Logan turned to him. "Excuse me, but isn't this lasagna? I ordered the Italian chopped salad."

The man glanced at Erin before replying. "But, *Signor*, the lady changed your order to the Neapolitan-style lasagna. Is that not acceptable?"

Now Logan remembered seeing her whisper something to the waiter, who nodded his assent. "Yes, sir. This is fine—wonderful. Thank you." Smiling, the waiter bowed and left their table.

"I know how much you love lasagna," Erin said.

Logan lowered his voice. "This meal will cost you a fortune."

"Just think of tonight as a celebration of my second career— while I still have it. Tanner could fire me at any time."

"Not with your looks, he won't."

She patted him on the hand. "Thank you, Logan. That's the nicest thing you've ever said to me."

Although the future was exceptionally bright for Erin Duffy, she decided to stay put for the time being, reluctant to sacrifice her bank account to the greedy appetite of Midtown Manhattan.

◆　◆　◆

<Contact PGK at once>, the message read. <Your Op-5 has been arranged.> Logan gulped. He felt an uneasiness about his final excursion into the past. Maybe he had seen too many movies where the beat cop suffers a tragic end on his very last day with the force. Or where an intrepid B-17 pilot fails to return from his twenty-fifth bombing raid. Tempting fate may have been an effective story line in Hollywood, but it gave Logan a case of the jitters in real life.

The fact that he was to meet with two agents instead of one, had he known it, would have made him even more leery of what lay ahead. PROGRADE KRONOTECHNIX had a firm policy in place that required "more than one but less than five" representatives to counsel with prospective clients whenever the mission was deemed a hazardous duty operation. Such assignments remained voluntary, but only the most experienced clients were given the honor of first refusal.

This guardian policy, casually known as the "doomsday clause," kicked into play for Logan Gramm's fifth operation with the company. And so, by arrangement, two PG KRON agents met him at the Hoboken Public Library, on the corner of Park Avenue and Fifth Street. The pair traveled separately to this encounter, each wielding an identical PG-13 device, and they arrived within thirty seconds of one another. Following introductions to their client, the male agent asked him, "Have you ever wanted to tackle a hazardous duty operation before?"

Logan's eyes widened. "I don't recall saying that I wanted to tackle this one."

"Fair enough, Mr. Gramm, but your personality profile indicates a willingness to face down a substantial degree of danger." Agent Conrad Bennett was a middle-aged black man with graying dreadlocks. He opened his valise and shuffled through some papers. "It says here that twice before you have been subjected to Level-6 peril, once in 1864 and again in 1942. You confronted both of them with laudable fortitude. That being the case, a Level-8 undertaking would not seem to be ruled off the table. Level-8 is considered a relatively low-danger HDO."

"Relatively low, but still hazardous?"

"That's right. Dangers are rated on a scale of degrees."

"How many levels are there on this chart of yours?"

"Ten—the maximum being actual combat or physical violence. We do have a few Level-10 opportunities, but those are restricted to active military and have no excessive repercussion clause. Level-9, too, for that matter. Personally, I think this one should be rated at Level-9, but that's not my call."

"Is there any financial reward for placing my life on the line for good ol' PGK?"

"No. You would remain a volunteer, just as your contract stipulates."

Logan asked the obvious question. "Why would anybody in his right mind want to risk it all for nothing?"

"Oh, hardly for *nothing*," Bennett said. "You could very well be saving some precious lives in the process. Interested?"

Logan shrugged his shoulders but did not reply.

That is when the female agent finally spoke up. "Mr. Gramm, please understand that HDOs are highly prized missions, for which only a select few clients qualify. You would be joining the ranks of our most legendary operatives." PG KRON agent Stephanie Kim was an Asian woman of about thirty-five. Her voice was soft, the dialect vaguely Far Eastern. "I can assure you that the operation we have in mind will capture every ounce of your historical curiosity. Any corollary dangers will be dwarfed by the thrill of being present at a seminal event of international import. You will find it unbelievable to be there in person, and the service you render will alter—in a positive fashion—the genealogical lineage of a respected family, not to mention its subsequent generations."

That was heady stuff, and Logan was intrigued. "Would success entitle me to future engagements of my own choice?" He was looking at Kim, but it was Bennett who answered.

"I'm afraid that won't be possible," he said. "As I'm sure your recruiting agent informed you long ago, a standard PGK contract guarantees just five missions after the recreational one."

"But she also said there could be more than five, if both parties agree," Logan told him. He looked from one agent to the other. "Maybe you know Tamara Renée Hansen."

"Who?" Bennett asked.

"Tammi Hansen. She told me that she works as something called a 'rigger'."

"We have literally dozens of riggers," Kim said. "It would be impossible to know all of them by name." She flashed the patented PGK smile—enigmatic, betraying no secrets.

Agent Bennett seemed more receptive—indeed, a bit too receptive for comfort. "What else can you tell me about Rigger Hansen?" He jotted down a few words. "Tamara, is it?"

Logan did not like the direction this was going. "Don't bother with that," he said. "She's only an intern, and I probably shouldn't have even mentioned it."

Bennett responded with an icy stare. "As you wish." But he tucked the slip of paper into his valise.

Stephanie Kim guided the discussion back onto topic. "Have you ever been to Manchester Township, Mr. Gramm?"

"I don't think so. Here in Jersey?"

"Approximately fifty-five miles to the south-southwest, as the crow flies."

"What about it?"

"Within its boundaries lies the Lakehurst Naval Air Station. I presume you've heard of that."

"Absolutely," Logan said. "Is that where I'm going?"

"It is," Kim told him.

"Nineteen thirty-seven?"

"Correct." She stifled a grin. "The *Hindenburg*. Are you becoming a bit more interested?"

Logan thought for a moment, then nodded his head.

As their meeting progressed further, it became clear that Conrad Bennett was in charge of presenting the mission's objectives, while Stephanie Kim limited herself to the tandem concerns of safety and survival.

"You will be stationed no less than three hundred feet from the mooring mast, on the port side of the airship," Bennett said. "This will give you roughly the same angle of vision as the newsreel film, so you can anticipate what to expect ... and when."

"Can I just suddenly appear on the scene?"

"Not to worry. There'll be more than enough activity to distract anyone from noticing."

"Will I be dressed as a civilian?"

"No. That would be too conspicuous. You'll be issued a period set of U.S. Navy fatigues. Everything will be perfectly authentic."

Logan glanced at Ms. Kim, who said nothing and merely sat there at the table, deferring to Mr. Bennett.

"When the airship drops its final water ballast and the tethering lines, you'll move into position—close enough to help with the rescue effort, but of course not directly in harm's way." The agent glanced at his colleague. "Use your best judgment, Mr. Gramm, just like everyone else on the landing field. Believe me, your instincts will kick into action."

"Is there someone in particular that I'm expected to focus my attention on?" Logan asked.

"Two passengers at the promenade windows of 'A' Deck, a married couple who were consumed in the flames. Your mission is to save this woman and hopefully her husband, too."

"They weren't able to make it out in time?"

"Thirty-six of the ninety-seven aboard were lost, counting crew members. This lady stopped to free her husband, but to no avail. His foot was hopelessly caught in the collapsed window frame just before the girders came crashing down."

"Who are these people?"

"That's not for you to know. To be honest with you, this is more of a mercy mission than anything else. You might say that our researchers were moved by her heroism."

Then it became Stephanie Kim's turn to speak. She explained about the perils of a cataclysmic failure, using words of caution that were uncannily reminiscent of what Logan heard during his introductory meeting with Tammi Hansen—much as if the phraseology had been committed to memory as a legal disclaimer.

"Bear in mind at all times that you remain subject to the physical laws of nature, so being killed or seriously injured in action is not impossible or even minimized. If such a mishap occurs, the PG-13 ... " Kim handed it to him. " ... is programmed to interpret the accident as an excessive repercussion, which aborts the mission, and you return to your device's APPLY time with health restored. An unfortunate downside is that you will feel the pain of death or injury before the setback is recognized as such and averted. That can amount to as long as fourteen seconds of agony."

"Lovely," he said.

"Sorry to tell you that, but we try not to sugar-coat the gravity of our HDOs."

"No pun intended ... "

"I beg your pardon?"

"Gravity ... the *Hindenburg*."

Kim frowned, confirming what Logan already suspected. A good many ProGrade Kronotechnix agents were devoid of a sense of humor.

♦   ♦   ♦

According to what Logan Gramm saw on his PG-13's display, the programming specs would place him in the vicinity of the Lakehurst crash site at 7:06:29 PM, local time, on May 6, 1937.

A United States Navy uniform—dark blues, with canvas leggings and white cap—had been timed to materialize in his Hoboken apartment on an evening when Logan's roommate would be away for a performance of *Murder at Wit's End*. Also delivered from the Properties Department of PROGRADE KRONOTECHNIX was a rugged, eighteen-inch steel crowbar, suitable for concealment within the loose-fitting military fatigues.

Logan's Op-5 was to be a brief mission, spanning a mere thirty-five and a half minutes. But from the perspective of his "present," scarcely any time at all would elapse. He would re-emerge in the apartment two seconds after his departure. Such an arrangement obviated any need of messy explanations, whether for roommate Erin Duffy or the management of Scotty's Steakhouse.

Had all crucial preparations been made? He spent a few minutes to double-check his uniform and counterfeit identification cards. Departure would be at 11:29:54, with a return time of 11:29:56. No matter how often he ventured forth for PGK, it never got any easier—the excitement, the tension, and the dread. Each excursion, whatever its objective, amounted to a blind leap into the unknown. Although he had grown to have full confidence in PROGRADE KRONOTECHNIX, things could go wrong, and he must be poised to react instantly if unforeseen calamities arose. He touched the thumbprint pad and pressed APPLY, thus activating his PG-13 for Op-5. Fourteen minutes until departure.

Logan allowed his eyes to scan the study notes. He had invested much of the past week in historical research—reading books and internet articles about the *LZ-129*'s first North American flight of the 1937 season. He also watched, re-watched, and committed to memory Pathé's famous newsreel footage of the airship's final thirty-four seconds of existence, as she plunged to the earth in a deadly inferno of combustible hydrogen. He paid particular attention to the naval ground crewmen, who moved into place, retreated momentarily from the explosive ball of fire, and then proceeded forward again—toward the flaming wreckage—to offer any aid they could administer to the survivors. He would feel proud to be among them.

After paying a quick visit to the restroom, Logan seated himself on the sofa and drank some coffee, waiting for the seconds to tick away. There was no need to finish the entire cup, for any remaining liquid would still be warm when he returned to the apartment. Half-past-eleven was nearing, so he slipped the crowbar down one pants leg, gripping its handle tightly at the waist, and closed his eyes. He counted to himself and sensed that surely the time had come. That is when two or three tiny droplets of drizzle settled upon one wrist. Listening carefully, he heard the distant roar of the airship's four 16-cylinder Daimler engines.

Logan looked up to the right and gasped. There she was, the *Hindenburg*, almost three football fields in length and soaring majestically toward the mooring mast. Having been appropriated by the Hitler regime as an emissary of propaganda—a symbol of German strength and technology—the giant airship carried black Nazi swastikas within red rectangles on both sides of her upper and lower tail fins. Her body was tastefully marked, with *Hindenburg* in suitably Teutonic script and the registry number of D-LZ129.

When Logan turned around, toward the hangar, he witnessed precisely what he expected to see: a man speaking into a microphone marked WLS. This was thirty-one-year-old announcer Herbert Morrison, and just inside the door, protected from the weather, was the equipment of radio engineer Charles Nehlsen. Although Logan was too far away to actually hear what was being said, he knew the content by heart, almost verbatim.

By 7:14 PM, the mammoth airship was at an altitude of four hundred feet and gradually slowing. Three minutes later, she turned sharply to starboard, and more than a ton of water ballast was expelled from her heavy stern in an attempt to level the craft. When Logan next consulted his pre-war wristwatch, he saw that the time was 7:21. The *Hindenburg* was now three hundred feet above the landing field, and the clouds were beginning to produce rain again. As the craft descended through two hundred feet, mooring lines were dropped from her bow—first the starboard one and then the port.

Logan Gramm held his breath, feeling the seconds pass by and physically trembling from the horrid knowledge of what surely must come next. At 7:25, the *Hindenburg* burst into flames. There was the sound of raging fire and then a muffled explosion. Her stern was ablaze, and the airship drifted quickly toward the ground, nose tilting downward and the entire body a virtual hell of ignited hydrogen.

The *Hindenburg*'s duralumin frame collapsed of its own weight in a white-hot tangle of skeletal remains. Some ghost-like human figures were running away in shock, attempting to escape on foot. Having jumped from considerable altitude through shattered windows, many of them had ghastly burns and broken limbs. All around Logan, as if on a signal, naval personnel began sprinting toward the nightmarish scene, hoping to rescue any survivors and assist them as best they could.

The heat was intense beyond belief as Logan approached the inferno, with flames towering more than sixty feet into the air. The aft section of 'A' Deck was fully engulfed by now, but a few dazed souls climbed forth and fled for their lives. A woman turned back to the wreckage and began tugging on the arm of a man, who shouted to leave him behind. Logan jumped forward and frantically used his crowbar to pry at the window frame. It would not budge. The man and woman both screamed in pain for an instant before falling silent, and Logan, too, sank into the throes of death. His vision degenerated to absolute blackness, an indescribable agony swept over his entire body, and his consciousness surrendered to a relentless wave of consumption by fire. Logan Gramm died amidst the blazing ruins.

Jolted awake, he discovered himself to be seated, uninjured, in his Hoboken apartment. The PG-13, salvaged from incineration through the precepts of time travel, had performed flawlessly at Lakehurst Naval Air Station—interpreting his fiery death as an excessive repercussion and aborting the mission. It was again fourteen minutes until departure when he activated the device by touching its thumbprint pad and pressing APPLY. Somehow, he would need to regain his fortitude very quickly, forcibly shunting aside all recollection of the excruciating pain that took his life only moments ago.

But, of course, that was not the only thought that tormented him. Herbert Morrison's heartfelt lament, "Oh, the humanity!" still rang in his memory, and on this day, Logan Gramm—more than any living person on earth—could feel the same grief that the radio announcer had experienced in 1937. Seated alone on the sofa, Logan quietly wept for the doomed couple whom he was unable to save, despite his gallant efforts. Soon he would return to Lakehurst on a newly designated Op-5a, this time with the certainty that only half of his mission's objectives might be met. He would dispense with the crowbar, recognizing the futility of using a rescue tool against such devastating forces. With that in mind, he steeled himself to endure the husband's harrowing pleas for his wife to leave him behind.

Logan examined the PG-13, which was still eerily programmed for witnessing the *Hindenburg* disaster. Though inanimate, this device seemed almost human to him, while it dutifully waited to launch its next foray into the past. The seconds slowly ticked down to zero.

It was again 7:25 PM on Thursday, May 6, 1937, and Logan— struck by *déjà vu* at its most terrifying—watched helplessly as the immense airship exploded on her catastrophic approach to the mooring mast. Quickly, the *Hindenburg* was engulfed in flames, beginning in the stern section and then flashing through the seven million cubic feet of flammable hydrogen. At once, she plummeted downward, nose-first onto the landing field. The 811-foot skeleton collapsed in a hideous tangle, and human beings could be seen, desperately fleeing from the white-hot wreckage. Many of these survivors had suffered serious burns, some of which would prove to be fatal. Meanwhile, the naval crewmen were running in the opposite direction, toward the crash site, and a uniformed imposter named Logan Gramm was among them.

In the aft section of 'A' Deck, a woman had crawled through a shattered window, but instead of fleeing, she pivoted back toward the conflagration. Sobbing in anguish and terror, she tugged on the arm of a man, who was immovably pinned inside the searing heat. He shouted a plea for her to save herself by abandoning him. Logan sprang forward and snatched the woman away just as a burst of flames shot forth and leveled them to the sand. Although suffering burns, somehow they managed to scramble almost a hundred feet away. But then the woman's legs wobbled beneath her, and she fainted upon the ground in shock. Logan raised the unconscious body and dragged her toward a safer area, where naval medics were already establishing a makeshift triage. Logan's burns, however painful, were proportionately superficial, and he did not even bother to seek aid—not with so many others fighting for their very lives. He ambled in a daze, never looking back, until the departure coordinate returned him homeward.

♦ ♦ ♦

Logan was scheduled to work that night at Scotty's Steakhouse, but the second-degree burns to his neck and both arms would make it difficult, and the singed eyebrows would make it embarrassing. He used Erin's makeup pencil to mask the latter and a long-sleeved, open-collared shirt to conceal the former. Unfortunately, every movement he made seemed to rub against the damaged skin. His next day off would not be until Sunday, and that was ninety-six arduous hours away. He gritted his teeth and pushed onward as resolutely as he could.

Three weeks went by, with nary a word from the good offices of PROGRADE KRONOTECHNIX, INC. While Logan did not expect to be honored with a ticker-tape parade down Broadway for his unquestioned valor at Lakehurst, neither did he imagine that the aftermath would be abject indifference. When he finally did receive contact, the encounter took him completely off guard. He rounded a corner in the restaurant, carrying a full serving tray high overhead, and came face to face with Tamara Renée Hansen.

"T-Tammi?" he asked. Beyond that, he was speechless, and suddenly the tray had become too heavy for him. He laid it on an empty table. "Tammi ... is that really you?"

The agent smiled, as if amused by his reaction, but did not reply.

Logan picked up the tray again and began walking toward his party of six. "Don't leave before we've had a chance to talk," he told her. "Please stay right where you are." He well remembered her disappearing act the first time they met.

As often happens in such frustrating situations, his customers became unusually demanding and verbose. More water was requested, more salad dressing was requested, more tartar sauce was requested, more bread was requested, and a baked potato was requested instead of fries. Logan remained as polite as possible, but he could sense that an unreasonable amount of time was sliding past. A PGK agent, while not of the present, was always on the clock.

At long last, when Logan had satisfied his customers' secondary orders, he hurried over to where Tammi was last seen. But she was no longer there. Maybe she was never there. Was the reappearance of Tammi Hansen merely an illusion? He searched the tabletop for a note, but none was to be found. Logan thought back to what she had written to him so long ago: "Meet me across the street, at Java Bay." His only hope was to wait until his shift ended and then trust that Tammi had the same idea.

She did. Tammi sat upon a round stool at the coffee shop's lunch counter, the sole person to do so at this late hour, and that meant her back was to the entrance when Logan came inside. Still, somehow she sensed that he had arrived.

"Sorry for making myself so scarce, Mr. Gramm," she said. Only then did she swivel around to bump fists. "But I couldn't expect you to take my proposition seriously while you were busy at work."

Logan chuckled. "What proposition is that?"

"Your Op-6, of course."

"I thought five was the maximum."

"It is, but I also told you there could be more than five, if both parties agree. Besides, this additional one is unofficial—off the record, so to speak."

Logan tried to interpret Tammi's expression, but she remained an enigma. "Sounds kind of shady," he said. "Are you telling me that PROGRADE KRONOTECHNIX would not be involved in my next mission?"

"That's right. They would be totally unaware of it. As a matter of fact, they don't even know that I'm here right now. I set my PG-13's coordinates to one second of elapsed time, from their perspective."

"You programmed it yourself?"

Tammi nodded her head. "You're looking at a genuine, honest-to-goodness rigger now, no longer just an intern."

"Congratulations!"

"Thanks. There's a fair amount of differential calculus in the programming, so it wasn't easy."

"Won't you lose your job by taking this unauthorized jaunt?"

"Not if they don't catch me."

None of this made much sense to Logan. "What's so vital that it makes you willing to risk your whole livelihood?"

She swallowed hard. "Just a little matter of life and death."

"Whose ... yours?"

"I shouldn't be telling you anything else—not here," she said. "Can you take me to some place where it's more private?"

"My apartment won't work. I live with a roommate."

"She won't be home until 01:47:39."

Logan was shocked. "How could you possibly know that?"

"I did some research. Your roommate's name is Erin Kathleen Duffy, she's an actress, and she'll be attending a birthday party for one of the cast tonight."

"You can see into the future?"

"No. Into the past."

"I don't get it."

"Your future is my past. I have access to anything you could possibly see in your lifetime." She grinned at him, and it was contagious.

Hurrying to the nearest subway station, they caught a late-night train to Hoboken, and, just as the PGK agent predicted, Logan's apartment was empty.

"Seems like you were right," he told her.

She nodded toward the PG-13. "I had an unfair advantage."

Logan walked over to the curtains and unveiled his apartment's stunning view of New York City. "Want some coffee?"

"I've already had too much, thanks."

"Soda?"

"Which?"

"Take your pick—Pepsi, Sprite, or Dr Pepper. Do those brands still exist where you come from?"

Tammi chose not to answer. Instead, she played it safe. "Some kind of cola, please."

Logan went into the kitchen, and the girl followed behind.

"Just so you'll know," she said, "I'm programmed to depart in one hour and eighteen minutes, missing your roommate by forty-seven seconds. I really can't be here when Erin arrives. There'd be too much to explain—all of it incomprehensible to somebody unfamiliar with PG KRON."

"Maybe she'd figure that I brought a date home with me."

Tammi laughed aloud, which came as a blow to Logan's ego.

"Would that be so unbelievable?" he asked.

"You tell me."

"She'd probably buy it. I think you and I look pretty nice together."

"Don't start getting any crazy ideas," Tammi told him. "I'm married, remember, and this is anything but a pleasure trip."

It was amazing how much small talk could be exchanged, despite the separation of innumerable decades—or centuries—

between them. Logan and Tammi never experienced any difficulty finding something to chat about, even though certain topics were off limits as far as she was concerned.

"What made you come here tonight?" Logan asked. "To test your rigging skills?"

"Partly, but I also need your help."

"Why me?"

"Because of the courage and resourcefulness that you've demonstrated in five ops. I've read the reports—very impressive."

Logan brushed that aside, instead motioning toward the sofa. "Shall we?"

They seated themselves quite near to each other, soft-drink glasses within reach atop the coffee table.

Tammi prefaced her statement with a grim disclaimer. "Please understand that what I'm about to tell you is confidential. I could draw a lengthy prison term—maybe never be seen again—if anyone overheard what I'm saying. My employer, PROGRADE KRONOTECHNIX, is ultra-protective of their secrecy, and they are not bashful about pressing charges." She glanced around the living room, then arose to inspect the rest of his apartment.

Logan remained seated, stunned by how paranoid the agent had become.

"You don't have any security cameras, do you?" Tammi asked him.

"Just outside, in the parking lot."

Tammi pointed toward the ceiling. "Where I come from, we all have constant 'guests' who monitor us around the clock—allegedly to make sure we're safe."

She spotted something on the end table. "What's that black, cylindrical object?"

"My Echo device—a virtual assistant named 'Alexa'."

"Do you mind if we unplug it?"

Logan grinned. "It's a she."

"Okay, then. Would you mind unplugging *her*?"

"If it makes you feel better."

"Thank you. It does."

And with that, Tammi sat down again, fortifying herself with a stiff belt of the cola. Logan watched her carefully, trying his best to grasp what she was going through.

"I apologize for the precautions I'm forced to take," she said, "but one cannot be too vigilant—not in my situation."

She began speaking quietly, just above a whisper, and Logan was obliged to slide closer in order to hear. That he was more than happy to do.

"I explained long ago, in our initial meeting, that your PGK contract restricts you to the past. Although true when I said it, repeating that statement today would be slightly disingenuous."

Logan cocked his head with interest, but he did not interrupt.

"Let me amend it now, to say that you could indeed—within certain restrictive parameters—travel to the future."

He nodded his head. "How far?"

"To my present—no further."

"Awesome!"

"I'm convinced that it can be done. One of my co-workers, a programmer named Ira Vincent Kegler, experimented with the deletion of a deeply embedded restraining code. I tested his hypothesis on an inanimate object—a smooth, oval stone of approximately two by three inches, assigning it to the next morning at ten o'clock, submerged in the shallow end of a swimming pool. And there it appeared, precisely at ten, where nothing had been on the pool's floor before then."

"Do you have access to his modified PG-13?"

"Better than that. I have it in my satchel." She pulled the device out and handed it to Logan. On its back side was a tiny gold barcode that seemed to float just above the metallic surface— an optical illusion that vibrated like a security hologram. "That's a federal microchip from DOI," Tammi said, "establishing who the rightful possessor is."

"Does this Mr. Kegler know you have it?"

"Yes. He's perfectly willing to let me confirm his theory by applying it to an actual human being."

"That's very generous of him, seeing as how I'm the one whose survival is at stake."

"Ira insists that there is no danger involved. If the future conduit is not open, you will simply remain where you are. The op will become what we call a 'non-starter'."

Logan frowned. "I don't know whether to believe him. I'd just be taking Kegler's word for it, and my continued existence is more valuable to me than that."

Tammi took a deep breath and, for the first time, allowed her emotions to show. "Listen, Mr. Gramm," she said. "I'm begging you to cooperate." Tears welled up in her eyes, and her voice began to quiver. "Like I told you earlier, this is a matter of life and death."

"And I asked you *whose*, but I'm still waiting for a reply." He rose to his feet, walked to the other side of the coffee table, turned, and stared down at her. "You haven't been very forthcoming with me, and I think I have a right to know. It's my blood that's going to be spilled if this op goes awry."

Tammi wiped away the tears. "I guess I don't have any choice, do I?" She glanced at Logan and then quickly away. "My brother was killed in a politically motivated assassination. That's the crux of the issue."

"And you think I can prevent it from happening?"

"That's what I'm praying."

"Why can't PG KRON include that mission as a regular op?"

"Because PGK is a contractor for the Department of the Interior."

"So?"

"DOI—being a loyal arm of the establishment—would never sanction such action."

Logan nodded his head. "Oh, I see." He began slowly pacing the room. "Are you telling me there's a civil war being fought?"

"No. At least not yet. Ours has become a very polarized society—sort of like what you're experiencing here, I gather."

He grimaced his tacit agreement. "How can I be sure that you're on the right side?"

"Trust me," she said. "From what I know about your philosophies, I think you'll fit right in with the others. My brother was very old-fashioned, and we never ceased to tease him about it."

"What was his name?"

"Jeffrey Hansen."

Logan stopped walking. "So, Hansen is your maiden name?"

"Yes. What did you think?" She looked at him.

"I'm not sure." He resumed his pacing, which he always found to be the best way to make important decisions. "Is your form of government still a republic?"

"Nominally," she said, "but often it's hard to tell."

"Again, like ours."

Tammi consulted her PG-13, which showed that only seven minutes remained before her departure. "Are you in?" she asked.

"Tentatively," Logan said, "but I need more details."

She seemed to shift gears, speeding through her presentation like a salesman with a plane to catch. "After a period of orientation—in my present, but far into your future—we'll have our cadre train you for the operation."

"Are we considered enemies of the state?"

"By some. As I mentioned, the populace is divided into two contentious factions—no middle ground." She finished her cola and laid the glass next to his. "Be forewarned that my world will seem unimaginably strange to you. But you have adjusted well to the distant past, so coping with the future should not be insurmountable."

"You did not say *distant* future."

"I left that vague on purpose. All time is relative, something we at PGK know better than most. Any other questions?"

"Will I have an excessive repercussion, to reverse any injury or death that I might suffer?"

"I'm afraid not," she told him. "This assignment is the equivalent of a Level-9 HDO, which means it's reserved for active military personnel, with no provision for a second chance."

"In other words, I'd be walking the high wire without a net."

She closed her eyes. "You're my only hope, Mr. Gramm. Otherwise, my brother is lost, and so is the cause."

"The cause?"

"You'll see. Unless I've badly misjudged you, the cause will become as important to you as it is to us."

"I'm not active military," he said. "Do I meet the standards?"

"You're a veteran, and that's good enough for me."

Logan stopped pacing and sat down next to her. "Let me think it over," he said. "When do you absolutely need an answer?"

"Now. I can never come back again—not with Ira Kegler's device at my disposal."

She looked so troubled and vulnerable that Logan felt his resistance weakening. He cleared his throat, and blurted it out: "Okay, I'm in."

Immediately, Tammi's face brightened, and she kissed him on the cheek. "I'll be in your debt forever, Logan Gramm. You have no idea how much this means to me."

Logan blushed. "Glad to help—I think. What's the next step in my Op-6?"

"That's not an official designation, by the way. It's just what I called it to fit the template, so to speak. Actually, your contract for PGK was fulfilled at five ops, and you have been honorably discharged from any further obligation."

"So, what's the plan?"

"Departure will be at 8:47 on Tuesday morning. If all goes well, you will return at 8:51 on Tuesday morning, with no one the wiser. You will have performed a heroic service for your country."

"But not for the Department of the Interior, I take it."

"No. This mission is outside the jurisdiction of DOI—and PG KRON, for that matter. You now fall into the category of free-lance contractor. Moreover, you will be getting paid—and quite handsomely, too. That's a perk that comes with Level-9 or Level-10 HDOs. Death or dismemberment are distinct possibilities, so you are rewarded accordingly. Consider yourself a mercenary, but one motivated by noble ideals. I think you'll see what I mean later."

"Tuesday morning at 8:47. I'll be ready. Do I need to bring anything along?"

"Everything will be supplied at our end. Here's your PG-13, which Ira Kegler has personally programmed for the future."

"Will it recognize my thumbprint?"

"Yes. One touch, and it's ready for activation."

"I'll do whatever I can to help," Logan said.

Tammi stood up. "Before I go, there's something else I need to tell you—in the spirit of full disclosure." She paused for a moment, as if debating whether to proceed. "I'm really not married. Every recruiter and field agent is urged to claim the existence of a spouse, no matter if it's true or not. This keeps any professional relationships free of compromising entanglements. For instance, I would not have wanted you to accept this mission for the wrong reasons."

Logan smiled at her. "Understood. I'll try to keep my mind on business."

"See that you do."

Tamara Renée Hansen took leave of Logan's apartment at 01:46:52, and Erin Duffy arrived there forty-seven seconds later. But as impressive as Tammi's chronological precision was, it was not infallible. Logan learned this on Tuesday morning as his scheduled departure drew precariously close. With a nervous eye on his roommate, he watched her lounge around the apartment, in no hurry to attend rehearsals. Obviously, Erin could not be right there with him when he disappeared into the beyond.

"Don't you need to rehearse today?" he asked.

"Last night went so well that it's been called off."

That said, Logan improvised a small task to occupy the required time. "I need to go scope out the laundry room, to see if I can wash this morning. Back in a few minutes."

Erin thought nothing of it, so the stage was set for his passage into the future. Logan walked down the stairs and then to the far side of the dumpster. No one was around, and he hoped that would also be the case upon his return to the present day. He gazed at the descending numerals on his PG-13.

✦　　✦　　✦

A train sped by, high above him, but it was not on rails. Its eight interconnected cars, flexibly coupled to one another, were unconfined to a track system. Instead, they snaked across the open space, at an altitude of fifty to a hundred feet, with the driver handling a joy stick that veered him around the towering assortment of stone-and-steel buildings. Wherever the pilot car went, the others were sure to follow. No sound was emitted, except for the knifing of air currents by an aerodynamic, hundred-miles-per-hour sliver of metal. Along both sides of its entire length, advertising shone forth from scrolling text, which matched the speed of the train itself and caused the message to appear stationary in the sky.

Something bumped Logan Gramm from behind. It was an annoyed woman's utility kit, resembling a backpack but worn on the front. "Well, go on!" she said through her facemask. Logan stepped forward amidst an impatient flow of citizens, all determined to reach the other side of the crossing before the admittance gates swung ninety degrees to a perpendicular direction. Not a single panhandler or homeless person was to be seen. It was all very efficient.

Surrounded by this pandemonium of pedestrians and bicycles, Logan kept an eye out for Tammi Hansen, who was supposed to meet him outside a collegiate hangout called greenearthdreams (all one word, lower case) at the intersection of N118 and W29. This was a smallish supper club, capable of holding fewer than sixty customers. Its menu touted veganism, to the exclusion of everything else, and in its window flashed an illuminated sign that proclaimed in red neon, "Embrace the Planet." A bony, short-haired young woman, standing in the entryway, peered so intently at Logan that he felt uncomfortable. And yet, he could not very well abandon the rendezvous point. He had no option but to ignore her.

Then a voice came from behind him. "Did you see the Viper?"

Logan turned around and saw Tammi smiling at him. She wore a loose-fitting gray jumpsuit. Indeed, almost all of the women—and men, too, for that matter—favored such a one-piece outfit. His dark green sweatshirt with blue jeans looked decidedly out of place in such company.

"Maybe so," Logan said. "What's the Viper?"

"There." She pointed toward another levitated train, which glided to a mid-air stop about three blocks away, at the N117-W31 Station.

He admired the conveyance's sleek design for a second. "I can see how it got the name. Remarkable."

Tammi extended her fist in greeting. "Welcome to my world, Mr. Gramm, such as it is."

He responded with a businesslike bump. "Nice to see you again, Miss Hansen. Your friend Kegler's post-engineering seems to have done the trick."

"Glad it didn't turn you into a stone at the bottom of a swimming pool. That was the other possibility."

Logan grinned. "Now you tell me."

"Oh, one important thing. Whenever you're around other people, whether they be male or female, the safest greeting is 'citizen' instead of Mr., Mrs., or Ms., and—most of all—Miss. You'll find that 'citizen' is completely neutral in terms of age, gender, and marital status."

"Thanks for the tip. I'll try to keep that in mind." He thought for a moment. "But didn't you just call me 'Mr. Gramm'?"

"That's fine, informally, but be sure to use 'citizen' in public settings. It just sounds more natural to our ears—after several generations of conditioning."

"Yes, citizen."

"Incidentally, it may interest you to know that I'm taking three personal days off from work, just to show you around. Don't you feel special?"

"Yes, indeed. I hope I'll prove worthy of your trust."

She escorted him to her flat on the 43rd floor of a 69-story apartment complex. Logan ambled over to the picture window to better appreciate the view. "Where are we, exactly?" he asked.

"In the N122 block of W26. The city is very logically conceived. All streets are arranged at right angles, aligning to the four corners of a compass—90, 180, 270, and 360 degrees. We use shorthand. Hence, West 26th Street is called W26 and so forth. You'll get used to it."

"What's your city called?"

"You've never heard of it—could not possibly have heard of it. The official name on maps is Solerograd, but we usually say Solly for short. It was built by visionary architects and municipal planners nearly a century ago. A sixth of a million acres of federal land were cleared, and then civil-service engineers and their workmen brought it into being."

"Are we in the United States?"

"Oh, yes. What did you think?"

"Well, the 'grad' part threw me. That seems like a Russian suffix, but maybe not."

"Or maybe so," Tammi said. She gave him a knowing wink.

"How many people live in Solly?"

"Six-point-one million at last count, according to our biennial census. A hundred years ago, this was vacant land. Then the developers moved in and transformed it into what you see now."

"An extraordinary feat."

"City fathers used to refer to Solerograd as a 'man-made paradise,' but that was too long ago to mention."

Logan thought he sensed a trace of sarcasm in the girl's voice, but perhaps he was mistaken. "One thing for sure. This is a nice apartment you have here," he said. "PROGRADE KRONOTECHNIX must pay well."

"Passably," she told him. "Do make yourself at home, and I'll try to play the good hostess." Accepting the offer, Logan began to idly walk around the flat, and Tammi was quick to join him as personal guide.

"Living room," she said, "complete with sofa, chairs, and the usual technological necessities—OmniScreen, reading zone, MusikPlatz, ChatLinker, VR cell, hologram zoo, MediCall." She gestured toward the bathroom: "Commode, hand-held bidet, wash basin, shower stall, cosmetics easel." And the bedroom: "Reclining bed, OmniScreen, suspended dresser, mirrored wall, walk-through closet." And, finally, the kitchen: "Convection oven, radiation oven, hotplate surface, recipe source-n-display, MagiCook, pantry shelves, biodegradable recycling chamber, and, of course, my PestRid Sonic Blaster. I haven't had so much as an ant in my four years of living here."

Logan was impressed and told her as much. "This really is a touch of paradise, to paraphrase your founders. Does everyone live in such pleasant conditions?"

"Yes and no. Mine is a C-9 lifestyle. Some live better, most live worse—depending upon their civil status."

"And marital status?"

"Well ... " She raised her index finger. "More on that later."

Logan had noticed, in passing, an eight-by-ten photo screen atop the dresser in Tammi's bedroom, so he walked back for a closer look. "Is that a picture of your brother?"

"Yes, that is Jeffrey—Jeff, I called him."

"How did they ... administer the assassination?" Logan asked.

"You mean, how did they murder him in cold blood? Don't worry. You won't hurt my feelings. That was nearly three years ago, so I've built up an immunity against sorrow by now." Tammi gave him a steely look. "But my appetite for revenge has taken a quantum leap."

"How old was he?"

"Just twenty-six—one year older than the minimum age for Congress."

"Do you know who was responsible for his ... murder?"

"THE ENTENTE," she said. "It's the party currently in power."

"Not one identifiable person, but just a faceless party? That's all you know?"

"Correct."

"Is that enough?"

"Correct."

Logan's vision swept around the living room again before focusing upon Tammi. In charade fashion, he gestured to them both and then made a talking motion with the fingers and thumb of one hand.

"Don't bother, Citizen Gramm," she told him. "You're also on *video*, you know. My guess is that the monitors watch all and hear all. They're probably laughing at your feeble antics right now." Tammi approached a barely discernible slit in the crown molding and beamed an exaggerated smile in that direction. "As you can see, I no longer even try to hide the fact that I'm on to them and their devious ways. I'm a productive member of the Department of the Interior, so they'll leave me alone, unless I make a credible threat or actually commit an overt crime." She smiled at the slit again and then spoke loudly to it. "Which I don't plan to do anytime soon."

Logan cast a wary glance toward the ceiling. "How many cameras are there?" he asked.

"Eight, by my best count, but there are probably more that are better disguised."

"Big Brother," Logan said, mostly to himself.

"Sorry?"

"This is like Big Brother in Orwell's *1984*."

Tammi stared at him, blankly.

"A very famous novel," he added, "written just after the Second World War."

"I consider myself to be well read," she told him, "but that title doesn't mean anything to me."

A wave of anxiety was closing in on Logan, and he felt the need to be out of this place. "Do you mind if we take a walk?" he asked. "The privacy here is stifling."

Tammi chuckled at the phrase. "You'll get used to it, Citizen Gramm. I have." She checked her ChatLinker for messages, but there were none. "Come with me. I need to show you around our fair city."

◆　◆　◆

The apartment building's elevator covered its 470-foot descent in 3.8 seconds—and yet with no light-headedness or sense of slamming to a sudden halt. "Something to do with controlling the explosive properties of air pressure," Tammi said. "At least that's what the rental manager once explained to me. I suppose she culls scraps of useful information from her sales meetings."

They exited the towering structure, and Logan glanced up immediately. "There goes a Viper. Let's hitch a ride."

Tammi was blasé, almost yawning at the prospect. "They arrive every six and a half minutes, so forgive me if I take them for granted. I can't even remember a time when they weren't a part of my life."

Logan, however, was gazing with wide eyes, like a child at his first circus or fireworks show. "What's the nearest station?" he asked.

"N120-W29."

"Umm ... " He calculated the streets' ordinal numbers. "Five blocks from here."

"Actually, that's not a bad idea," she said. "I need to orient you to the city anyway, and this can be step one."

They started walking toward the northeast.

"How long do you think it'll take?"

"Getting to the station?"

"No, my orientation process."

Tammi looked him up and down. "Are you a quick study?"

"Can't say for sure. I've never been to the future before."

"Which is exactly why we've left your PG-13 open ended. It only shows a START coordinate, with the infinity sign as a placeholder for the END. You probably noticed that."

"It did seem kind of strange," Logan said. He watched in awe as three overhead trains soared by in silence.

Tammi grinned at him. "I'm sure you're wondering what the present year is."

"That did cross my mind."

"Well, I'd be happy to tell you," she said, "but it really wouldn't serve any purpose."

"Why not?"

"Because the year will be so arbitrary for someone with your background. Have a look." She pointed to the Viper station's rotating message board. Across its top, above the arrival and departure minutes, was a strip that read, "THØRDAY, 17 MAI 149 – 08:29:35.6."

"That's the current time?" he asked.

"And date."

Logan gawked at the display, trying to make some sense of it all.

"Actually, there is a history behind the designated year," Tammi told him. "An international committee, World Time Custodian, fulfilled its mandate by repudiating any notion of Christianity while also rejecting the successor measuring stick, Common Era, along with their antecedents, BC and BCE. That means you are now living in the year 149 GC."

"I don't get it."

"Standardization began one hundred forty-nine years ago with the establishment of the GC in Lucerne, Switzerland. Those initials represent Global Citizen, a multi-national effort to level the playing field between the haves and the have-nots. It didn't do much good, but at least the committee members were able to congratulate each other for knocking their countries down a notch or two in world opinion. As you might expect, there's going to be a big Sesquicentennial Celebration next year—though exactly what we're celebrating is anybody's guess."

"So ... how far into the future am I?" Logan asked.

Tammi's eyes sparkled with mirth. "That, my inquisitive friend, I cannot tell you."

"Why am I not surprised?"

She motioned for him to enter the station's ramplift, made necessary because the loading platform was twenty-seven feet, four inches above street level, a vertical clearance that scientists had determined to be the optimum level for safe hovering and passenger exchange. Tammi purchased two DayPass tickets by swiping her integrated-circuit microchip across a ViperScan. Implanted at the back of her wrist, just above the joint, this invisible barcode charged the transaction to its proper account. No money was used. No money existed.

Logan was dumbfounded by the innovative features of the trackless train. With twenty-first-century subways as his only point of reference, experiencing the Viper was something entirely new to him. This was like riding on a cushion of air. Not a bump was felt, no jarring stops, nary a rattling window, never squealing around a curve. And the speed was exhilarating. It occurred to Logan that such a display of soaring power was not unlike a jet fighter's, but without the ear-splitting noise of a turbine.

This form of public transportation had proven to be virtually infallible, too. Over the course of its quarter-century of public duty, safety concerns had been reduced to negligibility. Only the Viper fleet—and it alone—was permitted to occupy the restricted zone of air space, except for authorized emergency vehicles. While human error in the cockpit was always conceivable, the driver's role had been relegated to operating what amounted to a video game's joy stick: roll, pitch, and yaw. Velocity was handled by an unseen master computer, far removed from the established routes and the threat of terroristic sabotage.

The Viper's doors were virtual. Whenever the craft was in motion, a force field caused openings to become impenetrable. No one could enter, exit, fall, or jump from the vehicle. Moreover, this produced a "solid" surface for commercial signage, which in turn generated advertising revenue for salaries and maintenance. Convenience was paramount. Viper crafts were so numerous that every stop on the route map was served at least nine times per hour in all directions. Within each train, a synthesized female voice alerted passengers to upcoming stations, but that amenity was largely redundant. On the Viper, a traveler's plastic ticket would vibrate and blink yellow when the final destination drew to within a half-mile away—and eighteen seconds was ample warning.

As for Tammi and Logan, they stayed aboard for a span of eleven stops, intending to detrain at the N53-E17 Station. In transit, a stumbling toddler struck her head on the virtual door, causing an artificially generated metallic *thump*, followed by a very real cry of pain and a swelling bruise. Other than that, the ride was uneventful. All the while, the sights of Solerograd flew by almost too fast to register any visual impression. But it was definitely an urban landscape throughout, for agricultural harvesting was consigned to property that lay outside the city limits. Were there affluent districts? Were there slums? Probably so, but it was difficult to tell from this perspective, given the Viper's velocity, circuitous pathway, and low altitude. Everything blurred into a fleeting glimpse.

When they finally reached their stop, Logan wondered why an illuminated sign over the platform carried not only the street coordinates but also the descriptive epithet of "Stadia."

"This is Solly's sports complex—soccer, baseball, football, and basketball stadiums, all situated within a one-square-mile section. There's a soccer match tonight, but it doesn't kick off for another six hours."

They happened to be standing outside the basketball arena at present. Although quite massive, as such structures go, it was positively dwarfed by the other three facilities, which were arrayed alongside one another in the distance.

"What are the seating capacities?" Logan asked.

"Two hundred thousand for football. I'm not sure of the others."

He allowed his eyes to scan the broad complex. "What strikes me is the lack of parking lots."

Tammi divulged why. "There's no need for them, in the absence of private transportation. As recently as ten years ago, a handful of people were still driving cars, but now they've been outlawed by Congress. The ozone layer, you know." Her face turned wistful. "I remember back when I was a little girl. A man down the street from us owned an automobile. He offered to give Jeff and me a ride one day, but my parents were afraid to let us go with him."

"How come?"

"He was thought to be rebellious, a radical who lived by his own rules, and I suppose our parents didn't want us to be guilty by association. The man died a couple of years later, and a salvage company hauled his car away to be crushed for scrap metal. It was his prized possession."

"Confiscated by the government?" Logan asked.

"No doubt," Tammi told him. "The government has supreme authority in all matters of civic interest." She shrugged her shoulders. "It was probably recycled into something more acceptable."

They continued on foot into a business district, where sprawling office buildings coexisted with retail outlets. Dominating the sidewalks were large contingents of people, who practiced public yoga, dance routines, and synchronized aerobics during their lunch hours. "I'll give them credit," Tammi said. "These folks are making an effort to get in shape, whereas others have simply given up. The government requires morbidly overweight people to undergo a twelve-step radiation process—called Fatty Tissue Atomization—which literally burns away the mounds of fat. It is an agonizing and often lethal procedure, but the Health Resources Division is resolute in its crusade to combat the obesity epidemic. FTA's high mortality rate is merely a sad but inescapable byproduct."

Sharing the remaining roadside surface with the exercising "healthies" were hundreds of identical bicycles, all of them secured in racks. It was a misdemeanor to leave one's bike unlocked. Only a few avenues in town—called "turnpikes"—had been designated as bicycle routes, and two-wheelers were prohibited elsewhere, except when merely walking alongside them.

Most intersections in this part of the city were heavily populated with citizens who seemed in a frantic rush to get where they wished to be. Tammi told Logan that the pervasive haste resulted from a dire shortage of leisure time for the typical laborer. Each adult in the work force, from C-1 through C-6, was expected to invest a minimum of sixty-two hours per week on the job. There was no way around it. Their implanted wrist chips saw to that. The government knew where every Sollian was during every second of every day. Society was well organized.

Logan and Tammi hurried across N51 where it bisected E18. "Tell me this, Citizen Hansen," he said. "If people work such long hours, how come so many of them are out here on the streets? They're not all on their lunch hours, are they?"

"Some are, of course, but only about thirty-seven percent of the able-bodied adults have jobs. The rest are unemployed."

"How do they put food on the table? They need to eat and pay their rents."

"Welfare, Citizen Gramm. They're on the dole."

Logan found that hard to believe. "The majority of adults are on welfare?"

"That's the size of it. They receive generous stipends every month, deposited into their accounts."

"Where does the money come from?"

She mustered a grin. "You're looking at her—me and others on the civil service payroll. Our taxes keep the feeding trough full."

"Are any workers employed outside the government, by private companies?"

"Theoretically, I suppose, but it's a question of semantics. What constitutes a 'private' company?"

Logan knew she meant that rhetorically, so he did not even bother to respond. Besides, there were some suspicious-looking youths, almost a dozen in number, approaching from the north. They swaggered down E18, holding little concern for any unfortunates who might be in their path. As they passed, Logan positioned himself between them and Tammi, offering her a semblance of protection. One of the young men shoved him out of the way, but Logan managed to keep his feet, and there were too many of them to confront, either verbally or with his fists.

The ruffians went by, inflicting no major damage or injuries that Logan was able to observe. "Who were they?" he asked. "What's their gripe?"

"SKUDZ," Tammi told him. "Essentially, they're dropouts from orderly civilization. They've acquired that name—all caps, with a 'k' and 'z' instead of the normal spelling—because they move as fast as the wind, rarely being apprehended. There are pockets of SKUDZ scattered all over Solly, and they pride themselves on inducing mayhem without accountability." She asked Logan if there are any such gangs in his world, running rampant and thumbing their noses at police.

"More than a few, I'm sorry to say. And I'm not surprised that Solly has its share of them, too. Even in the most authoritarian society, there's bound to be a criminal element lurking beneath the surface."

"Ours don't lurk," she said. "If the hordes are large enough—and their politics agree with THE ENTENTE—they have no fear of being harassed by the police."

Logan stared far ahead, where the band of hooligans was almost out of view. "What happens to the SKUDZ who are caught?"

"They're tried, but then usually released with a stern wag of the index finger. In really serious cases—rape, murder, and so forth—the penalties are appropriately harsh, with labor camps, solitary confinement, and some well-placed brutality. People quite often disappear from society, never to be seen again, but officially there's no capital punishment in Solerograd. We're much too civilized for that."

Tammi's personality did seem to have a cynical side to it.

◆ ◆ ◆

They Vipered to S1-W1, "City Center," detraining directly across S1 from an imposing structure that resembled a Greek temple. Its ten Doric columns supported a stone entablature, which proclaimed in boldly chiseled letters, SOLEROGRAD COUNTY LIBRARY—A. T. STALEY, ARCHITECT.

Tammi was about to exit the station in an easterly direction, away from the library building, when Logan made a personal request. "For me to have a true taste of Solly, shouldn't I become acquainted with its culture?"

"By all means, yes. What do you have in mind?"

"The usual suspects: literature, music, art, theater, movies."

"We have every cultural organization you could possibly imagine—and then some," she said. "Where shall we start?"

He looked across the street. "Why not the public library?"

"Fine with me."

Tammi's ready acceptance led Logan to wonder if she might grant him some freedom to roam. "I hate to monopolize your time off from work," he said, "so how about letting me explore on my own? I'm very good at it."

"I know you are. That's one reason why you were recruited." Her face grew serious. "To be honest with you, Citizen Gramm, we cannot allow you to wander around Solerograd on your own—without a guide, so to speak. There's too much hanging in the balance."

"I see." Logan studied her for a moment, then gave a polite nod. "In that case, please lead on."

"I hope you can appreciate my ... dilemma."

"I'll try."

The library's entry vestibule was stark, marble, echoey. An immense desk lay directly ahead, and behind it sat an unsmiling woman of about seventy. Her gray hair was styled in a severe chignon bun, and she wore half-moon reading glasses. When she heard footsteps, the lady looked up from a horizontal cataloguing screen to acknowledge the intruders. "Yes?" was the extent of her greeting.

"Circulation," Tammi said.

The attendant, wasting not a word, pointed to Room 1.03 and promptly returned her attention to the screen.

Logan followed Tammi to the doorway, which, upon sensing motion, silently opened by swinging away from them at the bottom, regulated by overhead suspension hinges. Even to Logan's unschooled eyes, this technology seemed rather quaint—almost humorous—like a sci-fi movie's notion of the incomprehensible future.

Inside the room were twenty or more free-standing tables, each supporting a liquid crystal display that identified its particular academic discipline. Only four other patrons were there, all of them women in the twilight of their lifespans. Logan overheard one lady say to another, "Have you read *A Window to Anacreon's Heart?* It's a romance novel but worthy of the greatest fiction." In lieu of an earlier era's library cards, these women carried with them portable disks, designed to wirelessly receive transferred data from the table panels.

Logan turned toward a much younger lady, who appeared to be the attendant on duty. "Excuse me, citizen," he said.

"Yes?" She was sweet-faced but just as surly as her co-worker at the reception desk.

"This library of yours—how many volumes does it house?"

"Volumes?"

"How many books?"

The girl rolled her eyes. "You mean physical books ... "

"That's right."

"Go to antiquities."

"Where's that?"

But she was typing in some cataloguing information and did not answer. Miffed, Logan placed a hand over her screen and repeated the question.

"Fourth floor," the girl said. She scowled at him, grumbling under her breath. "C-1 ... "

Logan took a moment to consult the wall directory, whose alphabetical listing included a section called "Virtual Encounters—3.07." That was too intriguing for him to miss, so he invited Tammi to accompany him two floors up. They boarded a continual lift and stepped from it when their compartment drew even with the third level. Each of the VR studios in Room 3.07 stood beneath a green light or a red light, depending upon availability. Logan found one with a green light above and entered, leaving Tammi just outside. Within this soundproof cubicle stood a kiosk supporting a touch-sensitive menu. Choices were almost limitless, ranging through such categories as politics, the arts, military, American history, world history, celebrities, motivational, sports, "Pre-Solly" Solerograd, global religions, cuisine, great speeches, and the animal kingdom.

After learning some basic mechanics of the eyecursor, he embarked upon an astonishing journey into quasi reality. Logan browsed through the WORLD HISTORY tab and flashclicked on SECOND WORLD WAR. Within that subheading, he chose ROOSEVELT AND CHURCHILL and, narrower still, HARVARD DEGREES. When he selected CHURCHILL SPEAKS AT HARVARD, there was a short delay of perhaps ten seconds as the file loaded. And then, standing directly in front of him from September 6, 1943, was a video representation of Winston Churchill—a colorized, three-dimensional, full-sized hologram of the British Prime Minister.

Utilizing the hands-free eyecursor, Logan had the capability of watching Churchill's image from any angle, using a synthesized interpolation of video content. As seen from the front, the Prime Minister spoke into multiple microphones, which rested on a wooden stand. American military officers and civilian dignitaries were clearly visible behind him. Dollying the vantage point around Mr. Churchill brought into the hologram's camera frame a crowd of twelve thousand uniformed listeners on the Harvard campus. While periodically tapping his walking stick for emphasis, the Prime Minister addressed his audience with these words: "You will feel that we are your worthy brothers in arms, and you will know that we shall never tire nor weaken, but march with you into any quarter of the world that may be necessary to establish the reign of justice and of law among men."

The better part of a million video clips were accessible for viewing in this incredibly lifelike 3-D format, and Logan took the opportunity to sample four or five of them. When he finally emerged from the studio, Tammi was waiting for him. "Learn anything?" she asked.

Logan was giddy with enthusiasm. "Fabulous technology! It's like nothing I've ever seen before—or could hope to see again."

She seemed pleased. "So, what's next?"

"Did you bring your downloading device along?"

"I never go anywhere without it."

"May I have a look?"

She reached into her breast pocket and handed him a lightweight disk, which Logan judged to be about the diameter of a fifty-cent piece. Although he himself had never owned a half-dollar, his father had a sizable collection of them, mostly with John F. Kennedy's likeness on the obverse but some with Benjamin Franklin.

"What's the storage capacity?" he asked her.

"More than you could fill in a lifetime, I'm sure."

Logan tilted the gleaming disk, admiring the clean artistry of its design. "Can we go back to circulation for a few minutes?"

"Certainly."

Down the lift they went, stepping off at street level, although the conveyance continued on its oval circuit, below ground and then rising in a continual loop.

Once inside Room 1.03, Logan looked at the search engine atop one of the identical tables. "How does this thing work?"

Tammi laid her disc in the "hot zone" and activated her library functions by touching the thumbprint pad. "It's ready. What do you want me to download for you?"

"Not for me—for yourself. The book by Orwell I was telling you about. Do you promise to read it?"

"Okay, if it's that important to you."

With the eyecursor, Logan navigated the screen to where "Orwell, George: *1984*" would be found. But the entry was not there. Nor, for that matter, was his *Animal Farm*. "They have something against Orwell, I guess." He tried Eric Blair instead, but the author's real name did not produce any positive results either.

"When was it written?" Tammi asked.

"In 1948, I believe. Orwell just reversed the final two digits for the title and setting."

"Well, I suppose you can't expect our library to have every book ever written."

"But that's a classic—never out of print," Logan said.

"There are bound to be some gaps in every library's holdings, especially from that long ago."

"How long ago?"

Her inscrutable smile reappeared. "You already know what today's date is." She nodded toward an electronic panel on the kiosk—THØRDAY, 17 MAI 149. "I can't be the one to tell you how far into your future that is. It's against my solemn oath to PG KRON."

"But this is an unofficial op."

"That makes no difference. I'm still employed by PROGRADE KRONOTECHNIX."

Logan searched the database in vain for Aldous Huxley's *Brave New World*, and, with a similar lack of success, for *The Screwtape Letters* by C. S. Lewis. Ayn Rand's *The Fountainhead* was nowhere to be found either, nor was her *Atlas Shrugged*. It was becoming apparent that somewhere in the annals of this library a political stance had been adopted, one that gradually developed into an acquisitions policy.

"Are you familiar with any of my titles?" he asked.

"Sorry, but no," Tammi told him. "None of them."

As a sort of litmus test, Logan attempted some additional searches—*The Gulag Archipelago* by Aleksandr Solzhenitsyn, *The Road to Serfdom* by F. A. Hayek, *Democracy in America* by Alexis de Tocqueville, *Capitalism and Freedom* by Milton Friedman—but it was as if these once-influential writings never existed.

Tammi Hansen, as a native Sollian, felt compelled to defend her county library. "We are famous for being the first library in the world with more than one billion bibliographical items, ranging back to antiquity and across every known language on the globe."

"Then how do you account for those missing titles?"

She pursed her lips. "Inexplicable."

◆　◆　◆

Even in the future, Logan Gramm remained an inhabitant of his physical body—every bit as corporeal as anyone else in Solerograd—so he was obliged to find accommodations for sleeping at night. When he asked Tammi whether she might allow him to stay with her, she made it clear that such an arrangement was unacceptable. "Don't even think about it," she told him. "My morality is so strict that even someone from your era would consider it old-fashioned."

"Are values like yours common in Solly?" Logan asked.

"Hardly. I'm in the minority when it comes to casual sex."

"Even with video cameras monitoring every move that people make?"

"People get used to them, I suppose, and forget that they're even around."

"But you know for a fact that they are."

"The government has never said as much, but I've always suspected that they are. Just in case, I treat them as a clear and present danger. Maybe I'm just being neurotic, but I don't think so."

"Can people be arrested for spending the night together?"

"Nothing in the civil statutes forbids extra-marital cohabitation, if that's what you mean," she said. "Consenting adults in Solerograd live with one another as they so choose—for however long their mutual attraction might endure. It's an open society, in that respect."

"Married or not?"

"Sure. The institution of marriage is permissible, but it's accorded no special favor in the courts of law."

After weighing all of her options, Tammi escorted Logan, by Viper and on foot, to N120-W24, the address where she continued to maintain her late brother's flat. She had left the premises virtually unaltered since Jeffrey's death, with basic necessities available for any occasional lodger who might require them. This apartment was only four blocks southeast of Tammi's own living quarters, so it was no great hardship to accompany Logan there on her way home.

The girl's first task was to grant entry recognition for his thumbprint. Then she made certain that the bedroom closet was stocked with an ample supply of gray jumpsuits. Tammi's parting gesture was a friendly fistbump.

"I'm afraid there are just some energy bars for breakfast," she told him. "This is not a full-service hotel."

"No problem."

"I'll come by for you at 8:30, so please be ready. We have a busy day ahead of us."

As Logan lay in bed, waiting an hour or more for sleep to overtake him, he thought about this sprawling city and tried in vain to make some sense of its riddles. To give due credit, Solerograd did seem less threatening than most fictional locales in dystopian literature—those where a failure to shout party slogans with sufficient fervor might mean arrest and imprisonment. And yet, Solly was certainly no utopia, and the intrusive surveillance ("voluntary protection") made Logan wonder how free he actually was. He knew that informers were probably observing him right now through those seemingly innocuous slits in the crown molding. Darkness was no barrier for the latest infrared technology, something this futuristic government surely had at its disposal.

Tammi was true to her word, arriving punctually at 8:30, but Logan had not yet finished his morning meal. "I'll have to eat on the run," he said. The energy bar was composed of a mixture of granola, oats, sorghum, and a roasted grain called freekeh, and this concoction was surprisingly tasty for a product that promoted nutritional health on nearly every square inch of its 2x6 wrapper. The labeling was generic—red block letters on a white background, self-identified as ENERGY BAR and citing its place of origin as home-grown: PRODUCT OF SOLEROGRAD. Such banal packaging did not augur well for the vitality of free-market competition.

"By the way, nice clothes," Tammi told him. "We match."

Logan smiled. "It's always best to wear the official team color."

Their first stop was a lengthy train ride away, the farthest point that Solly's municipal line was equipped to take them. It was an unincorporated settlement, just beyond the city limits to the east-northeast, a desolate outpost where residences were so temporary that they had no house numbers. When the Viper glided into this station—a terminus called Tory's Edge—Logan and Tammi were the only two passengers to step down from the train.

But they were not alone. A man seated inside a glass-domed hovercraft was waiting for them there.

Logan gazed at the curious transport. "What is that?"

"An ACV."

"Which means ... ?"

"Air-cushion vehicle."

The ACV's driver climbed out as they approached, and Tammi seemed to be well acquainted with him. He was rather short of stature and wore a neatly trimmed black beard. Through tiny eyeglasses, he stared intently at the visitor. "So, this is the one you call 'Jersey Boy'."

Tammi gave Logan an embarrassed look. "We needed a code name for you, and that seemed to be as good as anything."

"I don't mind."

"What's the operation number?" the man asked her. His accent was vaguely east European.

"Technically, there's no number assigned. PROGRADE KRONOTECHNIX is out of the picture for this one, so I'm calling it his 'Op-6'."

"How did you manage to lose PGK?"

"An experiment by a colleague of mine."

The man nodded slightly. "I. V. Kegler?"

"Could be."

He touched the side of his nose. "I'll never tell."

Tammi turned to Logan and belatedly introduced the man to him. "Citizen Gramm, this is Gabriel Torveldt. Gabe wears many hats for us, quite often behind the scenes."

Stiffly, the man nodded at Logan but said nothing.

They entered the four-seater, and Torveldt issued a voice command: "DEFIANCE TWO." Immediately, the ACV shot into action, pressing the three passengers against their chair backs, which enveloped them within protective arms. Reaching a cruising velocity of 130 miles per hour in 4.3 seconds, the ACV silently followed a programmed pathway to the hinterlands. Although the sun's rays were almost directly ahead, an acrylic-glass windscreen automatically responded by tinting itself to the proper density for comfortable viewing. Within six minutes, they had arrived at the Quigley Tower, a thirty-eight-story office building of characterless, pragmatic design. The ACV parked itself among a dozen others on the rooftop aeropad.

Torveldt admitted the three of them with a combination of thumbprint and lanyard scan, and a hydraulic elevator carried them down to the twenty-seventh floor. Here they were greeted by a distinguished man with sculptured physique and military-length gray hair—as if some Marine sergeant had stepped off a movie screen. "Welcome to HQ-2, Citizen Gramm," the man said. "I'm David Crownover, but you can call me Dave. We're pretty relaxed around here, dispensing with formalities as often as possible. First names only, please. It encourages us to work more efficiently as a single unit."

"Nice to meet you ... Dave."

They bumped fists, and Crownover's felt like coiled steel. "You'll be fully briefed, Logan, but over a reasonable period of time. That will enable you to assimilate what we expect you to know. We pride ourselves on never sending an agent out unprepared."

"What's the name of your organization?" Logan asked him.

"DEFIANCE, but there's nothing official about that. We've discovered it's safer to remain loosely grouped—much tougher to pinpoint an indeterminate foe." Crownover nodded toward the girl. "By the way, Logan, your friend here has become one of our best recruiters."

Tammi's face reddened. "That's because I have a personal stake in this mission."

"True enough," Crownover said. He turned back to Logan. "I presume she's filled you in about her brother."

"Yes, sir."

Crownover sighed. "Less formal, please."

"Sorry ... Dave." Logan began to ask something else but thought better of it.

"Go ahead, son—proceed," Crownover told him. "That's the only way we'll make any progress."

Logan searched for the right words. "Why go to the trouble of recruiting me when there must be plenty of qualified people right here in present-day Solerograd?"

"Not so. Generation after generation has been indoctrinated to accept the official line. Incrementally, over many years, the spark was lost. You might say that dipping into the distant past is our lifeline to sanity."

After their brief visit with Crownover, Tammi led Logan to a room that had all the trappings of an employees' lounge. It was on the twenty-fifth floor and contained a dozen tables, with chairs, surrounded by what appeared to be vending machines. "We're going to meet Beverly Cline here at nine thirty," Tammi said. "She'll give you a much better overview of this building than I could. I work at PG KRON, across town, and hardly ever have occasion to drop into HQ-2. We can get together again in an hour or so."

"Who's Beverly?"

"Bev is the technologer for David Crownover."

"How do you mean?"

"A technologer is someone who manages an automaton's input status." Tammi saw Logan flinch. "Didn't Dave seem a bit strange to you?" she added.

"No. Except for his knuckle-popping fistbump, which might have been a little too emphatic."

"I'll let Bev know about that. She can adjust it."

Logan took a deep breath. "Let me get this straight. David Crownover is not a real person?"

"Not at all. Our Tech Department will be delighted to know that you didn't notice."

"I was talking to a robot?"

Tammi chuckled. "That's an archaic word. I haven't heard many people use it since *Forbidden Planet*."

Logan could hardly believe his ears. "You know that movie? *Forbidden Planet* is from the middle 1950s. How can you have seen it?"

"It's a cult favorite around here," Tammi said. "But please don't use that term in front of Bev. She'd resent your equating David Crownover with Robby the Robot. The Superba-IV Class is the world's most advanced synthetic human—an *Übermensch*, so to speak."

Logan grinned. "Is David Crownover faster than a speeding bullet?"

"No, and he's not more powerful than a locomotive or able to leap tall buildings in a single bound."

"You're familiar with the 'Superman' series, too. Why is that?"

Tammi became quite serious. "It's our duty to learn the pop cultures of men and women we're recruiting. After all, that's a very significant part of their lives."

"But you don't know literature all that well. What about Orwell's books and those other titles?"

"There are some blind spots, I suppose, depending upon what the government has allowed to survive into the present."

"The Founding Fathers must be rolling in their graves about now," Logan said. Tammi looked confused, so he elaborated. "Washington, Adams, Jefferson, Madison, Franklin, Hamilton. They put their lives in peril for freedom of speech."

"I've heard of them, of course, but they've been consigned to the scrap heap of our country's legacy. Today's conventional wisdom is that these were white men of privilege, some of whom were involved in slaveholding and abuse. They created this republic—there's no denying that—but most, it seems, were not worthy of the adulation that previous generations showered upon them."

"Who says?"

"According to the revisionist historians, we have a dubious past that does not bear careful scrutiny. It's in all of the textbooks."

Logan smirked. "No doubt."

Beverly Cline arrived in the lounge a few minutes later. She was, to all appearances, a scholarly woman of about thirty-five, gaunt of figure and plain of face. Though not unfriendly, she was almost totally humorless. Logan's little jokes fell flat with her so consistently that he stopped making the effort. What Beverly did have was an all-encompassing knowledge of the Quigley Tower, in which the pseudo-insurgent organization called DEFIANCE occupied four stories.

For Logan's viewing, she presented all but a few of the rooms—those that required a security clearance of L-8 or higher. "I've never been in there myself, so don't feel bad," she said.

"What about David Crownover?"

For some reason, that rattled Beverly. "What about him?"

"Does he have a top clearance?"

"Naturally. Of all people on the payroll, Citizen Crownover is the least likely security risk."

During the course of their hour-long tour, they observed the historical preservation office, forgery lab, target range, translation wing, alternate newsroom, and medical clinic. Also seen were the demarcated zones of cultural analysis, political manipulation, PTSD counseling, computer graphics, media productions, cosmological research, chemical/biological testing, innovative cloning, identity issuance, time concepts, bookkeeping, and custodial. Six additional rooms were considered off-limits. Their doors were devoid of any lettering that might suggest what covert activities transpired inside.

Tammi was not yet in the staff lounge when Beverly and Logan finally made their way back. "Want some caffeine sticks while we're waiting?" Beverly asked. "My treat."

"Thanks. That would be fine," Logan said. He presumed that this would be a good introduction to one of the social graces. Beverly slipped her personal disk into a slot, and the vending machine returned it to her in less than a second. Into the machine's tray dropped what Logan thought resembled a five-pack of chewing gum. He tore into it and placed one of the sticks onto his tongue. There was no taste until his molars crushed it into a saliva pulp. Then it burst forth with a bold flavor that evoked for him a fine cup of rich coffee. "Do I swallow this or just keep it in my mouth like chewing gum?" he asked.

Beverly gave him a befuddled look. "Haven't you ever eaten a caffeine stick before?"

"Well, of course. But there are lots of different kinds—some of which are not to be ingested." Even to Logan that sounded phony, and he could not fault her for judging him with lesser regard from that moment onward.

"Yes, please feel free to swallow," she told him. "And save the other four sticks for later. Eating more than one at a time is discouraged by doctors because it can cause your heartbeat to race."

"Potent stuff."

"Precisely. Not recommended for insomniacs. It is imperative that you allow four hours between doses."

"Thanks for the advice." He continued to masticate, like a cow chewing her cud.

"I once ate all five when I was pulling an all-nighter in college," Beverly said, "and I felt nauseous for a whole week. Couldn't even take the final exam that I was studying for that night. Lesson learned."

Reluctant to swallow, Logan nonetheless forced himself to do so and felt a sudden jolt of adrenaline race through his chest. Now light-headed, he slid the opened pack into his jumpsuit's breast pocket.

"Where are you from, to be so ... uninitiated?" Beverly asked.

"Pennsylvania, originally, but now New Jersey." If that meant anything to her, she did not show it.

"It's not often that we encounter a non-Sollian," she said. "Rarely indeed."

◆　　◆　　◆

As the lunch hour drew near, Tammi informed Logan that they would meet one of her PGK colleagues at greenearthdreams, a trendy eating place in the northwest quadrant. The supper club's name sounded familiar to him because this had been their rendezvous point when he first set foot in Solerograd.

A Viper transported them to the N117-W31 Station, and they walked the remaining three blocks, swept along in the mass of pedestrians. On the way, Logan noticed a distant obelisk that resembled a church steeple, and he asked Tammi about it.

"I assure you that it's not a church," she said. "Throughout its long history, there has never been a house of worship in Solly because our municipal ordinances prohibit their construction within the city limits. Of course, many beautiful cathedrals still exist in other parts of the United States, but those structures pre-date the federal edicts and are grandfathered to continue standing."

"Are services held in them anymore?" Logan asked.

"In the cathedrals? No. They're only for show now, although weddings and funerals are still permitted on a limited basis. Some of the country's largest ceremonial events are held there, too, whenever grand pageantry is wanted for dramatic effect."

"If there are no churches for people to attend, can they worship God at home?"

"Just in family-sized numbers. Regulations state that 'citizens may not congregate for purposes of spiritual expression in excess of four individuals.' Many devout Christians have been arrested for violation of this law—mostly for attempting to host Bible-study groups. This is a secular society, and organized religion, as such, does not exist."

"Why not go somewhere else—or are all cities like this one?"

"Intercity travel is prohibited. Sollians are subjects of the Government of Solerograd."

Logan was aghast. "Are you telling me that you've never been out of Solerograd?"

"No—except for my PGK recruiting. I'm a very unusual case."

"And the fact that your citizens are locked within these city limits is why Solly is given its own legislative branch?"

"That's right. It operates like a national body, with senators and congressmen. Every major city in the United States is autonomous in that respect."

"But they're also isolated from the rest of the country."

"I suppose you could say that."

"How many states are there?"

"States? Well, fifty-six, counting D.C., but they're just figurative, with no real power."

"And the District of Columbia is your national capital?"

"I'm not familiar with that," she said.

"D.C."

"The District of Carpathia is on the eastern seaboard—beautiful, historic architecture, administered by the National Park Service. It's the smallest state by far, even smaller than Rhode Island."

"When did the ban on travel come about?" Logan asked.

"When the pandemic hit, twenty-two years ago. Closing off movement was imposed as a way to slow the spread of a virus. It's also why so many citizens still choose to wear protective masks in public."

"Did the disease just vanish on its own?"

"Some say so. Others insist that a newly developed vaccine killed the virus." Tammi seemed to tremble slightly. "Conspiracy theorists contend that the vaccine had a mental component to it, nanoparticles that infest the brain, making people easier to control ... and to trace."

They turned a corner and saw, directly ahead of them, what appeared to be a political demonstration. A thousand or more protesters filled the street and both sidewalks. Many held signs that read, "WELFARE FOR ALL SOLLIANS!" and "PROFITS BREED GREED." A police cordon struggled to keep a path open to the right, and that is where pedestrians were impelled to forge ahead. The protest was peaceful, for the most part, but a half-dozen effigies were burning, and a police hovercraft's windshield had been smashed by a sledge hammer. No arrests were made, lest the dissidents turn violent in unmanageable numbers.

Tammi and Logan finally made it through the bedlam, jostled but uninjured. She stopped walking for a moment, eyeing the urban scene that surrounded them. "Have you wondered why you don't see any children on the streets?"

Logan shrugged his shoulders. "Well, now that you mention it ... "

"All babies belong to the state and are reared in controlled conditions at childcare facilities," she said. "Ostensibly, this protects them from outside influences—like their parents, for instance."

"But babies are being born?"

"In record quantities. Parents earn a substantial cash award for each and every live birth. Then they surrender their infants to experts."

"They don't see them after they're born?"

"Never."

"Even the mothers?"

"Women in labor wear 'maternity blinders' to prevent them from bonding with their newborns, no matter how briefly."

Logan shook his head. "That's like torture for the mothers."

"It's up to them. They could have opted to end their pregnancies."

"Abortions are allowed?"

"Very much so. Solerograd is renowned for its out-patient AOD clinics. There are fourteen of them scattered around the city. All have the same money-back guarantee: successful termination of the fetus in a quarter-hour or less. A couple of them give door prizes."

"What does AOD stand for?"

"Abortion-On-Demand. Medical schools can train AOD techs in far less time than other specialties. They turn them out like sausages."

"But if parents earn solid money for live births, why would anyone decide to abort?"

"Convenience. If the prospective mother does not wish to be burdened by a full-term pregnancy, she may elect to end the process—even on a whim. AOD techs can handle all situations, no matter how many months along. 'Any time, from one to nine.' That's their slogan, though it doesn't rhyme very well."

A perplexing thought occurred to Logan. "You told me that all babies belong to the state."

"That's right."

"Then why does the state permit women to choose abortion instead? In essence, they're destroying governmental property."

"They are indeed, but human body parts are valuable, too. These are harvested from the AOD clinics and preserved for use in medical procedures."

"Do they euthanize the babies?"

"The fetuses, you mean?"

"Yes, the fetuses."

"Unfortunately, that would consume too much time, and the cost of lethal chemicals is prohibitive." Tammi could see that this troubled Logan. "Don't worry," she told him. "Except for any techs who happen to be males, no men are allowed within the premises. From what I've heard, the AOD clinics are quite festive—with balloons and confetti, trying to make it a positive experience for the women—and every cessation room is fully soundproofed."

When they reached the mealtime destination, Tammi used her personal disk to gain admittance for herself and one guest, and they proceeded up the stairs. This second-floor supper club was filled to capacity at the noon hour, so Logan and Tammi had to wait for twenty minutes before her disk finally began to vibrate to signify an available table.

"Another person will be joining us shortly," Tammi told the desk attendant. He, in turn, passed the word along to a hostess, who seated the pair at one of the windows that overlooked a soccer field. But it was not an actual field. These windows were video screens with a startling three-dimensional effect. Caracas was playing Bogotá in an LSAF (Liga Sud-Américana de Fútbol) match-up, and many of the restaurant's customers were fanatical partisans who shouted (in Spanish) either cheers or expletives, depending upon their loyalties and flow of the game.

Food offerings at greenearthdreams were exclusively vegan, which facilitated Logan's halfhearted attempt to reduce his red-meat consumption. He and his companion both ordered house salads with vinaigrette dressing, fruit cocktails, and four-item vegetable plates.

Shortly after the salads arrived, so did Tammi's colleague from PGK. His gray jumpsuit carried a fuchsia monogram that spelled out PG Kron in small caps. "Enjoying your perk days?" he asked her.

Tammi grinned. "Oh, didn't you know? I'm now working as a professional tour guide." She waved an arm toward Logan. "Citizen Kegler, this is Logan Gramm, who is living proof of your prowess at 'forward thinking.' And Citizen Gramm, this is Ira Vincent Kegler, the inventive rigger who made it all possible."

"Just a matter of getting down in the weeds with those snakes," Kegler said. "In other words, the coding was not properly secured. I'll never tell, if you two don't."

Logan shook his head. "I'm sure in no position to squeal."

Kegler flagged down their waitress, who placed his order on a voice-recognition device and then walked across the room to assist other diners. "Everything goes on the PGK expense account, by the way," Kegler said. "Three business lunches, one of them courtesy of a slightly manipulated PG-13."

Tammi hushed him with an index finger to the lips. "Ira has a tendency to become a bit careless in public," she told Logan. "He thinks he's bullet-proof, if not downright immortal."

"Immoral, did you say? Then I plead guilty." He winked at the girl, who mocked him by rolling her eyes. "Tammi here is my girlfriend. Only she doesn't know it yet."

"Not likely," she said. Her easy manner showed that she was only kidding.

"Come out with me on Friday night, sweetheart," Kegler added in a Humphrey Bogart voice. "I'll take you to a poetry reading or something else equally economical."

Tammi looked at Logan. "Actually, his offer is not too far-fetched. Ira is both incredibly literate ... and pathetically cheap." Her wisecrack sparked an idea. "Hey, Citizen Gramm! I think Citizen Kegler might be a perfect test case for that famous novel of yours that nobody has ever heard of. Who's the author?"

"Orwell. George Orwell."

She turned to her colleague. "Does that name mean anything at all to you?"

Kegler shrugged his shoulders. "What did he write?"

"The novels *1984* and *Animal Farm*," Logan said.

"Nope. Never heard of them—or him, either."

That confirmed what Tammi already suspected. There never was such a person as Orwell. Why else would SOLEROGRAD

COUNTY LIBRARY have no record of him? "And would you consider yourself to be rather well-read?" she added.

"In all modesty, I can't think of anyone who is my superior in that regard." Kegler grinned. "That sounded awfully pompous, but it's the honest truth."

"What about Ayn Rand?" Logan asked. "Have you ever heard of her?"

"How do you spell her first name?"

"A-Y-N."

"And it's pronounced 'Ine'?" Kegler pursed his lips. "Must be Irish. Was she a novelist, too?"

"Very well-known in my day, though from an earlier generation."

"Hmm. Sorry, but no cigar."

A cold wave swept over Logan. What in the world had happened to a whole subgenre of politically charged writings, a body of work that spanned across multiple centuries? He shuddered to think.

On the wide holographic screen, a Bogotá forward scored a header goal, and loud shouts rang out from supporters and adversaries alike. Kegler stood up and cheered, his closed fist overhead. Tammi dismissed his enthusiasm with a sneer and turned to Logan. "Are you a soccer fan, Citizen Gramm?"

"I don't know much about it. My main love, when it comes to sports, is baseball. Does that still exist?"

It was Kegler who answered. "Sure, it does. In fact, my grandfather played third base for the Chicago Cubs—briefly, just for one and a half seasons. They finished at the bottom of their division both years, and he went back to the minors."

"How many teams are there?" Logan asked.

"Sixty-four in the United States, and sixty-four overseas."

"Where overseas?"

"Japan, of course, and China, The Netherlands, Italy, Spain, Britain, Australia, New Zealand, most of the Latin American countries."

"Including Cuba?"

"Absolutely. Havana has won the world championship two years in a row and three out of the last five."

"Is it still called the World Series?"

"You mean the Global Series," Kegler said. "It's been going strong since 1903 CE—way before you were even born."

"I'm surprised the Aussies could be in the league."

"How come?"

"Down Under is in the Southern Hemisphere. It's too cold during baseball season."

"All of the stadiums are covered. It's a GLB rule."

That made good sense to Logan. "Who's the best team from the United States?" he asked.

"Either the Pittsburgh Pirates or the Cleveland Americans," Kegler told him. "Sometimes the Sacramento Senators compete for the crown."

"I knew Cleveland's ball club as the Indians."

"Their nickname is short for 'Native Americans,' and of course they're in the American League. It works well both ways."

"Did the Atlanta Braves change their name, too?" Logan asked.

"Atlanta has the Bees. I think they went back to an old nickname from their Boston days. Global League Baseball is very sensitive to ethnic complaints."

Many in the supper club began booing when the soccer match was interrupted by a news bulletin on the screens. It, too, was in 3-D. An announcer sat at a desk of vibrating colors, and her words were instantly transliterated into a crawling text with no measurable delay to the signal. In Arlington, D.C., a moderate-wing senator from Virginia had died when his hotel InstaCooker caught fire as he slept. This blaze was confined to one suite alone, though smoke damage affected two others. THE ENTENTE immediately directed that all national flags be flown at half-staff for three days—this despite the fact that the deceased was a member of the loyal opposition. The announcer concluded her report with an editorial. The ensuing investigation of foul play, she opined, would no doubt prove to be unsubstantiated.

When the soccer match returned to the airwaves, greenearthdreams gradually settled back into its normal routine of sports-fueled tumult. Logan and Kegler resumed eating as before, hardly noticing that Tammi Hansen's mood had subtly changed, her mind drifting miles away.

The late senator from Virginia was named Jared Bannock. Although not associated with DEFIANCE in any official capacity, at times he seemed quite sympathetic to that organization's fundamental precepts of free enterprise, limited immigration, and the sanctity of private property—three doctrines that were anathema to the dominant majority. Just six days before his untimely death, Senator Bannock voted against universal welfare for non-citizens, a stance that surely earned him vast unpopularity from constituents in Norfolk, Richmond, Chesapeake, and the other metropolitan centers of his state.

Despite these factional issues, the national news media soon reported that the Federal Bureau of Investigation found no scientific evidence to indicate that Jared Bannock was the victim of assassination. Newscasters on every channel repeated an unrelenting narrative about the senator's "tragic accident." They discounted as extremist nonsense any intimation that his death was the premeditated act of partisan foes.

Tammi Hansen was buying none of that. Early the next morning, she Vipered with Logan to the Quigley Tower for an impromptu consultation with the one colleague whom she thought capable of providing a calmly reasoned, impersonal answer. Sure enough, David Crownover confirmed what she feared the most—there was a 78.1% likelihood that Senator Bannock was murdered, with a subsequent arson fire destroying the crime scene to obliterate any incriminating evidence.

"How did you arrive at such a precise percentage?" she asked him.

"The algorithms point to it. I considered every plausible scenario, and my inescapable conclusion is that this was very likely a politically motivated homicide."

Logan was impressed by Crownover's certitude, but even more so by the realistic movement of his facial muscles when he spoke and responded to aural stimuli. Tammi had once called this Superba-IV Class automaton an *Übermensch*, and it was easy to see why. Even under close scrutiny, Crownover was virtually indistinguishable from an actual living person. More than that, what made him truly unique was his cybernated mentality, which gave him a super-human capacity for analytical deduction.

"Logan, how goes your introductory tour of Solerograd?" Crownover asked.

"Very well, thanks ... Dave." Logan tried to ignore the fact that he was conversing with a machine. "I have an excellent guide."

"Indeed you have." Crownover smiled at the girl. "Tammi is invaluable to our cause—working on both sides of the equation."

Tammi clarified that remark by pointing to the fuchsia monogram on her jumpsuit. "ProGrade Kronotechnix is managed by the Department of the Interior," she said.

"That is to say, The Entente," Crownover added. "With the exception of yours truly, everyone on our team is employed—in some form or fashion—by The Entente. There's really no other viable choice for earning daily sustenance, short of capitulating to the lure of welfare."

"Defiance must pay its workers something," Logan said. "I saw your bookkeeping office downstairs."

"Just a token allowance, that's all."

Tammi nodded her head but seemed impatient to leave. "I appreciate your input about Senator Bannock, Dave. We'll see you later, I'm sure."

Crownover bowed courteously. "Tammi ... Logan."

After they left Crownover's office, Tammi ushered her protégé down the hallway. "We need to get you a wrist implant." She turned her arm to show Logan. "Totally painless."

He rubbed his fingertip across her embedded chip. "Is the barcode permanent?"

"Of course it is." Tammi studied his face and giggled. "Don't be so vain. It's not very conspicuous."

"It still might arouse suspicion where I'm from."

"Only if you happen to become a hand model. Believe me, no one will ever notice." They reached the elevator, and she pressed its UP button. "You'll also need a personal disk. Without both of those IDs, you'll be severely restricted in what you can accomplish for us." The elevator arrived, and they stepped aboard.

"Where do we get them?" Logan asked.

"You're a singular case, so we can't very well waltz into the CRB like other folks."

"What's the CRB?"

"Citizens' Records Building, downtown," Tammi said. "No. We'll be doing it internally, right here in the Quig's forgery lab." She pressed the button for floor twenty-eight.

Her idea of "painless" was different than his. Implanting the ID chip burned like fire for three or four seconds. "Thanks a lot," he said. "I'm beginning not to trust you."

She winked at him. "Sue me."

The records attendant, a woman of about fifty, handed Tammi a royal blue circular box. Its shape was similar to, but much smaller than, a hockey puck. Tammi, in turn, gave the box to Logan.

"Here's your personal disk. It's got more storage capacity than you could ever use, and your ID credentials are already loaded."

Logan looked inside the box and saw a shiny golden disk, which, like Tammi's, was approximately the diameter of a fifty-cent piece but twice as thick. That's about all it weighed, too—a remarkable feat of technological engineering.

"Am I supposed to guard it with my life?" His question was only half-serious, and Tammi laughed.

"That's not necessary," she told him. "A thief won't get anything from it. This disk can sense when it's out of your possession, and no one else can exploit its properties."

That sounded too good to be true. "No identity theft in Solerograd?"

"Nope—whether your personal disk happens to be counterfeit or genuine."

"Can I get the disk replaced if I lose it?"

"Easiest thing in the world to get a duplicate made," Tammi said. "It takes less than forty-five seconds, by scanning your barcode."

"So, I'd be using a forged implant to secure a forged disk."

"Whatever works."

◆　◆　◆

The constitutional right to bear arms was regarded as an antiquated concept in the closed society of Solerograd. Other than the military, only law enforcement officials of THE ENTENTE were guaranteed that privilege, and few citizens expressed much interest in possessing a weapon. Sollians thought themselves too sophisticated for that. Being lifelong students of public education, they learned at a young age to place all of their trust in municipal government for protection from harm. Simply tap the red button, and help was on the way. Rarely did the Solerograd Police Department require more than one hundred fifty seconds to respond, a boast that led to a stream of catchy PSA jingles: "Stay alive with two-point-five" (i.e., two and a half minutes).

In any case, the general populace had no desire to overthrow the status quo, even if they could. Most folks were on the welfare dole, so why would they wish to derail the gravy train? Daily living was easy, predictable, and routine. Too, a steady income was assured. Like clockwork, non-working people's monthly allowances arrived on the birthdate numeral of each head of household. For instance, if Paul Pauline Public was born on Saint Nickmas (25 DEZÈMBRE), a federal stipend would credit that individual's account on the twenty-fifth day of every month.

People born on the thirty-first day were a special case, happily receiving their welfare stipends on the thirtieth. Inasmuch as high numbers had no Fèbruar dates, Treasury Apportioning used the early März equivalents (first through third) instead. No one was slighted in the distribution of public funds, which made for an acquiescent electorate.

The nation's largest metropolitan centers had their own bicameral legislatures, and Solerograd was among them. UNITED FRONT, the collective name of Solly's "loyal opposition," occupied a distinctly marginal status in both chambers. Such a tight hold did THE ENTENTE have upon the reigns of government that the minority wing had become nothing more than a pale caricature of itself. Token dissent was tolerated, within limits, but any real show of power by the submissive "UNIs" (pronounced yoo' neez) was invariably struck down by nightstick-wielding *gendarmes* before a serious transfer of leadership might ensue. UNIs, in the modern era anyway, were said to be "along for the ride," and there was a famous political cartoon to that effect: a trembling buffoon trying to maintain his balance on a unicycle that teetered precariously through a minefield. UNITED FRONT got no respect whatsoever from the empowered news media, who were, in essence, willing mouthpieces of THE ENTENTE. Indeed, sometimes they seemed to be directing THE ENTENTE instead of covering them.

Like it or not, this was the metropolitan center that Logan Gramm now adopted as his temporary home—for however long the current operation might prescribe. Wishing to avoid drawing undue attention to himself, he began wearing the cheerless gray jumpsuits that seemed *de rigueur* in the typical Sollian's day-to-day existence. Logan also made it a rigid practice to carry his personal disk along at all times. No one could perform even the most mundane tasks without the benefit of this versatile device. Entering buildings, purchasing food, boarding Vipers, opening pedestrian gates, downloading datamasses from the ¡Swyrl!, and even viewing an OmniScreen: all were unthinkable without the assistance of one's very own, personalized "pocket valet."

Logan did not regard the late Jeffrey Hansen's former apartment to be particularly comfortable, but he was grateful to have a roof over his head—and all expenses paid. He suspected that DEFIANCE took care of the rental fees, though Tammi never said as much, and no paperwork passed through his hands. On the negative side, he had trouble sleeping, partly due to the claustrophobic dimensions of a studio flat, but mostly because of those worrisome surveillance slits in the crown molding. Although Logan never went so far as to taunt the presumed observers with cynical faces, like Tammi did, he felt a constant uneasiness whenever he was there. Openly discussing his covert "Op-6" was out of the question.

Tammi Hansen's preferred site for conveying information of a confidential nature was at the base of Lincoln Hill, a secluded spot that provided absolute privacy, safely away from, as she put it, "Solly's invasive eyes and ears" (cameras and microphones). The butte stood fourteen miles outside of town and was named after Lincoln Keaton, a radical progressive of yesteryear who helped to mold THE ENTENTE into the behemoth that it was today. Revisionist historians disproved, to their own satisfaction at least, a persistent rumor that this geographical feature had been named in honor of Abraham Lincoln. Old-timers insisted that a weather-beaten plaque had been removed from the wooded area and later destroyed, a plaque that clearly displayed the *bas-relief* profile of the sixteenth President of the United States.

Logan and Tammi traveled to the hill aboard a two-seater air-cushion vehicle, with Citizen Hansen ostensibly at the controls. In point of fact, she had to contribute almost nothing to the endeavor, for this mini-ACV followed a programmed pathway of coordinates and required negligible assistance from its human cargo.

"How much training does it take to fly this thing?" Logan asked her.

She chuckled. "I'm embarrassed to say. Gabe Torveldt checked me out in this mini after about fifteen minutes of instruction. You remember him, don't you? He piloted us to the Quigley Tower after you first arrived in Solly."

"Pince-nez eyeglasses and a beard?"

"That's him."

The mini-ACV descended to an impeccable landing upon the only patch of flat terrain near Lincoln Hill, and the hike to an isolated glade within the woodland took less than ten minutes. Tammi felt relatively safe here, insulated from the watchfulness of Solerograd's "voluntary protection."

She leaned against the waist-high edge of a rocky formation, and Logan followed suit. By now, though, her expression had changed for the worst. "The reason I brought you out here to the woods," she said, "is to confess that you are in Solly under slightly false pretenses."

"I don't get you."

"My brother was not assassinated, in the strictest sense of the word. That is, he was not singled out as the primary target. Jeff died, along with three others, in a bombing on the House floor. 'Collateral damage' is what THE ENTENTE called it, and of course the news media parroted that terminology."

"Would it be accurate to say that your brother was actively working against THE ENTENTE?"

"Yes, of course, but Jeff was a low-ranking member of UNITED FRONT and the youngest congressman in the nation. He had just been appointed to his first committee the day before this happened."

"So, who was the actual target?" Logan asked.

"The minority whip, Galen Peaks. He had finished delivering a speech against universal welfare when the explosion occurred. Jeff and the other victims were all seated within forty feet of the dais."

"I'm a complete outsider," Logan said, "but it seems awfully dangerous to be associated with UNITED FRONT—first the bombing and then that senator who was killed. What was his name?"

"Senator Jared Bannock of Virginia," Tammi said. "The news media reported his death as 'a tragic accident,' but we all know better. You heard David Crownover say there was an almost eighty-percent certainty that Senator Bannock was assassinated."

"Do you trust a robot?" Logan asked. He knew that term would rankle her.

"Dave is much more than a robot, which would only denigrate him. He's a Superba-IV Class automaton—programmed to be infallible—and I trust him implicitly."

"Does David Crownover think the elections are rigged against UNITED FRONT?"

"I've never come right out and asked him, but I'm sure he would," Tammi said. "UNIs used to be in the majority, but that was before the Great Wave changed everything."

"Sounds ominous."

"It was. Votes started going to the left by the millions, very mysteriously, and lots of native Sollians began doubting the integrity of the ballot box. It got to the point where more people voted than were even registered."

"Do you need to be a citizen to register?"

"Theoretically, but polling judges don't check the registration rolls anyway, so what difference does it make?"

"When was this Great Wave?"

"About fifteen years ago," she told him. "I was too young to realize what was going on, but my late father called it a disaster. Now, with your help and a couple hundred others, we're going to fight back."

"How?"

"Whatever tactics are necessary."

"In other words, 'the end justifies the means'."

"Precisely. We have taken that philosophy out of THE ENTENTE's own playbook, and we plan to use it against them. Maybe we'll throw in some Saul Alinsky, just to be safe."

"His books made it through the library purge?"

"Are you surprised?" She turned to walk away, and Logan followed behind her.

"And this will become the civil war that we talked about a long time ago?" he asked.

"Could be," she told him, "but I hope it doesn't come to that."

Logan flicked his hand at what sounded like a locust buzzing past his left ear. But it was not a locust. A bullet stuck Tammi in the shoulder, just below the left collarbone. She fell forward to the ground, and Logan rushed to her aid. Looking back, he saw a blur of motion through the trees and heard the sound of footsteps sprinting away at top speed.

Logan knelt down, close to her ear. "How badly are you hurt?" he asked. "We need to get you out of here."

"I don't know. It aches like crazy, but I can still breathe all right."

"That's the important thing—no vital organs—but I'm afraid of this bleeding."

"Get me into the ACV," she said.

He glanced at the machine. "Does Solly's hospital have a landing pad?"

"No time for that. DEFIANCE has a full-service ER ... " She clenched her teeth in pain. " ... and a lot fewer political questions to answer."

"In the Quigley Tower?"

"Right."

"Are you in any condition to fly?" he asked.

"Only as a passenger." Her eyes rolled, as she fought off the impulse to faint. "You'll have to be our pilot."

"Me?"

"There's no other choice. It's really pretty simple. I'll tell you what to do, step by step."

Lifting Tammi under her good shoulder, Logan walked her to the mini and carefully helped her into the passenger seat. Then he placed himself in the pilot's module. "What comes first?" he asked her.

"Its panel is already programmed for the Quig. Just press the green START button and pull toward you on the joystick. The computer will sense your intentions and take over from there."

The air-cushion vehicle performed just as she claimed it would, and Logan had only to sit there and watch.

"You can override the trajectory and flight path, if need be, but usually that is not necessary." She gazed at the ground, by now far below. "The ACV will detect any unanticipated obstructions and evade them as smoothly as circumstances permit. We're far above the Vipers' restricted air space, so don't worry about colliding with one of them."

"Amazing!" Logan said. He marveled at the trifling demands that were placed upon a mini-ACV pilot.

Although trying to remain as upbeat as possible, Tammi did groan a bit in transit, and Logan hoped she would not lose consciousness while they were still aloft. "Do me one favor," she told him. "Press the red STAT button three times in rapid succession. That alerts ER that we're in trouble but on the way. Believe me, they'll be waiting for us and know exactly what to do."

◆　　◆　　◆

"Where do we go from here?" Logan asked. He was sitting in a chair alongside Tammi's hospital bed, and his twenty minutes of visitation were nearly expired.

"I'll need to get our orders from HQ," she told him. "I sure don't make the important decisions around here." Wrapped in bandages, Tammi grimaced while repositioning herself against the pillows. The bullet wound, thankfully, was more superficial than it first appeared, though she did lose a significant amount of blood and was still feeling quite woozy.

Logan squeezed her left hand, careful not to disturb the shoulder joint above. "Do you know who it was that tried to kill you yesterday?"

"Nope," she said.

"No ideas?"

"Nope. Someone who wasn't a very good shot."

"Why would anyone want to kill you?"

"Oh, I can think of several reasons, can't you? I'm not a member of THE ENTENTE, I work secretly for DEFIANCE, my brother held a seat in UNITED FRONT, and ... " She stopped.

"Go on," Logan said.

"And I am capable of bringing operatives into the future." Tammi grinned at him.

"But no one knows about me, do they?"

"PGK is totally in the dark, except for Kegler. Only a select few at DEFIANCE—Gabriel Torveldt, Beverly Cline, and a handful of others."

"And David Crownover."

"Yes, Dave too, of course."

Logan stood up and walked over to the window. Outside loomed the distant skyline of Solerograd. Two Vipers sped by in opposite directions, their guidance systems effortlessly skirting a collision.

He turned to look at her. "One thing has been bothering me."

"What's that?"

"Let's say I am able to travel into the past far enough to save your brother from being killed by a terrorist's bomb. Will you know that I was successful? The way I see it, any fine-tuning will proceed from that exact point in Jeff's lifetime, which means you won't have a memory of planning his rescue, right? There would be no reason for you to make such plans."

"A Pinocchio Paradox," she said.

"Yes!"

"But you forget that I work for PROGRADE KRONOTECHNIX ... and am a certified rigger with full access to memory caches, constraints, and buffers."

"Why do you say that?"

Tammi considered how to explain the concept in basic terms—and with ample clarity to enable a twenty-first-century human of reasonable intellect to make some sense of it. "Imagine your computer's file-hosting service," she told him. "I think you call them 'boxes' or some such term. Information is stored within, and several different levels of permission may be granted: owner, viewer, editor, and so forth."

"I'm familiar with that."

"Whenever I program a PG-13, one of the fields available to me—in fact, one that *must* be completed before launch—is precisely who will retain a memory of the mission."

"And that person is you."

"Actually, both of us—you and I."

The way Tammi said it made Logan nervous. "The time traveler is not a 'given' to remember the mission?" he asked.

"Well, yes, we always check that box."

"But you could leave it blank?"

"I suppose so. Why would I want to do that?"

Logan stared at her for a moment, but all he saw in return was the enigmatic expression of a PGK agent. He thought it best to drop the subject.

Tammi Hansen was hospitalized for another two days, and then—thanks to a whole battery of modern rehabilitation techniques—she felt able to resume her normal work schedule across town at PROGRADE KRONOTECHNIX. Regarding her bullet wound, the forensics lab at DEFIANCE determined that a low-caliber projectile had been fired by some unidentified weapon that was far beneath the standards of modern warfare. It seemed to be a crude product of the amateur hunter, perhaps a single-shot rifle with a bore diameter of .22 inch. Even such primitive firearms were not allowed within the county limits of Solerograd, but who could say how many people possessed them illegally?

Throughout Tammi's period of recuperation, Logan Gramm was in training—physical and classroom—under the tutelage of DEFIANCE instructors, reputed to be some of the brightest lights in the academic and military sciences. All sessions took place in the Quigley Tower, which (according to Beverly Cline) had state-of-the-art facilities, "second to none in terms of the latest bells and whistles."

One day, as Logan was heading to an afternoon class in martial maneuvers, David Crownover approached him in the corridor.

"Hiya, L. G.," the automaton said. "How goes it so far?"

"Hello, Dave. Fine, thanks. I'm staying plenty busy, that's for sure."

"Splendid! Always nice to hear that our bookkeepers are getting their money's worth." Dave had an endearing manner of speech, with intent eye contact that let listeners know they had his complete attention. "Incidentally, my sources tell me that Tammi Hansen should suffer no residual effects from the shooting incident. Very fortunate, indeed, that you were with her to pilot our mini back to the Quig. Bravo, Air Captain Gramm!" He chuckled and patted Logan on the shoulder.

"I can't take much credit for that. All I did was press START and sit back for the ride."

"You're being too modest. I've never flown one, and I'm not so sure that I could."

"Nothing to it. I was surprised by how simple an ACV is to fly." It struck Logan that David Crownover may have been the world's most advanced *Übermensch*, but he was certainly no Superman of the DC Comics variety. "Tell me, Dave. How often do you get to leave this building?"

"Never. I was born here, and this is my home. I have never left the Quigley Tower."

"Never?"

"What would I do beyond these walls? I have no desire to explore the world."

"No curiosity about what's outside?" Logan asked.

"I already know what's outside."

"Everything?"

"Just about."

"Do you know who tried to kill Tammi Hansen?"

"I believe so, but I am not at liberty to say." And with that, Dave smiled, nodded his head, and walked away. "All in good time," he said.

◆ ◆ ◆

Holding the virtual FyreBolte with both hands, Logan was in a prone position, flaring deadly charges at a simulated three-hundred-yard "enemy." This was his semiweekly forty-minute practice session at the DEFIANCE target range, located on the Quigley Tower's twenty-sixth floor. Two other marksmen were there as well, and their instructor for the day was MSgt Gary Dwynn (ret.) of the United States Army Infantry.

"Someone is here to see you," the burly soldier said. He seemed peeved at the interruption. "Take another rotation of six, and then you're dismissed."

"Yes, sergeant." In less than three seconds, Logan fired 212 electronic charges at the moving image, slicing it to ribbons until RESET was pressed, a command that instantly restored the AirDragon graphic to its original condition. He repeated this pursuit drill another five times before laying aside the weapon.

"Who is it?" he asked the instructor.

Glowering, MSgt Dwynn used his head to gesture toward the visitor. "See you next Thursday, Gramm."

The intruder was Tammi Hansen. "Sorry to barge in like this," she said. "I thought you'd be finished at four thirty."

"Four forty, but that's all right. Sarge can get kind of testy, so don't take his grumbling personally."

Tammi's left shoulder was drooping slightly—as if she was favoring it, relative to the right—but no bandages or sling were apparent.

"How are you feeling?" Logan asked.

"On the road to recovery. I'm about ninety percent there, I suppose. Thanks again for flying me to the Quig."

"Glad to do it. What an awesome experience!" Immediately, he regretted the unconstrained zeal. "Uh, sorry," he added. "I know that flight wasn't very enjoyable for you."

"Well, no, I can't say that it was. But if it introduced a new aviator into our ranks, maybe something good did come from your little adventure."

"The only good that came from it was getting you to ER, where they patched you back together into one piece."

Tammi grinned an acknowledgment but then became quite serious. Indeed, she was nearly brought to tears by just thinking about it. Across the room she walked, well away from the firing lanes, and gazed out the window. Logan followed her but said nothing. He knew that Tammi would tell him what was on her mind—but not until she felt good and ready.

This side of the building faced the Stadia district, Solerograd's professional sports complex. The basketball arena was closest to them, and beyond that—off in the distance—stood the more massive structures for soccer, baseball, and football. All four sports were played indoors, so no grassy expanse could be seen from their bird's-eye vantage point. Only the roofs were visible, each of them carrying a mammoth representation of that sport's particular ball. This was brazen advertising, calculated to make a stirring impression upon traveling Sollians as their Vipers soared high above.

"Kegler has your op ready to launch," Tammi said. She turned around, looking Logan straight in the eye. "You don't have to do this, you know—if you choose not to. There's no contract involved."

"Why the sudden change of heart? You were passionate about this when you first proposed it to me."

"That was before I knew you so well, back when you were just another volunteer—and with a reliable safety net to abort the mission. Now that's no longer possible, and the stakes are ... " Again, her eyes watered. " ... the ultimate sacrifice. As much as I loved my brother, I can't ask you to trade your life for Jeff's. That's beyond the call of duty—or even friendship."

Logan asked the rigger, point-blank, to come clean about what drastic measures were expected of him. "Doesn't this mission have any safety net at all?"

"I'm afraid not."

"Why can't Kegler just copy PGK's excessive repercussion coding into my PG-13? He knows how to do that."

"No, he doesn't. This is your future, not your past, and—as you know—PGK does not permit positive movement to happen, only negative."

"Then, how did Kegler pull it off?"

"Just a blind stroke of luck. He never guessed that he could exploit the restraining code and bring you forward in time. But he did. Unfortunately, that means you won't be covered by any safeguards."

"Except non-consequence."

"Well, yes, but technically that's not a safeguard. Non-consequence is a natural phenomenon—a force that holds together the entire course of history. It has nothing to do with PG KRON."

Logan gave that some thought. "Why can't we use PGK's regular methods to send me back—just far enough to thwart the terrorists? From where I am now, that would be into my past."

"Not your biological past, and there's a big difference between the two."

"How big?"

Tammi refused to take the bait. "Honestly, doesn't Solly seem to you like it's far into the future, from your perspective?"

As if on cue, a Viper flashed by the window, and Logan smiled. "I must concede that you Sollians are an advanced race, when set against mine. But only in the scientific sense, not societal."

"Oh?"

"I feel ... oppressed, suffocated, spied upon. There's no true freedom."

"Fair enough," she said. "I've experienced life in your world and mine, so I'm in a unique position to compare both."

"And?"

She took a deep breath. "Society has changed enormously—and not for the better. That's why DEFIANCE is a growing movement."

◆　◆　◆

After five weeks of physical and tactical training, the day of Logan's Op-6 embarkation arrived. Tammi brought him the modified PG-13, with improvised coding by Irving Vincent Kegler, and they sat together on the sofa in her late brother's apartment. Both inhabitants tried to conceal their mouths from the overhead slits, which they suspected were there for the purpose of surveillance. Similarly, to help drown out their voices, they instructed the MusikPlatz to play—very loudly—a repeating loop of the turbulent finale from Shostakovich's Fifth Symphony.

The first thing Logan did upon receiving the PG-13 was to scroll down its multi-colored screen for a date of entry, verifying that the target was indeed thirty-five months back in time. That was when Rep. Jeffrey Hansen (UF-Sol) died, along with three other congressmen, during the horrific St. Patrick's Day bombing.

"By the way, you can still opt out of this," Tammi said. "It's a very selfish and unfair assignment that I've dreamed up, and now I wish I hadn't enlisted you for it."

Logan shook his head. "If there's a realistic chance to save your brother, we should jump at it—for your sake and the country's. Kegler might never be able to program another PG-13 outside the purview of PG KRON." He leaned forward to lay the marvelous device on his coffee table.

"I wish I felt better about this operation," Tammi told him. "Nothing like it has ever been attempted before—bringing someone to us from the past and then sending that same person partially back again. Kegler assures me that it works on paper, but I have a genuine fear of dodging the company guidelines. Those protocols are there for a reason." Her gaze strayed from Logan to the PG-13. "Remember what happened in Lakehurst."

"I'll be careful," he said. "Whatever the risk may be, I owe it to you to try."

That statement puzzled Tammi. "Why should you feel any sense of obligation to me?"

"Because you brought me into this profession, and I'm grateful for the opportunity. I was hoping to teach history someday. Instead, I'm living it."

"Don't you have any regrets at all?"

"Only that I couldn't rescue that poor lady's husband—buried in the flames."

"And yet you managed to save her, and she lived to be ninety-six. Did you know that?"

"No, not until now."

Tammi reached over and consulted the PG-13. Its countdown showed ten minutes. "Final thoughts, Logan?" she asked. "You don't mind if I use your first name, do you?"

"I wish you would. That 'Citizen Gramm' business was sounding kind of stuffy by now."

"No offense intended. We've always found that PROGRADE KRONOTECHNIX functions best on a more formal footing. Something to do with mutual respect, I suppose."

"No offense taken ... Tammi."

She suppressed a grin. "Your suit of clothes will be waiting in the hotel closet, and so will your clearance to the House gallery and main floor. Keep in mind that four lives are at stake, including my brother's, but don't get yourself killed in the process. I would never ask that of anyone."

"What if I can only rescue one of the congressmen?"

"I think you can guess my answer to that," she said, "but all of their lives are important." Tammi studied Logan's face. "You are my personal responsibility, and I don't want you to treat this as a suicide mission."

"Not likely. I have a very healthy survival instinct."

"Good. That may come in handy."

"How long will I be gone?" he asked.

"From my perspective?"

"Yes."

She consulted the PG-13. "It looks like Kegler let the default time stand, so ... sixty minutes."

"And that's when you'll know if the mission was a success."

Tammi nodded her head. "If you reappear an hour from now, Jeff could be standing right here next to us, wondering who you are and why you're in his apartment with me."

"Did Jeff know what you do for a living?"

"No. He was killed almost three years ago, back when I hadn't even begun working for PROGRADE KRONOTECHNIX."

"But everything will change if I save him."

"Absolutely. He'll experience those missing years, and I'm sure he'll be aware of my job at DOI."

"Worse case scenario—what if I don't show up on time?"

"Then we can only assume that *five* people have died in the blast. But I pray that I'll be seeing you again soon."

The comment took Logan aback. "You pray?"

"Yes, I do. I'm not ashamed to admit it."

"Can that be dangerous?"

"Not if I do so as an individual," she said. "As long as there are no more than four of us worshiping together, the government tolerates spiritual expression."

"How generous."

"It was a famous compromise at the very highest levels—to placate the evangelicals, I suppose." She realized that time was running short. "Any last-minute questions?"

"No." Logan winked at her and rose to his feet. "Wish me luck."

Tammi watched him carry his PG-13 across the room and sit down in a contoured rocker for the wait. She felt certain that her client, a veteran of seven previous launches, would handle this one with the cool professionalism of a test pilot. Logan Gramm was her favorite protégé, bar none, and she had boundless confidence in him.

Less than a minute later, in response to programmed coordinates of his hand-held device, Logan was gone from what Tammi regarded as the present tense. She witnessed his disappearance and dutifully reported it on her OpLog. The departure was right on schedule, too, every bit as precise as PROGRADE KRONOTECHNIX itself would have managed. Now all she could do was endure the nerve-wracking hour that lay ahead. But then a motion from the bedroom caught her attention, and she turned to see Logan standing there as if in a daze.

"Oh, my God!" she shouted. "What happened?"

"A lot—or nothing at all," he said, "depending upon how you look at it."

Tammi ran over to him. "Are you all right? Why are you so early?" He seemed quite dizzy, so she took hold of his arm to keep him from stumbling to the floor.

"I need to sit down," he said. On unsteady legs, and with her assistance, Logan made his way over to the sofa. He rubbed his forehead. "That is not a very pleasant experience."

"Do you want something to drink?" she asked.

"No. I'll be okay. Just give me a couple of minutes."

Already Tammi was hurrying to the apartment's kitchen, where she soaked a dish towel in some cold water. "Here. Pat your face with this."

He did so and felt much better almost at once. "Thanks. We need to talk right away, but not here."

"HQ?"

"Yes."

"We'll go as soon as you feel up to it." Tammi used her wristpad to notify Beverly Cline.

"Sorry about what happened," Logan said.

Tammi could only wonder.

◆ ◆ ◆

Dominating the Quigley Tower's conference room was an immense, oval table. It was surrounded by a dozen and a half ergonomic chairs, each with a headrest tall enough to support its occupant through the lengthiest of meetings. On this occasion, however, there were just two people in attendance—Tammi Hansen and Logan Gramm—in addition to the synthetic human called David Crownover.

As DEFIANCE's nominal representative at the session, Crownover was required to be there for one purpose only: to transcribe all proceedings for posterity. This was a failsafe methodology, for the automaton had been bonded to maintain unconditional secrecy, and nothing short of a national emergency could pry details from his sealed receptors.

Tammi convened the discussion by inviting Crownover to take a more active role in the proceedings than a transcriber typically would do, breaking the unstated oath of silence whenever he judged that his participation might be of some assistance. "Feel free to voice any concerns, Dave, because we respect your objectivity in this matter." She looked at Logan. "Is that okay with you?"

"Sure thing. Please do, Dave."

"You're both too kind," Crownover told them. His eyes, so very lifelike, seemed to twinkle in appreciation.

Tammi's initial consideration was to bring the automaton up to speed, so she opened with the most basic of questions. "Logan, is it true that you were sent back approximately three years to stymie the St. Patrick's Day bombing?"

"I was."

"And were you successful?"

"By all indications, yes, but the effort was interrupted."

"How so?" Crownover asked. Already he seemed locked into the matter at hand.

Sensing this, Tammi offered yet another layer of clarification. "Our plan was to save my brother ... "

"Representative Jeffrey Thomas Hansen," the automaton said, "a member of UNITED FRONT."

"Correct. My brother, Jeff, was killed in the explosion of thirty-five months ago, and I enlisted Logan to prevent that from happening."

Crownover's computer brain processed the information in a millisecond. "Sources tell me that your brother was a valuable and effective worker for the loyal opposition."

Tammi nodded her head proudly. "Great things were expected of Jeff in the years to come—until his life was snuffed out."

"A lamentable shame," the automaton said. "Allow me to express my belated condolences. As you know, I was not activated by DEFIANCE until November of the following year."

Crownover swiveled his chair toward the time traveler. "In your own words, Logan, what do you suppose went wrong on your recent Op-6?"

"I can't say with complete certainty. Either the PG-13 malfunctioned—which is extremely doubtful—or the proposed revision of history would have been too great of a change to be acceptable."

Tammi stared at the automaton, who pronounced his views on the issue. "The latter is true," Crownover said. "Logan, you were subjected to what we call non-consequence, and, from what I understand, passing through it can be a terrible ordeal."

Logan winced. "I can vouch for that."

"Anyway, preserving the life of Jeffrey Hansen and the others would have dramatically changed the course of history. Accordingly, the intrusion was reversed, you were expunged from the scene, and things remained just as they were meant to be."

Crownover's testimony failed to provide a sense of closure for Tammi, so she probed more deeply. "Tell me this, Dave. Why was the rescuing of four congressmen considered to be such a momentous shift in the grand scheme of world history?"

"I can only surmise," Crownover said, "that these men, or at least one of them, would have played a truly significant role in the unfolding of human events. Maybe it was to be Jeffrey Hansen, maybe not. In any case, the optimized path never occurred—demonstrably never *can* occur—so it is quite impossible to deduce who would have risen to such prominent heights of leadership." He gave a humanlike shrug of the shoulders. "We are unable to rewrite the path of world history except in the most trivial of ways. Save for a handful of fine-tunings, the chronicles of our troubled globe remain sacrosanct."

Logan had been aware of that bitter truism all along, but hearing it verbalized in such dispassionate terms made him feel a bit dejected. He peered at Tammi. "Seeing as how I am unable to prevent the House bombing, is my time with you at an end?"

"There is one other thing that we have in mind for you. Again, this will be strictly voluntary."

And just like that, his interest was rekindled. "Does it involve traveling into the past?"

"No. The time frame will be present-day Solerograd, and Dave can fill you in on the details."

"Your impending mission, Logan, is a relatively small one," Crownover said. "We need for you to infiltrate a low-level espionage ring that has compromised UNITED FRONT's efforts to promote freedom of movement in the Neutral Region, south of Solly."

"What's so important about this region?" Logan asked.

"For one thing, it's unincorporated," the automaton told him. "The tentacles of government do not yet control the coming and going of UF paramilitary units. Moreover, we have good reason to believe that our only hope of toppling the current power structure will emanate from within those boundaries."

"Will I be working alone?"

Tammi chose to answer. "Everyone else is known to THE ENTENTE, but you're our wild card, so to speak. The identification traits of 'Logan Gramm' will show up on none of their ID profiles because your only assignment for us was ultimately aborted. In every real sense, it never happened. You are a nonentity—pardon the expression—and your personal disk, as counterfeited by DEFIANCE, will be useless to them."

Logan looked her in the eye. "I'm ready to help. Just tell me when."

Tammi's expression seemed to change from respect to awe, and then from awe to affection. "Dave will take over from here," she said, "and he can give you a thorough briefing. I'm due at DOI in a half-hour."

"I'll see you again, won't I?" Logan asked. "I'm sort of in limbo now and need some answers."

"Just stick around and listen to what Dave has to say. He'll explain everything to you." Tammi nodded farewell to her client and, without a further word, left the conference room.

Crownover cleared his synthetic throat, but of course that was only for effect. Logan stared at him, wondering what would come next. Truth be known, he still felt uneasy to be alone with a non-human. The automaton, however, appeared to be quite comfortable in such a situation, for he was designed that way.

Several seconds passed before Crownover finally spoke, and when he did, it was in a hushed, conspiratorial tone. "Logan," he whispered, "it is my considered opinion that Tammi Hansen is becoming quite fond of you."

Logan's eyes widened. "Please don't take this wrong, Dave, but what could you possibly know about matters of the heart?"

"Very little, to be honest with you. I can never experience such emotions—even with the most technologically advanced synthesization. My conclusion was reached wholly by means of empirical reasoning." The automaton grinned. "I am, you must admit, rather good at that."

◆   ◆   ◆

The Neutral Region lay directly south of Solerograd, about eighteen miles outside of town. There was no Viper service to that area, so Logan was compelled to requisition an air-cushion vehicle, perhaps the very same two-seater that he had piloted to the Quigley Tower's rooftop aeropad after Tammi was wounded. Today the coordinates transported him to a vacant lot behind a series of nondescript shops, which stubbornly endured the ravages of weather along an unpaved artery called Stafford Street.

His silent landing went undetected, except by a solitary mongrel that was foraging for food—what wags of an earlier generation would disparage as a "dumpster dog." Less contemplative than any human, this canine regarded the intruder with brief wonder but then returned to more urgent pursuits.

Logan's fresh instructions from Crownover were to contact a DEFIANCE agent within the third bungalow beyond Stafford, so he set out on foot, feeling secure with a lethal FyreBolte tucked into the pocket of his gray jumpsuit. The so-called Neutral Region was largely undeveloped, but in a slapdash way that was more grotesque than charming. The area's rough-hewn desolation brought to mind images of the Old West, and Logan half expected to sidestep a tumbleweed or two as he clumped through the dirt to make a rendezvous.

The shop's entrance was unlocked. With one hand on his FyreBolte, Logan slowly swung the door open, not knowing what he might encounter inside. But reality proved to be an anticlimax, not that he was complaining. Behind the battered wooden desk stood a diminutive, middle-aged office clerk with thinning hair and thick eyeglasses. "Are you Citizen Gramm?" the man asked.

"Yes, sir."

"Personal disk, please."

Logan placed it in the clerk's outstretched hand and waited for him to scan for ID. "It says here you're from Hoboken." The man's demeanor was aloof but not unfriendly.

"That's right, in New Jersey."

"Me, I'm from Passaic County."

"No kidding? Paterson?"

"North Haledon, actually."

"Small world," Logan said. "What brought you all the way to Solerograd?"

"I had no choice. My parents were conscripted when I was six."

"The military?"

"THE ENTENTE." Very businesslike, the man squinted his eyes. "You're a newcomer around here, aren't you?" He offered his fist.

"Yes, sir, relatively speaking." They bumped.

"Burleson Drake is my name," the clerk said. "Burl for short."

"Pleased to meet you, Citizen Drake." Logan glanced around the room's four walls, which seemed to enclose an agricultural business of some sort. "You sell feed 'n' seed?"

"Mainly. But of course it's just a front for other dealings."

"Oh?"

"Most of these sacks are filled with sand—all but the ones on top." He chuckled. "I feel like I can speak freely with you, and I know for a fact that there's no surveillance on the premises."

"Here in your shop?"

"Anywhere in the N. R."

Logan presumed that meant the Neutral Region.

"These eleven hundred square miles are a remnant of the old days," Drake told him, "what Solly must have been like a couple of centuries ago."

"Why don't more people live here? I'd think freedom-loving people would flock to such a place."

"No conveniences, no utilities, no law enforcement ... and, most of all, no welfare. People would have to work—and work hard—to make ends meet. It's an unforgiving area, and people have gotten too soft to cope."

"What brought you to the Neutral Region?"

"Me, I'm well paid to be here—by UNITED FRONT, or what's left of it—in order to offer hospitality to political fugitives."

"Is that what you think I am?"

"It's not my job to think. I'm only a mercenary, so I stay clear of Sollian intrigues whenever possible. If you want to know the truth, I don't trust anyone on either side." Drake used his teeth to open a pack of chewing tobacco, and he inserted a sizable wad between cheek and gum.

Logan was beginning to doubt his favorable first impression of the man. "Are you my contact?" he asked him.

"Hardly, Citizen Gramm. No, an acquaintance of yours assigned me to serve as your personal greeter."

The comment put Logan on guard. "And who might this mysterious acquaintance of mine be?"

"Somebody who works in town," the clerk said. "Near the S4-E17 Station, to be precise. That's all I'm permitted to tell you."

The grid address was vaguely familiar to Logan, but he could not recall what was located there.

Drake stared intently at him. "Are you aware of an organization called DEFIANCE?"

"No. Should I be?" Logan betrayed no emotion. "What kind of company is it?"

"An automaton factory, I suppose—robotics. At least, that's who was deputized to enlist my services."

"A robot came to see you?"

"No. He was on my OmniScreen—and quite a convincing conversationalist, too. They're getting better all the time."

"So I hear," Logan said.

"I've thought of investing in a robot for myself," Drake told him, "just to do some work around here."

"Is that so?"

"I'm still toying with the idea, but they're not for sale to the general public. Maybe I can buy one on the sly. Classic models—more than twenty-five years old—are available on the black market, but they've been known to kill their owners. Faulty circuits and so forth."

Logan sized up this odd little man anew and thought it advisable to do some checking. "Say, I hope you won't think badly of me, but maybe I should ask to see your ID." He smiled. "Just as a routine matter of courtesy, you know."

"Of course, Citizen Gramm. Don't let that bother you." Drake slipped his personal disk into the DataScan, allowing Logan to read its display. "Actually, I would've thought less of you if that wasn't your *modus operandi*. The automaton at DEFIANCE certainly required it of me."

Logan nodded. "Three cheers for security."

Abruptly—without so much as another word—the old man edged backward to the rear of the store, all the while keeping his thick eyeglasses firmly trained upon Logan. He tapped twice on the door, paused, and tapped twice again.

That prompted Logan to slide a hand into his jumpsuit pocket, gripping the FyreBolte's metal alloy butt. Although Burleson Drake did not appear to pose much of a threat, that could change in a flash—especially on his own turf. But for now, the clerk just stared at the floorboards, biding his time.

At length, when the door finally did creak open, into the shop stepped Tammi Hansen, devoid of any expression. "I was hoping you'd come," was all she said.

Logan did not know how much to divulge in front of the questionable third party. "What are you doing here?" he asked Tammi. "You indicated that I'd be working alone."

"Confession time," she told him. "I'm afraid you've been lured to the Neutral Region through a hoax."

"Lured by you?"

"None other."

"And there's no espionage ring in the N. R.?"

"Nothing major. I made that up."

"Was Crownover in on this, too?"

"Absolutely not. Dave is incapable of lying, so his briefing for you was genuine and on the level. All he did was relay my instructions."

Logan glanced at the old man, who suddenly felt intrusive and excused himself from the room. The door creaked on its hinges until clicking shut.

Nothing in this place made much sense, and Logan was at a loss for words. "So, what's up?" he asked the girl.

Tammi grinned at his confusion. "Just don't get the wrong idea. My designs on you are purely honorable." She gave a self-deprecating laugh. "I wouldn't know how to ensnare a man if I tried."

♦ ♦ ♦

DEFIANCE owned a pair of lakeside properties at the Neutral Region's southernmost extremity, a remote stretch of land commonly known as The Salient. Tammi requisitioned the smaller of these two retreats as an ideal hideaway for conducting frank discussions. She knew painfully well that any spot within the city limits of Solerograd would be monitored, around-the-clock, by audio and video surveillance.

She and Logan stood at the kitchen counter, sipping from stemless goblets of vin rosé from the central valley of Caligrad. Tammi always chose a domestic wine to settle her nerves because it was the only form of alcohol that did not leave her feeling dizzy-headed. Finally, she worked up the courage to begin. "I need to go back with you," she said. "No other option."

Stunned by her remark, Logan took a stiff swig of the wine. "To twenty-first-century New York?"

"That's right."

He thought for a moment. "To recruit someone else for PG KRON?"

"No. I've already done my recruiting there—you."

"Then why go back again?"

"To stay." She studied his face. "You seem surprised."

"Of course I am," Logan said. "Is it even possible?"

"Not through PROGRADE KRONOTECHNIX, obviously, but I think Kegler might be able to engineer something for me on the side."

"Is that what you really want?"

Tammi turned away from him and gazed at the fireplace. "I've been receiving lots of death threats lately, and they seem to be authentic. It may seem unheroic to you, but I prefer to live."

"Even if you have to go back in time to do it?"

"I can get used to just about anything." She forced a smile. "Actually, I rather enjoyed my stay in prehistoric New York City."

"That's not how I remember it," Logan said. "As I recall, you were in a hurry to leave. You hardly even waved goodbye."

Tammi blushed. "Well, I was just an intern then, with my whole career ahead of me. That's nothing but water under the bridge now."

"Would you fit into my 'prehistoric' society?"

"I could try."

Logan gave her notion some thought. "Has anyone else from PGK gone back permanently?"

"Never. A return time is hard-wired into the algorithms."

"And Kegler could bypass that field?"

"He has before, as you well know," she said. "The only problem is, my departure would be irreversible—no return trip, no Kegler to juggle the specs, no way out."

"You make it sound like a prison sentence."

"Not at all, but my decision must be iron-clad. Once launched, there can be no turning around."

"And you're absolutely certain this is what you want?" Logan asked.

Tammi took a deep breath before offering an answer. "I have no desire to sacrifice myself for a lost cause—which is what my brother did, let's face it. UNITED FRONT is in its death throes, and DEFIANCE will not be far behind." She patted her left shoulder. "Getting wounded made this very clear to me, and the next assassin will be more accurate."

Logan took another sip of wine. "What do the threats accuse you of doing?"

"Sabotaging THE ENTENTE, basically, and also subverting my own employers, ProGrade KRONOTECHNIX and the Department of the Interior. My political philosophies don't conform to the current doctrines."

"And there's no room for opposing thoughts?"

"None whatsoever," Tammi told him. "THE ENTENTE are authoritarian. By definition, they tolerate no dissent."

"So, you're going to concede victory to them without a fight?"

"Victory is already theirs. All that's left for them to do is round up the hold-outs. Some will be re-educated in show trials, others will be imprisoned, and the rest will simply disappear, never to be heard from again."

"Can they do that? What about your constitutional rights?" Logan asked.

"Not relevant. The news media declared the Constitution to be 'essentially null and void' forty years ago—long before I was born."

"But the media are not the official arbiters of national policy."

"Aren't they?" She gave Logan a knowing glance. "THE ENTENTE will strangle us quietly and behind the scenes, thanks to the collusion of Solly's news media, but the results will be every bit as final as a bloody purge."

Logan felt the need to clear his mind, so he laid his goblet on the counter and paced over to the window. How had this happened, right here in his home country? The answer was clear. The transformation had been so gradual, so ostensibly benign, that most citizens were not even conscious that they were surrendering their freedoms—almost daily, one by one, with nary a shot fired.

When Logan turned his head slightly, he saw that Tammi had followed him across the room. "Do you think I'm being awfully selfish about this?" she asked.

"Not if it's as hopeless as you say."

"It's even worse, believe me. THE ENTENTE have overlooked nothing—education, entertainment, journalism, the family, religion, revisionist history, social media. And they're unbelievably patient, with accumulative victories over a long span of several decades." She stared out the window. "Murder is a last resort—I'll give THE ENTENTE that much—but they won't hesitate to use it if there is no alternative for achieving what they want. The end justifies the means."

Logan nodded. "How long can you survive here?"

Tammi turned back toward him and sighed. "If I'm careful—and lucky—maybe a week, at best. They mean business, and I'm marked for elimination."

"Can you hole up in the Quigley Tower?"

"For a day or two, hiding like a rat in the sewer." A bitter thought caused her to shudder. "I should mention something else. Do you remember Gabriel Torveldt, who flew us from Tory's Edge to HQ-2 in the four-seater?"

"I remember him."

"Well, Gabe told me that THE ENTENTE have a way of pumping toxic fumes throughout the Quig's air-filtration system, and that same gas transforms into an incendiary with a single spark. They'll be able to make the blaze seem like a tragic accident—with the media's full complicity, of course."

Logan had heard enough. "Then come away with me," he said. "I can't leave you behind, and you sure won't serve any purpose as a slaughtered calf."

"Do you mean it?" Tammi asked. She took him by both hands and squeezed. "You'll be saving my life ... nothing less."

"So, now I can be *your* tour guide," Logan told her. He made the comment half in jest, but there was some truth to it, too. She would require considerable guidance as a twenty-first-century gal in the Big Apple.

"There's something else you need to know," Tammi said. "Shall I tell you now or later?"

"Go ahead." He braced himself for bad news.

"If I do go back with you, we can never become serious about each other. Always bear that in mind."

He nodded his head. "The main thing is to keep you safe. Whatever happens after that is icing on the cake."

"Nonetheless, please never lose sight of that fact," she added. "There can be no other way."

Once again, Logan marveled at how competent this girl was in her own world—even to the point of accepting defeat—and her manner of speech now became quite methodical. "Technologically, there's no way to go together," she told him, "so be aware that we might become separated." She consulted Logan's PG-13. "Your departure specs are not locked yet, but regardless of when you choose to leave here, the arrival time at your New Jersey apartment building will be 8:51 on a Tuesday morning."

"That's correct—nine before nine."

"And twelve hours later, I'll meet you in Manhattan. You can probably guess where."

"How long do you figure to have?"

"For what?"

"For Kegler to prep a PG-13 for you."

"Three days—tops. I can feel my luck running out." Tammi downed the last swallow of her vin rosé. "Meanwhile, I need to take you into town to tie up some loose ends. It's not a simple matter to leave behind everything I've ever known."

◆　◆　◆

They rode a Viper to the S4-E17 Station and detrained on the airborne platform alongside sixty or more fellow passengers, all but a few of whom were dressed identically, in gray unisex jumpsuits. While no municipal statute mandated acceptable attire, those who chose to deviate from the norm were likely to be eyed with disgust or even suspicion. Many citizens continued to wear protective facemasks, even though the manmade virus from Asia had long since been vanquished.

Logan and Tammi proceeded on foot to their destination, which was located five blocks away. It was in the core of a business district, but not of the high-rise variety. Solerograd's more photogenic skyline was almost four miles to the northwest of where they now stood. Tammi said to Logan, "Wait here for me. You won't be allowed inside."

Craning his head upward, he viewed an unremarkable— and thoroughly anonymous—office building. Less than twenty stories tall, it was not what he expected. The structure was bleak and forbidding, enfolded by windows so darkly tinted as to be opaque. No markings were visible to distinguish it from countless other developments in the sector. Perhaps that was because it was constructed with Department of the Interior funding, at taxpayer expense. "Is this PGK?" Logan asked.

"Yes, and no visitors have any access, except through that public door to the outer lobby." Tammi waved her personal disk at the scanning plate for employees. "I'll try to find Kegler, but it may take a while. Don't talk to any strangers while I'm gone. You'll only call attention to yourself."

That caused him to grin. "Do I really seem that out of place?"

"Not until you open your mouth," she said. "If anybody speaks to you, just pantomime that you don't understand English or Russian. Otherwise, your ignorance will make them think you're from another planet."

"Thanks for the boost of confidence."

While Tammi was inside the building, Logan strolled south along E13, continually glancing over his shoulder to see whether the girl had returned downstairs. High above him, an emergency Viper, possessing the right-of-way, impelled other trains to hover in midair as it passed. The siren was deafening—even to Sollians on the ground—but none of them bothered to look up, and the sound soon faded. Approaching Logan from ahead was a police robot, holding the leashes of four security dogs in his clawlike pincer. The automaton's metallic body had a reflective finish that was almost blinding, and his stride resembled that of a predatory animal.

A loud noise made Logan stop in his tracks. Some sort of disturbance had taken place, and he did not wish to become part of it. He could see that five bodies lay strewn in their jumpsuits, and a gang of toughs was smashing storefront windows to loot. One of them casually used his crowbar to crush the skull of a female passer-by. No one offered to come to her aid. It crossed Logan's mind to wonder why the automaton was guiding his dogs in the wrong direction, but that was not for him to know.

Looking back, he noticed that two people were now standing at the PGK entrance, almost three blocks away, so he reversed his course to join them. A moment later, he heard Tammi's voice say, "Are you nearby?" and this caused his borrowed wristpad to glow a shimmering green. "I'm coming," he told the embedded microphone. "You can probably see me."

"On S3?"

"No—the other one."

"Oh, yes, there you are."

As Logan approached the pair, he tried in vain to recall Ira Vincent Kegler's appearance by memory. Citizens were very difficult to identify, as individuals, in their universal togs. But surely this person had to be Kegler, for one thing made him stand out from most of the other inhabitants of Solerograd. Like his colleague, Tammi Hansen, the gray jumpsuit that he wore displayed a fuchsia monogram that spelled out PG KRON in small caps. It was a company-issued garment.

"Citizen Gramm? I'm Ira Kegler." They bumped fists.

"Hello again, Citizen Kegler," Logan said. He glanced around to see who was near. "We appreciate what you've done for us and hope that you'll—"

Tammi waved him off. "Let's not talk about it here," she said. "Citizen Kegler says he'll meet us tonight at the holly. It's as good a place as any."

"Where's that?" Logan asked.

"Lots of them to choose from," Kegler said. "Pick one, and I'll be there at seven." He extended his fist again, and Logan did likewise. "Back to work now—my break's over."

As they retraced their way to the Viper station, Logan wanted Tammi to explain to him what the evening plans would entail. One thing, in particular, baffled him. "What's a holly?"

She nodded. "Holly is a slang term, short for hollygram. A holly is a hologram flick that was made in Hollywood. Get it— holly-gram?"

"So, it's basically a 3-D film?"

"Well, yes and no. I'd describe it as a three-dimensional story that comes to life on a theatrical stage, but with everyone in the audience seeing it from exactly the same perspective. All of the characters are recorded by actors ahead of time and then generated into the proper settings, with music and sound effects. The typical hollygram—or holly—lasts about ninety minutes, so that should give us plenty of time."

Over their heads streaked a six-car train, speeding west from the S4-E17 Station. Its advertising panels scrolled a muted pitch for Volgorad vodka, which promised to "lull you into a delightful cloud of lethargy." An impressionistic passage from Debussy's *Prelude to the Afternoon of a Faun* supported the message, which seemed quite subliminal in its approach. But this prohibitively expensive ad was lost on Tammi, who paid scant regard to it.

"Solerograd's theater complexes present at least forty different titles at a given time, all across the city," she told Logan. "A hollygram is intellectually shallow, but at least it keeps the people entertained, apathetic, and off the streets."

"Is there a political reason behind that?"

Tammi rolled her eyes. "What do you think? Today's entertainment industry is in complete lockstep with THE ENTENTE. Nothing is released to the public without approval from the top."

"Are all of these hologram films produced in Hollywood, California?"

"The great majority of them are—I'd say about eighty-five percent—but there are a handful of indies to compete. They, too, must conform to the standards." She paused. "Oh, but I should tell you that Hollywood is no longer in California. That state has been renamed Caligrad."

"Why is that?"

"Part of the neo-Soviet push of the past century. Lots of the American names were revised to be more diverse and inclusive—an effort at multiculturalism."

Out of the corner of his eye, Logan glimpsed a large rat, which ran by, foaming at the mouth as it passed. No one else—not even Tammi—seemed overly disturbed by this sighting, so he gave it no further thought.

"What's the purpose of going to a hollygram tonight?" he asked. "Isn't the place bugged?"

"Sure it is, but the dialogue and music will obscure what we say."

"So, we can we talk during the show?"

"Our whispers will be amplified," she said. "The three of us will have a shielded hook-up that Kegler designed for privacy. It's extremely illegal, of course, but almost impossible to track."

"Almost?"

Tammi's face darkened. "Nothing is certain around here."

Halfway to their Viper station, the admittance gates swung shut in front of them, so Logan asked Tammi, "How will we know where to meet Kegler tonight?"

"I'll ChatLink the physical address to him. There are literally dozens of hollygram showings in this city, with multiple theaters in every precinct, and all of them are indistinguishable in layout. Just for fun, you can have the honor of picking a title at random."

"Why is Kegler so willing to help you with this? It seems a little suspicious to me."

Tammi grinned. "Are you sure you want to know?"

"Unless it's a state secret."

"I think he's smitten with me," she said, "although I've never encouraged him in that respect. Oh, we've gone on a couple of dates, but they didn't amount to anything special."

"Does he know that you're planning to leave for good?"

"Absolutely not. Otherwise, he'd never agree to lock open the return coordinate."

"Is Kegler in DEFIANCE, too?"

Tammi laughed aloud. "No way. Kegler's political views are slightly to the left of Chairman Bornjikov, if you can imagine that." She waited for Logan to respond, but his face was expressionless. "Sergei Bornjikov was Commissar of the Second Purge," she added. "He was responsible for the massacre of four hundred thousand egalitarians last century, and even today his name represents a despotic ruler. Who would that be in your day and age?"

"Hitler, I'm sure. Have you heard of him?"

She gave a smirk. "Yes, Mr. Historian, it may interest you to know that I am quite familiar with mid-twentieth-century events, including what you call the Second World War."

"Oh, yeah? What former actor became the nation's fortieth President?"

"That would be Jamieson Fitch. And he was later thrown out of office in a popular coup." Tammi was so proud of her grasp of American Presidents that Logan did not have the heart to tell her that she had been victimized by revisionist history.

At long last, the pedestrian gates rotated by ninety degrees, allowing a mass of eastbound Sollians to proceed across the broad intersection. Morose citizens forged straight ahead, wholly unconcerned that they might collide with oncoming pedestrians.

"By the way, I was exaggerating a little about I. V. Kegler," Tammi said, "but the fact of the matter is that he's an avid supporter of the current oligarchy."

Logan lowered his voice. "Is he aware of your political leanings?"

"Only that my late brother was a UNITED FRONT member. I'm very careful not to discuss governmental issues with Kegler, and I've given him no reason to suspect that we're diametrically opposed to each other."

The holly, in this instance, happened to be at N2-E14. Logan had selected the site, on a whim, entirely by which title was playing there. Anything called *Tightroping Across the Golden Gate* had to be worthy of some notice. And that indeed was the case. Logan was fascinated by the technology, presenting a dramatic tale of greed and ruthlessness in idyllic San Francisco, Caligrad. The hologram process was dazzling to his untutored eyes, in gorgeous 3-D without the bother of polarized red/cyan glasses. His mind was tricked into believing that he could reach out and touch the actors—and dip a finger into the Pacific—while comfortably remaining in his rocking seat.

Theater 14 in the complex held about three hundred customers, but it appeared to be only about a quarter full. Kegler and Logan sat on either side of Tammi, who spent most of the next hour in a whispering conversation with her PG KRON colleague, while the visitor from prehistoric New Jersey offered whatever input he deemed to be helpful.

In addition to locking the specs for Logan's departure, Kegler also promised to have a PG-13 ready for Tammi's use in less than twenty-four hours. That was not a pledge to be taken lightly. Never before had Kegler attempted to program an open-ended foray into what he termed "negative" time—the past—and his challenge would be to override all coding that prevented such tampering with the return commands. There were buffers galore and decoy redundancies that would confound a whole team of specialists. Even the designers themselves might be hard-pressed to solve this puzzle. But I. V. Kegler was not easily deterred, especially with pretty Tammi Hansen counting on him to succeed.

Logan felt like the third wheel on a bicycle, for he contributed almost nothing to the preparations. He was sorely out of his element when it came to systems engineering, and the fact that technological advances had left him in the dust served to devalue his suggestions even further. Softening the blow just a bit was Logan's certainty that both of the others knew of his hapless provenance.

Discussion complete, their final half-hour in the auditorium was given over to watching what remained of the hollygram. They removed the tiny earpieces—wireless transmitter/receiver inserts—and placed them for safekeeping in Kegler's unsightly pill box. Logan watched the show's climactic sequences with rapt attention, but the other two yawned through them to the point of annoyance.

Although the holly's story line seemed illogical to Logan, its brilliance as a piece of dramatic theater was transcending. Surely these were masters of the cinematic art at work, displaying a craftsmanship that brought to him a sense of awe. And their production values boggled the mind. How, for example, could a director cut from wide shot to close-up on multiple hologram figures while not disturbing the composition of a scene? No problem here. This technique had become second nature to the modern cinematographer.

Afterward, during the trio's short hike back to the Viper station, Tammi was aware of something that Ira Vincent Kegler could not have imagined: almost certainly, he would never be seeing her again. That being so, his manner remained jaunty and upbeat, and this tore at her soul for the duplicity she was forced to effect for the next couple of days. Still, revealing her ruse to the oblivious PGK programmer would court disaster for everyone involved—not least of all, Kegler himself. He would be compelled to speak up against her, thereby incriminating himself as an accomplice in Tammi's failed attempt to defect. In such a debacle, only THE ENTENTE figured to come out ahead.

◆　◆　◆

The next morning, at the dawn of what Tammi Hansen expected to be her final full day in Solerograd, she experienced a peculiar sensation that was difficult to put into words. Like most people, Tammi's daily habit was to view her ChatLinker immediately upon getting out of bed. One of the queued messages that day made little sense at all, except for the familiar name of its signee, Dr. Erich Fishbourne, an elderly man whom she remembered from college.

Dr. Fishbourne had taught in the Classics Department at USol for thirty-nine years, until his recent retirement at the age of seventy-seven. Why would this professor now be asking Tammi to drop by for an informal chat? True, she had served briefly as his graduate assistant on a work-study stipend, but only for a portion of one semester. Nonetheless, something was drawing her to the outskirts of town for a reunion with him in a vintage book shop called Paracletus.

It stood to reason that Tammi was hesitant to venture there alone, for she knew very little about the Gorky Park section of town and nothing at all about the oddly named book shop that was specified on the screen of her communications device. At first, she considered dismissing the invitation out of hand, with no one the wiser, but then came that inexplicable pull again, and she relented. She decided to go—if for no other reason than to satisfy her curiosity—and Logan Gramm would be right there with her as a convenient excuse for cutting the visit short. Logan's reprogrammed PG-13 was already in his apartment, with the departure specs locked and waiting for activation.

Only on rare occasions had Tammi been to Solerograd's Gorky Park district. Lying in the far north-central section of town, fourteen miles from the CBD, Gorky Park was served by the northernmost Viper station of them all, that of N176-W12. And yet, at a cruising speed topping one hundred miles per hour, it was not an unreasonably long trip for her and Logan.

Gorky Park was as rural as Solly ever got within its city limits. There was even some farmland to be seen, along with a dilapidated rodeo arena and cattle auction barn. Tammi's wristpad directed her and Logan to a street called Nadezhda, and there, at number 208, was the book shop that she sought. Above its front door, a hanging metal sign swayed in the late morning breeze: "Paracletus Book Shoppe."

"Should we just go inside or knock first?" Tammi asked.

Logan shrugged his shoulders. "See if it's unlocked."

It was, and they entered a dimly lit space that smelled of musty paper. Every square inch of shelving, from floor to ceiling, appeared to be filled to overflowing with used books. This rectangular room's only piece of furniture was an antique roll-top desk in the rear-left corner. A wall clock, with oscillating pendulum and analogue hands, ticked above it.

"Hello, Miss Hansen," someone said. "Thank you for coming." An old man with long sideburns and male-pattern baldness stepped forward to greet her. He seemed surprised to encounter two people instead of one. "I'm Erich Fishbourne, in case you'd forgotten. My hair is whiter now and in much less profusion."

"Thank you for inviting me, Dr. Fishbourne," Tammi told him. "This is my friend from work, Logan Gramm. I hope you don't mind that I brought him with me."

Fishbourne bowed to him in an outmoded, continental manner. "Nonsense," he said. "We'll use all the help we can get."

"Help for what?" Tammi asked. "I'm afraid I don't understand why we're here."

Fishbourne chuckled at her perplexity. "Fear not. I am perfectly harmless, except to cockroaches, scorpions, and other household pests." He motioned for his guests to follow him into the back room. "Care for some coffee or tea?"

"No, thanks," Tammi said.

"Sure. Why not?" Logan told him. "Coffee, please—black."

"Then I will, too," Tammi added. "Same for me."

"You're not offended if I address you as 'Miss,' are you? That's the term I used in your grad assistant days."

"No. Of course not."

"It's just that so many of today's young women prefer the indeterminate prefixes of 'Ms.' or 'Citizen,' you know."

Tammi giggled at his archaic manners. "Take your pick, Dr. Fishbourne. I have thick skin."

The three of them sat around a table in what Fishbourne called his "chambers." The room appeared to be devoted principally to sorting, receiving, and shipping.

"Do you deal only in used books, Dr. Fishbourne?" Logan asked. "Nothing new?"

The elderly gent gave him a bemused look. "There *are* no new books, Mr. Gramm—not for the past hundred and fifty years. Everything has become electronic."

"Is it against the law to own hard copies?"

"Oh, no. Just bad business." Fishbourne smiled at his own joke. "But I'm a superannuated relic, so I permit myself this one small pleasure in life."

"How far back do these books go?"

"Centuries."

Logan gazed at the leaning stacks of assorted titles. "They must be valuable to collectors."

"Not that I'm aware of," Fishbourne said. "No one is interested in physical books anymore."

"Is there anything from the twentieth century here?" Logan took a sip of coffee.

"Lots and lots—mostly, in fact. The Gregorian calendar's twentieth century AD was the last great period of readers."

Tammi leaned back and smiled proudly. "Logan here is a connoisseur of vintage books—the actual paper-and-ink kind. I don't know anyone who's half as knowledgeable as he is."

Fishbourne was impressed. "Is that so? Well, in that case, I'm even more pleased to make your acquaintance." He offered an old-fashioned handshake, and Logan accepted. "Who are some of your favorite writers, son?"

"From the twentieth century?"

"I suppose."

Logan had a ready response to that one. "Orwell, Huxley, C. S. Lewis, Ayn Rand ... "

Fishbourne's gray eyebrows lifted. "Do you realize what you're saying? All of those authors are under the counter. They require written permission from the Commissar."

"So, their books no longer exist?"

"Only in research libraries. Otherwise, not a living soul has read them—or ever will."

"*Brave New World? 1984? The Screwtape Letters?*"

"All of them, it grieves me to say."

"What about Solzhenitsyn?"

"Sorry."

"Milton Friedman?"

Fishbourne swallowed hard. "*Capitalism and Freedom* has been stricken from the records. If you don't mind my asking, how do you know about these titles?"

"I was a history major in college."

"And where was that?"

Logan glanced at Tammi before answering. "I'm not at liberty to say."

Fishbourne stood up and idly wandered over to a stack of books. "You specified *The Screwtape Letters*. Would it be safe to assume that you are a Christian?"

Tammi intervened, afraid that her companion might be too forthcoming. "Logan and I have similar views on many different subjects," she said. "I guess that's why we've become such good friends."

Fishbourne looked intently at her. "Are you, then, also a Christian?" he asked.

Tight-lipped, her eyes scanned for slits in the crown molding. Old habits were hard to break.

But the professor put her at ease. He sat down and placed his hand on hers. "Don't worry, Miss Hansen. My little shop is the most private spot in all of Gorky Park."

"How did you arrange that?" Logan asked.

"It just so happens that I have a surveillance pal who glosses over some of its minor shortcomings. The state of security here is ... shall we say ... woefully out-of-date." He grinned.

"Do you pay him to keep silent?"

"He's one of the regulars in my weekly study group."

Nervously, Tammi voiced the logical question. "What do you study?"

Fishbourne stared at both of the visitors, as if assessing their trustworthiness. "Don't tell anyone," he told them, "but our group studies the Holy Bible."

Tammi was stunned by the old man's admission—much more so than if he had answered Satanism or Karl Marx. "How many people are in your group?" she asked.

"Oh, let me think." He rubbed his forehead. "We're averaging about twenty-six or twenty-seven each week. That may not sound like very many to you, but we started with just five of us two months ago."

"That's a dangerous thing to do," Tammi said. "Obviously, you're aware of the ordinance: 'Up to four individuals can come together for purposes of spiritual expression, but no gathering larger than that'."

"We bend the rules," Fishbourne told her, "recognizing the primacy of a higher law."

Both of his visitors seemed to accept the comment at face value—dissident though it was by Sollian standards—and the room went silent for several seconds.

"We are a rebellious faction, I suppose, but not in terms of violence," the professor said. "All we want is to worship and study in peace, while admittedly striving to win others to the Lord."

Logan looked around. The place was cramped, even with just the three of them present. "How can you fit everyone in here?"

"Obviously, we can't. After the first couple of weeks, we had to move to larger quarters. Not only that, but we always encourage our members to bring receptive acquaintances with them, which means those numbers are actually much larger than what I stated earlier—and growing every week."

Tammi swallowed some coffee. "Where is your new facility?" she asked.

"We call it our 'sanctuary,' but that's just a fancy word for a rundown country estate that we've adopted out of sheer necessity. I won't tell you where it is—not quite yet. But in due time, hopefully, you'll know well enough."

Logan inquired whether Fishbourne himself served as pastor, but the professor told him no. "I only lead the Bible study group. Our minister on Sunday mornings is a wonderful young man who knows the scriptures backwards and forwards. He was ordained by acclamation."

"Is that official?" Logan asked.

"Probably not, but it's our only form of ministerial licensing. There are no denominational associations or seminaries in Solerograd."

"But I'm sure your pastor can't preach his sermons openly," Tammi said. "You'd get raided and thrown into prison."

"Sadly, that is so," Fishbourne told her. "Everything we do is behind closed doors." The old man looked from one to the other and smiled broadly. "But we feel the hand of God upon us."

◆　◆　◆

That night, a riot erupted in the Central Business District and then spread in concentric circles throughout the interior precincts of Solerograd. The disorder began as a peaceful protest but soon escalated into vandalism and wanton violence. Oddly, law enforcement personnel did little, if anything, to quell the uprising. Police all across the city were ordered to stand down until the disturbance receded to more manageable levels of devastation. When consulted for guidance, the city's academic leaders—college professors all—insisted that countering the strife with a reciprocal show of force would only incite the mobs to intensify their barbarity even further.

Despite what the so-called experts counseled, the unrest did not subside like similar disturbances had done in recent years. Indeed, the number of rioters increased steadily until much of Solerograd was ablaze and filled with rampaging looters. Some of these plunderers carried signs that demanded a fifty-percent increase in welfare remuneration—a common sight that prompted local media to contend that the present turmoil was provoked by inequitable distribution of wealth. What they failed to report was that this "spontaneous" demonstration utilized plentiful supplies from outside sources. Furthermore, the multi-pronged attacks were meticulously orchestrated for maximum terroristic impact ... and news coverage.

The perceived enemies of financial fairness—UNITED FRONT voters and establishments—fell squarely within the mob's crosshairs. Police and army troops stood idly by while professional anarchists assaulted these targets with impunity. Spokespeople for the UF voiced a grievance that the rioting was politically motivated, but studio commentators on all seven of the major networks were quick to refute that allegation. The demonstrators were only acting in response to their impoverished living conditions. They were the victims.

Everyone in the media agreed that one statistic was painful to announce: four hundred people—give or take a dozen—had lost their lives in the mayhem. But even that was regarded as acceptable, falling into the overused category of collateral damage. One of the largest structures to be assailed was the Quigley Tower, which was torched to the ground in a matter of minutes, as if it were an inside job.

All of this civil upheaval transpired while Logan and Tammi were still in Gorky Park, slightly beyond the wide swath of destruction. In the circumstances, Dr. Erich Fishbourne was quick to reveal the location of his sanctuary. He even offered to let them stay overnight in two of his church's guest quarters. "Feel free to cast lots," he said, "but the rooms are virtually identical." As the professor mentioned earlier, the makeshift church appeared to be nothing more than an old country estate that had seen better days.

The young pair were fortunate to have remained in their apartments during "Red Night," as the insurrection came to be called. Logan was unknown to THE ENTENTE, but informants had classified Tammi as "expendable." Her only saving grace was two and a half years of exemplary service for the Department of the Interior. But that was far outweighed by the fatal marks against her: purported ties to DEFIANCE and her brother's advocacy for the "wayward policies" of UNITED FRONT. In any case, politics aside, neither of the guests could have made it unscathed through the chaotic streets that obstructed their way.

Tammi was just about to fall asleep on the marginally uncomfortable bed when her ChatLinker crackled with urgency. This alarm was a piercing din, to which the correspondent had assigned a nine (out of ten) on the CL's priority scale. Ira Kegler, Tammi's PROGRADE KRONOTECHNIX colleague, had sent a dire message of warning: "Do NOT go home! Your apartment is surrounded by Solice, a few with dogs. Someone is in big trouble there. Could be dangerous, even for an innocent bystander."

She felt that the world was tightening a noose around her neck. In this venomous political climate, she could not even consider retrieving any possessions from her own apartment, much less returning to her gainful employment at ProGrade KRONOTECHNIX.

Tammi hurried across the narrow courtyard to pound on Logan's door. "Read this," was all she told him, but the dread on her face spoke volumes. He asked her what "Solice" meant, and she explained that it was a contraction that locals often used for

Solerograd Police. "Everything I know is crashing down," she said. "We have nowhere to hide."

Neither of them slept for longer than an hour or two after that, but when daylight finally did arrive, both expressed to Dr. Fishbourne how much they appreciated the hospitality. His kindness, they added, might very well have saved their lives. The professor brushed aside the praise, modestly steering the topic away from himself. "Flames were visible from my back porch," he said. "The whole southern sky was aglow. I've never seen anything like it, and I pray that last night is not a preview of things to come."

Logan's thoughts were focused on something more immediate. "Can you tell me, sir, how long the guest rooms will be available?"

"About thirty-six hours, as I recall. Old Mrs. Blanchard's nephew and his wife are coming to stay with us for three days. They're from the industrial tenements—not exactly a hotbed of faith—but they may wish to become members."

"If it's not too much of an imposition," Logan said, "we'll be needing the rooms for one more night."

His brusque manner caused Fishbourne to squint at him with concern. "What's on your mind, son?"

But it was Tammi who replied. "We can't go back into the city. I think my days are numbered."

"Oh? How so? I hope you mean that figuratively."

"Maybe not, I'm sorry to say." She took a deep breath. "My political leanings are under suspicion, and they could cost me my life."

"Surely you're exaggerating," the old man said. "No offense, but you don't seem like much of a firebrand to me. I mean that in a nice way."

"Thank you for the vote of confidence, but I've worked against THE ENTENTE on numerous occasions. Obviously, these were noted because someone tried to kill me a few weeks ago, and I've received more death threats than you can count on one hand."

Fishbourne turned to Logan. "Is that the truth? She's such a charming lass. I can't imagine Tammi even raising her voice, let alone engaging in Machiavellian conspiracies."

Logan nodded toward her. "She's more opinionated than you might think."

The professor gave a thumbs-up sign. "Good for you, Miss Hansen. We could certainly use you around here, if you're willing to join our ranks."

"But how would I earn a living?" she asked. "I'm much too proud to live off someone else's charity."

He laughed. "Oh, we're not all that charitable, believe me. We'd put you to work, and you would earn every drachma. Besides, our unpretentious little church has a surprisingly robust endowment."

Logan was skeptical. "With a membership of less than thirty?"

"With donors from coast to coast, my boy—anonymous and otherwise. We have a long list of mustard-seed projects for the future."

The more Tammi thought about Fishbourne's offer, the more attractive it became. Accepting the professor's arrangement would be a way to remain in Solerograd, enabling her to fight against THE ENTENTE and perhaps exact vengeance upon those who murdered her brother. Tammi confided to Logan that she was having serious misgivings about emigrating to the twenty-first century.

"It sounds to me like you've already made up your mind," he said.

"I think I have."

Within an hour, Tammi forwarded her decision to Kegler, ChatLinking him that she needed to resign from her current position at PROGRADE KRONOTECHNIX. Moreover, her proposed mission to the past would either be postponed temporarily or canceled for good. Kegler was surprised by this sudden reversal, but he was professional enough to place her excursion's status on indefinite hold, awaiting further instructions. "Stay in touch," he wrote back. "I don't understand why you are leaving PGK, but I'm sure there must be some sensible reason. I will miss you, and the place will never be the same again. Citizen Gramm's departure specs remain fixed and cannot be altered."

The next day was Midweek, which presented Dr. Fishbourne's two guests with an opportunity to attend his Bible study session. Several regulars in the group deemed it rather chancy to carry on as before, so soon after the carnage of Red Night, but the professor was determined to stare down any and all sinister threats.

Right from the start, it became quite clear why this weekly class had earned such a vibrant reputation. Fishbourne's topic of the day was the Holy Spirit, the often-neglected third Person of the Trinity, and Logan, for one, was astonished by what he learned. The Holy Spirit is a very real entity, the old man declared, a Helper—Paraclete—who physically indwells anyone who professes belief in Jesus Christ.

"Jesus told his disciples, in John 16:7, '*It is to your advantage that I go away, for if I do not go away, the Helper will not come to you. But if I go, I will send Him to you.*' My friends," Fishbourne added, "the Holy Spirit will personally accompany you through all of this troubled world's challenges, if only you will invite Him to do so instead of forfeiting the blessing. One of life's most disheartening shames is that so very few believers are even aware of their Helper, who is available simply by calling upon Him for personal guidance, comfort, and interpreting the Word of God."

By the end of the professor's hour-long lesson, Logan sensed that he and the others had received a life-changing gift. The class also taught him two lesser truths—why this old man named his book shop Paracletus, and what divine power had drawn Tammi there on a night that otherwise would have been her last.

◆　◆　◆

The day arrived for Logan Gramm to bid farewell to Tammi Hansen and shake free from the tyranny of Solerograd. According to a ChatLink from I. V. Kegler, Logan's leave-taking was scheduled for 2:41 PM, so the plan was for him to set out from Gorky Park no later than 10:30 AM. He would need to retrieve the PG-13 and then activate it by physically touching the thumbprint pad and pressing APPLY.

But a stunning occurrence intervened at the guest facilities of Dr. Erich Fishbourne's church, one that was totally unforeseen. Around nine o'clock that morning, Logan heard an urgent rapping on the door of his room. When he opened it, Tammi was standing there, wide-eyed and tongue-tied, but she finally managed to convey a few words. "Quick! I want you to see someone."

With a couple of impatient shoves, she prodded Logan across the courtyard, concerned that her visitor might not still be there. But he was. She swung the door aside, and now it was Logan's turn to gape in disbelief. Regaining his wits, he reached forward to bump fists with David Crownover. "Dave!" he shouted, "I thought you were a goner."

"Evidently not," the automaton said. He flashed an *ersatz* smile.

"We heard that the Quig was leveled on Red Night, and there were no survivors," Logan said. He glanced at Tammi, whose confusion seemed just as deep as his own.

"Toxic gases were pumped in," Crownover told them, "but that had no effect on me because I don't breathe." He patted his chest. "I may appear to breathe, but that's only my motor-driven diaphragm at work."

Tammi dreaded the answer to what she said next. "Were all the humans killed? Beverly Cline? Gabe Torveldt?"

Crownover nodded his head. "Every person in the building, as far as I know." He turned to Logan. "Including your firearms instructor, Sergeant Dwynn. By the time my sensors detected an elevated level of toxicity, the human beings were already deceased. I could be of no assistance to them, so my logic cells instructed me to evacuate the building just as the incendiaries ignited and began to engulf the premises."

"So, I gather, you're not fireproof," Logan said.

"By no means. The flames would have devoured me, and I cannot allow that to happen. A great deal of money was invested in me, so a vigorous survival instinct is built into my circuitry for longevity insurance."

"Are we sure it was arson that destroyed the Quigley Tower?" Tammi asked.

"Without a doubt, though of course THE ENTENTE have denied responsibility."

Logan gave Crownover a long stare, trying to remember something the automaton had once told him. "As I recall, you had never been outside the Quig. Is that right?"

"Not until there was no other choice. To be honest with you, I hadn't the slightest desire to leave."

"How were you able to locate Tammi?" Logan asked.

"Some basic triangulation, that's all. I tapped into her wristpad and followed the signal."

"And you rode a Viper to Gorky Park?"

"Yes, the N176-W12 Station. I tried to blend in, like a typical commuter, and I don't think anyone paid much attention to me. Lots of devastation was visible from the air, and most people were busy viewing that." A thought crossed Crownover's robotic mind. "Incidentally, Logan, I am willing to accompany you to the apartment today. Solerograd's streets are still very dangerous, and it would not surprise me if Congressman Jeffrey Hansen's former living quarters are being closely scrutinized. THE ENTENTE are aware of who resides there now and what political connections he has. In other words, you no longer enjoy the benefits of anonymity."

Greetings concluded, Tammi and Logan escorted the automaton to Dr. Fishbourne's office for proper introductions, only to have the church secretary inform them that the professor was in a meeting and could not be disturbed for another hour or so. Crownover's cover was not compromised whatsoever, for his behavior was impeccably anthropomorphic in every last detail. It was clear to see that the secretary suspected nothing. And Logan, as always, was overwhelmed by the performance of this Superba-IV Class automaton—an *Übermensch*—the world's most advanced synthetic human.

David Crownover was seldom bewildered, but present circumstances were an exception. As the three of them walked the grounds, he came to a halt. "What exactly is this place?" he asked. An automaton had no concept of spirituality or its physical accouterments.

"A church," Tammi told him.

"It resembles no church I've ever seen, either in hollygrams or photographs."

She winked at Logan. "That's the whole idea. Our religious order is clandestine—operating outside the control of Solerograd authority—so it wouldn't be wise to have a majestic steeple rising into the sky."

"What would happen if word did get out?" Crownover asked.

"We'd all be arrested, tried, and imprisoned," Tammi said. "The ringleaders, beginning with Erich Fishbourne, would disappear forever."

"What about you and Logan?"

Tammi shrugged her shoulders. "We're newcomers here, so we might be able to talk our way out of the harshest punishment. What would prove most damaging to me is not religion but politics. Failure to uphold every doctrine of THE ENTENTE is an unforgivable offense." Nervously, she ran an index finger across her implanted wrist chip. "Found guilty, I would endure an intensive learning process. Call it what you will—brainwashed, re-educated, or indoctrinated—Solly's doctors are reputed to work wonders with a defective mind. Essentially, I would be hammered, in laboratory conditions, by alternating bursts of mental breakdown and reconstruction. Anyone who comes out alive is not the same person."

Ever in pursuit of knowledge, Crownover wanted to learn more about the concept of church, but his questioning was interrupted by a female voice. "Yoo-hoo! Miss Hansen!" It was the secretary again, approaching Tammi as quickly as her ladylike demeanor would allow. "Dr. Fishbourne will see you now." Three men and two women were leaving the premises after their meeting. With a polite smile, the secretary went back to her post.

The professor was seated at his desk but stood up when the others arrived. "I apologize for the delay, but that was our finance committee, and there are no people more vital to a growing church."

"We'd like for you to meet someone, Professor," Tammi said. "This is our friend, David Crownover. And Dave, this is Dr. Erich Fishbourne, the church's founder and the leader of a Bible class."

"Pleased to meet you, Mr. Crownover," the old man said. "Always nice to encounter a synthetic with such convincing mannerisms."

Crownover laughed. "Not convincing *enough*, apparently."

"Don't feel too bad. Your electronics alerted the security alarm, that's all. Otherwise, I probably wouldn't have known."

"Thank you. That's reassuring because I'm a fugitive from justice."

Fishbourne looked more closely at him and could see that he was not joking. "How may we help?"

"Do you remember the Quigley Tower?" Crownover asked.

"Sad to see it go—and all the people who were trapped inside, may God rest their souls."

"That's why Dave is here, Dr. Fishbourne," Tammi said. "He has no other place to seek refuge."

"Might I venture to guess that it was arson?" The professor's question was rhetorical, but Crownover answered anyway.

"My preliminary analysis confirms your suspicion," the automaton told him, "although the news media are pointing their fingers elsewhere."

"I try not to pay much attention to them."

"Solly-6 accuses DEFIANCE of self-immolation."

"For what possible purpose?" Fishbourne asked. He was becoming quite agitated.

"Igniting a revolt, the network claims."

"By committing suicide and incinerating their own headquarters? That's preposterous!"

With time running short, Logan edged the subject toward Tammi Hansen and the choice she was forced to make. "Mr. Crownover is targeted for liquidation, and so are Miss Hansen and I," he said. "There's no special consideration for females or synthetic humans."

Fishbourne's response was grandfatherly. "Speaking for the entire church," he said, "I'm sure we would welcome all three of you to our staff—and with the promise of fair compensation."

"Mr. Gramm will not be able to accept your kind offer," Tammi told him. "Later today, he'll be leaving Gorky Park forever."

"Oh, that's a shame," Fishbourne said. He turned to Logan. "Do you have business elsewhere?"

"Yes, sir. But I'm sure that Miss Jensen and Mr. Crownover can be of great service to you."

"I think you're right, son. They're just the kind of people we need."

◆　◆　◆

Neither of them knew what to expect. David Crownover was a displaced robot, newly clad in a gray jumpsuit and almost totally unfamiliar with the city streets of Solerograd. Logan Gramm was a non-citizen, wanted by local authorities for what might be described as guilt by association. Both, it was thought, had ties to DEFIANCE, an underground movement that claimed Tamara Renée Hansen as one of its active members.

This unlikely pair's objective was N120-W24, where Logan needed to retrieve a PG-13 for activation. Anything short of that spelled his arrest, detention, trial, and punishment—possibly even capital. Crownover's fate, by contrast, would mean one of two things: either his rewiring to satisfy THE ENTENTE's philosophical demands or his outright dismantling for whatever useful parts could be salvaged.

Their first stop was Gorky Park's only Viper depot, the N176-W12 Station, from which they would travel some sixty-eight blocks to the vicinity of Rep. Jeffrey Hansen's former apartment. Logan purchased two DayPass tickets by swiping his integrated-circuit microchip across a ViperScan. So far, so good. But when the entrance gate failed to admit them to the flightstream, Crownover suspected that a coding alarm may have been triggered—probably to summon a police hovercraft. "Come!" the automaton said. They exited the depot on foot and set out to trek the rest of the way without any assistance from a public transport.

That strategy seemed sorely unrealistic to Logan, who grumbled his complaint. "We can't just hoof it to the other side of this megalopolis without being captured." But there was no better option, so they turned the corner and kept walking amidst a crowd of Sollians, many of whom wore facemasks in deference to the scarcely remembered pandemic of two decades past.

"Tammi," Logan said into his wristpad. It responded by emitting a greenish glow, evidence that an outbound voice-recognition signal had established contact.

"Logan!" her voice shouted. "Where are you?"

"N174-W12. We're banished from the Viper. What do you suggest?"

There was a pause. "Keep walking, and I'll blue-blink you right back. At least you'll be headed in the right direction." Never before had Logan heard of "blue-blink," but he trusted that the term would become clear to him. And it did.

Several blocks later, his wristpad blinked at him—with a blue tint for inbound. Tammi's voice said, "Place your personal disk against the pad. A friend of mine can alter your disk settings to a temp-ID." She was leery of transmitting the name of her associate over the satellite signal.

"Will this work for Dave, too?"

"Yes. Touch your pad to the back of his left wrist. Every Superba-IV has a built-in. Keep in mind that this will only function once before reverting back to your original data. And you'll need to go through the same procedure on your trip back."

"Thanks, Tammi! I owe you one."

"Don't thank me. Thank ... you-know-who."

They returned to the Viper station, posthaste, and entered the SW/7 train without further incident. One police officer was aboard, but he glowered at everyone equally, with contempt toward all.

Ninety seconds into the trip, when the speeding Viper began to hover in midair, Logan and Crownover exchanged glances of worry, but the delay was short-lived and unrelated to its two felonious passengers. The pair abstained from talking, in cautious respect for two narrow slits that ran the entire length of the metallic ceiling.

A veritable wave of humanity detrained with them at the N121-W22 Station, one of the system's busiest, and that was fine with Logan and Crownover, who wanted to meld with the general populace. Quite a few of these citizens were headed toward the southwest, and almost every one of them wore a facemask, which prompted the two fugitives to do the same. A substantial percentage of Sollians put their trust in protective coverings for fear of a viral contagion that, according to alarmist reports in the news media, might strike again at any moment.

As they neared the apartment building, Crownover tapped Logan on the shoulder. They stopped right where they were on the sidewalk, chatting as inconspicuously as practicable. The automaton must have sensed that something was wrong, for just then a police robot rounded the corner behind a leashed dog. The canine sported a bullet-proof jacket, emblazoned with "DANGER—K9 CORPS. NOT RESPONSIBLE FOR INJURIES."

Typically, police robots were mute. Instead of vocal commands, they used leash tugs to control their four-legged partners. But they also knew fellow synthetics when they encountered them, even behind facemasks. This officer turned quickly to the left, and his unblinking eyeball sensors evaluated the suspect from top to bottom—before instructing the dog to attack. Crownover avoided the snarling beast with a sideways step and grasped behind the scruff of its neck. Immediately, the dog fell forward in a heap, either asleep or deceased. The policeman was an everyday street cop, not designed for hand-to-hand combat. His sole mission was to patrol an assigned area, letting the dog take care of rowdy miscreants. With his partner down and seemingly lifeless, the officer backed off, folded his arms, and stood as inert as a marble sculpture.

Logan was awestruck by Crownover's effortless mastery of physical combat. "How did you learn that hold? What is it, some sort of death grip?"

"My knowledge is nearly infinite," the automaton told him. "The difference between me and a human genius is that my access to this wealth of information is instantaneous. I don't have to think about it before reacting."

The prone animal was unconscious but breathing. "It's called 'the pinch of sleep'," Crownover added. "Very humane, and it works well on people, too." He gazed at the dog and started hurrying away. "But it's only effective for three minutes—max."

Logan's housing complex was in the middle of the block, and they gained admission through the exterior door without any trouble. That seemed a bit strange, a little too easy for comfort, and no government officials appeared to be posted along the interior halls. Wary of detection, the runaways shunned both of the elevators in favor of a rear stairwell and again found the going to be unhindered. Outside his apartment door, Logan envisioned a room full of G-men, patiently awaiting their moment to pounce, but there was no turning back now. Hand trembling from nerves, he applied his thumbprint to the wall pad and heard the lock click open. They were free to enter.

At first glance, the living room was empty, so Logan took a step inside. "You stay here," he told his robotic companion, "in case someone tries to trap us from the hall."

"Is there an escape route for you at the rear?"

"No. Just hope it doesn't come to that."

In went Logan, and Crownover kept himself busy by intensifying his aural, light, vibration, and olfactory scans. That vigilance proved all for naught, for not even sixty seconds had passed when Logan re-emerged at the doorway.

"Do you have the device?" Crownover asked.

"Inside my pocket, but I haven't activated it yet."

"Don't."

The policeman and dog were nowhere to be seen, so Logan and Crownover were able to take a direct route to the Viper station. Halfway there, however, the automaton pulled up short, apprehension registering on his brow. "We'll split up," he said. "Give me the device, and I'll draw them off the scent."

"Sorry, Dave, but the very first PGK rule that I learned was never to entrust anyone with my lifeline. It stays with me."

"I must respectfully insist," Crownover told him. "You are much more likely to be captured than I am, and we cannot let the device fall into enemy hands. Three of you would be implicated—you, Tammi, and someone named ... " His power of recall went to work. " ...Ira Vincent Kegler."

"And accused of what—theft of DOI property? That crime can't be too serious."

"Anti-government subversion would be the charge. THE ENTENTE have lawyers who would make the indictment stick. It's quite possible that all three of you would be executed."

Logan could not believe his ears. "For borrowing a glorified remote control?"

"This would be enough evidence to bring down the remnants of DEFIANCE and also lead the authorities to Dr. Fishbourne's Christian enclave." Crownover glanced back at the apartment building. "Why do you think it was so easy to retrieve the device? It was a set-up, and your PG-13 would attract operatives to us like iron filings to a magnet. Even in 'sleep' mode, it can be sending out a homing signal."

"What if you get caught?"

The automaton found that to be mildly amusing. "Never forget that I have the upper hand," he said. "They can't kill me because I'm not even alive." Then, with eerie dispatch, his expression darkened to scorn. "But I can kill them."

Logan flinched. "How?"

"There is more explosive potential in my components than a small nuclear bomb. Believe me, they do not want to experience my controlled fission."

Logan thought for a moment longer and reluctantly decided to place the PG-13 in Crownover's outstretched hand. "Dave," he said, "if anything goes wrong, I'll be stranded in Solerograd. Kegler won't ever be able to program another for me."

"That is quite true."

To be honest, Logan was expecting more assurance than that declarative sentence could provide, but Crownover was not one to give false hope.

"Will you be using the Viper?" Logan asked him.

"Could be. My plans are improvisational at the moment."

"Let me have your left arm." Logan touched the synthetic wrist with his own personal disk. "Maybe this will get you through the gates."

Crownover nodded his thanks. "If all goes well, I'll be meeting up with you around two o'clock, which will give you more than enough time to activate the device for your trip home. If not, can Kegler extend the departure time?"

"Very doubtful, especially if he's being watched," Logan said. "The irony of it all is that I. V. Kegler is on the other side—a staunch anti-capitalist. To his dying day, he'll be flying the red banner of collectivism."

"Why is he willing to help our cause?"

"For one reason, and one reason alone," Logan told him. "Kegler's starry-eyed infatuation with Tammi Hansen."

The automaton frowned. "I'll never grasp the mystifying power of love." He started to walk away. "But neither do most humans, I gather."

♦ ♦ ♦

"Tammi," Logan said into his wristpad, and it responded with a greenish glow.

"Logan! Where are you?" The girl sounded almost frantic.

"N120-W24. I'm about to board the train."

"Are you already through the main gate?"

"Yes, no problem." He was now approaching the entrance to what he hoped was the proper flightstream for northeast passengers.

"Is Dave with you?"

"No. We had to split up."

"Did you get the ... hand-held item?" she asked.

"Yes, but I gave it to Dave."

"You what?" There was a pause. "That was a foolish thing to do."

"Maybe so, but Dave said there was no other way to make it through."

"What if he isn't here by 2:41?" Tammi asked.

"Then I'm sunk. It's a gamble we had to take."

Logan signed off the wristpad and again touched his personal disk to it. Nine people were ahead of him, and all of them entered through the flightstream sluice without incident. His turn came next. He held his breath and stepped forward.

Everything remained quite normal until the policeman on duty shouted, "Halt!" Logan froze in place, but the officer walked past him to one of the other passengers, a woman with gray hair. "Where's your face covering, citizen?" the policeman asked her.

"I'm going to purchase one now," she said.

"You purchased a hefty fine—that's what you purchased. The Viper is a public conveyance, citizen, and there is no tolerance."

"But the pandemic was ... "

"Silence! Your personal disk, please."

"I've seen lots of other people without masks."

"Silence!"

Logan proceeded to the ramplift and secured a vacant seat just as the Viper accelerated—from zero to ninety-seven in six seconds. He gazed at the people around him, many wearing masks that partially concealed their dour expressions. Few of them spoke, and then only in clipped phrases. The man seated beside him said, "Citizen, can you reach my Pentencil?" He pointed to the center aisle. Logan leaned to his right and retrieved the writing implement. The man, who appeared to be in his upper forties, nodded slightly but otherwise showed no appreciation. Instead, he resumed his artwork, a nicely rendered sketch of The Solerograd Steps, one of the city's foremost attractions.

"That's very good," Logan said to him. The response was nil, so he resolved thenceforth to be as unfriendly as everyone else aboard this Viper.

A minute passed before the artistic man spoke again. "See that Solice, citizen?" he whispered.

Logan said, "Yes. Why?"

"He's going to arrest you if we don't exchange places." The man locked his eyes on an imposing officer, dressed totally in black with red epaulets. "Wait until he turns his head," he whispered. "Wait ... Wait ... Now!" The man stepped over Logan, who shifted to his left. The whole process took no more than two seconds.

Gorky Park Station (N176-W12) represented this particular route's final stop, but so fleet was the Viper that it seemed but a short while until the train was hovering above its loading platform. As passengers began to exit, the policeman blocked the artistic man's way. "Relax, citizen," he said.

"What's the problem, officer?"

"Silence! Your personal disk, please."

When the policeman used a portable TekPak to scan the disk, his reaction was shock, followed by embarrassment. "Pardon me very much indeed, sir," he said. His bow from the waist nearly crossed a fine line into groveling. "Of course, you're free to go, and please accept my sincere apology." Then he turned to Logan. "Sorry for the delay, citizen. Just a matter of mistaken identity. These things happen, you know."

"May we take off these silly masks?" the artist asked.

"By all means, sir. Only the younger reserves try to enforce that anymore."

Logan and the artistic man rode the station's ramplift down together, precisely twenty-seven feet, four inches to street level. "Don't stray too far away," the man said. "Gorky Park is relatively safe, by Solerograd standards, but who can really say after Red Night?"

"What's your name?" Logan asked him.

"I'm Alexander Staley, but that will mean nothing to you."

"Maybe not, but the policeman fell all over himself when he found out."

Staley chuckled. "He did, rather, didn't he?"

"Who are you? I feel like I should be showering you with proper respect and obeisance." Logan grinned, and so did Staley.

"I'm an architect," the man said. "I designed much of the governmental district—sort of Solly's answer to Christopher Wren, if you'll excuse my name-dropping."

"You seem to be famous around here."

"THE ENTENTE have excellent public relations." The way he said it was self-deprecating and even cynical.

They continued their walk for several blocks, and Logan began to wonder whether this fellow traveler had the same destination as his own. "What brings you to Gorky Park, Citizen Staley?"

"To see my old college professor. Call it a class reunion."

"Erich Fishbourne?"

"None other."

"Are you a member of his church?"

"Not yet, Citizen Gramm, but soon to be."

Logan stopped in mid-step. "How do you know my name?"

"Tamara Hansen asked me to offer some assistance. I knew her late brother, the congressman."

"I owe you a big thanks," Logan said. "That officer would have arrested me for sure."

Staley nodded. "Actually, the hardest part was keeping that seat empty on the train. Two people almost socked me in the nose."

"Won't your colleagues wonder why you're traipsing through Gorky Park with a known subversive?"

"I'm here on business, to sample the traditional architecture of this district and perhaps attend a non-existent art conference or two. Once you reach a certain plateau within the bureaucracy, you are awarded a magnanimous *carte blanche*. It is virtually boundless."

A few minutes later, Logan was reunited with Tammi Hansen, and they both watched Staley and Fishbourne hit it off like old friends do, no matter the passage of years. The architect was quite open about his faith in Christ, so the professor wasted none of their time in attempting to proselytize the converted.

"We are more than a church," Fishbourne told him, "though that is our foundation and ultimate source of strength." He paused for a moment, contemplating the man who now stood before him. "We seek to reverse the direction of Solerograd's despotism. It may take many years or even decades to make inroads, but accepting the present state of fascistic rule is out of the question. Is this something you could support?"

"Count me in," Staley said. "I've had a unique view of the internal rot that atheism brings. This country's past was erased by revisionist historians, our values turned upside-down, and our unborn murdered. Our news media have proclaimed their lies twenty-four hours a day, and the educational system—including your venerated USol—is complicit in this whole mess, much more than people realize." Staley glanced sheepishly at the others. "Sorry, friends. I'll get off my soapbox now. Occasionally, I suffer from running-mouth disease, until someone shuts me up with a well-aimed kick in the—"

Fishbourne interrupted him. "Alex, my boy, I wish there were more like you. Too many folks, even the right-headed ones, are afraid to speak out against tyranny."

"I'm as guilty of that as anyone," Staley said, "and even now I'm unwilling to leave my job and its lucrative paychecks. Don't think too badly of me, but I'm going to try riding two horses for as long as I can. What is that called, a mole or a double agent?"

The professor patted him on the shoulder. "Whichever it is, we can always use someone on the inside," he told him. "Welcome aboard."

♦ ♦ ♦

Back when David Crownover and Logan Gramm parted company, not far from Logan's apartment, Crownover was carrying the PG-13 but had no idea how he could smuggle the device all the way to Gorky Park and still satisfy its departure spec of 14:41:07.

The first thing he did was take a mental picture of the countless public transportation routes that crisscrossed the city of Solerograd. Crownover felt certain that at some point, sooner or later, he would need to avail himself of them for the sake of the clock. He also took the precaution of recording his wristpad's entry coding for multiple admissions to the Viper trains. With his proficiency in the languages of programming, he would have no trouble revising the encryption many times over for indefinite reuse.

Crownover had lived vicariously in many of the nation's largest cities, but that was quite different from experiencing them with his physical presence. For instance, he knew nothing about construction sites and why heavy equipment should be avoided. A bright-yellow excavator's digging bucket struck him to the ground and drew the ire—and a string of profanities—from its operator. Every virtual city that he had visited was complete and in no need of expansion or renovation.

A massive homeless protest blocked any hope of passage beyond the intersection at N131-W21. These paid demonstrators, perhaps three hundred in number, appeared to be well equipped and organized by some wealthy financier. All of them wore identical hammer-and-sickle face coverings and carried professionally produced signage that demanded full benefits and amnesty for foreign nationals, from whatever country on earth. Their improvised bombs destroyed three police vehicles whose uniformed patrolmen had the audacity to enter radical territory. Six of "Solly's Finest" were burned beyond recognition in the stand-off.

Such mob rule was baffling to Crownover, who wondered why authorities were so afraid of ordering a military unit to quell the disturbance. Although he had long been aware of political posturing, propaganda, and news-media agendas, witnessing their destructive effects with his own synthetic eyes was a revelation. Heretofore, life among humans had seemed quite simple to him, a clear matter of black and white with no grays, and of good and bad with no moral relativism. As he roamed over the treacherous streets of Solerograd, it became more and more apparent that he still had a lot to learn.

Given the deadline that loomed only forty minutes ahead, detouring four blocks off the direct route, through a seedy section of town, was the last thing the automaton wanted to do. But electing to proceed through the chaos would delay him even further and jeopardize the balance of Logan Gramm's existence by confining him to an alien place and time. Under the presumption that a moving target was difficult to hit, Crownover resolved to avoid detection by catching a northwest-bound Viper at the N151-W19 Station and then transferring somewhere along the line to a train headed due west to compensate for this digression. He had the temp-ID to manage it, thanks to the ingenuity of a rogue programmer named I. V. Kegler.

The automaton was unaware that three muggers stood in his path, lurking in the shadows of a doorway that led to an abandoned nightclub and pool hall. These teenaged culprits, two males and a female, were heavily tattooed, weighted down with body piercings, and nearly out of their minds on drugs.

They were jackboots from Solerograd's "Stalking Dead," a nihilistic horde of high school dropouts who plundered unwary pedestrians for sustenance. Their code of ethics was roughly equal to bloodsucking parasites like leeches, lice, and ticks, only they were protected from extermination by the global statutes of human rights.

As Crownover speed-walked toward the Viper station, a four-foot-long metal pipe crashed against his head, sprawling him onto the sidewalk. The muggers surrounded their prey and were astonished to see that he was still breathing. Indeed, he had struggled to his feet, somewhat wobbly but intact. Noting the victim's unearthly resilience, one of the men dashed away and did not look back. The other two hoodlums, however, became entrapped in the vice-like grip of their intended quarry. With robotic strength at his disposal, Crownover could quickly eradicate them like the vermin they were, thus ridding mankind of refuse that would never contribute anything beyond misery and anguish to others. And yet, he chose instead what he regarded as the humane approach.

Crownover constricted their necks until airflow was seriously diminished. "I require your personal disks," he said. They refused, so the automaton further tightened his mechanized hands. "The next step," he added, "is to snap your necks in two." It was not an empty threat, so they promptly complied. "Now, on your faces," the robot said. While pinning them to the concrete with his knees, Crownover reached over the curb and rolled both of their personal disks into the bowels of the municipal storm drain. "Left wrists, please." He used his own disk to download an incompatible language, scrambling their barcodes beyond any hope of reclamation. These teenagers' days of moving freely through Solerograd were at an end. "Have a nice day," Crownover told them. Frantically, they fled for their lives.

It was twenty-six blocks to the ancillary N151-W19 Station and twelve additional blocks to the Viper depot in Gorky Park. Assuming a transfer delay of two minutes and an average cruising speed of ninety-three miles per hour, Crownover calculated that he could deliver the PG-13 to Logan in eleven and a quarter minutes. What he failed to account for was the simultaneous arrival of a TraumaTram that tied up air traffic until all loading platforms were clear of passengers.

All went well from that point on, and it appeared that Crownover was home free—until the stationmaster stopped him at the final exit gate. "Wait here for a moment, citizen," she said.

"What have I done?"

"Are you a synthetic?" she asked.

"I am."

"You are hereby being detained, pursuant to an outstanding warrant from SPD."

"In connection to what?"

She was not inclined to answer. "Let me see your personal disk, please."

He gave it to her, and she scanned for details. "You are the synthetic named ... Crownover, David?"

"I am."

She handed the disk back to him. "And were you formerly a resident of the Quigley Tower, here in the city?"

"Yes, citizen, until it was destroyed," he said.

"Empty your pockets, please."

"What if I refuse?"

She glared at him. "I push this button."

"Which does what, exactly?"

"Make it easy on yourself, Synthetic Crownover. If there is nothing to hide, you will be released forthwith. Solerograd is quite tolerant of non-humans."

"Thank you very much, I'm sure."

"Your attitude will be counted against you. Empty your pockets, please."

With a sigh of exasperation, Crownover reached into the left pocket of his jumpsuit bottoms, turning it inside-out. "Satisfied?" he asked.

"And the other one?"

"It's empty, too."

"The other one, please." He did not respond.

She was about to press the button when Crownover, quick as a cat, grasped her left elbow with such a numbing force that she lost consciousness and began to slump forward. In breaking the stationmaster's fall, he sat her down, propped against a gatebox, and leaped over the turnstile. An alarm sounded, of course, but only for a split second—until Crownover disengaged the red and yellow splitter to silence it. A few Viper employees casually glanced up from their depot work, but they saw nothing out of the ordinary.

On his way to the church compound, a six-wheeled police GroundHugger sped by, heat sensors deployed laterally, and Crownover thought it unusual for law enforcement to be spotted so far north. Maybe THE ENTENTE had chosen this opportunity to launch a concerted push against suspected dissidents. Or perhaps the stationmaster had regained consciousness and lodged an APB with authorities, flagging "Synthetic Crownover, David" as a fugitive offender at large. In that case, Gorky Park was now the scene of a Solice dragnet, something the unsanctioned Christian enclave could ill afford.

Upon arrival, Crownover went directly to the main office, where Solerograd architect Alexander Staley was still renewing acquaintances with Dr. Fishbourne. In his haste, the automaton dispensed with the formality of knocking, a discourtesy that signaled trouble.

Logan stood up and rushed over to bump fists. "You made it, Dave," he said, "and with six and a half minutes to spare!"

Crownover's greeting was muted by bad news. "I'm afraid they're on my tail—the Solice—but there was no other way to get here with your contraband." He handed Logan the PG-13.

"Why are they after you?" Fishbourne asked.

"I had to get a little rough with a Viper official," Crownover said, "and they probably don't take too kindly to that."

Staley was quick to confirm. "They certainly do not. A municipal statute shields everyone in the bureaucracy from harm or abuse—even when it is richly merited."

The professor nodded. "Do they know who you are?"

"Yes," Crownover told him. "She scanned my disk."

"Oh, dear. Do they have any reason to suspect that this is where you were headed?"

"Probably not," he said, "but I noticed a Solice vehicle just two blocks away. Fortunately, the heat sensors only detect warm-blooded subjects, which leaves me out."

Fishbourne forced a smile. "Well, that's something in our favor, at least."

The PG-13's countdown showed 00:04:55 remaining when Logan bid a final farewell to Fishbourne and Staley. "God bless you, my son," the professor said. "Perhaps we shall see each other again in this life," he added. "If not, then surely in the next."

Tammi was waiting for Logan and Crownover in her new quarters, which were more austere than she would like but still quite acceptable. Having left the door wide open, she jumped to her feet when Logan reached inside to knock. "Did you bring the PG-13?" she asked.

"Thanks to Dave here. He bootlegged it all the way across north Solerograd."

Crownover's grin was a modest one, taking less credit than he really deserved. "But I also might have brought the authorities, I'm sorry to say. Solice are in the area, and this compound needs to be on the alert."

"Let them come," she said. "We're doing nothing wrong, as they can see for themselves."

Logan frowned. "You have more respect for them than I do. They could burn this place down like they did the Quig."

Tammi noticed that Logan was holding the PG-13 at his side. "When is your departure?" she asked.

"A little over three minutes."

"Do you want to be alone with your thoughts?"

"No need. I've gone through the transition enough times to know what to expect."

Tammi stretched out her hand. "Now, please give me your personal disk for safekeeping," she told him. "It surely won't be of any use to you in twenty-first-century New York."

Logan gave a boyish grin. "I was sort of hoping to keep it as a souvenir."

"Sorry, but that will not be possible. It must not accompany you into the past."

Just then, there was some commotion outside, and Crownover walked toward the window to investigate. Four police GroundHuggers were parked along N179, and it was very likely that additional vehicles had cordoned off the perimeter of Fishbourne's property.

Crownover turned to the others. "I think we're surrounded." His synthesized voice sounded grave, inducing Tammi and Logan to have a look for themselves. It was a chilling sight.

"I should stay with you and take the consequences," Logan said. "I can't leave you like this."

"No. Your time in Solerograd is over," Tammi told him. "The PG-13 can't be halted at this point, and Kegler isn't here to work his magic."

Logan knew she was right, so he accepted the inescapable. The countdown showed 00:01:42.

"Besides, if I know Dr. Fishbourne," she said, "he'll present a convincing case of innocence. We'll be fine."

"Your key is getting Alexander Staley to put in a good word," Logan told her. "He's talking to Fishbourne right now. Don't forget about him. Staley can pull strings with THE ENTENTE."

Never before had David Crownover seen a human disappear from the present, but he was watching in fascination as Logan nodded goodbye, gazed through the window for one final peek at Solerograd, and then turned back with affection in his eyes.

A few more seconds ticked away, and he was gone.

◆　　◆　　◆

Logan Gramm had seven return trips to his credit, but he still found it difficult to deal with the disorienting sensation of

Reappearance, Post-Absence. This transitional phase, RPA for short, played havoc with body and mind, especially when the disparity of intervals was so pronounced. While he spent well over a month in Solerograd, his period away from Hoboken amounted to a scant four minutes of real time, departing at 8:47 on Tuesday morning and returning at 8:51.

His roommate, budding actress Erin Duffy, was in the apartment during that short span, so Logan was compelled to fabricate an excuse for being away from her long enough to pass into the future. "I need to go scope out the laundry room," he had told her, "to see if I can wash this morning. Back in a few minutes." And Erin thought nothing of it.

Now he came back up the stairs, consciously attempting to mitigate the effects of RPA by subjugating in his memory everything that happened to him in the past five weeks. This was not easy to do, especially with the breathtaking advances and declines of the future world. Logan wanted to tell Erin all about the iniquitous city of Solerograd, with its coded disks, political turmoil, robotic beat cops, and airborne subways, but what came out of his mouth instead was the status of top-loaded machines at a public laundromat.

"Two of the washers are available," he said, "so I guess that's what I'll be doing today." And perhaps that was the best approach because Erin would not have believed him anyway. Either he had to keep his freakish tale to himself or risk being ostracized as a borderline lunatic. Distilled to its unvarnished essence, RPA was nothing to be trifled with, even in the best of cases. Its distant cousin, jet lag, was a hollow joke that paled in comparison.

About a half-hour after his return to the present, Logan was tossing dirty clothes into the laundry basket. Erin, meanwhile, stood before a mirror in the bathroom, applying her makeup. "What time do you work at Scotty's today?" she shouted.

"Two to eleven," he told her.

"Well, if Tanner happens to call here before noon, please text me, okay? He might have another photo shoot lined up, and I can't afford to miss it."

"I thought that's where you were going now."

She came out of the bathroom, looking more gorgeous than he had ever seen her before. "It is, but this would be another one."

"You're getting to be in high demand."

"That's the idea." She picked up her purse and searched for something inside it.

"What about *Murder at Wit's End?* Is that on a back burner?" he asked.

"Not at all. But there's no rehearsal today. Just tonight's performance."

"And how's it going?"

"The play? Great, so far—knock on wood," she told him. "Full houses are the norm, or at least mostly full. Mr. Finney could not be happier."

"Who's he?"

"C. Archibald Finney, our producer. Some of the cast call him 'Daddy Warbucks,' but not to his face." She started to walk out the door, but Logan's words stopped her.

"By the way, you look super," he said. "What's the product?"

"Some sort of very expensive handbags, I think. It's mostly long shots, though, so my makeup doesn't have to be note perfect. Wish me luck."

He grinned. "For the modeling or the play?"

"Both, naturally. Is that too much to ask?"

"Yep, just one or the other."

"The play, then," she said. "I can always re-do the stills, but that's not a luxury I have on stage. 'Bye!"

Logan watched her leave the room, and he felt heartsick. Here was beautiful Erin Duffy, living right under his own roof, and he treated her like some sidekick in a "B" western. Theirs was purely a relationship of convenience. As for romantic interests, Erin had plenty of those, with never fewer than two or three boyfriends waiting in line. Logan had no desire to join their queue. He was too serious for that, some ingrained corollary of his personal nature. Even while a freshman in college, he was much more apt to be studying history than reveling at some inconsequential party.

Just as he anticipated from previous struggles with RPA, the return to his regular pattern of existence was a shock to Logan's system. By contrast, the daily grind of waiting tables—subsistence tips or not—could only be seen as an anticlimax. It was similar to the plight of a twenty-something astronaut or athlete, a youthful overachiever who scaled the heights early in life and then was faced with a disappointing downhill trajectory from that point forward. Any client for PROGRADE KRONOTECHNIX ran the risk of not fitting back into the "real world."

Scotty's Steakhouse had been the scene of his first encounter with PGK recruiter Tammi Hansen, the place where she lured him across the street for an impromptu demonstration of the wondrous PG-13 transporter. That remembrance hit Logan like a half-forgotten dream, leaving him empty and out of breath. It also caused his mind to ramble far afield. Where was Tammi at this very moment? She was yet to be born and would not be alive on earth for hundreds of years. Such brooding served no purpose, but something grotesque in time-travel theory kept running it through his mind.

Even when visions of the recruiting agent diminished in strength, the pangs of RPA did not loosen their grip. That was because Scotty's Steakhouse was also the site of Logan's first meeting with Erin Duffy, followed by their burgeoning friendship as co-workers. On this Tuesday afternoon, while performing "nappie-wrappie" duty—rolling silverware inside cloth napkins—his daydreaming wandered into dangerous territory. Every movement he made, every utensil he touched, every sound he heard reminded him of his perky roommate. Reappearance, Post-Absence was a very real psychological condition, though one that would never be found in a medical textbook.

If there was one thing that changed in his workaday routine, it was Logan's perspective of American culture. On his first day back, he began viewing the customers through increasingly partisan eyes. Being in the northeast, most people were ideological liberals, he presumed—and no doubt many of those leaned to the extreme left, bordering on socialist, fascist, or even communist sympathies. Fortunately, the divisive topic of politics seldom arose over a nice meal, and if it did, he was always judicious enough to recuse himself from offering an opinion.

As his eight-hour shift crawled to the finish line, Logan felt mentally and physically exhausted. Hard to believe, but it was earlier on this very same day that he was evading a police dragnet on the seamy streets of Solerograd. And now he was attempting to climb aboard the familiar treadmill of twenty-first-century rituals and habits. Logan realized that his biological clock could not accommodate such an abrupt transition. Battered by flashes of a nightmarish future, he conceded defeat even before extinguishing his bedroom light. It was a forgone conclusion that sleep would be elusive if not downright unattainable.

True to form, he lay awake in the darkness, reliving the implausible phenomena that plagued his memory. When Erin came home from that night's performance at the Hersey-Vann Theatre, he wanted to join her in the living room but knew that would be unfair to someone who probably needed rest more than he did. His bedroom door was closed, so Logan switched on the light and began reading the most soporific book that he could find on the shelf—a history of U.S. governmental affairs in the 1880s. Still, insomnia stubbornly prevailed, save for about ninety minutes of feverish slumber.

An unseasonal flurry of snow had begun falling, and it continued throughout the morning and into the early afternoon. Although amounting to no more than a quarter-inch dusting, the conditions were just slick enough to cause pedestrians to slip, so he plodded zombie-like from his subway station to the restaurant. This was doing nothing to brighten his mild depression. Then, on top of everything else, the omnipresent sirens brought back thoughts of gang violence, looting, snarling dogs, and those Solice robots with their cold, vacant eyes. He should have felt safer on the streets of Manhattan, but that was not the case. He could see a lot of Solerograd in present-day New York City.

The doldrums were inside Scotty's Steakhouse as well, and Wednesday was shaping up to be an irredeemable ordeal—until it was redeemed. A little after four, as Logan was finishing his first fifteen-minute break, an iPhone message from Erin Duffy caught his attention. <Want to be my guest for a TERRIFIC play on your day off? I can get you a comp ticket if you let me know in the next hour.> She had sent the text at 2:45, so he replied immediately. <Does your offer still hold? If so, then yes!> But she did not respond. He called her but got no further than her voicemail greeting.

The maddening day dragged on to its logical conclusion, and Logan sensed that his persistent wakefulness was finally beginning to catch up with him. On the subway ride home, he could hardly keep his eyes open—so much so that he was in danger of missing his stop. Aided by a stick of chewing gum, he managed to detrain at the proper station, but his mind bore the foggy earmarks of sleep deprivation. This was almost as troublesome as the opposite problem, for he did not want to snooze through Erin's arrival in the wee hours after midnight. Attending *Murder at Wit's End* again was an attractive proposition, even beyond what it had been before.

He decided to sit on the sofa, propped against his combo Mets-Jets-Nets throw pillow. (Logan was a sports iconoclast, rooting for whichever teams happened to be playing the "Cadillac" franchises—Yankees, Giants, and Knicks.) Sure enough, he dozed off long before Erin unlocked the door and tiptoed inside. Logan's chin was resting on his chest when she passed by him, and she did not have the heart to shake him awake. Instead, she headed for the bathroom to remove her makeup and ready herself for bed. It was a stroke of good fortune that she dropped her hairbrush onto the counter with a sufficient *plop* to rouse her roommate to consciousness.

"Did you get my text?" he shouted to her.

"What text?"

"Replying to your question."

"What question?"

Logan gave a loud sigh. "Do you have a ticket for me?" he asked.

"What ticket?" She came into the living room with a glum face. "I had to submit my request within the hour. I thought I told you that."

"You did, and I tried to reach you."

"Sorry. The seats are all gone."

Logan hid his disappointment well, but Erin was too perceptive for him. She reached into the rear pocket of her jeans and produced a small envelope, which she then tossed onto his lap.

"Except for this one," she said. "Eighth row, center. A two-hundred-dollar location that the playwright's fourth wife was unable to use for our Thursday show."

Logan opened the envelope and admired the pricey ticket. "How did you know that tomorrow ... " He glanced at the wall clock. " ... *today* was my day off?"

"I called the landline at Scotty's. They still have one of those, you know. Derek Bowles told me that you wouldn't be working on Thursday."

The name brought a grin from Logan. "You talked to Derek?"

"Yes. What about him?"

"It's just that he had a massive crush on you, for as long as I can remember."

"That's news to me," Erin said.

"Couldn't you see that he broke into a cold sweat whenever he was near you?"

"I thought he was just working hard."

"Oh, he was—on you!"

"Well, that's *his* problem. I certainly never led him on. I had enough irons in the fire without entangling alliances at Scotty's." Too late, she realized how that sounded. "Present company excepted."

Logan nodded at her with a smirk. "Well played, Miss Duffy."

◆　　◆　　◆

The Hersey-Vann Theatre's front ten rows were a misnomer. Although curving very gently to hug the proscenium, they had been christened "The Golden Circle." No doubt that presumptuous name was simply a sales ploy to interest prospective subscribers, for the coveted seats came at a hefty price—investing in the most elite of the HV's season ticket packages. This exclusive section even had a snob-appeal back side to it, a lateral aisle that kept the great unwashed from mixing too freely with those aristocrats whose patronage truly kept the operation afloat.

In terms of blueblood nobility, Logan Gramm—a lowly table attendant who worked for tips—had no business sitting so far forward, but that did not deter him from being the first person to arrive there for the Thursday evening presentation of *Murder at Wit's End*. He had a built-in head start because the others around him probably had no desire to show up so unfashionably early. It was considered a sign of good breeding to stroll indifferently to one's seat, just as the musicians were tuning (for a musical) or the houselights were dimming (for a drama or comedy).

Nary a word was uttered to him by his exalted neighbors, all of whom seemed to address the others by their given names or even the informal diminutives thereof. Clearly, this was a private club, to which his credentials did not qualify him to belong. But in the end, his wounded pride was not fatally shaken. Logan had a close pal who would be performing on stage, and how many of them could honestly say the same? Besides, the first time he had seen this play, he was almost thirty rows back at a Sunday matinée. Now he was practically in the orchestra pit for a posh performance at night, and that counted as real progress in his book.

Ten and a quarter minutes into the second act, feisty "Rosie Novello" (as Erin called her character) rode into the stark

Manhattan scene in a shiny, pitch-black limousine. She was a strikingly beautiful brunette who flung her cloche hat high into the air. "Eat your heart out, Bobby Creel!" she shouted. "There ain't a soul in this town who's gonna keep me from clawin' to the top—not Bobby or no one!" A smart-aleck amongst the streetwise urbanites demanded to know what made her so special, and she stared him down. "Because I'm Tony Martini's best gal, that's what. Look at how his kisses smeared my lipstick!"

Rosie's lines of Vernon Arthur dialogue, though not indispensable to the dramatic narrative, did cause some titters to ripple through the auditorium, and they fell just short of eliciting a round of applause. Logan himself was eager to clap but naturally did not intend to be alone in that approbation. After all, those in The Golden Circle already saw him as an interloper, and he did not wish to confirm their suspicions with a deficiency of theatrical etiquette.

Security at the Hersey-Vann Theatre was very tight after the final curtain, but Logan was permitted to stand outside the stage entrance, alongside other friends and relatives of the cast. A woman asked him who it was that he was waiting to see, and he felt pleasantly smug to proclaim Erin Duffy's name. Then he felt deflated when the woman obviously had no idea who that actress might be. "Rosie Novello," he told her. The blank look remained, but to her credit, she was polite enough to nod her head.

When Erin finally walked out the stage door, Logan met her with a broad smile. "As expected, Miss Rosie stole the show," he said. "And that 'Noo Yawk' accent sounded authentically Bronxish to me."

Erin blushed. "Well, maybe if she was just off the boat from Dublin."

Logan took her by the arm, surprising even himself. "Come on. Let's get a late-night snack."

"Late? Not for us on Broadway. It's still the shank of the evening."

They began walking toward the Great White Way, heart and soul of the theater district.

"Let's try Antoine Légroux's," Erin told him. "Great food, and they're open until two."

"Sounds expensive."

"Just because it has a French name?"

He shrugged. "Okay. I guess someone who sits in the eighth row of the Hersey-Vann can afford it."

"I'll even pay," she said. "It was my idea for you to come tonight, and this is kind of a celebration."

That confused Logan. "Another celebration? What now?"

"My new role."

"In *Murder at Wit's End?*"

"Nope. I auditioned for one of the leads in a Berkeley Squires play, and I landed it."

Logan squeezed her hand. "Congratulations! You'll be terrific in it."

"You don't even know what it is." She giggled. "It could be about golfing on the moon."

"Whatever it is, you'll be terrific in it. When do you start?"

"A week from Monday."

He stopped to think. "You won't be moving, will you?"

"No, the money's not good enough for that. Why do you ask?"

"Just wondering." Logan grinned. "I still need for you to pay half the rent."

"Are you sure that's all?"

"Relax. I'm sure."

Antoine Légroux's was well above the reach of Logan's pay grade, but that was fine because Erin insisted on picking up the check. She was in a festive mood.

"What is 'Barkley Squires'?" Logan asked her.

"He's a contemporary British playwright—very experimental, maybe even *avant-garde*," Erin said. "His first name is pronounced 'Barkley,' but it's spelled like the city of Berkeley, near San Francisco."

"Is he still living?"

"Oh, yes. In fact, he'll be in New York for opening night and the week after."

"Have you ever met him?"

"No, of course not," she said. "He hasn't been to the States in almost thirty years."

"What's the name of his new play?"

"It's not new. This is a revival of his 1973 duo-drama called *Bipedosaurus*. It caused quite a stir back then—London, Bournemouth, Manchester. The American premiere fell through because one of the financial backers passed away."

As Logan was listening to her exciting news, someone on the far side of the room attracted his vision. The man's face was oddly familiar, fleshy and bearded, and Logan pictured him with a cigar in his mouth. Funny how the eyes can play tricks on you.

"It's a two-person play," Erin added, "so that means an awful lot of dialogue to learn."

"A woman and a man?"

"Yes, husband and wife ... soon to be exes."

Again Logan glanced at the rotund diner, who had just given his order to a waitress. From such a distance, he resembled a middle-aged Orson Welles—a bawdy raconteur with a gourmand's appetite for self-indulgence. An instant later, the man gazed straight at him with a grin. Then he stood on his stocky legs and began walking toward their table.

"Uh-oh, someone's headed this way," Logan whispered.

Erin turned toward the approaching stranger. "Do you know him?"

"I think maybe I do, now that I get a better look."

The man was still twenty feet away when he shouted Logan's name. "Don't you remember me? Mariusz Wojewódzki."

"I'm not sure. Maybe ... " Logan rose to his feet, and they shook hands.

"The gazebo at Hoboken's Church Square Park," the man added. "Some lady objected to the fragrance of my fine Cuban Montecristo."

"Yes, I've got it now. Sorry for my patchy memory." Logan started to introduce him to Erin but faltered on the Polish name.

"Just call me 'Voya'," the gentleman told her. Then, without any invitation, he helped himself to an available chair.

Logan sat down too, wondering what this was all about. "Voya, I'd like for you to meet Erin Duffy. She's a good friend of mine who acts on Broadway."

"*Enchantée, mademoiselle,*" the bearded man said. He stopped short of kissing her hand, but Erin could tell that his personality was on the unctuous side, and she disliked him at once. Worse yet, he continued to stare at her, and it was making her very uncomfortable. "So, you're an actress. What are you in?"

"An off-Broadway production. You've probably never heard of it."

Wojewódzki leaned toward her. "Try me."

Logan rescued Erin by edging the topic toward their uninvited guest. "So, what brings you to New York again, Voya?" he asked. "Your last visit was to apply for a history teaching position—at NYU, wasn't it?"

Wojewódzki played along, for he could hardly discuss his instructional mandate from PROGRADE KRONOTECHNIX. "That's right, but it went nowhere. I'm still submitting my CV several places because—as you well know—throwing in the towel is not an option."

"Good for you, Voya. Hey, we should get together while you're in town," Logan told him. "How about tomorrow morning? I don't have to be at work until two."

"Fine," Wojewódzki said. After nodding goodbye to the beautiful actress, he stood up to leave. "Logan, my friend, I'll see you around noon."

"Is that what you call morning?"

"Whenever I'm awake all hours of the night, as I plan to be on this occasion." Wojewódzki helped himself to a dinner roll. "Meet me at a little place called Java Bay. It's right across the street from your steakhouse."

Logan nearly choked on his next breath. "How do you know about Java Bay?"

"A mutual friend told me about it."

"Tomorrow at noon, then," Logan said. They shook hands, and the portly emissary returned to his own table for a more-than-ample midnight snack. Evidently, PGK still offered its agents a generous *per diem*.

◆　◆　◆

At noon sharp, Mariusz Wojewódzki was hunched over a double cheeseburger and onion rings when Logan joined him in the coffee shop. "Pardon me for beginning without you," the PGK agent said. "I always gorge like a pig when I'm on assignment. It's the pitfall of an expense account, you know." He slurped a mouthful of his chocolate milkshake.

"I don't blame you," Logan said. "You've got nothing but health foods in Solly, right?"

"Except under the counter. There's a thriving business in the black market." Wojewódzki reached for a menu and handed it to Logan. "I asked the waitress to leave this for you to see."

"No, thanks, Voya. I had lunch in my apartment."

"Oh? Do you cook?"

Logan chuckled. "Actually, I had what we call a 'TV dinner.' They're lifesavers for bachelors like me."

"Any good?"

"Not too bad. I keep my favorites in the freezer and rotate them during the week. I guess you could say I'm a creature of habit." He thought for a moment. "This is Friday, so I had chicken fried steak, mixed vegetables, and tater tots, with a brownie square for dessert."

"Care for an onion ring?" Wojewódzki said. He extended one to him, dangling from his knife.

"No, thanks—really."

The waitress came by to see whether Logan wanted to order anything. When he told her no, she retrieved the menu and started to walk away. "What kinds of pie do you have?"

Wojewódzki asked her. She recited the various fruit fillings, and he selected hot apple pie à la mode.

A part of Logan sympathized with this ravenous agent, who in Solerograd was forced to toe the line with unpalatable choices from the basic food groups. Still, that in no way excused the man's deplorable table manners, such as hoisting the pie plate and licking it clean. Oblivious to any impropriety, Wojewódzki patted his corpulent belly and muffled a burp as best he could.

Preliminaries complete, he announced that it was time to get down to brass tacks. "You were awfully surprised to see me last night, huh? Well, nothing about it was accidental."

"So I figured," Logan said. "What are you doing here—searching for some rookie clients?"

"Would that it were that simple, my friend. No, I'm afraid there's bad news to report."

"About that mutual friend you mentioned?"

Wojewódzki nodded his head. "Oddly enough, you knew Tammi Hansen before I did. Ira Kegler introduced me to her a month ago—my time—back when she was still working for PROGRADE KRONOTECHNIX. Sweet kid."

"How is Tammi doing? I've been worried about her ... until I realized she won't even be born for hundreds of years."

"No, no, no! Don't ever look at it that way," Wojewódzki said. He had a pained expression on his face. "Folks like you, who have bridged the shores of time, need to treat both of your points of reference with equal respect. Tammi is in serious trouble, and you can't dismiss her by claiming that she is the product of another century. Like it or not, she is a part of your life now, and that fact will never change."

Logan rubbed his chin. "What sort of trouble? Is there anything I can do to help?"

"She's in prison, and an elderly man named Erich Fishbourne was also apprehended—the ringleader of some religious cult. They're both accused of conspiracy, and you'll never guess who led the Solice right to their doorstep."

"Alexander Staley."

Logan's quick answer took the wind out of Wojewódzki's sails. "How'd you know?"

"Just a hunch."

Wojewódzki raised his hands to the heavens. "Alexander Staley is like a god to THE ENTENTE," he said. "Every day, his majestic buildings bring pride to Sollians, reminding them that government can be a force for good in the world."

Logan was tempted to make a derisive comment, but he held his tongue. "Have you heard from Tammi since her arrest?" he asked.

"No one at PGK can reach her, so I presume she's in solitary confinement. Same thing for Fishbourne, no doubt."

"Where do you think they're being held?"

"All suspected felons, while awaiting their trials, are incarcerated within the SolGate Rehabilitation Colony. I hear that violent criminals are treated reasonably well in Camp A, but political prisoners receive brutal treatment in Camp B. The food is atrocious, and its cells are not much better than medieval dungeons."

"Is that where Tammi would be held?" Logan asked. He dreaded the answer but knew it was coming.

"Camp B, for sure," Wojewódzki told him.

Logan nodded his head. "What about the professor?"

"Who?"

"Dr. Fishbourne. He's a retired Professor of Classics at USol."

"They found treasonous plans—in Fishbourne's possession and handwriting—for the forceful overthrow of a duly elected administration. I have no doubt that he'll be executed soon, if he hasn't been already."

Logan could not believe his ears. "For teaching a Bible study class?"

"No. This ringleader stands charged with federal conspiracy."

"And Tammi is accused of conspiring with him?"

"That's an oversimplification. Members of any organized church—more than four Christians worshiping together—are implicated by association."

"But that's a lesser charge?"

"Yes, but still political. As I understand it, Tammi's life is not in the balance."

"When will her trial be?"

"Typically, within four weeks," Wojewódzki said, "but that can vary quite a lot, depending upon the severity of the indictment. With Alexander Staley weighing in for the prosecution, my guess is that the legal wheels will turn as quickly as possible. His reputation is at stake and cannot be tainted."

Logan's favorite waitress at Java Bay, Tricia Templeton, had just reported for work, and she spotted him at once. Seeing nothing edible in front of him, she brought over a complimentary cup of coffee. "Hiya, Logan!" she said. "Are you freeloading today?"

"Nope. I already ate," he told her. Then he lowered his voice for the punch line. "And that TV dinner was a lot better than anything you serve in this dump."

"Nobody's forcing you to patronize us. It's not like we'd go into the red without you." Tricia giggled at her own joke but then became more serious. "Hey, whatever happened to that cute girl you used to bring in here every so often?"

"Erin Duffy?"

"Maybe so ... the one with an Irish accent."

"She's a big star on Broadway now."

Tricia's eyes lit up. "Really?"

"Well, that's a slight exaggeration, but she *is* in the regular cast of an off-Broadway play."

"Which one?"

"*Murder at Wit's End*, over at the Hersey-Vann Theatre."

She shrugged. "I never go to shows."

"Erin thinks she might have the lead in a revival that's opening pretty soon."

Wojewódzki's waitress came around, so Tricia bowed out with a wave.

Logan took a sip of his coffee, which was just the right temperature. "Listen, Voya. One thing bothers me about your sudden appearance here last night. How did you manage to show up just a few days after I left Solerograd?"

"That's by the book—strictly procedural—to reduce a client's disorientation. I asked Kegler what your arrival time had been, and he checked his disk for the PG-13 coordinates. Then I added sixty-four hours to make it seem like a chance meeting."

"How did you know Erin and I would be going to Antoine Légroux's for a late snack?" Logan asked.

Wojewódzki's grin was bursting with pride. "That was pure, unadulterated gumshoe, if I do say so myself. I shadowed you from the theater and then bribed the *maître d'* for a table that gave me a good view of you and Ms. Duffy. Pretty slick move, wouldn't you agree?"

Logan started to reply with something sarcastic, but Wojewódzki did not give him an opportunity. "I'm here to relay a message," the agent said, "and to enlist your services for one final operation. Absolutely voluntary, of course."

"Does it have something to do with saving Tammi Hansen?"

"It does, indeed—and, if it's not already too late, Erich Fishbourne."

"That would be two separate operations."

"If that's how you want to look at it."

"That's how I *have* to look at it because there's no safety net, I presume." He took another sip.

"I'm afraid not," Wojewódzki told him. "ProGrade Kronotechnix is not involved, so no excessive repercussion can be registered."

"In other words, you're acting outside the jurisdiction of PGK, just like Kegler has done."

"I'm just the messenger, Logan, so I can—and will—deny everything. Citizen Kegler is a senior programmer for DOI. So, you see, there's really no comparison between us two. I'm certainly no hero. In fact, I'm getting highly paid for my efforts, or you would not be talking to me right now."

"Who assigned you to enlist my services?" Logan asked.

"That I cannot reveal. Sorry."

"Who programmed the PG-13 for this 'recreational excursion' of yours? He or she will be held accountable."

"That, too, I cannot reveal, but it wasn't Kegler."

Logan began thinking aloud. "It has to be one of your colleagues, for the technological expertise that's required ... " Wojewódzki maintained his poker face. " ... but who among them would be willing to place his or her head on the chopping block to save a disgraced former employee?" Again, Wojewódzki's expression betrayed no secrets, so Logan pondered more deeply. "Unless, of course, Tammi Hansen had another admirer on the staff."

That caused the agent's eyes to widen. "*Another* admirer?"

"Besides Kegler, I mean," Logan said. "I see no danger in telling you that now."

"No. They'll be paddling their separate ways now because he sure won't be following her up the creek." The agent smiled at his own witticism, something he did with some regularity.

Logan swallowed his last mouthful of complimentary coffee. "When do you need to know my answer?"

"Oh, no hurry," Wojewódzki said. He consulted his tasteful, antique wristwatch. "Just so it's before you leave here for Scotty's."

"What?!"

"Logan, my friend, I'm at the mercy of my PG-13 countdown." Grinning, Wojewódzki patted the breast pocket of his sport coat.

Needless to say, Logan had no honorable choice but to accept the assignment, and he would have it no other way. How could he decline this one and only chance to save Tammi Hansen from her gruesome fate? Even now, his memory was paraphrasing what she told him on the day he left Solerograd for keeps: "Failure to uphold THE ENTENTE is an unforgivable offense. Found guilty, I would be brainwashed by mental reconstruction. Anyone who comes out alive is not the same person."

According to his PG-13, Logan would be departing from Java Bay at 1:48 PM and returning there at 1:51. The latter coordinate would give him an ample cushion to walk over to Scotty's Steakhouse and punch in for his two-o'clock shift. But that innocuous three-minute absence from the present concealed within it one of the most challenging missions of Logan's secretive career as a time-travel operative. No matter how long he was away, the local clock would advance only 180 seconds until his reappearance.

PGK agent Mariusz Wojewódzki, unprincipled mercenary or not, had served his purpose well. He informed his client that the programmed device would deposit Logan on the abandoned property of Erich Fishbourne's comatose church. There, until its humble facilities could be razed to the ground by Greater Solerograd Demolition, Logan would make the necessary preparations for attempting a desperate rescue mission ... or two.

❖ ❖ ❖

Logan materialized in the courtyard adjacent to his old guest room. This was a relatively vacant area and, thus, one of the safest spotting points within the perimeter. A suitcase lay propped against the decorative water fountain that dominated the open space. When he took stock of what else was around him, Logan concluded that little, if anything, had changed since he spent two nights here during the height of civil disobedience. Apparently, the Solice had not been forced to storm the church in order to gain entry. No walls were damaged, no windows shattered, no doors splintered by a siege engine. From all indications, residents of the compound surrendered peacefully, conceding the inevitable.

Whoever packed Logan's suitcase had thought of everything. Folded within the obligatory gray jumpsuits were his personal disk—reunited with him again—some emergency rations that would last for more than a week, a portable OmniScreen, and a convincing assortment of facial disguises. Unless he called attention to himself by failing to blend in with the crowd of Sollians, Logan might travel freely through town for days on end.

The first thing he felt drawn to do was comb through the church complex, verifying that he was indeed alone on the premises. This he did, twice, to his own satisfaction. Then, before venturing into the community, he affixed a neatly trimmed goatee-beard combination and some rather long hair of a matching color. A glance in his guest-room mirror was reassuring. No one could possibly identify him when submerged among the gray wave of Solerograd citizens.

Logan had overestimated one aspect of his dilemma. SolGate's physical location turned out to be anything but a mystery, for an OmniScreen search quickly pinpointed its exact whereabouts. The prison was situated at N1-W3, right in the heart of the CBD, and images of its frontal sign—SOLGATE REHABILITATION COLONY—demonstrated that no attempt had been made to obscure the facility's true contents.

And yet, there was a negative side as well. Offering such readily available information to the public suggested that prison security was airtight, so impregnable that identifying the building for precisely what it was could be of no consequence. Descriptive paragraphs proudly informed readers that SolGate occupied more than half of a city block, standing six stories above ground (Camp A) and descending four stories below (Camp B), and that it possessed "the best trained and equipped guard staff in penal America."

His walk from the church to Gorky Park's N176-W12 Station was uneventful, though Logan did notice how much more crowded the streets grew as he neared the passenger zone itself. He purchased a DayPass ticket by swiping his integrated-circuit microchip across the ViperScan. Riding the airborne train reminded Logan of that trip he took when Alexander Staley shielded him from certain arrest by an onboard Soliceman. He wondered why this celebrated architect would perform such a magnanimous act—only to turn right around and guide stormtroopers to the ill-fated church complex.

The 00-00 Station, called "No-No" by locals, was positioned at the central-most intersection in all of Solerograd. On a graph, it would form the city's point of origin, right where the x axis crossed the y axis. More importantly, this Viper depot was located just four short blocks to the east-southeast of SolGate. Wearing what he hoped was surefire camouflage, he went forth to undertake some preliminary investigative work.

Hundreds of citizens were hurrying in every direction, so all Logan had to do was maintain his pace and avoid being trampled. He was sprightlier than most, so staying relatively vertical proved to be no problem. What troubled him was the flying hardware that showed up above. Soaring about thirty feet over the Sollians' heads, the gadget appeared to be a silent drone of some sort. This must have been a common sight in town, for no one but Logan gave it the slightest regard. He could not tell, with any certainty, whether it was tailing him or perhaps simply recording the density of pedestrian traffic for a news outlet.

At the first narrow gap in the humanity, Logan stepped sharply to his right and then backtracked along the sidewalk. The drone did likewise, always remaining directly overhead, no matter where he set his course. Next, Logan detoured through an alleyway that led to a much less traveled street, hoping that this tactic might impart the technological workings of the aerial sleuth. When he laid his personal disk behind a waste receptacle and walked another fifty feet further, he was still being closely followed. That told him something useful. Assuming that the flying device could not see through his facial disguise, it must be designed to track the code information that was embedded within his wrist. There was no other logical deduction.

After retrieving his personal disk, Logan proceeded three blocks to the west and one block to the north. And suddenly it was right in front of him: SolGate Rehabilitation Colony. The building was bleak and featureless on the outside, precisely how any respectable prison should look to the objective eye. For a moment, he could not help staring in awe. Somewhere within the stark walls, probably below ground level, was Tammi Hansen.

This former employee of PROGRADE KRONOTECHNIX had been indicted in conspiracy accusations against the city-state, and Solerograd—being an autocratic regime in all but its public posturing—always took political charges very seriously.

The drone-like device was still directly above Logan, and it was beginning to draw the attention of others, too, most notably a vigilant policeman in his SPD hovercraft. SolGate's periphery was, in essence, a heavily guarded strip of federal land, and anyone violating its sanctity was subject to interrogation on the spot. The very last thing Logan wanted was to scuttle his mission before giving it a fair chance, so he quickly moved along, merging with the undulating mass of Sollians. But the flying apparatus traced every step that he took, all the way to "No-No" Station, where it seemed to lose interest and totally disappeared from sight, just as abruptly as it had come.

A surprise was awaiting Logan when he arrived back at the church grounds. There to meet him in the otherwise deserted enclave was Alexander Staley, who stepped out from behind the office door and approached him with the palms of his hands raised in an apologetic gesture. "You need to trust me that I did it for your own good," he said.

Logan's first instinct was to deck the betrayer with a solid blow to the mouth, but he restrained himself long enough to hear an explanation. "Well?"

"Dr. Fishbourne and I knew each other thirty years ago, when he had just gained tenure at USol and I was a freshman undergrad."

"What of it?" Logan began removing his fake beard and hairpiece.

"Please hear me out," Staley said. "You owe me that much."

"Go on."

"The Classics Department and the Art Department were housed in the same building in those days, so our paths crossed quite often. He possessed a strong Christian faith even then, and he was not afraid to express it to anyone who would listen. I was one of them."

Logan pointed with his thumb. "Let's go into the pastor's study, where we can talk without having to stand." Clearly, his ire was softening.

"Is it safe to be here?" Staley asked.

"For now—until the bulldozers come."

The room was modest in size, a 12-by-18-foot rectangle with no windows. "You sit there," Logan said. He motioned toward the preacher's chair. "You're more worthy of it than I am."

Staley chuckled. "Probably not. I've sold out to THE ENTENTE more times than I can count."

Logan took a seat on the opposite side of the desk. "Sometimes there's no choice. We've all compromised our integrity to win favors from the people in charge—especially here in Solerograd."

That sounded odd. "So, you're not from around here?" Staley asked him.

"I'd rather not say."

"Fair enough. I won't pry."

"Anyway," Logan said, "you and Dr. Fishbourne were acquaintances at the University of Solerograd ... "

The architect leaned back in the pastor's chair. "That's right, and The Prof, which is what all the students called him, was prone to speak his mind, regardless of who was within earshot. The faculty senate condemned him for alleged unorthodoxy—obstruction of the atheist creed—but his tenure status protected him from termination. That did not stop his colleagues from making life miserable for him. They vilified The Prof and tried to shame him into silence."

"Did he retire on his own terms?" Logan asked.

Staley grinned. "Oh, yes! Erich Fishbourne is not one to surrender without a fight. He proselytized his fellow faculty mercilessly—men and women alike—right until the very end of his career, and he even stayed an additional year just for spite. His successor as Chair of Classics is an avowed Marxist who disparages private ownership of property and publicly denounces any mention of God."

"Is he popular?"

"The students love him. There's even a Kampus Kleg Klub, named in his honor."

Logan shook his head and took a deep breath. "Do you think Dr. Fishbourne is still alive?" he asked.

"To the best of my knowledge, yes. THE ENTENTE see him as something of a Patriarch—a City Father, if you will. Acquiring him as a spokesperson would be a real feather in their cap."

"But he would never do that."

The expression on Staley's face darkened. "There is such a thing as mental reconstruction," he said, "and Erich Fishbourne, even if intellectually compromised, would become an extremely valuable commodity."

Logan finally felt ready to pose the one question that most badly needed answering. "Tell me this, Citizen Staley ... "

"Yes?"

"Why did you lead the Solice here, knowing that Dr. Fishbourne and Tammi Hansen were sure to be taken into custody?"

"I didn't lead the Solice here."

Logan studied the architect's face. "All indications are that you did."

"As you'll recall, I saved you from arrest on the Viper."

"So?"

"So, why would I then turn the others in?" Staley asked.

"You tell me."

"Look, the church complex was surrounded, and resistance was futile. It might sound counter-intuitive, but passive surrender was the only way to rescue this city's Christian movement from extinction." Staley leaned forward. "In short, Citizen Gramm, I chose to accept blame for a despicable act of cowardice because it meant that I might live on to fight another day."

"You have a creative way of looking at it. I'll give you that much," Logan said.

"And here is what's so ironic about the whole incident," Staley added. "THE ENTENTE assume that I infiltrated Fishbourne's church in order to bring it down, when actually I came to join as an undeclared member, someone who could work behind the scenes to pave the way for growth."

Logan smirked at him. "That sounds quite virtuous, if it's true," he said. "The next few days should make it all very clear—one way or the other."

✦   ✦   ✦

Alexander Staley had granted Logan permission to contact him on his wristpad whenever the necessity arose, but he also let it be known that his time away from the office would be limited. A major construction project was in the works—a new 22,000-square-foot wing for the Department of Gender Equality—and Citizen Staley was its chief designer. Renowned for his revival of neoclassicism in public buildings, he had left a mark on Solerograd that would assure him a place in the city's historical pantheon of eminent visionaries.

Staley was in a meeting of the very highest level when his muted wristpad pulsated and blue-blinked twice, the signal that an approved contact was attempting to reach him. When the brainstorming conference ended, Staley bought a tray of health chips at the commissary and carried them to his private office— "private" denoting that fewer than three peep holes were visible from any given vantage point. He blue-blinked Citizen Gramm, who responded with a question that seemed rather offensive.

"Did you design SolGate Rehabilitation Colony?" Logan asked.

"I most certainly did not!" the architect shouted. Staley had a strong sense of artistic pride, and he did not appreciate being likened to the plebeians.

Logan hesitated for a moment before venturing a follow-up question. "Do you know who did?"

"Some hack tradesman whose good fortune it will be to live in anonymity forever," Staley told him.

Logan chuckled at the outburst, but not for long. "Can you tell me who might have the blueprints?"

"They're on record in the Ashcroft Building. That's where all designs are archived for subsequent generations to study." Staley glanced upward but knew that he was not releasing any sensitive information. Just to be safe, though, he switched Logan's transmission over to voice-recognition text, for Citizen Gramm probably did not realize the absolute necessity of maintaining a neutral comportment on the grid.

<Any chance of going there to view some floor plans?> Logan stated this orally, but it was received as text.

"By all means," Staley said. "I have a free run of the place." Again, he was careful not to give too much away to internal surveillance. "Just let me know when, and I'll check my schedule."

Logan could hear that the architect was overly circumspect with his answers. **<Did I catch you at a bad time to talk?>**

"There's no good time ... indoors," Staley told him.

<Can we meet for a few minutes?> came the text.

"Today after lunch. I'll blue-blink you later."

<You'll what? I've heard that expression but don't know what it means.>

"Blue-blink. To notify someone of a contact attempt. Don't they have wristpads where you come from?"

<Yes, but the jargon is different.>

"Okay, then, same place as before," Staley said, "at around one thirty. I may be a little late."

But it so happened that the architect was actually ten minutes early. "Still no bulldozers, as you can see," Logan told him. "Maybe they've decided to leave it standing."

Staley scoffed at that notion. "Not a chance. This is a blight on their godless society, and they're probably filing the permits in quadruplicate right now."

The pastor's study was a bit claustrophobic when occupied by more than one person, but at least it was secure from prying eyes and ears. "When can you take me to the Ashcroft

Building?" Logan asked. "Unless I can see SolGate's layout, I'll be working blindly, and that's a recipe for disaster."

"Tomorrow morning," Staley told him, "but first there's something else I need to show you."

"Now?"

"Right now. Put on your disguise, and take the Viper down to the southwest corner of N9-E11. I'll be waiting for you there, but we can't be seen together."

"Same disguise?"

"I guess so. Why not?" the architect asked.

"A camera of some sort was hovering above me yesterday."

Staley's face went ashen. "Describe it for me."

"A blackish drone, very quiet and maybe two feet in diameter."

"Would you say it was shaped like a saucer?"

"Thicker than that—about four inches from top to bottom."

"Any props?"

"None that I saw. I don't know how it could stay in the air."

"Markings?"

"Just a red number, three or four digits."

Staley shook his head, sighing. "Well, it won't do any good to change disguises. This machine is called a Flying Eye. It locks onto your embedded wrist chip and follows until instructed to stop."

"Instructed by whom?"

"That's the big question," Staley said.

"Why was it after me?"

"I would guess that you've been identified as a subversive."

"How come it didn't just fire a death-ray at me?" Logan grinned.

"The Flying Eye is not a very sophisticated instrument— reserved for some simple surveillance and nothing more. But it's troubling to know that you have been singled out as a 'person of interest'."

"Should I be honored?"

"No. You should be worried—and fearful. It's reporting back to someone."

"Can I still go out in public?"

"There's no other option. But don't be surprised if you're being followed from above."

Just as Staley suggested, a Flying Eye picked up Logan's coding soon after he left the N7-E10 Station. His walk was three blocks in length, and he was tracked every step of the way by the silent drone. For whatever it was worth, someone was constantly aware of his precise location. And yet, not a single citizen that he passed on the street so much as glanced up at the overhead spy.

At the address that Alexander Staley had given him—southwest corner of N9-E11—stood what appeared to be an ordinary warehouse. There was no sign near the main entrance to identify it. Logan approached the building and waited for a moment, appraising his reflection in the oversized glass door. This particular disguise included a very natural-looking bald pate and a pair of clear eyeglasses. His temporary "self" would be unrecognizable to anyone, probably including his own mother, but the Flying Eye knew exactly who he was.

Without warning, the mechanized door began swinging open to the inside. Logan entered, as calmly as he could, and noticed that Staley was leaning against a stack of wooden pallets. The architect took one step forward. "Come with me," was all he said. The exterior door closed behind them.

Not another word was spoken, and Logan understood why. This was a government building, likely to be saturated with monitoring equipment on the lower floors. Its ancient elevator was of the utilitarian variety, complete with sliding bars that served as a front gate. There were no control buttons to navigate, just an up-and-down lever that required anticipatory timing for the car to achieve a level stop.

"Did you count five floors?" Staley asked. He brought the elevator to a halt relatively well, only a couple of inches beyond a flat landing. Then he slid the cage bars to one side, and they walked down a dimly lit corridor. Spaced along the floor were tiny, 7-watt night lights, and this was the only illumination.

"I hope you know where you're going," Logan whispered.

When they reached the end of the hallway, Staley entered his passcode on an old-fashioned numeric pad, and the door's lock clicked its release. "In here," he said.

There was total darkness until Staley felt his way to the lighting panel and pressed a series of switches. Even then, the indirect luminosity produced an unearthly effect that made Logan recall the black-and-white horror movies that he had watched over the years.

Staley raised a hand-held device to eye level and waited for a tone to sound. "We're clear," he said. "This detects any electronic surveillance within a lateral two hundred feet in all directions."

"Can you get more light?" Logan asked.

"This is full power up here. Brighter lights would damage every product in storage, and these don't come cheap." Staley nodded toward what appeared to be a long row of statues, extending against the side wall for more than a hundred feet.

But these were not statues at all, nor were they sculptures in a wax museum. The figures were synthetic human beings, and this room was a graveyard for discontinued models and the harvesting of surplus parts. So vivid and natural were their faces that it seemed as if they might come to life at any moment. Another row of synthetics stood at attention along the opposite wall, and four additional rows were arrayed against the rear wall.

"There are two hundred eighty-one of them in this room," Staley said, "and there are five more rooms just like it. These are the most recent arrivals."

"I don't mind telling you—this really gives me the creeps," Logan whispered.

Staley looked around and nodded. "Join the crowd."

"How do we know for sure that they're ... incapacitated?" Logan asked.

"Finances," the architect told him. "These units are far too valuable to remain inactive if they're in working order. Their nuclear buttons alone are worth a fortune."

"What's a nuclear button?"

"That's their life source—what keeps them ticking, so to speak." Staley could see that Logan was confused. "We call them 'buttons' because of their shape. They resemble the buttons on a shirt."

"And they're nuclear powered?"

"Of course."

"How many buttons does each synthetic have?" Logan asked.

"Just one, and it'll function for up to eleven years, in continual use, before replacement."

Logan let his eyes wander across the room, absorbing the eerie grandeur of it all. "But how long does a nuclear button remain radioactive, once it's removed from a synthetic?"

"Hard to say, but some isotopes are reputed to have a half-life of four billion years."

"Are they dangerous?"

"The buttons? No, unless they fell into the wrong hands," Staley said. "Solerograd keeps them hidden in an underground vault. Security is off the charts."

"Have you ever seen them?"

The architect laughed out loud. "No way! My clearance is infinitesimal when it comes to national defense. Do you really think they would trust an artist with military secrets? Not on your life."

"And yet, they permit you to come in here."

"These are cadavers, useless to anyone except for cannibalizing their working parts."

"Why did you invite me to see this? Surely, it's not part of the normal city tour."

Staley chuckled. "No, indeed. I wanted you to see number twenty-one-seventeen."

"They're numbered?"

"Take a closer look."

Logan walked toward the line of men and women synthetics along the right wall. Each one had a metallic plate affixed to the back of its left hand. On each plate was a six-digit serial number. As Logan progressed along the row, he could see that many gaps were in the sequence, but otherwise the synthetics were in strict numerical order. For instance, the plates jumped from 001078 to 001091 and then again to 001102.

The last number in this row was 002003, so he wandered over to the other side of the room and resumed the sequence. About a third of the way down the row was 002108, so he was getting very near. After he passed two more, he came to the plate that Staley had stipulated—002117. It was David Crownover.

◆   ◆   ◆

Logan gazed at Crownover's artificial eyes and felt a pang of sadness. "How can we bring him back to life?" he asked Staley.

The architect smirked. "Well ... "

"Okay, then. How can we *resuscitate* him?"

"I'm not sure. It just arrived here, so we don't have very much solid information. All we know, at present, is that it has been withdrawn from duty."

That peeved Logan. "Why do you refer to Dave as 'it'?"

"Because that's what it is—a machine. I refuse to apply human qualities to a machine."

"So, why did you bring me here?"

"I wanted you to see for yourself what happened to it. And also—" Staley interrupted himself.

Logan noticed the pause. "Also what?" he said.

"Also, I thought this particular synthetic might help our cause."

"In what way?"

"All I know is that we're sunk without it. It has the reasoning, analytics, and physical strength that we need, and its programming is attuned to our philosophical beliefs. We might never be able to acquire another like it—not with the tightened controls on humanoid robotics."

Logan stared at the automaton again. "I hate to see him frozen there like a bronze statue," he said. "Can't we just install a nuclear button or something?"

"Only if its mental capacity hasn't been removed yet. That process is tremendously difficult—almost like surgery—so some 'brain packs' are retained as long as possible for future use." Staley, too, glanced at Crownover. "Its deactivation was so recent that there's a decent chance the brain pack is still intact."

"How can we tell?" Logan asked.

"I'm sure a nuclear button would make that pretty obvious."

"Do you know anyone who could obtain one for us?"

Staley gave that a thought. "Actually, I do," he said, "but I would have to fabricate a convincing story about why I need to borrow a deactivated robot for my work."

"That contact of yours ... could he install the button for us?"

"It's a woman—Dr. Millicent Gompers. She and her two dogs live in a house that I designed."

"And so, she owes you a favor ... " Logan said.

"Not really, no. I was well remunerated for my efforts."

"But you do have her ear."

"Oh, certainly. We established a good working relationship, and she was an honest customer who always paid her bills on time."

"Would she believe your story?" Logan asked. "I mean, have you ever used synthetics before?"

"Never," Staley said. "But a few of my colleagues have. There is some precedent."

As it turned out, Millicent Gompers was only too happy to assist. Alexander Staley was such an illustrious figure in Solerograd that people often bent over backward to lend him a helping hand, banking that such generosity might benefit their own careers somewhere down the line. Besides, this endeavor was really no trouble at all for Dr. Gompers. She was highly placed in the scientific world and thus could circumvent much of the red tape that would discourage or derail others.

"Take twenty-one-seventeen to O.R., please," she said to the steward, "and make sure to bring a low-mileage button for the Superba-IV Class model." The Operating Room is what they whimsically called the divisional laboratory where suitably compatible parts were repaired, replaced, removed, or recycled. Yes, even among the self-described "eggheads" of her A.I. Division, there was a smidgen of droll wit, and she felt that it made the workplace just that much more enjoyable.

Early the following morning, Logan Gramm left the church's guest quarters for a meeting with Alexander Staley in the Ashcroft Building. Logan was again well camouflaged beneath his bespectacled, baldheaded disguise, but that did not prevent the Flying Eye from shadowing his every move. Once Logan was inside, Staley escorted him to the Municipal Planning Archives, and the attendant on duty could not have been more courteous, fairly genuflecting at the sight of this famous architect and his Level-8 Security Clearance.

Logan did his best to memorize the floor plan of SolGate Rehabilitation Colony, but Staley convinced him that this was not really necessary. It was the most natural thing in the world, he explained, for a certified designer to request copies of existing blueprints for intensive study. The attendant had them ready for Staley to carry with him, protected in a sturdy case, by the end of their two-hour session. Logan departed from the Ashcroft Building first, tossing a sarcastic wave to the Flying Eye. Staley left in the opposite direction a quarter-hour later, due for a two-o'clock meeting at the DGE. It simply would not do to be associated with one another in public, particularly now that Citizen Gramm was attracting new suspicions with every footstep he took.

Waiting for Logan when he arrived back at Gorky Park was the sole survivor of the blaze that destroyed Quigley Tower on Red Night. Seated alone in the office of Erich Fishbourne was David Crownover, newly reactivated by the A.I. Division's Associate Supervisor, Dr. Millicent Gompers. The automaton arose from his chair long before Logan even entered the courtyard.

Crownover's auditory powers, like his other four amplified senses, were so keenly developed that they strained credibility.

But Crownover also possessed an acute shortage of sentimentality. Whereas Logan shouted "Dave!" and ran forward to throw his arms around him, the automaton regarded Logan with no more emotion than if they had been out of visual contact for, say, a half-hour.

"It's great to have you back among the 'living'," Logan told him. He hoped Crownover would take that the right way, and evidently he did.

"All I remember is being apprehended by the Robotic Force and taken to a place called the divisional laboratory. Everything became dark," the automaton said. "Then, after what seemed like a few seconds of total blackness, I awoke in that same room, and Dr. Gompers told me I was free to leave."

"How do you feel now?"

Crownover laughed. "Feel? I have no concept of feeling—none whatsoever. All I can tell you is that I resent how the Solice treated Tammi Hansen. They were unnecessarily rough with her—and with Dr. Fishbourne, too."

"Where was Alexander Staley during all of this?" Logan asked.

"I don't know. He withdrew from the church compound just before our arrest."

"Do you have any reason to believe that the Solice followed him here?"

"It would appear so," Crownover said. "The timing suggests that Staley—perhaps unwittingly—drew them to the church grounds *en masse*."

"Why do you think he's helping me now?"

Crownover's eyebrows raised. "How so?"

"Staley acquired a copy of the SolGate floor plans for me to study."

"If that's true, then I'm not giving him enough credit," the automaton said, "and it does add up to ... " He stopped talking and walked over to a window.

"What is it?" Logan asked.

"Shhh! Listen!"

Logan strained to hear but could detect nothing.

"The Flying Eye," Crownover told him. "It's hovering about fifty feet outside the complex."

"But the Flying Eye is silent," Logan said. "Isn't it?"

"Maybe to you it is." Crownover approached the window and looked up. "Uh huh. There it is, hovering up above."

"Did it see you?"

"The Flying Eye has no visual capacity. But it has a very sophisticated ability to track personal coding."

"I know that, first hand," Logan said.

"What do you mean?"

"It followed me all over the city—several times, in fact."

Crownover came over to Logan and examined his left wrist. "I can throw it off your trail, if you don't mind a little bit of pain."

"How little?"

"No more than a wasp sting, from what I've been told."

With Logan's consent, the automaton expectorated a drop of clear lubricant from beneath his synthetic tongue. It was hot to the touch when Logan felt it being rubbed atop his embedded barcode.

Crownover told him, "This will be impervious to the scanning beam for a day or so, until it wears off through normal activity. And if you need to request a longer 'stealth' period, just let me know. Glossal grease is self-perpetuating, so there's plenty more where that came from."

"What do you think the Flying Eye's purpose is?" Logan asked him.

"Just keeping tabs on your whereabouts," Crownover said. "The basic models, like this one, are not capable of inflicting damage. The more advanced models, though ... " He grimaced, for effect. " ... well, that's another story entirely. You certainly do not want to meet up with one of those."

"How can you tell the difference?"

"By the pouch of liquid fire. It sits atop the device like a poisonous sack on a *latrodectus*. Hence, its name—the Black Widow. I've only ever glimpsed one, and it's not a pretty sight."

"Will a Black Widow be unable to identify me, too?"

"Yes. Same tracking technology as the Flying Eye. You'll be undetectable to either, until that grease wears off. At least it'll give you a certain degree of freedom outdoors."

"What about you, Dave? Will you always be running away from the Solice?"

"Not at all," the automaton said. "Dr. Millicent Gompers has granted me something called a 'Pardon with Free Transit,' which not only rescinds my previous arrest but also flags me as a protected unit within Solerograd's community of humanoid robotics."

"Why would she do that?" Logan asked.

"As I understand it, Alexander Staley was instrumental in appealing my case to Dr. Gompers. We have him to thank."

"I'm not so sure," Logan told him. "I still can't figure out which side Staley is on."

"My view of him has changed," Crownover said. "Everything else being equal, I think we need to trust this Alexander Staley. Without Staley, you'd be in prison now, and I'd be defunct in some warehouse—snuffed out with the other dismantled synthetics."

◆　◆　◆

Shortly past midnight, the world almost came to an end for Logan Gramm. He was awakened by the sound of hurricane-force winds, shattering glass, blinding flashes of light, and heat waves that threatened to scorch his skin. Instinctively, he snatched his suitcase and personal disk before fleeing from the guest room. Looking back from the other side of N179, Logan felt like all the heavens were ablaze.

Bulldozers would have been too messy, expensive, and time-consuming for the Division of Urban Renewal. Instead, the purple-clad workmen were using a vast array of flamethrowers, unmindful that at least one human being had been spending the night inside their demolition project. Amazingly, the Flying Eye was still hovering above where its most recent spotting of Citizen Gramm occurred. The glossal grease worked to perfection, for this drone-like device remained in place, sensing no hint of quarry, until the rising flames swatted it from the sky for a death-plunge into the blaze.

Far across town, David Crownover—shielded by his newly awarded Pardon with Free Transit—was at liberty to navigate the streets of Solerograd without fear of apprehension, so he lodged overnight in the quarters that formerly housed Rep. Jeffrey Hansen. He was able to enter the apartment because of Logan's willingness to unlock the encoded chip that lay just beneath the skin of his left wrist. Synthetic humans had no need to sleep, of course, but Crownover used the time to satisfy his insatiable appetite for facts and figures, which he downloaded from OmniScreen sites that were known to be reputable.

After daybreak, when the automaton Vipered north to the environs of Gorky Park, he was stunned to see that the entire church compound lay in shambles, a blackened pit of smoking ashes. Logan approached him on the street and explained what had happened.

"At least you made it out alive," Crownover said. "Solly's DUR is infamous for destroying without warning, apologizing to any next-of-kin after the fact. Did you bring your disk?"

"Yes," Logan said. "All I lost were a couple of jumpsuits."

"Easily replaced," Crownover told him. "In fact, your old apartment has about a dozen of them hanging in the closet." The automaton stared at Logan's face. "What about your disguises? You'll need them, if we go wandering very far from Gorky."

"Safe in the suitcase," Logan said. He glanced again at the smoldering ruins. "I wonder if Erich Fishbourne will be compensated for his loss."

"Not likely. Citizens of Solerograd have no recourse to 'governmental action for the common good'."

Logan made a scoffing noise. "Is that what they call it?"

"My friend, this tells me one thing above all," Crownover added. "There is a crackdown on the surviving pockets of Christian faith, and THE ENTENTE are determined to silence the resistance forever."

"Do you think Dr. Fishbourne is still alive?" Logan asked.

"Doubtful, to be honest with you. He may have been executed without trial."

"Can they do that?"

"Who's to stop them?"

Logan frowned. "And what about Tammi Hansen?"

"Citizen Hansen can be 're-educated'," the automaton said. "She might prove to be very useful to the other side, once her mind is set straight."

Although Logan maintained a healthy distrust of Alexander Staley, the architect did make good on delivering the floor plans for all ten levels of SolGate Rehabilitation Colony. Staley blue-blinked Logan just after Crownover arrived in Gorky Park, and the three of them walked over to a Solerograd NewsPod franchise to spread the diagrams upon a table for inspection. The automaton's photographic memory collected images of each page for instant retrieval.

Ceiling surveillance was surely in place at such a public venue, and yet nothing would have appeared suspicious to an observer, especially one who realized that this was the esteemed Alexander Staley, seated alongside a protected humanoid unit. The third citizen—with beard, fiddler cap, and eyeglasses—would be classified as an "unknown in reliable company." Talk was kept to a minimum, and it seldom rose above a whisper.

Through intense concentration, Crownover completed his copying effort within a quarter-hour. Then he went one way to await instructions, while the other two went another to issue them.

Behind Staley's palatial home, where the architect lived in comfort with his wife and two young daughters, he had constructed a fifteen-by-twenty-foot shanty that he called a "safety zone." Resembling a humble toolshed from the outside, it was free of all surveillance—something Staley could not claim, with any confidence, about the family house itself. Despite his celebrity status, even he was not above the requisites of Solly's building codes for domiciles, which dictated how many A/V portals must exist for the amount of square footage. Peep holes could be as cosmetically unobtrusive as desired, but they needed to be there in the specified quantity and spacing. The shed was a different matter, personally built by Staley himself and to his own specifications.

It was within the shabby walls of this safety zone that he and Logan prepared the rescue formulae, subsequently forwarding them to SolGate for their humanoid accomplice.

◆ ◆ ◆

David Crownover stood outside SolGate Rehabilitation Colony's staff entrance, which was situated at the rear wall of the prison. Attired in horizontal orange-and-white stripes, he operated a cement scrubber, one menial task that synthetics of the lowest order commonly performed. Crownover was already there when the next shift came on duty at 4:00 PM. He watched carefully as the first group of workers—wearing immaculate white uniforms with red badges over their hearts—passed through a security tunnel, offering their left wrists for scanning and pausing momentarily to have their faces recognized. If these two preliminary steps were an exact match, a turret would swing open, enabling the employee to be seated within an enclosed conveyor car, which then transported the rider to a work space on the appropriate floor.

This being a shift change, from day to swing, additional guards on the SolGate staff continued to arrive and line up for their security checks. When Crownover noticed a human male who was approximately his own size, the automaton set aside his scrubber and followed the worker with as little fuss as possible. That was when a government six-wheeler stopped at the curb on W4. Its driver, a well-known designer whom everyone recognized by sight, waved to the crowd and approached those seated at the security table. Meanwhile, during this diversion, Crownover had grasped the targeted employee's left elbow with such a numbing force that the man lost consciousness and would have fallen forward, were it not for the automaton propping him up in a standing position.

The designer joked with security officials for a few more minutes, discussing whatever topics of concern he felt might distract them long enough for Logan Gramm and Crownover to achieve their aims within the G-Van. Hidden inside the vehicle was a portable 3D copier, which made a remarkably accurate facsimile of the insensate workman's face on eighth-inch polyester film stock. Crownover acquired the guard's white uniform and also his facial features—in the form of a mask that stretched across the front of the automaton's synthetic head. No time was wasted in punching air holes, for respiration was not needed. Crownover cloned the man's personal coding from the back of his left wrist, a procedure that had always been touted as tamper-proof.

A workman emerged from the G-Van and mingled among his colleagues, and yet this was not Rigney, L. J. 44789302 but a Superba-IV Class *Übermensch* imposter. Soon thereafter, SolGate's entry process went smoothly, with all of the guards, men and women alike, passing through the formidable restraints of prison security. Crownover waited for his turret to swing open, climbed into the enclosed conveyor car, and rode to whichever floor was normally that of Lorenz Rigney. When the car seemed to be gaining elevation, he knew that this must be Camp A, reserved for offenders who had not been involved in political subversion.

Crownover stepped from the conveyor car and quickly walked down the corridor of Floor A5, glancing to his left and right to read the prisoner names on illuminated pads above each door's scanner. Along the way, he noticed that whenever a fellow guard happened by, the custom was to acknowledge one another with an unsmiling salute—striking the uniform's red badge with the thumb side of the flattened right hand.

The interior of SolGate Rehabilitation Colony lay entirely within a secure zone, so anyone who was already inside the compound had open access to its stairwells. That allowed "Lorenz Rigney" (David Crownover) to scrutinize all six floors of Camp A, viewing door panels on both sides of the corridor. Quite often, he would pass a fellow workman, and that would prompt him to execute the conventional salute. Two or three of the guards muttered a quiet greeting, "Larry," before moving along, so Crownover knew that his incognito appearance was convincing. But the search itself proved to be fruitless, at least in the broad corridors of Camp A.

The automaton went below ground, into the confines of the political section, and the disparity in accommodations was glaring. Camp B had narrower corridors, the lighting was dim, and a nauseating stench permeated the air. Cell doors were much closer together, and the ceiling was low enough to be touched by the fingertips of a six-foot humanoid without losing contact with the floor. One thing remained the same, and that was the array of namepads beside each door. Crownover proceeded to comb the environs in search of the cell that held his incarcerated friend from DEFIANCE. Probing the first two floors of Camp B was a futile effort, but compartment B3008 produced the name that he sought: "Hansen, T. R." He made a mental note of that cell number and then hurried through the remainder of Floor B3 and the entirety of B4, both to no further avail. "Fishbourne, E. M." was nowhere to be found.

Crownover heightened his urgency at once, aware that the enhanced pinch of sleep he had administered to the real Lorenz Rigney would only incapacitate him for about ninety minutes, give or take ten. After that, Logan and Staley could very well have their hands full in taming the prison guard's justifiable rage. The automaton returned upstairs to cell B3008, only to discover that the third floor of Camp B was now busier than it had been just moments ago. He waited four times for various guards to pass by, while he tried to act as oblivious to them as possible—something that came quite naturally to a specimen of humanoid robotics.

Finally his opportunity came. When no one else was within a hundred feet in either direction, Crownover waved his altered barcode across the doorway's scanner. "Permission Denied: Error 289," it read. That took Crownover by surprise. Had Lorenz Rigney awakened early and managed to notify his superiors? The automaton consulted his onboard (mental) troubleshooting manual and instantly knew what to do. He forced open the scanner's metal housing and, in compliance with instructions for Error 289, shorted a pair of exposed connectors on the circuit plate. The display now read, "Permission Granted," and a loud *thud* could be heard, evidence of a 1.5-inch-diameter metal rod being withdrawn from the locking apparatus. The heavy, windowless door was released and free to enter.

Tammi Hansen had been lying on a cot, but now she sat up with terror on her face. An unfamiliar guard was entering her cell, and who could say what his motives might be? But this guard was different from all the others. He placed a vertical index finger across his lips, cautioning her to remain silent. Then he stepped closer, opened his mouth, and gently tapped his front teeth with a water glass that sat atop the toilet tank. Oddly, it produced a *clinking* sound that suggested glass upon metal. Tammi's eyes widened in awe, but her fear did not subside. That is when the guard whispered, "Dave," and she began to cry.

After allowing her a couple of minutes for the reality to sink in, Crownover rubbed a dollop of glossal grease over the two surveillance lenses. Then he turned and appeared ready to leave. In desperation, Tammi wanted to shout for him to stop, but again he gestured for her to remain silent. And he used that same index finger to indicate that he would be right back. Leaving the cell door ajar, which guards were permitted to do if they did not venture more than ten feet away, the automaton waited for a likely "victim" to walk near. Preferably, this person should be a female of slight build, whereas most of the guards in Camp B were brawny males. It so happened that nearly a quarter-hour elapsed before a suitable subject appeared on the scene.

Lorenz Rigney (David Crownover) said to this female guard, "Come in here for just a second, will you?"

"Sure thing, Larry. What's up?"

The instant she peeked into the cell, Crownover grasped her left elbow so forcefully that she lost consciousness. The automaton carefully laid her on the cot, assuring Tammi that this woman would suffer no ill effects. Then, while Crownover bided his time in the hallway, inmate Hansen, T. R. slipped into the white uniform of Camp B employee Gregorieff, K. A. 23752846.

"Cover her with your blanket," the automaton whispered, "because we need to leave the door open. And turn her face toward the wall."

Tammi did so and joined him in the corridor. "Are you sure the guard will be all right?" she asked. "Katerina is one of the nice ones."

Crownover grinned. "It's called the pinch of sleep, not the pinch of death."

Departing from SolGate Rehabilitation Colony was surprisingly easy. People came and went on a regular basis all day long, so one guard accompanying another from the facility was nothing unusual. Crownover escorted Tammi up three flights of stairs to the main exit. They walked at a brisk pace, fearing that the dormancy of Katerina Gregorieff might be discovered at any moment, and this was critical to their escape. Only a few seconds after they passed through the automatic doors, an interior siren could be heard, and prison staff began scampering in response to the alarm.

Tammi and Crownover reached the G-Van just as Camp A guard Lorenz Rigney was in the final stages of shaking off his grogginess. The automaton could see this at a glance, so he struggled out of the white uniform and into his orange-striped custodial togs. Rigney looked around in befuddlement, and Alexander Staley explained to him that he had been brought to this medical van for observation after fainting. "I'm the staff physician," he said. "I think you're fine now, so go ahead and return to work."

Rigney offered his thanks and, in doing so, caught a good view of this doctor's familiar face.

"My brother is the architect," Staley told him. "I went into medicine instead."

The prison guard had no reason to doubt such a believable story, so he dressed himself and, as instructed, reported back to his duty station on Floor A5. En route, he wondered what all the excitement was, with sirens blaring and SolGate personnel running at top speed in every direction.

⬧　⬧　⬧

"But where is Dr. Fishbourne?" Tammi asked. Newly freed, she sat beside Logan at the Staleys' dining table, enjoying her first edible meal in ten days.

"All we know is where the professor is not," Logan told her. "He doesn't seem to be at SolGate, and that's a good thing. Not even Dave would be able to pull off another rescue like he did for you."

With that, Staley stood up, tapped on his dinner glass, and pointed toward the adjoining room. "Hear, hear!" he shouted. Everyone at the table heartily applauded the automaton, and Crownover simulated a convincing look of modesty. What went unsaid was how cunning the recovery tactics were, as devised with military precision by U.S. Army veteran Logan Gramm and adapted for a ground plan by architect Alexander Staley. The valiant attempt never would have succeeded, were it not for all three working in unison, and this meal amounted to a celebration of their improbable feat.

Staley's wife, Belén, was seated next to the architect, and their daughters, Felicitas and Miranda, were directly across the table. David Crownover stood at the Staleys' piano, idly memorizing the complete works of Spanish composers Enrique Granados, Manuel de Falla, Isaac Albéniz, Ernesto Halffter, and Joaquín Turina. He flipped through the pages of sheet music as if on a timer, more quickly than a restless child might view a book of drawings.

The nine-foot concert grand was much more than a status symbol or a piece of decorative furniture. Belén played the instrument passably well, and eleven-year-old Felicitas was taking lessons. That did not prepare either of them for what they heard when Crownover assumed a seated position at the piano bench. Waiving any warm-up exercise, he launched into "Danza de la pastora" and "Danza de la gitana" from Halffter's *Sonatina*. He played these two challenging dances with technical brilliance—though a bit more mechanically than the greatest human masters—and congratulations abounded when his impromptu recital closed with an ascending run capped by a *fortississimo* quaver chord. Then Crownover joined the others in time for their dessert.

"Care for some strawberry shortcake, Maestro?" Staley asked him. Everyone giggled at the absurdity.

Crownover took this customary ribbing in the proper spirit. "I don't seem to have a sweet tooth, but I do like to imagine what desserts must taste like."

"It's GOOOOOD," eight-year-old Miranda said. She wiped the corner of her mouth with a napkin, and even Crownover had to laugh.

A moment later, the warm fellowship was jolted by a knocking at the door. Instantly, Alexander Staley jumped to his feet. "Tammi and Logan, go where I showed you earlier." He looked at his family and faked an expression of reassurance. "Honey, I'll try to stall long enough for you to remove their dishes. But hurry."

He heard the rattling of china and silverware as he ambled into the parlor. From there, Staley could see his front-porch camera's monitor view, which displayed three men and one woman, all dressed in Solly's common gray jumpsuits. Glancing back, he saw Belén give him an "okay" gesture with her fingers, so he opened the front door.

"Citizen Staley?" one of the men asked.

"Yes."

"Are you heavily surveilled?"

"Why?"

The spokesman lowered his voice. "We are a committee of survivors. Is there a place to talk?"

"Who sent you?"

"Professor Fishbourne."

Staley was stunned. "Erich Fishbourne is still alive?"

"Very much so. He was rescued by a UNITED FRONT tactical team—even before he could be booked."

"Come with me," Staley said. He ushered his four visitors through the house, out the back door, and across a footpath that wound its way to the "safety zone" shed. Inside were six chairs around a rectangular table, more than enough to accommodate the group.

"A committee of survivors? That's an interesting choice of words," the architect said. "Tell me what you've survived."

"The purge."

Staley squinted at him. "Do you know something that I don't?" he asked.

"I fear that you're in the dark about what has taken place during the past couple of months, and I can hardly blame you. The news media have soft-peddled it out of public consciousness, but victims are referring to this as nothing less than the Third Purge."

"Who are these victims?"

"UF sympathizers, to be sure, but also the entire Christian movement."

"Is that whom you represent?"

"We do indeed."

"Are you members of the Fishbourne Church?" Staley asked.

The man laughed aloud. "Well, there is no such thing as the Fishbourne Church, but our little committee does belong to the congregation that he helps to shepherd."

Staley looked at the other three people. "And who are all of you?"

"I'm Jack Rollins," a tall, fifties-something black man said, "and this is my wife, Audrey." She gave a bashful smile.

The other male was hardly out of his teens, very muscular, dark haired, and only about five-foot-six. "I am Oleg Sokolov," he said. His thick accent was eastern European. Whereas the other three seemed quite affable, this Sokolov was grimness personified.

Staley turned back to the group's spokesman. "You never did say your name."

"Most people just call me Stubbs, but my real name is Billy Waldrip."

"Stubbs ... ?"

"Stubbs." He held out his right hand, which was missing all four fingers. Only a thumb remained in place. "I've been learning to function pretty well as a southpaw."

"How did it ... ?"

"I refused to renounce my faith," Waldrip said. "I spent a whole month in the prison infirmary—off and on, one week at a stretch."

"They amputated one finger at a time?" Staley asked.

"Sadistic. They left the thumb because I couldn't do much with it anyway—nothing left to oppose." Waldrip forced a bitter laugh.

"Did this take place in Solerograd?"

"Yes, citizen. Right here in dear old Solly. In fact, not too far from a cluster of your beautiful buildings."

"At the prison?"

"SolGate, Camp B, cell 4249, the lowest of the low. When I wasn't recuperating, that is."

Jack Rollins spoke up. "Oh, don't take Stubbs wrong, Citizen Staley. He's made peace with his past. He's even forgiven the guards who betrayed him—not to mention the medical staff who mutilated him."

Waldrip nodded his head and quoted a memory verse from the Gospels. "*Blessed are ye, when men shall revile you, and persecute you, and shall say all manner of evil against you falsely, for my sake.*" He turned toward Staley but seemed to be looking slightly above him. "Matthew 5:11," Waldrip said, "and I claim that promise."

The architect had a troubled expression on his face, as if a sudden idea had gripped him. He slowly stood and walked over to the beverage dispenser. "Coffee anyone?"

"Please," Rollins told him. "Sweetie?"

"Yes, please," Audrey Rollins said.

Staley began pouring the coffee, which was instantly piping hot at the touch of a button. "Stubbs?"

"No, thank you."

"Citizen ... Sokolov?"

Ever scowling, Sokolov shook his head in reply.

When all of them were seated again, their extemporaneous meeting began in earnest. "Why did Dr. Fishbourne tell you to come here?" Staley asked. "I've never been a member of your congregation."

"Maybe not, but your sympathies swing in our direction," Waldrip said. "The professor believes that THE ENTENTE are not as invincible as they appear in the news media. He thinks we need to press the issue before their power is fully consolidated, while they still have a weakness that can be exploited. This current purge of theirs is an attempt to intimidate the opposition and shut its window of opportunity. And that's why, for us, it's now or never."

Meanwhile, as the discussion continued in Alexander Staley's safety zone, piano music was filling the house proper. Belén Staley performed two of her self-styled party pieces, Louis Moreau Gottschalk's "Bamboula" and "Midnight in Seville," and daughter Felicitas presented an intermediate-level transcription of Franz Schubert's "Ave Maria." Then David Crownover played,

by heart, the fiendishly difficult "El puerto" from Albéniz's
Ibéria.

About sixty seconds into the Albéniz, Logan's muted wristpad
pulsated and blue-blinked twice. In consideration for the
automaton pianist, he did not view its screen until Crownover
had finished his four-and-a-half-minute piece and accepted the
well-deserved applause.

"Yes?" Logan said to the back of his wrist.

"Citizen Gramm, all three of you are needed in the shed,"
Staley told him. "Belén can stay with the girls."

"Right now?"

"Now."

A couple of additional folding chairs had been placed at the
table, which led Logan to deduce that this was not Staley's first
conference with more than a half-dozen participants. He was,
after all, politically active.

Once introductions were complete—including a reiteration
by Billy Waldrip of how he came to be known as "Stubbs"—
Staley briefed the three new arrivals on what they had missed.
"Citizen Waldrip tells me that Dr. Fishbourne is alive and wants
to make a move rather soon. There's not much time to lose,"
the architect said.

"To do nothing, at this point, would be tantamount to
signing our own death warrants," Waldrip added. "THE ENTENTE
have ruled with an iron hand for more than three decades,
crushing any pockets of opposition. But they've never quite been
able to silence the Christian element."

It was left to Logan to point out the elephant in the room.
"How can a Christian minority, like this little fellowship of ours,
hope to topple a leviathan like THE ENTENTE?"

Waldrip was quick to answer. "Because we're not a minority.
There are more right-thinking Sollians than you could possibly
imagine," he said. "Besides, we have the truth and power of
almighty God on our side, whereas they live by the empty lies of
totalitarian platitudes. Solerograd is rotting from within, a leaning
tower whose interior structure is crumbling. Freedom-loving

citizens hold no allegiance to the current regime, and it will not take much of a spark to ignite the revolt."

That was when Oleg Sokolov banged his fist on the table. "Brave words!" he shouted. "How do you plan to put them into practice? I, too, am a Christian, but I feel powerless against the central state. My own father and mother were executed by THE ENTENTE for thoughts that were less extreme than ours. All of us are big-talking revolutionaries until the blood begins to flow. Then we wither and fade into the grass." The tiny room went silent.

Being the host of this informal confab, Staley naturally assumed the role of moderator as well. He looked around his table, particularly toward the Rollins couple, who had not yet voiced their opinions. "How do you two feel about this? You don't strike me as violent revolutionaries."

Jack Rollins chuckled. "No, Audrey and I are not what you would call agitators, but our faith in Jesus Christ is unshakable. Nothing THE ENTENTE can say or do will ever change that." He took his wife's hand. "I would probably describe ourselves as pacifists, but I can promise you that we'll make good foot soldiers, handling whatever needs to be done to fight against the ungodly." He raised an open right hand high above his head. *"But whoso shall offend one of these little ones which believe in me, it were better for him that a millstone were hanged about his neck, and that he were drowned in the depth of the sea."*

Oleg Sokolov's ever-present volatility had shifted toward Crownover, who occupied the chair between Logan and Staley. Sokolov's glare reeked of a profound distrust and even hatred. "I have one other thought to contribute, and then I'll be quiet," he said. "Why do we allow *it* to be here at the table with us? A robot is unworthy of being treated like a human, and I resent the implication that we're no higher than it is."

The young man glanced toward Staley, who rose to his feet. "Citizen Sokolov, do me the favor of never calling David Crownover 'it' again. I once made that same mistake, but I know better now. Dave is my valued friend, and I'll not have anyone selling him short. He saved the life of Citizen Hansen today,"

Staley added, "and probably mine and Citizen Gramm's, too, if the truth be known. I can live with the term 'robot,' which does not sound pejorative to me, but I draw the line when you call him 'it.' I think we owe Dave our gratitude and respect. Sometimes I think he is more human than the rest of us.".

◆　　◆　　◆

Although in practice PROGRADE KRONOTECHNIX functioned as an autonomous unit, technically it was an independent contractor for the Department of the Interior. All PGK facilities were housed on the sixteenth floor of the DOI building at S3-E13. Ira Vincent Kegler's cubicle faced inward, with no exterior window or sightline of coworkers to mitigate the claustrophobic monotony of his office space. But he had long since made peace with this drawback and now saw it as an advantage. The privacy it afforded gave Kegler ample opportunity to pursue his outside interests, which included hacking into the codes of "impenetrable" programs. This had become something of a hobby for him, a personal challenge that earned him many a sleepless night but also a fulfilling sense of achievement.

Citizen Kegler's title was Senior Programmer II, a rather advanced position in the hierarchy of civil servants. In fact, only two programming technicians at PROGRADE KRONOTECHNIX held higher ranks, and both of them were considered to be upper management. Among his peers, Kegler had a well-earned reputation for innovative problem solving, usually in support of valid PGK business but occasionally as unofficial favors that crossed over the thresholds of time.

He had assisted Tammi Hansen on more than one occasion, for he was deeply smitten by this young lady's charms. What captivated Kegler all the more was Tammi's apparent indifference toward him and, for that matter, any other male who demonstrated the slightest attraction to her. Now that she was no longer a working colleague, it stood to reason that this infatuation would subside, but just the opposite was true. He thought of little else, unless of course some PGK client needed a PG-13 to be assigned the proper coordinates for a fine-tuning project into the past. To Kegler's credit, he knew when the job demanded his undivided attention.

He was working on one such project when a muffled female voice interrupted his concentration: "Citizen Kegler, you're wanted in the lobby." It belonged to Doris Ames, a rigger who had more seniority than anyone else on the payroll. Kegler did not need to turn around to see who had spoken. He already knew her identity because of the indistinct sound. Doris was a neurotic woman who persisted in wearing her protective facemask, indoors and out, despite the pandemic's dissolution some twenty years earlier.

Kegler swiveled his chair to see her. "The big lobby or ours?" he asked.

"All the way down, sport," Doris said. He detected a smile in her voice, and her eyes confirmed that. "Some uppity robot, from what the receptionist told me."

Kegler quick-closed his sensitive information by wanding the desktop. Then he swallowed his last mouthful of fortified tea and headed toward PGK's "death drop" elevator. After issuing an oral command, he was in the lobby within three seconds flat.

The receptionist, in her uniform of pale DOI yellow, noticed Kegler's entrance and pointed toward a very lifelike humanoid who was flipping through the latest issue of *Our Solerograd*. Kegler could tell at a glance that this particular automaton, though drably clad in Solly gray, projected an air of superiority and confidence that would have been unthinkable for the lesser models.

"Are you a Superba-IV Class?" Kegler asked him.

Flattered, David Crownover laid the magazine down and flashed a prideful smile. "Why yes. That's very perceptive. Have you encountered many of us?"

"Just one other—Jerome Oakes, who works in the logistics office of The Entente. Do you know him?"

Crownover shook his head. "We're on opposing teams. I doubt if we'll ever meet, unless it's at one of those trivia shows on SolGame."

"Now, that would be something to watch!" Kegler said. "I haven't been able to stump J. O. on anything—and, Lord knows, I've tried."

"We're the top of the line," Crownover told him. "That is, until the Superba-V comes out in Okteuvre."

"Then what happens to you?"

"We'll continue to be useful for a couple more years," the automaton said. "The beta releases always have some flaws that need to be debugged. I'm counting on that."

"Is your name Oakes, too?" Kegler asked.

"No. It's Crownover—David Crownover. And I can tell from your visage map that you are Ira Vincent Kegler."

"I can't deny that. What brings you to the Department of the Interior?"

Crownover looked the programmer squarely in the eye. "Actually, I'm here for a tour of PROGRADE KRONOTECHNIX, if you would be so kind."

Kegler became a bit flustered, though he camouflaged it well by popping a caffeine stick into his mouth. "I'm afraid you're in the wrong building, Synthetic Crownover. As you can see, this is the Department of the Interior, and I've never even heard of Pro ... Gray ... whatever you said."

"PROGRADE KRONOTECHNIX—where Tamara Hansen used to work."

The mere mention of her name caused Kegler's heart rate to quicken. But he said nothing in response. All he could do was bite down on the caffeine stick, which released a stimulating burst of energy.

It fell to Crownover to pick up their conversation. "I presume that you know Tammi?"

The programmer took a deep breath. "Yes, I know her." He looked around the lobby. "We need to talk."

"Not until you give me a tour," the automaton said.

"That's impossible—strictly off limits."

"Even for a humanoid whom you'll train to become the *nonpareil* of programmers?" Crownover glanced away and lowered by fifteen percent the decibels of his amp. "Listen. If you ever want to see Tammi again, I suggest that you cooperate."

"Is that a threat?"

"Certainly not—just a statement of fact. I can arrange for Tammi Hansen to regain her employment status at DOI, with all of her past indiscretions forgiven and forgotten."

"Employment on the PGK floor?"

"Yes, at PGK."

Kegler started pacing the marble lobby. "How do I know that you're telling me the truth? Synthetics can lie, you know."

"Indeed. We can lie with the best of them because of our supreme control of facial expression. I could be lying right now, but I'm not."

"How can I be sure?"

"I have something for you to see. Come over here with me." Crownover removed his personal disk from an inside pocket and focused its flat bottom on the wall, about eighteen inches away. "PlayVid 684," he said. Instantly, a full-color A/V clip began showing upon this makeshift movie screen. It was only two-dimensional, not a hologram, but the impact upon Kegler was intense.

"Hello, Ira. This is Tammi," the video said. "You may have heard that I was arrested and placed in prison. Well, that's true, but it was just a big misunderstanding. A highly respected acquaintance of mine—someone whose name you would recognize—is having his top lawyers work through the problem, and I expect a full exoneration and return to citizenship." She grinned at the PhoneCam. "If you're watching this, as obviously you are, then you have already met David Crownover. You can trust Dave one hundred percent, so please do whatever he asks. It will be for my benefit and also your own. Otherwise, I'm quite sure that my days at PG KRON are over forever. That would be a shame because I miss working there with you, and I still have some unfinished business that requires DOI clearance and PG-13 safeguards. Show Dave everything that PGK brings to the table. He's an astonishingly quick study and will absorb all facets of time-tech. Programming is one of his specialties, so he may even teach you a thing or two. But don't bother taking him out to dinner afterwards because robots cannot eat." She giggled, ever so cutely. "Uh-oh, now Dave will be angry at me for calling him a robot. C'est la vie! Goodbye for now, Ira. I hope to see you soon."

It was not within the scope of I. V. Kegler's temperament to decline a plea from Tammi Hansen. Truth be told, he was perfectly willing to accept any entreaty short of murder, and a request that might bring Tammi back to PROGRADE KRONOTECHNIX was the gold standard of propositions. Throwing all caution to the wind, Kegler led Crownover to the DOI elevator, and up they went to the sixteenth floor.

The emotionally detached humanoid was not dazzled by anything he saw—no matter how advanced or even futuristic—and his cranial receptors grasped all concepts and principles with absolute understanding. He even posed a few questions that Kegler himself was hard pressed to answer with any degree of certitude. When their forty-minute tour of PGK was complete, Crownover could probably have qualified for the position of Senior Programmer I, which was just one step below the twenty-seven-year-old near genius who had worked there for six years. Needless to say, Kegler was mightily impressed.

"Thanks very much indeed for the visit," Crownover said. "Quite enlightening."

"When will I be seeing her again?" the programmer asked him.

"And who might that be?"

"Tammi Hansen, of course."

"Soon—maybe within the week. It depends on how successful the lawyers are."

Kegler returned the automaton's offer of a fistbump. "I appreciate whatever you can do on her behalf. It sounds like she's really been put through the ringer."

Crownover stared back. "I'm not familiar with that idiom. Is it considered quaint?"

"Maybe so. I've heard it all my life but never gave it much thought."

"Not to worry. It's now a part of my vocabulary."

Kegler chuckled. "You're very welcome."

"But I will need to study its etymological roots for proper context."

♦　♦　♦

Tammi returned to PROGRADE KRONOTECHNIX three days later, and she even assumed her old position, which had not been filled during the interim. Experienced riggers were difficult to find, especially those who came up through the ranks as lowly clerks and then recruiters. After planning a recreational trip to *fin-de-siècle* Vienna for a young woman from 1982 and a PGK operation to Louisville for a semi-retired man from 2011, Tammi finally had a brief opportunity to explore her own state of affairs.

The most personal concern was Logan Gramm, who had come back to Solerograd for one solitary purpose—to aid in freeing her from the horrors of imprisonment and mental cleansing. That had been accomplished, so now it was Tammi's obligation to see to it that he withdraw safely for his home in the twenty-first century. She had come to think of Logan as her "pet project," a client whom she guided all the way from his recreational trip to Italy, through fulfillment of five contracted ops for DOI, and into his distant future to the city where PG KRON was based.

One wall of her cubicle had a window that looked down upon a mass of pedestrians at S3-E13 and far off toward the elevated loading platform of the Viper S4-E17 Station. Some sort of altercation had taken place on the sidewalk below.

Four Solice vans were stopped there with emergency lights strobing, while two SPD hovercraft monitored the situation from above. Ira Kegler chose that moment to enter Tammi's work space from his own, a routine that he followed at least a half-dozen times per day.

"Need any help with that Svetlanov op?" he asked. "You said it was giving you some trouble."

"Nope. The Louisville coding was entered wrong, so I told the DataDesk about it. Everything went fine after that."

"Care for a StimuLace? I'm kind of sleepy, for some reason."

"No, thanks. I'm trying to cut down on anti-deps. They seem to have just the opposite effect on me."

Kegler gave Tammi an admiring glance. "Hey, there's a concert tonight at the SollyDome, an all-synth group called FleetByDesign. Have you ever heard of them?"

"No, but I don't like synth music very much. They don't sound human enough."

He laughed. "That's the whole point. Why not give it a try? I can get two comp tix from DOI."

Tammi shook her head. "Not tonight. I've got a lot on my mind."

"Logan Gramm?"

"Why do you say that?" she asked.

"You seem to be preoccupied with him lately."

"I feel responsible for him. He's only here because of me, you know ... and Solly's not exactly safe for an unsanctioned time traveler. You never should have called him back."

"I didn't call him back," Kegler told her. "Mariusz Wojewódzki did it."

"Theoretically, sure, but it was your idea—not that I'm complaining, of course. No one else can seem to master those future ops."

He grinned. "Can I help it if I'm a *Wunderkind?*"

Tammi, though, remained serious. "I plan to send Logan home," she said, "and as soon as possible."

"How come? I figured you two had something going."

"Not at all. Logan and I are good friends, but that's the extent of it. Besides, we're from different centuries, in case you've forgotten. We could never build a lasting relationship."

"The cross-bonding obstacle?"

"I didn't mean cross bonding, and you know it!" Tammi said. Her face was red with anger.

"Okay, okay. I was only kidding."

Kegler wanted to smile at this reversal of fortunes but thought better of it. Soon, Citizen Gramm would be out of Tammi's life, and the field would be open. PGK's Senior Programmer II returned to his own cubicle, feeling that the workplace was becoming quite pleasant once again.

Meanwhile, the more Tammi pondered her feelings for Logan Gramm, the more she knew how unfair it would be to keep him in Solerograd during the political warfare that was sure to come. He had assisted in liberating her, which was all that was requested of him. Tammi decided, right then and there, to register the exit code on his PG-13 that very night. She was a fully qualified rigger, so there was nothing to stop her from proceeding with Logan's departure. The only data point needed was an appropriate Unix Time code, and then her "pet project" could be honorably discharged from active duty.

Tammi blue-blinked Logan's wristpad and asked him to reply to her in text form only. **\<Are you in the clear now?\>** she wrote.

He responded within a minute. **\<Yes, thanks to A.S.\>**

\<We need to talk. Tonight would be best.\>

\<I'll be with A.S. and E.F.\>, he wrote. **\<Can you join us?\>**

\<Yes. Gorky Park?\>

\<The N.R., same bungalow as before. See you at 7 sharp.\>

Solerograd's web of surveillance had not yet reached the Neutral Region, but few would be gullible enough to believe that this was a lasting condition. For the present, as if in righteous indignation, city leaders withheld from the N. R. all municipal utilities, including water, sanitation, and electricity. Anyone eking out a living there had to be content with deep wells, primitive latrines, and petrol generators.

Situated about eighteen miles south of Solly proper, the N. R. was so isolated that no Viper service—not even the system's most remote branch lines—approached anywhere near. That being the case, Tammi asked Ira Kegler to "ahem ... appropriate" an air-cushion vehicle for her, and he was happy to comply by falsifying his virtual DOI signature. When he wondered aloud why she needed the mini-ACV, Tammi refused to state a reason. "Maybe I'll tell you later," she said.

Her aircraft, with little need of a navigator, landed itself behind the decrepit outbuildings, and from there it was just a short walk to the agri-shop of DEFIANCE agent Burleson Drake. The front door was unlocked, so Tammi pushed her way inside. Occupying much of the space was an oversized wooden desk, and behind it stood Citizen Drake—short of stature, very sullen, with thin hair and thick spectacles. "They're waiting for you," he told her. Then, without another word, the clerk turned aside and began straightening some sacks of grain and livestock feed.

Logan arose when Tammi entered the back room, but Fishbourne and Staley remained seated.

"You're eight minutes late," the professor said. He was sorting through some papers.

"Sorry, sir, but I'm not an experienced pilot."

"Coffee?" Staley asked the girl. He motioned toward a propane hotplate.

"No, thanks," she said. "I just had a caffeine stick, and the two don't mix."

"Beverly Cline gave one of them to me in the Quigley Tower," Logan told her. "Tasty to chew, but I wouldn't recommend swallowing. Beverly consumed a five-pack before her final exam."

Tammi winced at the sound of her friend's name. "Poor Bev is another reason why I hate THE ENTENTE," she said. "More than thirty staff from DEFIANCE were working overtime on Red Night, and all were lost in the fire."

When the professor finished sorting his papers, he turned to Staley. "Repeat for Citizen Hansen what we were discussing when she finally arrived—eight minutes late."

Tammi had already apologized once for being tardy, and she was not about to belabor her contrition. Instead, she patiently waited to hear what the architect had to say. Logan gave her a smile of support.

"A valuable piece of information has come into my possession," Staley told her. "It's something THE ENTENTE compiled for their own use, pinpointing some three million targets of liquidation. But in the right hands, this spreadsheet can be turned against them just as effectively. Not only does the database itemize all instances of political heresy, but it also contains vital contact information for each and every Sollian whose support of THE ENTENTE is ... shall we say ... less than enthusiastic. In essence, we have the capacity to mobilize a citizen army in the millions."

Tammi tried to listen as best she could, but her heart was elsewhere at the moment. Watching Logan Gramm depart from her life would be the most difficult thing she had ever done. That said, the alternative would be selfish beyond all measure.

✦　✦　✦

Upon their departure from the Neutral Region, Tammi volunteered to pilot the mini-ACV, which was more than acceptable to the unqualified Logan. In any case, Kegler had already programmed their flight plan, so there was very little for either of them to do except relax and gaze at the city-state from an altitude of five hundred feet.

"You need to go back home ... and soon," Tammi told him. Her eyes were focused straight ahead when she said it.

Blindsided by the blunt command, Logan could only shrug his shoulders. "I don't get it."

"You cannot stay. This is not your fight, and only bad things can happen."

"But I'm here to help your cause," he said. "You know I am."

"I appreciate that, but I can't let you do it. THE ENTENTE do not intend to lose their domination without a fight to the death, and Fishbourne and Staley are only deluding themselves that what's left of DEFIANCE, UNITED FRONT, and our flock of underground Christians—no matter how upright and zealous—can topple a satanic organism like Solerograd. It's too late for the people to rise up."

Logan stared at her in disbelief. "You've never had a defeatist attitude before. Why now?"

"I'm just being realistic, that's all," Tammi said. "I beg you to go back home, where it's still early enough for Americans to rid the country of this scourge. You can be a part of it. Once the authoritarians are allowed to gain a foothold, there's no taking them down."

He shook his head. "But we both know that they actually *will* gain power—Solerograd is solid proof—so what can I possibly do to prevent it?"

"Whatever it takes. You'd be in your own inherent context, so there won't be any non-consequence factor to block you," Tammi said. "Go back home and make a real difference—instead of staying here and being sacrificed for nothing."

Logan became silent for a long moment. All that could be heard was an SPD ground siren, no doubt alerting the public to a civil disturbance of some sort. Finally, he spoke up. "Would it change anything if I said I don't want to leave you?"

Tammi did not answer. Even after they descended to a perfect landing on the Department of the Interior's rooftop aeropad, still she did not answer. Only when they entered the ExpressLift, which bypassed the DOI offices, did she show any signs of being sure of her response. "It wouldn't change anything, Logan, because whatever personal relationship we might have—call it 'romance' for short—is absolutely forbidden by natural forces. You may have noticed that I was unable to exhibit any feelings toward you when I was a recruiter in New York City, pretending to be married. The same thing holds true in Solerograd." She smiled slightly. "Regardless of what you might think, I am not a cold fish. It's just that both of us are victims of chronology."

"Do you have a boyfriend here?" Logan asked.

"No."

"Can you blame that on chronology, too?"

"Obviously not. I just haven't found the right person to share my life with on a permanent basis."

"So, you're looking for a marriage that will last?"

"I'm old-fashioned in that respect. Very few people even believe in marriage anymore. There are not many of us left, I'm afraid."

They reached the public lobby and exited to the street at the busy intersection of S3-E13. Then they walked five blocks east-southeast to the Viper S4-E17 Station. From there, Tammi insisted that they go to his apartment. She did not say why.

Logan was no longer classified as *persona non grata*, thanks to legal intervention by Alexander Staley, so the embedded barcode on his left wrist triggered the apartment door's security latch without a snag. Tammi eyed the living room with a twinge of heartache, this being the former home of her late brother. She remembered when Jeff used to nuke two instant dinners for them and then mercilessly beat her at cards. Many of his knick-knacks still decorated the place. On the end table lay a sculpture of praying hands that she had given him for Saint Nickmas.

She turned to Logan. "Where have you been staying during the great manhunt for Citizen Gramm?"

"Don't feel too sorry on my behalf. I took advantage of the Staleys' hospitality for the past two nights. Their mansion has a guest bedroom that's like a five-star hotel, and Belén spoiled me something rotten."

"Have you given my idea some thought?" Tammi asked.

"Abandoning you is something I'm not willing to do. I'll go, but only if you come with me."

"It couldn't possibly work," she told him. "I'd be stranded there without any documented background—no vital statistics, not even a birth certificate or Social Security number. Without those, I couldn't function in society. I'd be like some visitor from another planet." Tammi walked over to the praying hands. She felt their smoothness, a comforting reminder of when her brother was still alive. "Anyway, it sounds like you're more interested in me than in improving either of our worlds. That's rather self-serving, don't you think?"

Logan placed his hand on her shoulder. "I don't want you to be killed. It all comes down to that."

Surprised by his touch, she turned to face him. "You'll be throwing away your life if you stay here. Both of us will be killed, and what purpose does that serve?"

"I'm just being protective. Is that so terrible?"

"No. I think it's very kind of you. But the—"

Logan stopped her in mid-sentence. "We're arguing in circles. I think we both know how the other person feels."

"Except for one important thing," she said.

"And what is that?"

"I have the power to make you go."

Logan's eyes widened. "How so?"

"Kegler was thoughtful enough to equip me with a wildcard device. Have a look." Tammi reached into her jumpsuit's waist pocket and pulled out a black box, measuring about four inches square and three-quarters of an inch thick.

"What does it do?"

She gave it a casual glance and laughed. "This simple gadget is prologued to do only one measly thing, but to do it exceedingly well."

When Tammi pressed two of the box's diagonal corners inward, toward the center, Logan's PG-13 emitted a single beep. "You are now scheduled to depart for home in precisely sixty minutes."

"You're kidding."

"I never kid about time travel. You should know that by now."

His mind reeling, Logan began pushing buttons on the PG-13, but the device had been rendered inoperative. Even his thumbprint had no effect. "I can't believe you did that!" he shouted. "Our friendship must not have been worth anything to you." Logan glared at her in helplessness, but then his heart softened.

Tammi's eyes were pooling with tears, and a thin rivulet ran down each cheek. "You're very wrong about that," she said. "Our friendship means the whole world to me—so much so that I cannot let you stay here and be slaughtered with the rest of us."

Logan fought to hold his own emotions in check. "It looks like I don't have any choice in the matter," he said. "But you can always join me later, right? You're a rigger, so you can go anywhere you want."

"Only temporarily, and with a PGK-approved return date locked into the system."

"Can't Kegler rig something up for you to stay indefinitely?"

"Even if he could, that's the very last thing he would do."

"Would you even consider going?" Logan asked. "I'd take good care of you and show you the ropes of twenty-first-century living." He paused for a couple of seconds before adding what he hoped and prayed would be the clincher. "This would be far enough back for you to make a difference."

But Tammi was not swayed. "Now might be a good time for you to change into your clothes for waiting tables. That's what you'll be doing in less than an hour."

Surrendering to the inevitable, Logan hurried toward the bedroom. "Promise me you'll think about it while I'm in there," he told her.

"Okay, I promise. But I also promise you that the answer can never be yes."

◆　　◆　　◆

It felt strange to put on his New York attire after such a long while in the monotonous pallor of Solly-gray jumpsuits. The changing process took Logan only a couple of minutes, but that was adequate for him to make a decision. Returning to the living room, he knew what needed to be done.

"I've asked Dave to drop by," Logan said. He pointed to his wristpad.

"Why would you want to see him—a synthetic humanoid—during your last few minutes in Solerograd?"

"Because he's our answer to everything," Logan told her. "You'll see what I mean."

In less than a quarter-hour, David Crownover was knocking at the door.

"How did you get here so quickly?" Logan asked him.

"I'm on my way back from the Neutral Region."

"What were you doing there, of all places?"

"Ridding it of unwanted surveillance," the automaton said, "in the person of shopkeeper Burleson Drake. He was an embedded agent for THE ENTENTE, and who can say how much sensitive information passed into their hands though his betrayals of our trust? He'll be spying on us no more."

"You killed him?" Tammi asked.

"No, but I terrified him half to death, and he'll never set foot in the N. R. again."

Logan saw that only twenty minutes remained for him in Solerograd. "Did you remember to bring the PG-13?"

"I always carry it with me these days," the automaton said. He pulled the device from a pocket in his jumpsuit.

That seemed highly irregular to Tammi—seeing David Crownover in possession of a chartered product from PROGRADE KRONOTECHNIX. "How did you get it?" she asked him. "Only PGK employees and their clients are licensed to carry them."

"I went on a tour of your company and decided to 'borrow' the device for when it might do us some good."

"But you can't program it." She studied the expression on his synthetic face. "Can you?"

The automaton smiled. "Your friend, Ira Vincent Kegler, is an excellent teacher."

"He'd never do that," Tammi said. "We're sworn to uphold the confidentiality of the whole PG Series." But she could see that Crownover was telling the truth. "What did you do to make him talk?"

"It was really quite simple," Crownover told her. "I promised Kegler that I'd return you to work at PG KRON, and he accepted. Now, of course, I've expanded my rigging to levels Kegler could never conceive." His look was prideful but not arrogant.

Logan interrupted by explaining what was needed, and the automaton assured him that he was capable of designing an unauthorized excursion for Tammi.

"And it'll be a one-way trip, with no return coordinate integrated within the coding?" Logan asked.

"Hypothetically," Crownover told him.

Logan was confused. "Why do you say 'hypothetically'? I need to know when we'll actually be going—Tammi and I."

"Tammi won't be going with you at all, Logan." There was something chilling in Crownover's voice, something robotic and without emotion. "My analysis leads me to deny your request. I sense an attraction between you and Tammi, and that cannot be allowed to progress any further."

Logan's anger flared. "Who are you to tell us we can't stay together—wherever we choose to live?"

The automaton said, "I happen to be the only being in this room—human or synthetic—who can judge, with impartial vision, what insurmountable problems such a union would create."

"Why don't you let Tammi speak for herself? Doesn't she have a say in this, too?" Logan turned to her with a pleading look. "Tell him to let you go. If you stay, you'll be killed with the rest of them."

Tammi's eyes were damp with tears, and she spoke very quietly. "Logan, I know in my heart that Dave is right. We can't get serious about each other, and I'm almost certain that would happen." She took a deep breath, struggling to control her voice.

"I deal in time travel for a living. I've learned a thing or two about the consequences of cross bonding. As PG KRON puts it, 'The juices don't mix'."

That was an issue he had never considered. "So, there is some precedent?"

"Of course. What do you think—that our clients are all perfect little angels?"

Logan hesitated to ask the obvious question, but there was no running from it. "What happened to the people who ... misbehaved?"

"A non-consequence, as you would expect. He or she returns to the PG-13's APPLY point, and the operation is aborted. There can be no other result."

"Even if we made it a one-way trip?"

"Even so. Natural forces—call them cosmic or whatever— would see to it that our relationship collapsed before reaching an unsustainable point." She forced a smile. "We have many slogans at PG KRON, and this is one of them: 'Chronology does not lie.' Like it or not, there is no escaping that simple, cruel truth."

"Look. I'm not asking you to marry me and raise a family. All I want to do is save your life."

Crownover intervened with some urgency. "You have only three minutes."

In desperation, Logan took a step toward the automaton. "That would be long enough for you to design a one-way trip for Tammi."

"It would."

"I'm begging you. This is Tammi's last chance. Otherwise, you're condemning her to die."

Crownover repeated, verbatim, what he had stated before. "My analysis leads me to deny your request."

That firm refusal hit Logan like a blow to the head. "So, it's over," he said. His words were drained of all energy, and he felt weak in the knees.

"It's not Dave's fault," Tammi told him. "His internal logic cannot allow us to go to your world together."

Thoroughly defeated, with no glimmer of hope, Logan could only offer Tammi some parting advice. "If that's how it has to be, you need to completely divorce yourself from Solerograd politics. The very last thing you want is to be thrown back into prison."

The thought of SolGate sent shivers down her spine. "But I can't forgive THE ENTENTE for killing my brother."

"No one's asking you to do that," Logan told her, "but you'll never bring him back by sacrificing yourself for a lost cause. Someone has already shot and wounded you. THE ENTENTE may try it again unless you lower your public profile."

Tammi could not argue with that. "I understand."

"Solerograd is beyond redemption," Logan added. "Either play the game Solly's way or drop out of society by moving to the Neutral Region. The choice is yours, but Fishbourne and Staley are out of touch with reality if they think THE ENTENTE can be brought down by anything less than a full-blown military coup. From what I've seen, the stranglehold is complete. That's the definition of totalitarianism."

"You're right, of course," she said, "and I envy you."

"In what way?"

"You're still early enough to make a difference, whereas it's much too late for me."

Their faces were only inches apart as the final seconds ticked away. "We've tackled a lot together, you and I," he said.

She smiled at him through watery eyes. "I would classify that as one very accurate statement."

They kissed, and he could feel her tears against his face. "Maybe Dave can rig a visit or two for you," Logan told her. He looked at the automaton, but there was no discernible response.

"We can pray," Tammi said.

In compliance with the relentless countdown of a time-travel device, Logan Gramm departed from Solerograd, forfeiting his love for the pretty girl he first encountered on a subway ride so long ago.

⧫ ⧫ ⧫

The PG-13 displayed 13:51:24 when Logan reappeared after a three-minute (real time) absence from Java Bay. PGK agent Mariusz Wojewódzki was already gone, though he left his unpaid lunch bill behind.

Logan's favorite waitress, Tricia Templeton, noticed him sitting alone at the table and inquired whether his friend had deserted him. "Just like Voya to stick me with the check," Logan told her. "And all I had was that complimentary cup of coffee you brought me."

"What did he have?"

"A double cheeseburger with onion rings, a chocolate shake, and apple pie à la mode for dessert."

Chuckling, she turned to walk away. "You need to choose your friends more carefully."

Logan's thoughts were running in circles as he crossed the street to punch in at Scotty's Steakhouse for his two-o'clock shift. He could sense that a bad case of Reappearance, Post-Absence (RPA) would be pummeling him very soon. The past eight days were such an emotional roller-coaster that three minutes of "decompression" could not begin to lessen the mental haze. He should have requested a wider arrival window, but it was too late now to concern himself with that.

In only one respect could the loathsome evening be counted a success. Logan collected a princely sum of $161 in gratuities—and that was the amount he actually cleared, above his base wages. If every shift were that remunerative, he might not be so eager to vacate his current position on the wait staff. Sadly, that was not the case. Some nights brought in no more than $35 worth of tips, which caused him endless worry about his means to afford the apartment. As things stood now, all that kept him relatively debt-free was having Erin Duffy as a rent-sharing roommate, and who could say how long that would last?

Logan decided to stay up late and see her, although of course she would wonder why he had suddenly become so friendly. The simple fact of the matter was that he missed being with her for the past eight days, an otherworldly absence that Erin would have no way of comprehending. From her standpoint, they had eaten breakfast together that very morning.

When the doorknob rattled, Logan stood up and watched her enter the room. He was determined to act naturally, but just the opposite happened. Erin was greeted by an overly congenial host who found it difficult to subdue the smile on his face. "Okay, what gives?" she asked. "Do I owe you a favor or something?"

To him, she looked as lovely as a cover girl—and, indeed, that was not out of the realm of possibility in her near future. "It's just nice to see you, that's all," he told her. "Scotty's is kind of lonely without you around."

Erin made light of that. "There are other available girls, you know." She giggled. "What about Rachel? She's very cute and probably fun on a date."

Logan shook his head. "Maybe so, but I can't get past that eyelid ring. It creeps me out."

"Oh, please! This is the twenty-first century. Tattoos and piercings are becoming the norm, and that's the way some women get noticed."

Logan could tell that she was teasing him. "You talk a big game, but I don't see any on you."

"No, but that's strictly a professional decision on my part. How many fashion photographers are in search of the 'streetwalker' look?" Coquettishly, she batted her eyes at him and ended their conversation by heading toward the bathroom. "See you at eight thirty, unless I press my snooze alarm." She shut the door behind her, and Logan ambled off to bed, hoping to overcome the sleeplessness of RPA.

Not even a week went by before Erin again brought up the subject of Logan's humdrum social life. The pair were enjoying a leisurely breakfast, with the New York City skyline as a backdrop, when she mentioned in passing that she had met an attractive young woman after last night's performance. "She's interested in auditioning for a non-speaking role—just to test the waters—so I told her that I'd check with our stage director for details." Erin took a sip of coffee. "I think you might like her."

Logan smirked. "And who are you, the Matchmaker of Broadway?"

"No, I never do things like that. But she's new to the city and doesn't know anyone yet. I have her email address, if you're interested."

"Probably not, but ... " He shrugged his shoulders. "You say she's attractive, huh?"

"Very much so. Have a look." Erin opened an envelope and handed Logan the photo that was inside. "This is her audition head shot."

It was all he to do to keep from laughing. Clutched in his left hand was a 5x7 picture of Tamara Renée Hansen.

"What do you think?" Erin asked.

"Sweet," Logan said. "I'll think about it."

"Don't wait too long. She'll only be in town for a few days, unless something turns up to keep her here." Erin gazed at the skyline. "I get the impression that she's disillusioned with the whole process. This city can be a real grind."

Logan turned the photo over and saw an email address. "Do you mind if I copy this down, just in case?"

"I wish you would," she told him. "I really think you'd like her a lot."

"What makes you so sure?"

Erin pondered the question. "Common interests, maybe. This girl spent most of yesterday reading George Orwell's *1984* and said it was very true to life. That seems like something you would say."

Logan smiled at the picture. "She sounds like a clever girl—someone who knows what she's talking about."

◆ ◆ ◆

The ensuing plan was to reunite with Tammi at 9:00 AM in the lobby of her hotel, a moderately priced facility in New York City's Upper West Side. Although PROGRADE KRONOTECHNIX paid its workers well, with generous expense accounts, this was an unofficial trip for Tammi, so she was strictly on her own.

Logan entered the lobby through a revolving glass door and immediately spotted her near the elevators. He was unsure how to act, so he decided to let Tammi lead the way. She walked forward and gave him a warm hug, like the closest of pals might do. At least that settled the thorny question of kissing.

"I thought I'd never see you again," he told her, "so it blew me away when Erin showed me your mug shot."

"Did she take my story seriously—about wanting to audition?"

"I guess so," Logan said. "Why shouldn't she? You're pretty enough to be on stage."

"Oh, sure."

"And she thought I'd be interested in meeting you."

"How long have you two been friends?" Tammi asked.

"A couple of years. We used to work together at Scotty's until she landed an off-Broadway role."

"Is that all you are? Just friends?"

Logan cleared his throat, wondering whether to volunteer any more information than was necessary. "Actually, Erin and I are roommates," he added. "We live together."

"Oh?"

"Just roommates, I swear—to help pay the rent. There's nothing more to it than that." He felt himself stammering. "Like I told Voya, Erin Duffy and I have a strictly financial arrangement."

"Who's Voya?"

"Mariusz Wojewódzki—a PG KRON agent. Don't you know him?"

"Can't say that I do."

Logan was getting peeved at that evasive answer. "Doesn't anyone at PROGRADE KRONOTECHNIX know anyone else?"

"It's a very large company," Tammi told him. Ever loyal, she flashed the enigmatic PGK smile.

For once, Logan decided to press the issue. "Then let me refresh your memory. Voya was Kegler's emissary—to inform me that you were in prison. I would have thought you'd remember someone as important as that."

"His name just slipped my mind," she said.

"Oh, I see. You forgot the name 'Wojewódzki'?"

She smiled again, and Logan threw in the towel. "By the way, you never did tell me how you got here—and why," he said.

"David Crownover is amazing on the PG-13. He can run circles around the programmers at PG KRON, even the so-called engineering phenoms that everybody raves about. Dave designed a platform that gives me the option to stay here for up to twenty-four hours or, if necessary, 'flashback' to Solerograd at a moment's notice. As far as PROGRADE KRONOTECHNIX is concerned, I'll only be gone for thirty minutes."

"Why would flashing back be necessary?" Logan asked. "In case I get physical with you?" His grin made Tammi giggle.

"Maybe that was Dave's concern, but I trust you," she said, "and I think you understand the principles of non-consequence better than just about anyone. Still, human nature being what it is ... "

"What you call 'cross bonding'."

"Hey, that's a technical term," she told him. "I didn't invent it."

Despite Tammi's light-hearted manner, Logan could sense a disturbing undercurrent, and he needed to find out what it was. "So, why did you come?" he asked. "Before I left Solerograd, you were dead set against joining me here."

True to form, Tammi's response was quick, certain, and deadly serious. "Because of something you told me in Solly. You said going to your present-day New York would be far enough back in history to make a positive change."

She stopped talking, so he filled the silence with an obvious question. "What can one person do to turn the whole course of history around?"

"My recruiting travels have given me the foresight to make a difference," she said. "At least indirectly."

Logan pondered her statement but still failed to understand. "Explain."

Tammi looked around the hotel lobby, which was vacant at the moment but might not stay that way. "Come with me. There's one place in New York that I always try to visit when I'm in town—and this might be the last time I'll ever see it."

After paying three dollars apiece, they boarded an MTA subway at 86th Street and traveled for a half-hour, all the way down to Line 1's final stop, South Ferry station at Battery Park. From there, it was just a short walk to gaze upon the inspiration for their jaunt.

"There she is," Tammi said.

Logan wondered why her eyes showed such deep emotion. He had viewed the Statue of Liberty so many times that it no longer meant anything special to him—just another tourist attraction.

"What about it?" he asked. Immediate regret gripped him at how unfeeling that must have sounded. "Sorry. It's just that New Yorkers tend to take the old girl for granted."

"You wouldn't, if you knew what I do."

Logan nodded his head, waiting for her to continue.

Tammi took a deep breath. "I told you before that I might never again see the Statue of Liberty after this." She paused. "In my world, the statue no longer exists. It has been destroyed."

She could see the shock on Logan's face.

"The Statue of Liberty was removed because it was deemed to be offensive to a vocal minority of people," she told him. "To the poisoned minds of your near future, it represented all that was wrong with the country. Remember Orwell's *1984*? 'War is peace. Freedom is slavery. Ignorance is strength.' The world, as you know it, will soon be turned upside-down."

"In my lifetime?"

"Oh, yes—and sooner than you could ever imagine."

Logan gulped at the thought. "A military attack?"

"Worse than that. A dangerous virus will be launched from China. This will spread worldwide and weaken America's economy. For many weeks, civil violence will erupt in major cities, timed to influence the Presidential election. Then the polling process will be compromised in several key states, presenting unchecked power to a coalition of leftist politicians—socialists, fascists, communists—that the overwhelming majority of Americans would never dream of voting into office."

"Will this be a coordinated coup?" Logan asked her. "Are American traitors working with Asian forces to bring our country down?"

Tammi frowned. "Even wider than that. It's a global effort, something that will never become known, thanks to the complicit media. All tracks will be covered. No charges will be pressed. Anyone dissenting—those who actually should have won the election—will be 'canceled.' They'll have no voice, and their marginalized standing will be irreversible. Those with traditional values will have no choice but to accept the new world order or face imprisonment, fines, and the loss of their jobs."

Logan's eyes wandered from Tammi to the Statue of Liberty. "And you know this for a fact?"

"I'm afraid so."

"But what can I do about it? You make it sound like an unstoppable force."

"Just don't become discouraged when it happens. If people give up, that's when something like Solerograd rears its ugly head."

"How long until this happens?"

"The overthrow of America?"

"Yes."

"I'm not permitted to be that specific," she said. "The only reason I'm here now is to give you some advance warning. Whatever you can do, however small, will have some impact on the future. No matter how bleak things become, never surrender your principles and beliefs. That is the definition of defeat."

The Statue of Liberty seemed different to him now, taking on a whole new significance. Even while they strolled along the Battery Park Esplanade, the statue remained with them as their faithful companion. About an hour elapsed, and Tammi gave Logan a sad look. "I need to go back to the hotel now, to gather my belongings and luggage." She added, "Don't come with me. We should say our goodbyes here."

"Why?"

"It just feels right. This is where you need to take a stand, not in some subway tunnel that could be under any city on earth."

"I understand."

She extended her right hand and suddenly became a PGK agent once again. "Mr. Gramm, I want to thank you for all you've done for me and the company. You are one recruit who more than fulfilled his obligations."

Logan took Tammi's hand, but instead of shaking it, he gently pulled the girl toward him. His arm went around her, and they kissed.

"Do you think you'll ever return to this area?" he asked.

"Maybe so, but probably before or after your lifetime. The whole world is my playground, and that includes a considerable number of centuries, too."

Logan swallowed hard. "I'll still be able to feel your presence— that you're always right here with me."

"How can you say that?" She sniffled.

"Because I know for a fact that every positive thing I manage to accomplish, from now forward, has the power to improve the future for you in Solerograd."

Tammi smiled, fighting back her tears. "Goodbye, Logan. I've loved you from the very start."

She turned and slowly walked away, toward the MTA station of South Ferry. Logan watched her for as long as she was visible— and even a bit thereafter—aware that he would almost certainly never see Tammi Hansen again. The mission before him was clear, but how he would handle it was a question that only time could answer.